REMEMBRANCE

REMEMBRANCE

❋❋❋❋❋❋❋❋❋❋❋❋❋❋❋❋❋❋

JUDE DEVERAUX

G.K. Hall & Co. • Chivers Press
Thorndike, Maine USA   Bath, Avon, England

This Large Print edition is published by G.K. Hall & Co., USA and by Chivers Press, England.

Published in 1995 in the U.S. by arrangement with Pocket Books, an imprint of Simon & Schuster, Inc.

Published in 1995 in the U.K. by arrangement with Simon & Schuster Ltd.

U.S. Hardcover	0-7838-1171-3	(Core Collection Edition)
U.S. Softcover	0-7838-1172-1	
U.K. Hardcover	0-7451-7829-4	(Windsor Large Print)
U.K. Softcover	0-7451-3667-2	(Paragon Large Print)

The text of this Large Print edition is unabridged.
Other aspects of the book may vary from the original edition.

Set in 16 pt. News Plantin by Rick Gundberg.

Printed in the United States on permanent paper.

British Library Cataloguing in Publication Data available

Library of Congress Cataloging in Publication Data

Deveraux, Jude.
    Remembrance / Jude Deveraux.
      p.   cm.
    ISBN 0-7838-1171-3 (lg. print : hc)
    ISBN 0-7838-1172-1 (lg. print : sc)
    1. Large type books. I. Title.
  [PS3554.E9273R46 1995]
  813'.54—dc20   94-42981

Part One

Part One

1

New York City

1994

You can't be happy in this life because of what happened in your past lives.

What would you think if someone said that to you? You'd think, "It's hopeless, why bother trying." Right? Or would you think, "The woman telling me this is crazy and I'd better get me and all my worldly goods out of here"?

Or would you be like me and think, "A story! Everyone's into time travel now and nobody's doing past lives, so maybe I can ask a lot of questions and make a story from this lady's answers."

This last is what I thought when I first met Nora because I am a writer inside and out. There isn't one molecule of me that isn't geared toward, How can I use this in a story?

People are always asking me how I came to be a writer. I'd like to have an answer that would please them. I'd like to say that I was walking through a meadow full of tiny blue flowers when a beautiful woman in a silver dress appeared and bopped me on the head with her wand. She had a golden voice and said, "I am giving you the gift of writing. Go forth and write."

Sometimes I think that people want to hear that I was "chosen," rather like a prophet. But you know, whenever you read about prophets, they *always* cry to God, "Oh Lord, why me?" Sometimes I think being "chosen" isn't a gift, it's a curse.

At any rate, I have just told you why I became a writer. I make up stories about everything. Absolutely everything on earth. I see something, hear something, read something, and my mind starts creating a story.

Storytelling is natural to me. When people ask me how I came to be a writer, what I want to ask in return is, What is in your head in place of stories? What do you *think* about while listening to a terminally boring speech? While driving a car? While putting the sixth load of wash in the machine? To me, this is the real mystery of life. I already know what's inside my head, but what is inside other people's heads if not stories?

Well, anyway, now that I am a full-fledged writer (that means I need no outside job to pay the bills) I find that we writers have a little club that we're all supposed to be loyal to. The Hippocratic oath is nothing compared to this.

Since I don't want to lose my writing membership, I'll say what I'm supposed to. *It's bloody hard work writing.* What is that thing someone said about opening a vein and spilling your blood onto the paper? Well, it's true. Writing is really, really hard work. By golly, I bet I sit on my fanny six to ten hours a day. I pace the floor thinking about "what happens next." I have a publishing house that sends me flowers and money every time I turn in a book.

Now, really, does it sound like a writer suffers more than, say, a secretary? She has to be awakened by an alarm clock (I wake when I want to), get the kids and hubby off, work for a boss who never praises her, then do another shift of work when she gets home. And no one ever says, "Wow, you're a secretary. How did you get to be one?"

I guess we all do whatever we can. If you can drive a truck, you do that. If you can hassle people without conscience, you become a lawyer. If you have stories in your head you write them down. To me being a writer isn't any different — and not nearly as important — as most other professions. But it seems that the world doesn't agree with me. The world at large has decided that writers are smarter, more astute, more enlightened, more whatever than other people, so they treat them with awe and reverence.

My opinion is that we should have a National Profession Lottery and every year about ten professions would be drawn from a hat, and for that year all the praise would go to the people in those professions. They should have best-seller lists, receive fan letters, have autographing parties, and have something like a publishing house to praise them and give them gifts.

See? There I go again with a story. Give me a keyboard and I can't stop.

However, about these ten professions to be chosen, I want to make it clear that there is one "profession" that is too evil to be included in this lottery. Book reviewers. Specifically, romance book reviewers.

Maybe I should tell you right now so, if you are offended, you can stop reading this book. I write romances.

There, I've said it. It's out in the open.

For all the joy of my life, there is one aspect of it that is really and truly quite awful. Shockingly awful. And that is the way the world looks at romance novels, at romance readers, and, above all, at romance *writers!*

Isn't the world a weird place? I saw a man on *Oprah* who was admitting that he'd had sex with his daughter several times when she was a child. Nearly every actor/singer tells the world he/she has done every drug known and hurt or driven away most of the people in their lives.

And how are all these people greeted? With love, that's how. With love and understanding and sympathy.

But here I am and what do I do? I write funny little romantic stories about men and women who fall in love with each other. The wildest thing they do is make a baby or two. No drugs. No incest. No one boiling anyone and doing heaven only knows what else to them. I don't even have people plotting clever ways to kill someone. I just invent stories about what we all dream about: having someone to love who loves us in return.

You'd think that the very thought of a romance writer would bring a smile to people's lips. Ah, how nice. Love. Making love. Laughter. Kissing.

But no, the world is upside down as far as I can see, and romances and their writers are ridiculed, hissed, and generally spat upon.

And for what reasons? One of my favorites is that women who read them might get mixed up about reality and imagine a man is going to rescue them from Life. According to this theory, women are so stupid that they can't tell a story from reality. Is anyone worried that the *men* who read spy thrillers are going to go after their neighbors with an automatic weapon? No, I don't remember anyone thinking that. Nor do I remember anyone worrying about murder mysteries or science fiction. It just seems to be dumb ol' women who might think some gorgeous, thoughtful, giving hunk is going to rescue them.

Honey, if any woman thought a gorgeous hunk was going to rescue her, romance novels wouldn't be forty percent of the publishing industry.

Anyway, back to the reviewers. These smart young people graduate from college with dreams of working on some magazine of intellectual merit, and what happens to them? Some old man who no longer has stars in his eyes decides to teach the young whippersnapper a lesson about life so he gives this child the lowest job in all the in-

11

dustry: *reviewing romance novels!*

Guess who bears the brunt of the newly grad-uated person's rage? Eighty grand spent on ed-ucation and they are given a book to read that has a nursing mother cover (so called because of the size of the you-know-whats and the ob-viously about-to-be-lowered bodice [Quiz: do you think a man or a woman invented these covers?]).

Anyway, this person takes her/his rage out on me, the romance writer. The lowest creature on earth. A housewife with a bank account.

Rule number one for reviewing a romance novel: compare the book to the *best* book you've ever read. If it does not live up to Jane Austen, then use about sixty grand of your education to cut this writer down in the nastiest way possible. If, however, you should make the error of liking the book, write that "Readers of Hayden Lane should like this one." Whatever you do, don't stick your neck out and actually say *you* liked the book. If you allow anyone to think you like romances, you'll never get promoted to reviewing the "good" books.

So, anyway, what does all this have to do with the subject of past lives? It has everything to do with it because, you see, I'm thirty-nine years old; I'm about to hit the big four-oh, and I'm trying to figure out some things about my life. Sometimes I think I'm as curious as my readers as to how I became a writer. What *does* make us what we are today?

All in all, the most interesting thing to analyze

is people. Why does the lady down the street dress with military precision? Why does someone have a fear of knives or fire or high places? What about those people who are too afraid to leave their houses?

There is, of course, the theory that every fear in your adult life was caused by something awful that happened in your childhood, preferably something you don't remember so that a therapist can see you hundreds of times and charge you thousands of dollars to help you remember this dreadful thing. So after therapy you're poorer and have some more rotten memories as well.

During a bad time in my life (what can cause a woman a "bad time" except a man?) I went to a therapist. She told me that I had stories going through my head because I wanted to go to bed with my father. When I recovered my power of speech, I said in great indignation, "I did *not* want to go to bed with my father!" "Oh," she said calmly, "then you suppressed it."

Seeing that I couldn't win — and winning has always been important to me — I didn't return after that visit.

But I have tried to figure out why I write and why I write what I do. You see, all writers want one thing. They want immortality. That's why we're so vain that we think someone else will want to read what we put down on paper. We writers hear of Mark Twain dying in poverty and feel no sympathy because ol' Mark attained the goal. He will live forever. Our families would no doubt choose for us to be writers who make lots of money, but we writers would take eternal recognition over wealth every time.

But that's the problem. No one comes to you, sitting on a pink cloud, a clipboard in hand, and says, "We're giving you the gift of writing. Do you want the kind that everyone sneers at or the kind that people remember after you're dead?" Talent is not like a used car. You can't take it back if you don't like it. You can't say, "I'd like to trade in my talent for an Edith Wharton model."

My talent happens to be in writing romantic novels, and they get laughed at and ridiculed. In any movie, if the director wants to show that a female character is stupid, he puts a romance novel into her hands.

Early on, I decided that I was grateful for any talent at all. Those who can, do, and those who can't, review. As Anthony Trollope said, "Only a blockhead writes for anything except money." Or there abouts. Anyway, it's true. You can't very well sit down at your computer and say, "I'm now going to write my way into history." It doesn't work that way. You don't decide what lives on after you, other people do.

So, anyway, I still wonder how I came to write romantic novels and I look back at my life to see if I can figure out what made me such a writer. In fact, I'd like to know what made me like I am in every aspect.

Until I was seven years old, I was the happiest

child on the planet. My parents and sister and I lived next door to two houses filled with cousins and aunts and uncles and a couple of sets of grandparents. It was heaven. I was the ringleader of the bunch, ordering everyone about, telling them what to do and how to do it. My creativity was truly appreciated.

Well, maybe not appreciated by everyone. There was the time I saw my grandmother twist the head off a chicken, so I told my cousin we ought to help Nana and twist the heads off all the chickens. There we were, no more than five years old, chickens tucked between our scraped knees and twisting and twisting and twisting. My grandmother came out of the house with a load of wash and there were all her chickens, their heads cocked to one side, listing drunkenly about the yard. Looking back on it and thinking of the ferocious temper of my grandmother, I don't know how my cousin and I escaped alive.

But those wonderful years ended soon enough when my mother decided she'd had enough of her mother-in-law's renowned temper. My mother (who could defeat any temper with her rock-hard stubbornness) on one fateful day informed my father that she had bought a piece of land and he was going to build her a house on it. In my parents' household we all liked to pretend that my father was the one who made the rules. I think the rule he made was, Give Mama what she wants or she'll make life hell for all of us. Whatever his thoughts, he wasn't fool enough to say no to my mother when she had *that* look in her eye.

Whatever the philosophy behind it, the result was the same: We moved. In that one day I lost all those cousins and grandparents; I lost the chickens and the cows and the possum that lived in a barrel in the barn. I lost blackberry bushes that gave me chiggers and I lost apple trees to climb. In one day I went from being the champion of all, a person of prime importance, to being the child-who-must-be-kept-down.

In a matter of hours I went from having the most exciting life in the world to having a life of supreme dullness. My mother and sister were cut out of the same cloth. They were good. Good, good, good.

What is more boring than good? My mother was always saying, "Don't eat too much chocolate. It'll make you sick" or "I can't look at that right now. I have too much work to do" or "Hayden, you cannot read that book now. You haven't finished cleaning the bathroom." On and on she went. There was a right time and a wrong time for everything. But as far as I could tell the right time for exuberance never came.

Didn't people ever want to do something that wasn't on the schedule? Was I the only one in the world who actually wanted to eat as much chocolate as I could hold and damn the consequences?

Looking back, I think that some people are afraid to break out of the rules. Maybe they're afraid that if they break the rules, they'll lose all self-control and become something horrible — in my mother's case that would be a woman with a dirty bathroom floor.

Whatever was behind it all, again the result was the same: I was put in a bubble of isolation and left there alone. I had to try to remember to sit up straight, walk sedately, and never, never be rambunctious. I tried, but it's difficult to control yourself when you're a child. I guess an awful lot of me slipped out because I heard the phrase "You know how you are" a few million times. Sometimes I got the feeling that my parents thought that if they didn't keep me under rigid control every minute of every day that I'd lose it altogether. Maybe I'd start eating chocolate and laughing and just plain *never stop*. Maybe they feared not being able to reel me back in if they just let me go ahead and *be myself*.

Now that I'm an adult and know all about adult things (uh-huh, sure) I know that my parents were not creative and I was. If they bought something that needed assembly, they read the box and put it together in the way the manufacturer wanted them to. If I bought something, I felt that reading the instructions was cheating. And if I couldn't put it together easily, it was quite ordinary for me to jump up and down on the box and say all the dirty words I knew — which, thankfully, weren't many.

My punishment for box jumping or any infraction of the peace rules was to be talked to "for my own good." Never in my life have I understood that phrase. When someone says this is "for your own good" it always, always, *always* means that someone is trying to make you openly acknowledge his or her superior power.

So, anyway, how did I survive these spirit killers? How did I survive being dragged to the preacher so he could talk to me because I was "different"? How did I survive hearing my mother ask my relatives if they had any idea what she could "do" with me?

I did the best I could by escaping into a land of stories.

I read incessantly. When my mother made me vacuum the bedroom I shared with my sister, she was more concerned with the length of time I spent vacuuming than with how clean the floor was after I was finished. All she ever checked was to see that the light bulbs were spotless, so I learned to clean the bulbs, then I'd get in the closet with a book, a flashlight, and the vacuum and sit down for a forty-five-minute read. Since my mother had the ears of a bat, I had to make sure the suction was going on and off, so I sat there putting various parts of my face to the hose, sucking and reading, sucking and reading. I did learn that one must make sure the hose end is clean or one's face gets awfully dirty, then one's mother makes one actually clean the room. Gag!

So, anyway, I learned to get round the work, work, work, clean, clean, clean ethic of my mother's house and make time for the books I loved so much. I read nonfiction even then. I read about heroes, about men and women who had done things and accomplished things in their lives.

There was Daniel Boone and Jackie Cochran and, oh sigh, Captain Sir Richard Francis Burton. There was the most magnificent queen who ever lived, Elizabeth I, and there were girls who dressed as boys and became spies. Oh, but the list was endless.

I didn't realize it then but what I was doing was researching. Yes, that's right, researching. Now I receive reader letters saying in awe, How do you ever do all the research necessary to write historical novels? Okay, let's have a reality check here. This woman has written me that she has a full-time job and three children under the age of five and she wants to know how *I* research a romantic novel. I want to ask *her* how she survives each day.

I guess I'm explaining so much about my life to make you, my readers, think I'm a normal, sane person because something happened to me that isn't normal and maybe not even sane.

You see, I fell in love with one of my fictional characters.

Up until I started writing a book titled *Forever*, I liked to think I was a perfectly well-adjusted person. Maybe I did have a lot of stories running through my head, but to me, the people who don't have these stories are missing something.

Anyway, I like to think I was happy and relatively well adjusted. I was thirty-seven years old, had a great career, had friends, and best of all, I had met a wonderful man named Steven.

Steve was a dream come true: smart, funny, talented, caring. If I'd made him up he couldn't have been better. And he adored me. He laughed at all my jokes, thought I was beautiful, smart. You name it, everything was perfect between us. There was no question that finally, at last, I wanted to get married. When he asked me to marry him, while riding in a hansom cab through Central Park, I threw my arms around his neck and said, "Yes, yes, yes!" with such enthusiasm that I embarrassed Steve.

But that night, actually, early Sunday morning, I awoke at 3 A.M. with an IDEA. That's unusual for me. When I first started to write I was plagued with Ideas, and I was so afraid that I'd forget them when I awoke that I got out of bed and wrote all night. But after I'd written about ten books, I'd wake up with an Idea, then fall back asleep.

But that night of my marriage proposal, with my left hand weighted down by Steven's ring, I had an IDEA. It was so big that I couldn't relax against Steve's warm body and go back to sleep.

So, tiptoeing, I got out of bed and went to my computer to write down my thoughts. What I was really thinking about wasn't so much a story but a character. Well, okay, a man. A wonderful man, a man unlike any I'd ever written about before. A man who was more real to me than any other man I'd created.

In my books, I write about one family, the Tavistocks. When I first started writing, every time I finished a book I'd get depressed because I knew that I'd never again see the characters in my book. So one day I had the brilliant idea of writing four books about four brothers in one family. However, I had not taken into consideration that when I finished the series I would be quadruply depressed. When I reached this point, the only way I could figure how to recover was to write more books about the same family.

At the time I didn't realize what I was getting into. As the number of books about this family increased, the mail brought me thousands of requests for family trees. And people kept pointing out that I'd have a man and woman with a little boy in one book and in the next book their child would be a girl. I had to buy professional genealogy software to keep up with all of my people, since within a few years I had over four hundred characters, all related to one another.

Over the years I had come to love my Tavistocks and their cousins, and they had become very real to me. So on the night of my engagement it wasn't unusual for me to start writing about a man named Tavistock.

I named him James Tavistock, to be called Jamie, and he was a great big gorgeous sixteenth-century Scotsman running around in the Tavistock plaid, and the heroine was a modern woman of today who travels back in time to meet him.

When Steve awoke the next morning I was still at my computer, trying to get down dialogue and notes for the book. He'd never seen me like this because over the years I had learned to treat writing like a nine-to-five job. I took off weekends and holidays just like everyone else. I found that this worked better for me than the lunacy of "waiting for inspiration." The rent I pay each month for my apartment is all the inspiration I need.

Steve was very understanding. He's an investment banker (no, I do not allow him to handle my money; I said I was in love, not insane) and was a bit fascinated by the creative process. So he ordered his own breakfast from the delicatessen (in the real world the woman fries eggs for her man; in New York we dial the telephone for our men), and I kept typing.

After a while he got bored with hearing the keys of my computer, so he tried to get me to go out with him to see a movie or walk in the park. But I wouldn't go. I couldn't seem to stop writing about Jamie.

Steve said he understood, then decided to leave me to my work; he'd see me the next day.

But I didn't see him the next day, or the next. In fact I didn't see him for nearly two weeks. I didn't want to see anyone; I just wanted to write about Jamie.

I read books on Scotland until the wee hours of the morning and everything gave me an idea about Jamie. I thought about him, dreamed about him. I could see his dark eyes, his dark hair. I could hear his laugh. I knew what was good about him and what was bad. He was brave and honest; his honor was such that it was a life force. He was proud to the point that it hindered him. But for all his many virtues he was also vain and at times as lazy as a cat. All he wanted was me — I mean, the heroine — to wait on him.

After two weeks I went out with Steve, but I don't know what it was, but it was as though I couldn't really *see* him. It was as though I was seeing all the world through a Vaseline-coated lens. Nothing seemed real to me. All I could seem to hear and see was Jamie.

Over the next months my obsession with this man only deepened. Steve did everything he could think of to get my attention. He talked to me, pleaded with me to stop working and start paying attention to him.

"Where is the woman I fell in love with?" he asked with a smile, trying to make light of what was hurting him so much.

I couldn't really answer him. I just wanted to get back to my computer and my research books. I don't know what I was looking for in the books; maybe I hoped to "find" Jamie in them.

I have to say that through all of this Steve was wonderful. He really did love me. After about four months of complete inattention from me, he begged me to go with him to a counselor. By this time I was feeling guilty. No, correction,

I was feeling that I *should* feel guilty; what I was actually feeling was that I wanted everyone on the earth to go away and leave me alone with Jamie.

For three months, Steve and I had weekly visits with a therapist, talking about my childhood. I was completely uninterested in any of it. I sat there and told them what they wanted to hear, that my mama didn't love me and my daddy didn't love me, et cetera. The truth was, in the back of my mind, I was thinking only of what I wanted to write about Jamie. Had I fully explored the way the sunlight played on his hair? Had I described the sound of his laughter?

Steve knew very well that I was paying no attention to any of the therapists, so, after eight months of receiving nothing from me, he told me he wanted to break our engagement. In a scene that I felt as though I were looking at from a distance, I gave him back his ring. The only thought that was in my head was, Now I can spend *all* my time with Jamie.

When I first told my friend and editor, Daria, about my obsession with this hero, she was thrilled. Obsessed authors write *great* books. The authors who fail are ones who call their editors and say, "What do you want me to write next?"

Daria was the only person on earth who wanted to hear about this man as much as I wanted to talk about him. Of course to be honest, Daria had learned to listen to authors while line editing other people's manuscripts, eating a bagel, and directing her assistant about covers and cover copy. Daria has one humdinger of a brain.

But then something odd happened. After about three months of my talking nonstop about this book, Daria said, "I want to see what you've done."

"No!" I snapped at her request. Now this is very odd. Writers act as though they have lots of self-confidence, but we all have clay feet. We are in awe of the power of our editors, those first people who see our work. Daria *always* raves about the first section of a book I turn into her. Later she may tell me it all needs to go into the trash, but not at first. It's like, you can't tell your best girlfriend that the guy she's madly in love with is a creep. *After* she breaks up with him, you can tell her.

Anyway, I usually sent Daria my book in fifty-page clumps and started pestering her for her opinion (i.e., lavish praise) before the express service had even picked it up from my door. One book, I sent her the whole five hundred pages in ten-page segments. Wisely, Daria refuses to have a fax machine in her apartment or else all her insecure, praise-hungry authors would be faxing her their books page by page then demanding an hour's praise for every paragraph that they hope is wittily written.

By all of this you can see how unusual it was when I didn't want Daria to see what I had written. I told her I wanted to finish the section I was writing before I sent it to her.

The truth was, I didn't want her — or any other woman — to set eyes on my Jamie.

Even after months, I still refused to allow Daria to see any of the book, and she began to be concerned. Some writers lie about how much they're writing, but I knew Daria didn't think this of me, since I write because I love it — correction, I write because I must, because I am driven to it.

Daria grew more concerned when, a month after it happened, I told her that I had broken my engagement to Steve. "You didn't tell me this?" she asked, aghast, for we were truly friends, not just business friends. She seemed a little worried when I said that the broken engagement didn't matter, that I hadn't been very upset by the breakup.

Months went by and I kept writing. When I write, I keep a file named Scenes, and whenever I have an idea about possible bits of dialogue that I might be able to use in the book, I stick it in this file. Being very frugal, I almost always use every word I put into this file.

But I had written so much about Jamie that the Scenes file was over six hundred thousand bytes, over four hundred pages, and I hadn't yet really started the book. I kept telling myself that I needed to do a bit more research or needed to know just a tiny bit more about Jamie before I could actually start writing the book itself.

I had Jamie and my heroine, who was named Caitlin, in every possible situation. I told myself

I was "exploring possibilities of their characters." Twenty-five books I had written, and I'd never before felt this need, but then I'd never before felt this way about a character I'd made up. Oh, I often felt as though I were "in love" with a hero, but it was nothing compared to what I felt about Jamie.

Months went by and still I kept writing notes for my book. Jamie was no longer a Scotsman but an Englishman in the time of Queen Elizabeth I.

Daria was more than annoyed with me as I *still* wouldn't allow her to see anything I'd written. She reminded me that I was past my due date; it had no effect on me. She sent me a copy of the cover and talked to me about all the people at my publishing house who were depending on me, something that I usually cared a great deal about. But I didn't care about anyone or anything, just Jamie.

I think it was the wedding invitation I received from Steve that made me realize that I had a "problem." I know it was probably a bitter, hurtful thing he did, sending me that pretty, engraved invitation, letting me know that I had truly lost him, but actually it was the best thing that could have happened to me.

I realized that I had discarded a real, live, utterly wonderful man for a character I had created on paper. I realized that I had not talked to any of my friends in months and that the romance trade papers were running little gossip bits about, What ever happened to Hayden Lane?

But realization cannot stop something that's bad. All smokers know they should quit, but that doesn't make them able to stop the habit.

But when I was able to admit to myself that I did indeed have a problem, I decided to get help. I spent three months going to a therapist every day. That was useless. No one had even conceived of a case like mine. At first I tried to keep it from her that the man I was obsessed with was a figment of my imagination, but I have a big mouth and I'm not good at intrigue, so she soon found out. Her advice was to get out more, see people. I tried, but that didn't work because I bored everyone to death with "Jamie says" and "Jamie likes" and "Jamie does."

When therapy didn't seem to be working, I started trying other methods of figuring out what was wrong with me. In New York, there's a palm reader, a psychic, a tarot card reader, some esoteric something on every corner. I went to several of them. I guess I hoped that someone would tell me that within a week or two I'd be back to my old self. But not one of them told me anything helpful. They told me I was rich and famous and had a star in my palm that meant I was "special." They told me the people at my work were beginning to think I was crazy and had decided to treat me as though I were nitroglycerine about to go off.

In other words, they didn't tell me anything I didn't already know. At home, I cried a lot and yearned for Jamie all the time. I didn't just want to write about him, I wanted to feel him, touch him, talk to him. I wanted to follow his long legs down country paths; I wanted to bear his children.

I don't know what would have happened, or how long all of this would have gone on, if I hadn't met Nora. Like a spider sitting in the midst of her web, she had an office across from my hairdresser's with a huge red neon sign that said ASTROLOGY. As I sat there with foil in my hair (my hair is white blonde and I get downlights to make it look more "natural" — weird, huh?) I thought, I think I'll go have my chart done.

I say that Nora is like a spider because I soon learned that she knows even less about astrology than I do. She put the sign up to attract people. Nora really is a clairvoyant, and as soon as I sat down and asked for my chart to be done, she said, "How about a psychic reading, instead?"

I said, "Sure," and that one word was the beginning of everything.

2

"You're not supposed to be here," the astrologer cum clairvoyant, Nora, said. "Where are you supposed to be?"

"At my computer?" I'm always making jokes, but then *she* was the clairvoyant, not I. Shouldn't *she* be divining where I was supposed to be?

"You are in love with someone, deeply in love with him, but something is wrong. Something is blocking that love. What is it?"

I sat there in one of my rare moments of speechlessness and stared at her. She was a little too close to the truth, but even toothpicks under my nails wouldn't have made me give her any help. In the last months I had had too many so-called psychics guessing what my problem was.

First of all, I don't think this woman had read the fortune-teller's handbook.

Nora didn't *look* like a fortune-teller. Palm readers et al. are supposed to shave off their eyebrows, paint them at random elsewhere on their faces, wear earrings the size of hubcaps, and drape cheap, garish rayon scarves about their shoulders. Nora did none of these things. She had a sweet, round face, big brown eyes, dark hair worn in a short fashionable cut and Connecticut lady-on-the-weekend clothes. She just looked normal, pleasant. Not in the least bizarre.

I could understand that she didn't know the dress code of witches but why wasn't she saying what she was supposed to say? She should be telling me that I'd meet a tall, dark man, etc. etc.

Above all, she should *not* be asking me questions.

I took a deep breath. "I do not know what is blocking me because I am *not* in love with anyone." I let my voice drip sarcasm. Lots of therapy in the last months had convinced me that I could not love a person who did not exist. And, basically, I hated Nora's approach of telling me, not that I was going to meet someone who I would love, but that I already did love someone. I knew that was not true. There was no man in my life, not a flesh-and-blood one anyway. I decided that she was the *worst* psychic I had ever been to.

With some anger at having been duped — knowing I should be assertive and demand my money back — I gathered my things and started to leave. "Thank you so much," I said rather nastily, "but —"

"You do not know you are in love with him because you have not met him yet."

I sat back down in the chair. Now we were getting somewhere. Now we were reaching the tall, dark stranger part. Better yet, this handsome stranger was preloved. Maybe he was the man who was going to take Jamie out of my mind and heart. And maybe Nora did know how to play the game after all.

"When am I to meet this man?" I asked, for *I* know how to play the game.

Nora just sat there staring at me, wordless, while I stared back. I was glad I wasn't paying her by the hour.

"Sorry," she said then looked away. "Just reading thoughts."

This statement made my mind reel. What *were* my thoughts? Could she read anyone at any time? What went on in the heads of people? Could she sit next to a guy on the bus and know he was planning a murder? I was sure there was a story in this.

But then, of course, a person couldn't read other people's minds, could she?

While I waited, Nora ran her hand over her face (proving she wore no makeup, something I truly envied; my hair and skin are so pale, remove the makeup and I look like a rabbit). "You are a very unhappy person."

I drew in my breath sharply. No one had ever before said that to me. I am successful, self-confident, pretty, smart, etc. I am what I hoped I would become.

I gave Nora a raised-eyebrow look. "I am a

very successful writer." Damn! I thought. Rule number one: Never tell psychics anything; let them tell you.

"Money means nothing in life," Nora said. "Success means nothing. You could be a queen and be a failure in life."

The British royal family has proven that, haven't they? "What constitutes success?" I asked, deciding to forgo sarcasm in favor of hearing another opinion.

"The giving and receiving of love," she answered.

Love, I thought. Love is what I write about. Specifically, giving love to a man. But at the moment a human man was something I didn't have.

"I have friends," I heard myself saying. "I love many people and they love me." I sounded like a petulant child.

"No," she said. "For you there is something more."

Maybe I looked frustrated or maybe I looked as though I were going to start crying — about how I felt. I have a tendency toward self-pity anyway, and her telling me I wasn't happy had rung some bells inside me. I had heard that Steve's wedding was beautiful.

"Maybe I should explain," Nora said. "Many women can be happy with any of . . . well, perhaps one man in twenty. But then they don't ask much. They want a nice man, someone who'll support them, who plays with the children. They —"

"Every woman wants that." I have a dreadful

habit of interrupting people. Only in New York, where people talk on top of each other, do I fit in.

"Yes, that's what I said," Nora answered, eyes boring into me, pointing out my rudeness and showing she had more spirit than I originally thought. "Most women want a man who is good to them and they choose him based on compatibility, race, money, education, things like that."

After that she just sat there, saying not a word. Yes, okay, I thought, so you told me the prologue, but where's the story? I searched my mind for what I was supposed to say, since she seemed to be waiting for me to speak.

Sometimes my brain works like lightning but sometimes it just sits there. "Oh," I said at last. "What do *I* want?"

Nora smiled so sweetly at me that I felt as though I were back in first grade and had just received a star from my teacher.

"You," she said, with twinkling eyes, "want everything. You want a Grand Passion. A Great Romance. You want the stars and the moon. You want a man who is brilliant and strong, as well as soft and weak, a man who's handsome and talented and . . ." She paused, looked hard into my eyes and said, "You want a man who can love. Love with all his being, just the way you'd love him in return."

I collapsed back against the chair and stared at her. In months, therapists, self-help books, palm readers, astrologers, all of them combined had not figured out as much about me as this woman had in minutes.

"Yes," I managed to say. "I want it all." I was so full of emotion I could hardly speak.

Unfortunately, what Nora did then was give me a very stern look. "You ought to settle for less."

My head started to clear. *What* were we talking about? My sense of humor was beginning to come back to me. "Okay," I said, smiling. "I'll settle for half. You have any good-looking cousins? Except red-haired men. I don't like red-haired men."

Nora didn't so much as crack a smile. "No. No one will do for you. You will know him when you see him."

I lost my humor. Yeah, right. One of those, I'll-know-him-when-I-see-him gags. What I wanted was an address, or at least a telephone number. I wanted someone who would drive Jamie from my head.

Nora was looking at me in that reading-thoughts way. Let her look into my mind all she wanted. Whatever was in my mind had already been put on paper and sold to my publishing house. And if she "saw" Jamie I could truthfully say that he was just another of my paper heroes.

"So," I said a bit nastily, "do you tell futures? Or do you just tell me what can't be?"

"Your future is your present. If you wish it to be."

Damnation! but I hate cryptic speech. I hate

stories full of mystical claptrap about what the sun said to the moon. If I wrote something like what Nora had just said in one of my books, Daria would laugh at me, then point out that what I'd written was meaningless you-know-what.

I thought I'd introduce a little logic into this conversation. "One minute you say there is this fabulous man for me and the next you say all the rest of my life will stay the same. I assume that means I don't even meet this man. But then you say my life is as I wish it to be, so I assume that means that if I do meet this man I might be stupid enough to turn him down."

"Yes."

Aaargh! I meant to force her to explain herself, not agree with me. I looked at her hard, wanting to pin her down. "When and where am I to meet this marvelous man?"

She didn't hesitate. "Three lifetimes from now."

I didn't think and certainly didn't speak but just sat there looking at her.

She seemed to guess that she'd shocked me. When I asked about my future I meant, well, maybe ten years from now.

"You will be very happy together," she said as though this might console me. "But you have many things to learn before you find him."

I recovered enough to laugh. "What library do I go to to learn these things? If I pass the test early can I have the man for Christmas?"

I was beginning to think Nora had no sense of humor (which is my description of a person who doesn't laugh at my jokes) because she continued to gaze at me without a smile. When she continued not to speak, I said, "I can't have a man because I haven't learned things and because I'm blocked, is that right?"

She nodded.

"Do you have any idea what is blocking me?"

"I would have to do more work."

At that I smiled. Oh, the silver-crossing-my-palm routine, I thought. Now she tells me I must pay her thousands of bucks a week and she'll "find" this man for me.

At my smug little smile and I guess maybe at my thoughts, Nora turned red. Red as in angry. "Do I look wealthy to you?" she snapped. "Do you think I charge people enormous amounts of money to help them? I can feel that you are a very troubled woman, so you have come to me and asked me questions yet you will believe nothing I say. Truthfully, you do not want to know for yourself. You want to do something with what I say in order to make yourself more money. It is *you* who are interested in making money, not I."

Talk about feeling small! I could have slid under the door. So maybe I did intend to use the information she gave me as research for my next book. And so maybe I was sitting there sneering. Had she been someone else, I would have paid her for helping me research, but because she had been branded a charlatan by society (before she'd ever been tried) I was being, at the very least, unprofessional.

I took a breath and apologized. "Yes," I said. "You're right. I am always looking for new material for my books." I relaxed a bit and asked her a few questions about her most interesting clients. She wouldn't tell me a word. Nothing about them.

"If you want to know what I do and how I work we should look at you. I believe your problem is in your past lives."

I had to bite my tongue to keep from laughing. People don't believe in past lives, didn't she know that? As my head whirled with things that were wrong with all of this, the clearest thought was something my beloved and brilliant editor said to me once: *It doesn't matter if it's true or not, it's a great story.*

Past lives, I thought. Two people in love, then great tragedy, then meeting again and again. Great romance! Great story! Jamie and I could — No, I mean, Jamie and my heroine could —

Suddenly I saw my whole problem as "not having a plot for my book." It wasn't that I was obsessed with a paper hero, it was that I needed something new and different to write about. What better than past lives?

So I gave Nora a check for a couple hundred bucks, chalking it up as money well spent for research purposes, made a whole week's worth of future appointments with her, then went home to have a gin and tonic to celebrate.

Already I was envisioning the *New York Times* best-sellers list and trying to come up with titles.

But that night I didn't celebrate. Instead I found myself staring out the window at the glass-fronted high-rises around my apartment, as usual, Verdi's (now *there's* a man who went to heaven) *La Traviata* wafting through the air and thinking about what Nora had said.

People are always concerned with appearances; they believe what they see. If you walk into a lawyer's office wearing a Chanel jacket you can be guaranteed that she's going to double her hourly fee. If you go to a writer's conference and people see the hype about you — nineteen *New York Times* best-sellers in a row — they think, Oh, wow, she's the happiest person in the world. If only I could achieve her success all my problems would be solved.

How I wished it worked like that. How I wish that old saying about laughing all the way to the bank was true. Most people believe that enormous wealth would solve all their problems, but at the same time they avidly read stories about the miseries of rich people.

But I knew what was missing beneath the surface of my life. I have a great career; with proper application of cosmetics I'm even pretty, and thanks to thousands of hours in the gym, I'm thin. I'm everything the books say I should be if I want to be happy. I can validate myself with the best of them. I know how to do things for myself, take care of myself. I give myself treats and praise.

As for men, I can hold my own with any of them. No little-girl games for me. I tell a man exactly what I want when I want it.

I have made myself into the heroine of a self-help book. I am what women who read self-help books want to become.

So what is wrong with me? Why aren't I happy?

And, more important, why did I let a great guy like Steve go? How could I have let a man like him slip through my fingers? He was so wonderful that another woman snatched him away from me while he was still warm from my bed.

Yet, sometimes, I look back on Steve and think that he was a little too perfect and the two of us together were a little too perfect. We were like a couple out of a magazine article that described what a relationship *should* be like.

Sometimes I felt that what I really wanted was a man like, well, like Jamie. If Jamie had awakened and found me ignoring him at my computer, he wouldn't have been understanding, he would have demanded my attention.

Sometimes I think my problem is laziness. Steve and I used to work out together, we were faithful to our trips to the gym, considering it a religion to keep ourselves in tiptop shape. Up until forty it's been almost easy to maintain my looks and my health, but now there's a part of me that just wants to give up. Am I going to have to deny myself chocolate cake for the rest of my life in a doomed-to-failure attempt to keep my thighs looking like a twenty-three-year-old's? When do you get to rest from being inspected by a man to see how you compare to centerfolds?

For many years I was contemptuous of my parents' marriage. It was so boring. I wanted excitement and romance. I wanted a man who was a great lover, a great friend, someone powerful in the world of business.

But now I remember my father handing my plump mother a piece of pie à la mode and her saying, "I can't eat that. I'll get fat." Then my father would wiggle his eyebrows and say in a lascivious tone, "Yeah, fat." Then they'd giggle together and my mother would eat her pie and ice cream.

Back then the whole scene was disgusting to me. And the fact that my parents had been married twenty some years, my mother was about fifty pounds overweight, and yet they were still giggling, made me further sick.

Now the scene doesn't make me feel ill. Remembering it makes me want to weep. Where's the man in my life telling me I'm beautiful even though I'm overweight and my eyes have a thousand tiny lines around them? Where's that boring man coming home to me every night and asking what's for dinner? Where are those kids yelling, "Mom, did you iron my blouse for me?" and "Mom, guess what we did today?"

All in all I know I'm very lucky. I have my writing, which is even more satisfying to me than

I could have ever imagined. I have friends and colleagues who I respect and admire and love. I have a good life, in many ways a successful life.

But, success or no success, it all comes down to the same thing: I am nearly forty years old and there is no love in my life.

Only, no one knows that. To the world I am a spunky, give-'em-hell woman who writes about give-'em-hell heroines who find fabulous men to love them *forever*. In my books my heroines say rude, cutting, even emasculating things to a man, yet he knows she's the one for him. He not only comes back for more, he proves to her that he's worthy of her.

But nothing like that has happened to me. Today it seems that men have the choice of any woman in the world, so you have to be nice, nice, nice to them. One wrong move and they will leave. There no longer seem to be people saying to each other, "I will love you even if you get fat, even if you become obsessed with a book, even if you ignore me for months at a time."

Men no longer seem to have to make any effort to win *you* because there are so very many available women out there. So here I am, I've proven to myself and to the world that I can do anything: earn money, manage money, live alone. I'm utterly independent.

But somewhere along the way, I had messed up, and now I was alone.

What was it Nora had said? "You want a Grand Passion. A Great Romance. You want the stars and the moon."

Yes, I thought. I would like that. I'd like to live out one of my romance novels with all the fireworks and magnificent sex. Maybe I wanted a man who was so magnetic, so, I don't know, so powerful that I just plain couldn't fall in love with anyone else, not a real man and certainly not one on paper.

I finished my gin and tonic and kept looking out the window and after a while I began thinking, Maybe my readers are feeling the same as I am. Maybe they're about to hit forty and feel Passion and Romance have passed them by. Or maybe they're twenty-five and married with two kids and are wondering if this is all there is to life.

Whatever, maybe they'd like to read a story about a woman who delves into her past lives in an attempt to find out what's wrong with this life. When I went to bed, I felt good about my next day's appointment with Nora. I felt that a whole new area of exploration was opening up to me.

But whatever I did, I knew that getting my mind away from both Jamie and Steve would be the best thing for me.

3

"You can't be happy in this life because of what happened in your past lives."

Those were the first words Nora said to me when I entered her office the next day. Nice antique reproduction furniture and not a crystal in sight.

I took the seat opposite her. She didn't look so good today. Her eyes, the day before the size of saucers, were sunken into her head and were ringed with black. There was a definite slump in her shoulders.

"What happened in my past lives?" I asked.

"I don't know."

At that statement I wanted to take her by her shoulders and shake her. But then I reminded myself that none of this was true so there was no reason for my anger. On the other hand . . .

"What do you mean, you don't know?"

"Everyone has many lives and it is difficult to find the specific lives that are causing trouble."

"Oh," I said. "So last night you flipped back

through my lives, rather like going through a deck of cards, but you couldn't find the one or ones that have the Great Passion in them."

"Right," she said tiredly.

Obviously this whole concept of past lives was not as fascinating to her as it was to me. "Mind sharing a few cards with me? I bet I would recognize Great Passion if I saw it." I was doing my best not to jump up and say, "Tell me, tell me, tell me and tell me *now!*"

She peeped at me through the fingers she was rubbing her eyes with, and I felt that she knew very well that I was excited — and she was enjoying my anticipation as much as an actor loves the moments before the curtain goes up. Vain, I thought, using my unpsychic powers of observation. She's quite proud of her talent and loves making people drag things out of her.

"Which life do you want to know about?" she asked.

I sent her my thoughts on that remark and managed to make her smile.

"You have written before, in France."

"Who? What was her name?" Visions of a biography (autobiography?) danced through my head. Also, the horrors of trying to learn to read French.

Nora waved her hand in dismissal. "I don't know. She doesn't matter. Your karma lies with the man."

Karma — I thought but didn't ask Nora to explain this word, but later I looked it up. Karma is: You get what you deserve. The theory is that if you hurt people in one life you'll be hurt in the next one. I think this is also a law of physics — for every action there is an equal reaction. Also in the Bible: Whatsoever ye sow, so shall ye reap. In fact, I think the law of karma just might be everywhere in lots of different forms.

Nora was going on and telling me more about my lives: one in Vienna (very unhappy), several in England, a bad one in Italy.

She said, "You have a friend now . . ."

I was still smarting over her remarks yesterday about my life of no love so I rattled off about twenty names of people I considered my friends.

Nora gave me a look of disgust, letting me know that I couldn't bamboozle *her*. "You have only two real friends."

"Yes," I answered, trying not to blush in embarrassment at being caught being a snob. Daria, young gorgeous legs that started at her earlobes, men drooling over her. And Milly, an overweight romance writer I'd met years ago, not pretty, not sexy, unmarried, only thirty-five but looking fifty, with a heart as big as the earth.

"Yes," I said, "I have two friends: Daria and Milly."

"You have known them many times. They are your true friends and they wish you only happiness."

"I take it this isn't usually the case."

A look of profound disgust crossed Nora's face, letting me know of the awful things she usually

46

saw in people's heads. I can hardly stand to look inside my own head, much less anyone else's. What filth must lurk inside a child molester's mind?

"What were these women to me in the past?" I asked.

"The young one designed something for you. I don't know what, and the older one was . . . I believe she was your mother yet not your mother."

Nice, concise, pinpoint information telling me absolutely nothing, I thought. I tried to encourage her. "Wasn't I ever a gunslinger's girl? A real femme fatale or some sultry singer in a bar? Something . . . I don't know, something very different from what I am now."

"No," Nora said, then proceeded to tell me about the "rules" of past lives.

Pardon me, I hadn't reconciled myself to the idea of there *being* past lives, much less to the idea of "rules."

Nora explained to me about character. Character — or as we often call it, personality — doesn't change. What you are now is what you've always been. At least in terms of character.

If in this life you're a stay-at-home, then you were a stay-at-home in the past. Mousy little women were *not* flamboyant seductresses in a past life, no matter what charlatans may try to make you believe. She also said that talents you have in this life may have been developed in another life (in that case I have *never* played the piano).

Countries you want to visit may be places where you had a happy life. Your style of dress, the furniture you like, pretty much your taste in everything is influenced by your past lives.

She went on to tell me that what a person likes to read and, in my case, write, are often based on past lives.

I interrupted at this. "Is this why I write books set in the Middle Ages with such ease? And why I hate pirate books and books about Vikings? And why I love just about everything Edwardian?"

Nora's answer was, "Probably." She'd have to "see" more about where I had and had not been before she could answer for sure. Personally, I wasn't sure a person could be "sure" about something that may not exist.

She went on to say that tastes and sounds and smells were very strong senses and they remained with you throughout time.

"For instance," Nora said, "there are certain smells that make you ill. People's bad breath, I believe."

She really *had* been snooping! But she was right and I'd never told anyone this in my life. When I am confined with a person with very bad breath I become quite ill.

"And there is an animal you like."

"Dogs?" I do like dogs but I don't have one.

"No," Nora said, concentrating, her eyes boring into mine. "An animal from the jungle."

"I had a boyfriend once who in Chinese astrology was a tiger," I said helpfully.

She didn't smile but then looked up in recognition. "You eat off the animal."

I did some quick — and imaginative — thinking at that one. Then I smiled. "Monkeys!"

"Yes," she answered, smiling back at me.

I've never figured out why I love monkeys. I have monkey candlestick holders, dishes, lamps, potpourri holders, et cetera, all over my apartment. It's not enough that people say, "Wow! You sure like monkeys, don't you?" when they walk into my apartment, but a few people know and give me gifts now and then, thereby making my collection grow.

"What else?" I asked eagerly. "Where did I live? What did I do?" I think I forgot about whether this was real or not. My hands were dying to get hold of a research book. I'd write an in-depth biography of someone, something I'd always wanted to do but I'd have greater insight because the character would be me. I guess. Sort of.

She frowned in thought. "What is the name of that jeweler you like so much?"

"Cartier? Tiffany? Harry Winston?" I could have added to that list all day.

"No," she said, annoyed. "The jeweler you really like."

I really like Cartier, I thought, but decided to, for once, forgo the sarcasm as I tried to think if there was a special jeweler in my life. As far as I was concerned, all of them were special.

"Oh," I said after a moment. "Fabergé."

"Yes." She didn't say so but I could tell she was proud of me. It must be reassuring to someone like her to find that we mere mortals can sometimes use our one-dimensional brains to advantage. "If you will read about that jeweler you will recognize yourself."

Another one of her why-the-sun-loves-the-moon statements. Personally, I'd prefer a name and date, but I could see that "Fabergé" was all I was going to get out of her.

We were out of time by then so I bid Nora good-bye and immediately caught a taxi downtown to the Strand. This place is billed as the largest used bookstore in the world, but it could also win the titles of dirtiest, rudest, and strangest check-out personnel. One day at the Strand I, as an amateur costume historian, became so fascinated with the rings in the nose, lip, and cheek of the young woman ringing up my books that she had to ask me four times for my charge card.

But whatever else the Strand is, it's a great place to buy out-of-print books. I bought a copy of each book they had on Fabergé, grabbed a cab, went through ten minutes of explaining my address to the non-English-speaking driver (while the meter was running of course) and got back to my apartment pronto.

For all that reviewers think romance novelists are worthless, one thing we learn to do is research. Heaven help us, we have to be good because our readers have memories that would make a computer data bank weep with envy. One screwup and they write you about it. I don't just mean dates, I mean things like scissors. Readers will write you that you had your heroine using scissors before scissors were invented. You can't have a hero say "Wait a minute" until after clocks were in common use. And food! *Don't* make errors with tomatoes and potatoes or you'll hear from them.

Of course these are the same women the reviewers and the general public think have the intelligence of carrots and the mental stability of Sybil.

Anyway, if there's one thing I can do it's research. My eyes and fingers can flip through a book with a key word in mind and find just what I need in seconds flat.

Twenty minutes after dumping my old/new, very dirty books on the living room rug, with the Jasmine song from *Lakme* surrounding me, I'd found her.

There were five women who were responsible for Fabergé's success. Two were Russian. No, that wasn't me. I've never felt any sense of recognition while plowing through *War and Peace*. I can't even make it through the movie. One woman was American and very rich. I liked this idea but then I read that she was a great philanthropist, opened charity hospitals, did lots of good for others. Unfortunately, this is *not* me. I put all my money into securities and hold on to every penny.

One woman was the Princess of Wales, later

Queen Alexandria. I'd already done too much research to believe she and I could have the same character. Alix was beautiful but not very bright and retaliated against her philandering husband by being late at every opportunity. Not my style.

The last name on the list sent a chill up my spine. Lady de Grey. Years ago I avidly watched the series on *Masterpiece Theatre* about Lillie Langtry, and all through it I was fascinated by her friend Lady de Grey. I even bought a few books on the Jersey Lil to try to find out more about this woman, but there was nothing more than a few sentences.

Just liking the name wasn't enough to make me think I was the reincarnation of this woman. In the index of one of the Fabergé books I found another page with a reference to Lady de Grey.

Here I found a little story about how all the society ladies hounded Fabergé to make more and more articles for them, never allowing him to sleep or eat.

"But none of them was worse than Lady de Grey," the author wrote. "She was an utterly charming and brilliant young woman, but when she set her mind to something nothing on earth could stop her. One evening when Lady de Grey entered the shop at dinnertime, Fabergé tried to escape out the back but her ladyship had a second sense about people and she caught him. Between her charm, her humor and her indomitable will, Fabergé knew he'd not be going home to dinner that night."

That description was so close to home that reading it left me feeling a little queasy. I sure liked the "brilliant" part but I could do without the "indomitable will." It reminded me just an itty bit too much of all the things my mother said to me when I was a kid.

But then I reminded myself that none of this was real and that there weren't past lives, so it didn't matter if this woman did have an "indomitable will." Nothing to do with me.

The index listed a photo credit of a piece of art owned by Lady de Grey. Frowning, annoyed at this whole character-stays-the-same garbage, I turned to the color photo.

There, on plate XVIII, was a picture of a beautiful jade carving of a sweet-faced little monkey.

I fell back onto the carpet and said out loud, "What have you stuck your nose into this time?"

4

The next day at 2 A.M. Nora called and told me that she had to leave town immediately. She didn't seem to think that two o'clock in the morning was an odd time to call so I didn't point it out. Even though she looked quite normal, she did live in a world of past lives and "reading thoughts" so I guess she was allowed a few idiosyncrasies.

Even though I was two-thirds asleep, I remembered to ask whether her trip was personal or business. There was a long silence on the end of the line and I knew I had overstepped the bounds of nosiness. However, this did not make me backtrack. Cowards never learn anything interesting they can use in a book.

After a while, she said, "It is business." My head filled with questions. What in the world could be "urgent" to a clairvoyant? A ghost of a former self hanging around the bedroom? A former lover come back to get you? Maybe a man about to kill a woman he'd already killed in a past life.

At these thoughts I was beginning to wake up and maybe Nora sensed it because she was off the phone in a flash.

I lay awake for a while and thought about what a clairvoyant could possibly see and started thinking about a plot in which I had a heroine who could read minds. I wonder what she would see in Jamie's mind, I thought. Would she be the blushing kind when she saw what was making his eyes so hot? Or would she say, "How dare you?" Or would she be like I would be if *I* saw Jamie? I'd put my hand to my forehead, say, "Take me, I'm yours," then swoon gracefully into his strong, masculine arms.

After that I decided to get out of bed and cool myself off. Better not watch late-night cable shows or I'd never get to sleep. In the end, I had a tiny glass of my favorite liqueur, Mandarine Napoleon, and wrote a truly hot sex scene for the book about Jamie — you know, the one for which I still didn't have a plot.

The next morning I went to the library to see what I could find out about myself, er, Lady de Grey.

Due to my superior ferreting abilities, I was able to find her in no time flat. In my mind, researching is so easy. I think where people go wrong is that they think of history in terms of the boring stuff they had to learn in school. Specifically, I mean wars. It seems that in school, history means wars and nothing else. You don't even hear about the time between wars. Who knows what happened between World War I and World War II? Maybe you heard about economics but certainly nothing else.

I have written several million words, all set in historical time periods and I know nothing about wars. I have a rule in researching: Don't read anything that isn't interesting. I figure that if it isn't interesting to me to read about, it won't be interesting to write about and therefore my reader will be bored.

So when I research I read about the good stuff. I read about clothes and food and how people thought about things. How did they treat their kids? How were women treated? Those sorts of things.

To find this information, I never read encyclopedias or those books with three hundred biographies in one volume. I like specific books, such as books about eyeglasses or the history of dentistry. I own over four hundred books on the history of costume, with all of them cataloged and cross-referenced so I can find things. I truly hate reading a novel in which the author says, "Lady Daphne was wearing the very latest fashion." *What* was the latest fashion? Was it a color or a sleeve shape or a new type of hat? I want to know.

One of my favorite authors, Nora Lofts, once said in an interview that people really want to know two things about a time period: how people earned their money and how they went to the bathroom. I have tried to follow that advice and put those things into my books in a subtle and relatively tasteful way. One time I laughed hard at a "medieval" book in which the idiot author thought the garderobe was a closet. Readers know that it was the toilet, but this dumb author kept having people sitting on the floor and discussing things. Very funny scenes actually.

Anyway, I had learned how to research long ago. Go for the specific, not the general. I headed straight for the genealogy room at the New York Public Library and had them hand me their oldest copy of *Burke's Peerage*. Unfortunately, the New York Library has so much thievery, they can't allow open stacks, so I try to use what I can find in the least amount of time.

It took about five minutes to find her. Rachel de Grey, died 1903. That would be about right for Fabergé. Her husband was the third Earl de Grey and the first Marquess of Ramsden.

I wrote down the tiny bit of information from that book, then hit the humongous card catalog in the library, all of it in difficult-to-read black books. Right away I found a book about the first Marquess of Ramsden. With my breath held, I turned the request card into the desk. Always, working at the New York Library is like skeet shooting because half the books have been stolen or "misplaced."

Thirty minutes later, my number was placed on the board and I had the book. Minutes later I had found the two references to the man's wife in the entire book. After all, how important can a man's wife be? All she has to do is be there for him whenever he fails, then tell him he's the best in the world so he has the courage to continue. Hasn't anyone yet realized that there's a reason single men are rarely ever a success?

Anyway, I was so very pleased to read what the author had written about me . . . her, that I soon forgave him.

"Lady de Grey, despite her delicate health, was the most helpful of helpmates. Her sweet and buoyant temper completely matched that of her husband, and from the day of their marriage their life was one long honeymoon."

Now that's more like it! I thought. None of this indomitable will garbage. If this was what finding out about past lives was like, then I should have done this sooner.

I went on to read that Rachel and her husband were married for thirty-five years and had two sons; one died while in Turkey (set upon by brigands) and the other was named Adam and inherited the title. I spent the afternoon reading about "my" husband, lapping up every word it said about his dear, sweet wife who helped him every step of the way. When my — her — son died, she erected a beautiful chapel in his memory.

By the time the library closed, my head was whirling with hunger and lovely facts. I fairly floated out of the library. Rachel had found the right man for her; she'd found her Jamie. And when she did, she was his faithful, constant companion for thirty-five years, inspiring love wher-

58

ever she went with her gracious manners and her retiring attitude.

By the time Nora returned to the city the following week, I was swollen with pride in myself at my unparalleled ability to find anything that was buried in a library. And I was smug at having lived such a wholesome, good life. I was so full of myself that it was a wonder I could get through the door of Nora's office. I was willing to bet that she'd never had a client who could find out so much so fast.

With all the arrogance I felt, I placed photocopy after photocopy on her lap. I even had a photo of this lovely lady. I'd made an intricate chart of dates, dressed it up with lots of different fonts to show off my skill with a computer, and I handed this to Nora with a flourish as I told her everything I had found out about myself.

Nora sat there and looked at me, blinking for a few moments. Then she nearly sent me into a rage worthy of one of my heroines because she started laughing at me. That's right. She *laughed* at me.

She didn't have to tell me why she was laughing because I knew. It was the same laugh my mother used after I'd promised her that I'd behave myself and not get into trouble. I used to promise not to open my mouth and give my opinions on things. I promised to "act like a lady." I promised all sorts of things but I never seemed able to keep my promises. Life was so very exciting and I wanted to participate and people who participate

59

in life cannot "act like a lady."

"You don't think this is me?" I said meekly, thinking how unfair this was. Every person I'd ever heard of who'd had her past lives done always came out as someone exciting. My current life was quite exciting enough, thank you. What I wanted was to read that at some time in the past I had loved a man for thirty-five whole years, that we'd had a life that was one long honeymoon.

Already, I was getting used to Nora reading my thoughts. "You have loved greatly in the past," she said gently, no longer laughing at me because she could sense that I was truly hurt. "But you are not a woman who . . ." She hesitated.

"A woman who stands quietly in the background," I said, feeling as though there was no hope. What was wrong with wanting to be the kind of person who everyone liked?

I no longer felt full of ego and pride. "What's wrong with me?" I asked. "I write love stories for a living. It seems that love is all I ever wanted out of life. Most people who meet me think I'm hard and cynical but I'm not. I just want what other women have but something is wrong with me." There were tears at the back of my eyes and I realized that I was being more honest with this woman than with any other person in my life. "Something is wrong with me. I'm defective or something. I seem to be different from everyone else. I had a wonderful man who was in love with me. He was perfect yet I just threw him away. I let him walk out of my life and

60

now I have no one. Just a man on paper. A man who doesn't exist."

The tears started coming then, great drops of self-pity, and Nora waited while I got myself together before she spoke.

"In the past," she said softly, "you loved a man very, very much. You loved him so hard that throughout time you have not been able to forget that love. No other man lives up to the love you had for him, so when you meet a man who you could love, you push him away because you still love this man from your past."

I blew my nose. "Fat lot of good that does me when I climb into an empty bed at night."

Nora smiled at me but said nothing.

I sniffed and my brain started working again. "If I still love him, how does he feel about me?"

"He loves you as much as you love him."

There were so many thoughts in my head that my tongue got tangled trying to get them all out. "You mean that somewhere out there is a man who loves me just as much as I love him and it's all based on our past lives? Is he looking for me? How do I find him? Is he turning down other women while he waits for me? What do I do?"

Nora's face had a sad expression on it. "I have told you."

I am a can-do type person, not one of those acceptance people. I never believe that a person has to accept what is; if you don't like it, you should do your best to change it. But I could see that Nora was an acceptance-type person.

I took a deep breath. "Can you give me more information about all of this? Maybe if I know more facts, I'll be able to understand more clearly." And then I can figure out what to *do* about this problem, I thought. If there was a man out there who was mine, a man who I just knew was the personification of Jamie, then I was going to do whatever I could to find him.

Nora smiled in a way that I found quite annoying, as though she knew what was in my head, as she started telling me about soul mates. At that term I groaned. If there was ever a more overused word in the world it was *soul mate*. It ranked right up there with my two most hated words in the world (right after *rewrite*): *utilize* and (gag!) *snuck*. I'd like to erase both of those words from the face of the world.

Anyway, after nearly an hour of back and forth, I think I got the hang of what a soul mate is in psychic terms.

Question: What is a soul mate?

Answer: It's one of those words some Californian out promoting a book made up. Like *lifestyles*. As in, one brainless actor says to an adoring interviewer: "My lifestyle includes my soul mate, Bambi." Three weeks later, of course, they're divorced.

In psychic terms a soul mate is the other half of you. Remember in the Bible where it says God made Adam, then took a rib and made Eve? According to Nora that's how all the first souls

62

were made: one spirit split in half, one male, one female. The very first clones, so to speak. I guess it's true that there's nothing new under the sun.

The theory is that the person is your *perfect* mate. You can be happy with other people but no one is quite like this person. Your soul mate "fulfills your spirit," as she says.

In theory soul mates should be together every lifetime, but over the centuries things get messed up. Schedules get out of sync. Boys get killed more often than girls. A couple of soul mates are born living next door to each other in Greece, but he falls off a horse and breaks his neck when he's eighteen; she lives to be eighty. After he's dead he's reborn as a Roman gladiator, which makes her old enough to be his mother, as well as their now being quite far apart. So about a hundred years later the time evens out and they're born living next door to each other again but the fathers have a falling out and won't let the kids-in-love marry. Etc. Etc.

You can see how soul mates get separated. I have trouble coordinating my Filofax with friends, so I can't imagine Heaven Control Center trying to get soul mates together over the centuries and around the world.

Considering the impossibility of all this, how do soul mates *ever* get together? It seems that being put with your other half is a great Gift from God. You have to: (1) *ask* for your soul mate; (2) *deserve* this person; (3) *accept* this person in whatever form he/she happens to be in at the moment.

Considering all this information, how do I personally come into this? According to Nora I have been praying to be given my soul mate for years. With a straight face I said, "Preferably gift wrapped in ribbon and left under the Christmas tree."

It had taken Nora a while to get the hang of my sense of humor, but we were beginning to spend a great deal of time together. She says that people who come to her are *very* serious. Considering that people come to her after they've given up on therapists and suicide counselors, I could see why they wouldn't be exactly a jolly little elf.

But I find humor everywhere and I didn't have to look very hard to see the idea of my praying for a soul mate as quite amusing. My mother impressed on me that good little girls prayed *only* for world peace.

Anyway, good girl aside, if I'd prayed for a soul mate I would have been afraid I'd receive some hairy LA guy who swore he was a producer and could make me a star. I assured Nora I had *not* been praying for a soul mate.

So here's where Nora shocked me. We always believe our minds are our own private territory, unassailable, but then a psychic comes along and tells you what you've been thinking and dreaming for the last three years.

She calls it praying but I prefer to call it wishing.

I have been *wishing* I could find *the* man who'd suit me more than any other man. I remember rather fiercely thinking, There must be one man for me. One man who is better than the others. A man I could love as hard as I wanted to love and he'd love me as much in return. I wanted a man I wouldn't have to play games with and pretend I didn't care when he hurt me. I wished for a man I could yell at yet he'd still love me. I wanted a man who made me feel *safe*. I wanted a man who I deep down inside *knew* loved me. Not because he told me he did but because I felt it, because just his existence made something deep within me vibrate.

Nora said that my books were blueprints for this man.

Nora told me all of this, making my face turn red at having my most private thoughts seen. People who knew me thought I was cynical; my sarcastic humor proved that. No one saw that inside I was mush.

What else Nora pointed out to me was that I'd said I'd take this man in any size, any shape.

It took me a while to remember what she meant. There was one night when I was all alone and I'd had a healthy gin and tonic that I remember with deep embarrassment. Sometimes loneliness and despair can drive a person to new lows. That night I "wished" very hard for this one man and I especially remember thinking that since I was a writer and could travel I'd take him from any country, any state of health, any anything.

So after Nora had told me all this and I felt that I understood it, I felt a little hope. Where was this soul mate of mine? How did I find him? Put an ad in the paper?

Unfortunately, once again, Nora gave me a look of despair. She told me my "spirit guides" had led me to come to her so she could tell me the bad news. Well, actually, Nora said it was good news. I was slated to be given my soul mate three lifetimes from now.

It was all I could do to keep from screaming. Did any part of this woman's brain live in the real world? There was no such thing as past lives and there sure as hell weren't any "spirit guides."

Her obstinacy, her unflappability made me grit my teeth. "I want Jamie and I want him in *this* lifetime," I said. "I am an American and I want instant gratification!"

She did laugh at that. "You could have him if you could change the past," she said, smiling. "But if you met him this afternoon you wouldn't love him, you'd hate him. You'd hate him at first sight. You'd hate him so much you would never want to see him again."

I just sat there as she told me that our time was up long ago and she had other clients coming. "Why don't you find the real Lady de Grey? There must have been more than one of them."

"Yes," I muttered, collecting my things and heading for the door. All of this wasn't real so I might as well do some more research. For all that Rachel de Grey was a nice lady, she wasn't heroine material. I needed to find a feisty woman who was a match for my Jamie.

I headed for the library, grabbing a hot dog from a street vendor on the way there. No more arrogance, I thought. This time the digging was for real.

5

Once I calmed down and conquered my own ego, I was able to see right away that Rachel couldn't have been the Fabergé Lady de Grey. Even in terms of personality, Rachel seemed too dedicated to her husband to truly care about perpetuating the art of a great man like Fabergé.

Okay, so now that I'd found out that Rachel wasn't "me" I could indulge in a little sour grapes. "My" Lady de Grey wasn't a frivolous woman who spent too much, she was a "patron of the arts."

Since the Lady de Grey I was looking for did not have the good fortune to be married to a famous man, she was quite difficult to find. It is a disgusting but true fact that women were fairly insignificant unless attached to the coattails of a man. On the other hand, to be fair, there were some famous women whose husbands are not remembered. But, to be even more fair and honest, most famous women never got married, so they didn't have to ask a man's permission to do whatever it was they wanted to do.

Anyway, my Lady de Grey was indeed difficult to find. Her name was Hortense but I couldn't find a birth date on her because in the Edwardian times it was considered impolite to tell a woman's age, even in a book on the family history. Personally, I wish a little of these manners could extend to the present age. Especially to *People* magazine. They are incapable of writing about anyone without putting the age of that person beside them, as though age were everything. (I began to hate this custom on the morning of my thirty-fifth birthday.)

When they announced the closing of the library, I was still searching for anything about her. All I could find were the basic facts. She had married Rachel's son, Adam, in 1904 and had died in 1907, four years after Rachel died.

According to the information I had found, both Hortense and her husband died on June 8, 1907, so I wondered if they had both been killed in an accident and made a note to look up the date of the sinking of the *Titanic*. After Adam's death, the title was retired, since there was no one to inherit.

By the time I got home, I felt sad. Writing romances and spending as much time as I do with my nose in history books, I know how important an heir is. As I listened to the divine voice of Frederica von Stade on the stereo, I thought of the great tragedy of this young earl and his countess not producing a son to carry on the family name.

I know this is absurd, but I began to feel guilty about this because I just knew it was *my* fault. I'd never told anyone this but about ten years ago I'd had a boyfriend who I'd thought was *the* one, so, feeling it was an okay thing to do, I'd not used any birth control for a whole year. I'd not become pregnant and I think that was a contributing factor in ending that almost-union.

Maybe if what Nora said was true and character did stay the same, I wonder if a woman stayed barren over the centuries? After all, she, Hortense, and her husband were married three whole years but had no kids. And it couldn't have been any problem with Adam. As every romance writer and reader knows, there are virile names and there are nonvirile names. There are even virile letters of the alphabet. There's a reason you aren't going to find too many heroes with names beginning with the letter *O. L* is also difficult. The best letters for heroes are *R, S,* and *T.* However, Adam and Alexander are good names, and every romance writer has at some time named her hero Nicholas.

Anyway, I knew that with a good virile name like Adam, it couldn't be his fault; it was Hortense's fault that the title had died out from the lack of an heir.

The next morning I was at the library early. During the night I'd had a brainstorm: If one of the other patrons of Fabergé was Queen Alexandra, maybe I could find my Lady de Grey in books about her.

All in all, I wish I'd never had such a good idea. I found Hortense in books on what was called the Marlborough Set. The house where the Prince of Wales lived, the man who was later to become Edward VII, was called Marlborough House, and the wild, fast people who frequented it were called the Marlborough Set.

Something that makes me crazy when dealing with people today, people who do not live eighty percent of their lives in the past as I do, is that when you say someone in the past was wild and fast, they smile smugly. Every generation thinks it is the one to have invented sex. Honest. This is true. People think their parents didn't know anything about sex "back then," so how in the world could people like the Victorians have known about sex? So what in the world could the Marlborough Set have done that was "wild," right?

I do wish I could, through my books, make people today understand that every generation has liked sex. Today the electricity goes out or there's a big snowstorm and nine months later the news reports that there's — ha ha — a big increase in the number of babies born.

So why hasn't anyone ever put two and two together and figured out *why* the people of the past had so damned many kids?

End of lecture, but the truth was, the Marlborough Set *was* fast. Every weekend they moved en masse to someone's huge country estate and the hostess had to put little cards on the doors of the rooms telling who was where. This is so lovers could find each other. There is one funny story of a jealous man mixing up the cards so a duke found himself in bed with his own wife! How did this story get round unless it was told by the two involved and why was it considered amusing unless everyone was going to bed with everyone else?

You can see that these people figured out what to do with themselves without a television to suck their brains out of their skulls. Instead of sitting in a dark theater and watching the latest Hollywood beauty undress for some Hollywood hunk, the Edwardian man lay in a bed in a candlelit room and watched his wife remove some eight layers of clothing. He got to see a body that no one else in the world had seen because, unlike women of today, the Edwardian female didn't dress in T-shirt and jeans. Also, he hadn't seen one centerfold to compare his wife to. He wouldn't even know that cellulite was something a woman should not have! Ah, the good ol' days.

As I read about the Marlborough Set, I found a few references to Lady de Grey and I began to become glad there weren't too many such mentions. It seems that in a fast set, Lady de Grey was the fastest. She had many, many affairs with other men, so many, in fact, that she was almost ostracized by the prince's set.

However, she wasn't ostracized because she'd gone to bed with lots of men, but because she'd broken the cardinal rule: No affairs until *after* the heir is born. It was believed that a man who owned a huge estate and had a title generations old had a right to know for sure that his eldest son was his. So after the man married some nubile eighteen-year-old, he took her to the country and did his best to impregnate her immediately. As soon as she was pregnant, he, of course, went back to town to have a good time. After the first kid was born, he went back to give her another one. After producing two children, then her ladyship was free to live her own life.

In Edwardian society, it was imperative that the first two children look like the woman's husband. After that it was a matter of endless speculation as to who the other children resembled.

One woman, in her memoirs, told how on her wedding day just before she was to be whisked off into society, her mother gave her one piece of advice: Never remark on who the younger children look like. Many years later this woman found out that her "uncle" Harry was actually her father.

It seems that Hortense had broken this rule and had started having affairs before she'd produced an heir. The only reason I could find for this transgression was that it was believed that she hated her husband. This, however, was not believed to have been any excuse for her actions.

I hated to admit it but reading this story made me feel quite depressed. Unfortunately, this did sound like me. What if my parents had forced me to marry a man I didn't like? I have never been one to play by anyone else's rules, and I know that if I am unhappy, I can do some awful things — none of which I am about to reveal to anyone. But I doubt very much if there's any thirty-nine-year-old woman who hasn't done one or two things that she'd rather not remember.

So Lady de Grey was married for three years to a man she didn't like and had lots of affairs. Was she trying to find love? Was she striking out in anger at people who'd forced her into this situation?

I would have to do more digging, but now it was time to see Nora again, so I gathered my things and left the library.

Nora had that hollow-eyed look that I was beginning to secretly (are there secrets you can keep from a psychic?) enjoy. It meant she had stayed up all night looking into her crystal ball or whatever trying to find out about my past lives. I tried to contain my eagerness as I waited for another installment of the story. This whole thing was like reading an enormous novel, a novel that I couldn't put down. The difference was that I couldn't just snuggle on the couch with a glass of lemonade and read it straight through. I was finding out things piece by piece, day by day.

"In Elizabethan times, many bad things happened to you and this man," Nora said.

"My soul mate?"

"Yes. Both of you committed suicide."

"Why?" Why is always important to a story.

Saying there was a murder holds no interest, but telling the emotions that led up to the murder holds people's attention — and in my case, pays the bills.

"You did not trust each other and there were curses involved."

"Curses? As in someone saying dirty words?" I wasn't being flippant. Whether or not to use bad language was a *big* issue in the romance world.

She didn't answer, just stared at me, waiting for me to understand.

"Oh. You mean those things like in a Sicilian movie? Or in really bad romance novels? Someone about to be hanged makes up a complex riddle that affects the next seven generations? That sort of thing?" From the look on Nora's face she'd not read a few thousand romances as I had.

I took a breath. "Are you saying that these two people, just before they killed themselves, cursed each other? Something like, May you never know happiness until a bald son marries a red-haired cat, then generations later there comes along some girl named Cat and . . ." I trailed off because obviously Nora had no idea what I was talking about. There are jokes that only other romance people truly appreciate.

"What were the curses?"

I knew what she was going to say before she answered. "I don't know."

I started to complain but then I guess specific words get lost over centuries. "So they didn't trust each other, cursed each other, then committed suicide?"

"Yes."

"And this is why today, hundreds of years later, I do something stupid like allow a great man like Steve to get away?"

Nora smiled at me, as though she knew some secret that I was trying to hide.

"What?!" I snapped, tired of trying to guess what she seemed to have found out about me.

"You didn't like this Steve. He bored you. You wanted to get married because you are afraid time is running out. You don't want to be alone any longer. You want a husband to grow old with." Her voice lowered. "You would like to have a child or two."

She did hit hard. When I went to therapists and talked for weeks about my parents and my parents, and well, uh, my parents, all I felt was that I was wasting money. But here this woman was telling me what even I didn't allow myself to look at. Yes, I was becoming afraid of my age and my rapidly disappearing youth. Yes, I was afraid of being alone. For years it had been enough to write books and be a great success, but now it wasn't enough. I was tired of validating myself. I wanted a great big, loud man hanging around and telling me I was the greatest.

And yes, I thought, Steve *had* bored me. Steve was perfect. That would have been great if *I* were perfect too, but I'm about as far from perfect as you can get. There were many days when I wanted to eat ice cream instead of going to the gym. There were days —

I didn't want to think of Steven anymore. He *was* a great guy and I knew it and thinking anything else was lying to myself. I treated him badly but I didn't know why. I couldn't imagine that Nora's medieval curses had much to do with it but *something* was wrong with me.

"I'm thirty-nine years old," I said, barely audible even to myself. "It's a little late to find a man and have kids. Men my age don't want infants — unless they're eighteen and wearing a bikini," I said, trying, as usual, to make a joke.

The way Nora looked at me made me sure she didn't foresee me as having kids. What was it she'd said? Your present is your future. I am as I'll always be, I thought. Alone with only a bunch of paper heroes to love me.

"Isn't there anything I can do? *Sure* you don't have a non-red-haired cousin or two who'd like a nice romance writer for a wife?"

Nora didn't smile. "I think he has cursed you to love no one but him." She looked at me very sadly, as though she were glad no one had put this curse on *her* head.

This startled me. "You mean that . . . I mean, assuming there is such a thing as past lives, that I have never loved anyone since the sixteenth century? That life after life I've been alone?"

"You have married and —"

"Kids?"

"Not many. You are not a fertile woman."

77

Gee, I thought. I think I'll go back to the therapist who told me I wanted to sleep with my father. At least she gave me some hope for the future. Nora didn't even give me hope for the *past*. "But I didn't love these husbands of mine?"

"Not the way you loved the man who is the other half of you. His spirit will not allow you to truly love anyone but him."

"And I've never seen him since the Elizabethan Age?"

"Oh yes," she said as though I'd missed the point. "Your jewelry lady was married to him. She —"

"What? Do you mean Lady de Grey was married to this man I love?"

"Yes."

"But as far as I can find out she and her husband hated each other."

"Love. Hate. It's the same thing."

Not in my book, I thought. I hated a guy I used to work with who was always trying to put his hands inside my clothing. I haven't yet ever hated anyone I loved.

"*Real* hatred," Nora said, "is the other side of the coin from love. Hate lasts centuries, just as love does."

"If we hated each other why did we get married?"

"Because you loved each other."

"Do you have any gin?"

She smiled. "Don't worry. Everything will work out soon."

"Soon. As in three lifetimes from now?"

"Yes. You see, you are writing about him, about this man on paper . . ."

She trailed off to let me supply a name.

"Jamie," I whispered. "Jamie is . . . is my soul mate?"

"Yes. He is just like you, isn't he? He is strong but not always sure of himself. And he needs you, does he not?"

"Yes." I didn't say another word or I might have started crying.

"You are beginning to forgive him for betraying you."

"*Did* he betray me?"

"You thought he did. You thought he did not love you as you loved him so you —"

"Killed myself."

"Yes."

"And then he killed himself too."

"On the same day, in the same hour."

I have never thought suicide pacts were romantic. The whole thing at Mayerling makes me ill. But if Nora were correct then I had been part of a suicide pact with a man I loved — and hated — enough to affect my life for the next four hundred years.

"So," I said, "let me see if I understand everything. I loved this man in the Middle Ages, but he may or may not have betrayed me, so I — we, killed ourselves out of . . . Out of love. Or was it out of hate? I seem to be confusing those two."

Nora shrugged to signify there was no difference.

"Okay, we died and since then we've had some chances to straighten things out but we've messed them up, so now, after four hundred years I'm starting to forgive him. Proof of this is that I've forgone a real live love for a man on paper who is the man I really love, who I will not see again until three lifetimes from now. Is this right?"

Nora smiled and said, "Yes."

"So, Nora, which one of us is crazy?"

We laughed together at that because the whole thing was really ridiculous. My throwing Steven over probably had more to do with something in my childhood than some lunacy that happened centuries ago.

In fact, I told myself, none of what Nora was telling me had anything to do with me. It was just a story, that's all, and I was paying her to help me research and that's all there was to it.

I said good-bye to Nora and went home.

6

The next morning there was part of me that said I should shelve this whole idea and write something else. Maybe a nice safe cowboy novel. Besides, I had to think of marketing. Maybe my readers weren't going to be interested in a past life book, and if there was one thing every publishing person knows, it's that you can't make a reader buy what she doesn't want to read. (I use a universal *she* here because eighty percent of all books are bought by women. Think about it: How many women do you know who read and how many men do you know who can pull themselves away from football and beer long enough to read a book?)

I thought all of this while I was getting dressed and heading for the library. Since I didn't have an appointment with Nora that day, I had many free hours ahead of me.

About one o'clock, I found what I needed. Lady de Grey's very best friend, Countess Dyan (*no coincidence that my best friend's name starts with a *D*, I'm sure), wrote her memoirs, making several references to Lady de Grey.

As I read the first tidbit, I almost stopped breathing. Lady de Grey was a major patron of the opera. She loved opera and had Nellie Melba and Caruso come to her house to sing at every opportunity. "For all that others pretended to like opera," Lady Dyan wrote, "Lady de Grey truly loved it. I think that if it were possible she would have listened to *La Traviata* while in the bath."

I slumped back in the wooden chair of the library reading room and let my breath out slowly. When I was fourteen years old, I received a portable radio for Christmas. I wanted it very much because I wanted to be in the know about who was who in the music world, that is, the world of something called the Top Forty. I wanted to walk around the halls of my high school snapping my fingers and knowing all the words of all the songs, just like the other kids did. I guess it was part of my lifelong attempt to conform.

But on the way to finding that Top Forty station, I heard a man sing and I was transfixed. I was transfixed until my horrid little brother (do little brothers come in any variety other than horrid?) started laughing at me and told me with much sneering that I was listening to, gag, gag, *opera*.

From that day forward I hid my love of opera and classical music as though I were secretly doing drugs. I practiced turning the dial to the Wacky

World of Whatever it was that I was supposed to like until I could do it with the speed of a Nintendo player.

Many years later I found out that some people think that enjoying opera music means that one is, well, I don't know, more intelligent or refined than other people or something. That seemed, to me, just as silly as people sneering and gagging at it. The truth was, I just plain old-fashioned *liked* it. I liked the music, the voices, I liked the passion in a story like *Carmen*. After all, opera is just a bunch of love stories set to divine music. To me, it's just another form of what I write.

An aside here: Isn't it ironic that romance writers are reviled for writing love stories, but set one to music and you're revered? But who am lowly I to question the superior intellect of reviewers?

So here I was reading that Lady de Grey loved opera. Loved it so much she wanted to hear it while she was in the bath. Imagine that!

As I continued to read Lady Dyan's book, I found other references to Lady de Grey. She was insatiably curious, loved to ask people questions and find out about them. She was as at home with the dust man as with the king. She had a great sense of humor and told the most amusing stories; people always wanted to sit next to her at dinner because she kept them laughing.

By the time I got to the end of the book I was shaking. If I'd ever seen myself on paper, I was seeing it.

I was about ready to shut the book when I noticed that there was an epilogue. I almost didn't read it because in my continuation of finding-myself-infinitely-fascinating I haven't said much about Lady Dyan. She had two sons, one of whom was a well-read and much-loved poet at an astonishingly young age. The other son had written a novel before he was twenty-one. Both of her sons were killed in World War I.

My best friend, Daria, once said that she had a theory that the problem with the aristocracy of England today was that all the best of their ancestors had been killed in World War I.

The epilogue had a paragraph at the end that said that many people had urged Lady Dyan not to mention Lady de Grey because of what had happened just before she disappeared. She was not someone she should comment on in her book. But Dyan wrote, "Lady de Grey was my friend, a truer friend no woman could have. She was the first to wear the dresses I designed for her and she came to me whenever I needed her. My fervent prayer is that her spirit does not haunt Peniman Manor as people say it does. I pray that she is at peace and is now in heaven looking after my sons until I get there. I stand by what I have said: She was my friend."

I don't know why this paragraph sent chills up my spine as it did. Maybe it was the idea of a ghost, I don't know. But I closed that book with a snap and got out of that library fast.

7

I spent that weekend closeted in my apartment. Usually, when I wrote a book I was at least somewhat detached from it. Oh, maybe I was "in love" with my hero and maybe I got very, very sad when the book was finished, but still, I knew it was a story and not real life.

But now I was getting mixed up. I couldn't seem to remember whether I was Lady de Grey or Hayden Lane. I sometimes couldn't remember whether Jamie was real or on paper.

The things Nora had told me hit me much harder than anything a therapist had ever said to me because there was so much truth in them. With every word I read about Lady de Grey I seemed to "remember" more. I seemed to remember the way Jamie turned his head. Was this something I had made up or was I "remembering" what he was really like?

By Monday I still wasn't in the mood to leave the apartment. In fact, I didn't seem to be in the mood to live. I didn't wash my hair; in fact

I didn't bother to dress. I sat in my bathrobe, ate quart after quart of frozen yogurt (in keeping with my illusion that this was "healthier" than ice cream) and watched TV.

An aside here: Why is it that I always seem to meet women who say, "I was so depressed that I ran five miles?" I could say, but don't, "I was so depressed that I lay on the couch for three days and ate a deep-fried side of beef accompanied by a vat of fries and six quarts of ice cream." When I get depressed I haven't the energy to stand up, much less run. All I can do is chew.

Anyway, I ate and watched daytime TV, specifically, American talk shows — which fascinate me like a cobra is fascinated by that moving flute. Why in the world anyone would want to parade their own hatreds and prejudices, not to mention their own peculiarities, before the entire country mystifies me. I sat through "Sisters Who Hate Sisters," then "Men Who Want to Be Women," then one about a man who took a life-size rubber doll with him everywhere and his daughters were embarrassed (the man, however, wasn't and showed the audience "Elaine's" entire wardrobe).

At 6 P.M., when my brain was pretty much sizzled, I saw a show about past life regression. It was about people who have been hypnotized so they can see who they were in past lives.

I sat on the edge of my seat during the whole show. I'd like to be able to say that I stopped eating but in reality I ate at double speed. Something Nora had said was haunting me. *You could have him if you could change the past.*

I was on the phone to Nora almost before I could swallow the last of the butter pecan yogurt, then had to try again and again to get through to her. I'd rather try to get the President of the United States on the phone than Nora. What kind of problems could people have that made them need a psychic so desperately? (Wisely, I did not look into my own situation in this thought.)

When I did get her, it took me only minutes to explain what I wanted to know. Under hypnosis, could I go back in time and *see* Jamie?

Her long silence made me so nervous that I started talking at about a hundred words a minute. I told her that I really needed to do this in order to write my book. I had so many questions: What caused Lady de Grey to disappear? Why did her husband die on the same day? Why didn't they have any children?

I rattled on and on, as much to myself as to her. In the midst of all the lunacy of what I had been learning in the past weeks I wanted to inject some logic. There was no such thing as past lives, of course, so no one could "go back," but if they could maybe I could do it for scientific research. Well, okay, maybe romance novels aren't exactly "scientific" but a good story is worth a lot, isn't it?

"You must not do this," Nora said at last.

"What? Do what?"

"You are too unhappy to return."

I swear this woman was going to make me crazy! "I'm not talking about 'returning.' I just want to hover around and see . . ." Jamie is what I wanted to say. To just look into his eyes. To see what it was like to look into the eyes of a man who was the other half of me. "I want to see what the Edwardian age was really like. I want —"

"If you go back you might want to remain there," Nora said. "You have nothing to pull you back to the present time."

"I have a book contract and due dates and a desk covered with bills that need to be paid," I said, joking.

But Nora didn't laugh. "You must not do this. You must promise me. It is dangerous."

"But there's a possibility that she's a *ghost!*"

"Ghosts are very unhappy spirits and you are not the one to deal with them," she said sternly.

Thirty-nine years old and I started whining. "But I saw a talk show on TV and lots of people have done it. It's ordinary. In California —"

"*You* are not ordinary," she said with quite a bit of spirit. "What has happened to you in the past is not ordinary."

She took a breath and calmed herself, and secretly I was a bit glad she'd lost her cool. "Hayden," she said, "I know you do not believe me when I tell you these things about karma and curses, but they are true. You must let nature take its course."

"I'm to wait three lifetimes until I get to see

88

Jamie, is that it? I'm to spend this life and the next and the next alone without him?" There are times when sanity plays no part in one's life and this was one of them. I was like a child begging its mother for a piece of candy. I want Jamie and I want him *now!* is what I was demanding of her.

"Come in tomorrow and we'll talk. I'll explain things more fully to you then. Until then just rest and" — she paused — "and stop eating."

At that I stuck my tongue out at the telephone and hung up. There should be rules to govern psychics; they would be allowed to look in some areas of your life but not in others. Eating habits would be definitely off limits.

Ill manners aside, I didn't feel any better than I had before I talked to her. However, I did decide she was right about the eating. I decided to make myself a salad. I took down my largest serving bowl then cleaned out the refrigerator, adding high-calorie Chinese sesame noodles to the bowl along with enough lettuce to feed a couple of rabbits. Nuts and tiny pieces of fried bread added to flavor, then I smothered it all with half a bottle of dressing.

If I didn't do something to break this mood soon I was going to have a bit of a weight problem I thought as I dug in and went back to the TV.

I think everything would have been all right, that is, I would have obeyed Nora, except for two things happening. One was that I tripped over a book and the other was that Milly called.

I can assure you that if you are near me, tripping over a book is a given. I own thousands, and I mean that literally, thousands of books. They are everywhere: on shelves, tables, on the floor, under tables. Everywhere. For the most part, people are horrified by the number of books scattered around me. Except for Daria. When Daria comes to visit, I have to straighten up or she'll spend all her time rummaging through my books and pay no attention to me.

So, anyway, tripping over a book that caught on my bathrobe was nothing unusual. But when I picked it up I saw that it was a book I'd bought years before in a town in Wales that, in an effort to bring in tourists, gave itself the title of Most Bookstores in the World. I'm sure that slogan would draw tourists in America, right?

The book was an 1898 copy of Debrett's *Peerage*.

So far I hadn't been able to find out too many details about Lady de Grey's husband and his family — or her family for that matter — because the title had become extinct. But in 1898 it was still active.

Eagerly, I tore through the book to find the family title. Sometimes Debrett's told how people died; they frequently gave dates that other books didn't. Maybe in here I'd learn some truly useful information.

What I found was not what I'd expected. What I found just about knocked the wind out of me.

Right there in black and white, on page 645 was something that shocked me. But it was shocking only to me.

Lady de Grey's husband's full name was Adam Tavistock, Lord de Grey.

8

What happened after that was all Milly's fault. She, along with ninety-nine percent of all romance writers, lives somewhere in Texas. I say "somewhere" because I figure life is too short to try to comprehend Texas. When I want to go to Texas for some romance writers get-together I call my publicist and she sends me a ticket. I get on a plane and land somewhere in Texas. There are only two cities in the state: one called Houston and one called Dallas. One city has a mall called the Galleria and one doesn't.

Basically, I'm not sure where Milly lives. It's outside the city that does *not* have *the* mall, which I'm sure is why I met her in the first place. Otherwise I would have been shopping.

Nora said that in a past life Milly was and was not my mother. I can believe it. On our passports, I'm older than Milly but she is what Nora calls an "old soul." She lives alone and writes the sweetest, gentlest romances you can imagine.

Her heroines are noble and good and live on farms and enter pies in the county fair, as opposed to my heroines who ride black stallions and wave swords around.

I called Milly and started telling her what was going on in my life. My two friends, Daria and Milly, are so different. Daria has a lightning-quick brain and the attention span of a three-year-old. To make her laugh you have to be genuinely original, with a fast and perfect delivery. Anything less bores her. Daria keeps you on your toes.

Milly's more the let's-make-cookies-and-talk-about-it type. So that night after I found out that my "soul mate" had the same name as all the divine men I've written books about, Milly suggested I come visit her in her Texas city.

A few days later I went to Milly's house. That's when she told me she'd invited a few friends to dinner. I must say I was a bit hurt by this because I wanted Milly's undivided attention to listen to *my* problems about *my* life and *my* book. I'm ashamed to say that Milly's limitless kindness always brings out my most selfish side. Unfortunately, shame doesn't stop selfishness (I'd learned that on *Oprah*).

However, I did cheer up a bit when Milly told me that she'd invited to dinner a man who does past life regressions.

Have you ever done something in your life that you *know* is wrong before you do it yet you still can't stop yourself?

I hadn't told Milly all of my story; in fact I'd told her very little in the few days it had taken to arrange my trip to visit her. I'd sort of, well, left out the part about Nora. It was one thing to visit a psychic in private and hear all about soul mates and love that is actually hate, but it's another to say the words out loud in the light of day.

I'd sort of skirted the issue and told Milly a story about Jamie, then researching and finding this man named Tavistock, then seeing a past life regressionist on TV. I could have told the true story to Daria because she's more into entertainment than truth, but Milly believes anything anyone tells her.

But now I was going to be spending the evening with a hypnotist and there was no Nora around to tell me not to do this thing that I wanted to do so much. If I saw Jamie — I mean, Adam — I could warn him about . . . I don't know what I'd warn him about because I knew little more than the date of their deaths, but I knew that I'd love him. If I saw Jamie I would love him, not hate him as people said Hortense hated her husband.

While Milly and I waited for the man to arrive, I could hardly keep my mind on what she was talking about, which was contracts and money, of course, what *all* writers talk about. I kept looking at the door and thinking I heard the bell.

When he and three women finally did arrive,

I was beside myself with excitement and had to work to stay calm enough to eat dinner. I thought the meal would take forever and by the time we left the table I was ready to scream.

For the sake of brevity I'm going to forgo writing how I think New Yorkers and Texans are the same people but with different accents — it's why they hate each other.

Nora once told me that in order to be hypnotized all one had to do was *want* to go under. By the time Milly's regressionist got started I desperately *wanted* to see Jamie.

As I stretched out on the Victorian chaise in Milly's living room, the man, wearing jeans and cowboy boots, said, "Is there a special life you'd like to look at?" His eyes were twinkling in that way that let me know he knew something he'd sworn not to tell but couldn't resist letting me know he knew. Sweet, well-meaning, trusting Milly sometimes had a big mouth.

"There is . . ." I took a breath and bucked up my courage. "There is a man I want to see."

"Ah . . . ," he said in that smug, all-knowing, all-hateable way men have. They are all convinced that all a woman really wants in life is a man. I guess we women could prove them wrong by running the world without them, but then we'd be a world full of fat, hairy women and who wants to look at that?

I kept my mouth shut as I lay back on the chaise and thought how much I wanted to see *him.* I wanted to see Jamie. I wanted to see the real Tavistock.

As the man's voice lulled me into another world, I thought, I want to see . . . I want to see . . . Tally.

9

It was a delicious feeling, leaving my body behind and just floating. I'd read a lot about out-of-body experiences but they'd never really appealed to me before, but this did. No worries, no pain, no anger, just sort of drifting along.

I was pulled up short when suddenly there was a bright light and I found myself in a bedroom that looked liked something out of one of my books. Or maybe out of one of my dreams of heaven. It was English country decorating at its best: a four-poster bed dripping mossy green silk, walls covered with hand-painted Chinese wallpaper, and furniture that was new antiques — new where I was but old now.

I looked down because I seemed to be hovering up in a corner of the room and I had no body. I was just sort of energy. And I figured the less I thought of that the better. Think of it as a movie, I thought. You're not crazy, you're watching a movie.

There were three people in the room, all of

them with their backs to me. One was a maid dressed in a pretty little black dress with a white apron. She was silently and efficiently helping a woman standing in front of a long mirror into an Edwardian morning gown, something a lady put on before she put on the other six or so gowns she would wear that day.

To my right was a girl, about fifteen or so, her long chestnut hair hanging down her back, and wearing a cute little dress designed for a child of no more than about six. Truthfully, it was refreshing to see a teenager in something other than black leather and heels.

I wanted to absorb all that I could see. I wanted to soak it up, like getting into a tub filled with hot water and sweet-smelling oil.

But as I was looking at everything, trying to memorize it to use in my next book, the woman in front of the mirror turned and looked straight at me. I didn't think she could see me, because I didn't seem to be able to see myself, but she sure *felt* something.

I held my breath as she looked toward me and I looked at her. Can you imagine what you'd feel if you could see yourself in another time period? Wouldn't you be overwhelmed with curiosity?

I was.

In the books I'd read about the Marlborough House set, I'd read that Lady de Grey was a great beauty. But what that meant was that she was a beauty compared to the other society women. What about some shop girl who would have made it in a big way if the Edwardians had had high-fashion modeling and movie starlets?

All in all, I was disappointed with "myself." As a child I hated my looks. I am blonde to the point of being colorless and much to my mother's very vocal ill temper, I started wearing makeup at about age twelve. Just a bit at first but I gradually increased the amount until I would rather have been seen naked than without three shades of eye shadow, dark pencil, and lots of mascara. Now, I could see that "my" lashes had been darkened and there was a bit of color to this woman's lips but to my eyes her face was still too pale. Cindy Crawford had no worries.

Oh well, I thought, it wasn't any of my business. I was an observer and nothing else.

"Catherine?" I heard the girl say, "are you all right?"

"Yes," the woman who was maybe me whispered, but she kept looking toward where I was and I knew she felt me very strongly.

Where is Jamie? I wondered, because he was the one I really wanted to see. It was all well and good getting to see myself but now I wished she'd leave the room and go see *him*.

But no one looked as though she was going to move. The maid was staring at Catherine — I thought her name was Hortense — the girl was also looking at her, and Catherine was looking at me, but I couldn't be seen.

Then, suddenly, several things began to happen

at once. A few other people seemed to enter my head at the same time. First of all I could hear Milly's Texas hypnotist calling me to return.

"She's really under deep," I heard him say. "Hayden? Hayden? Can you hear me? Milly, why don't you call her to come back?"

I heard Milly's sweet voice entreating me to return, but there was something else in it that let me know that she wanted me to do whatever made me happy. If it had been Daria calling me I would have been back in that Texas living room in a flash. Daria would have said, "Where are your pages!?" and if that didn't work, she would have said, "Hayden, how about a new contract?" and then, for sure, I would have returned.

But instead, I heard Milly's voice and I felt no urgency to return. I had come to see Jamie and I meant to see him.

At the same time that I began to hear Milly and the Texan, I felt the oddest little pulling from the blonde woman, who was staring at me. I felt that this woman was asking me to help her. She seemed to be telling me that she needed me.

And there was something else. It took me a while to figure out the emotion I was feeling, but she was afraid of something — or someone.

Not this, I thought. Not someone needing help and being afraid. The combination is something I can't resist. For all that I try to keep my image of being strong and crusty, I am a sucker for the underdog. How many new, frightened authors have I taken under my wing, then gently kicked their behinds until they were asking for more money and more publicity from their publishing houses? (Daria got extremely annoyed with me once when I did this to one of *her* authors, so now I only do it to authors from other houses — much to the delight of my dear publisher, William Warren.)

Anyway, I could feel that this woman needed me, so I sort of allowed myself to drift toward her. After all, wouldn't it be great for my books for me to see what was inside the head of a real, live Edwardian woman?

I drifted and she pulled and I felt Milly's voice growing weaker.

And then it *happened!*

As best I can describe it, my mind merged with hers, and for those first seconds, it was heavenly. I wonder if this is how Nora feels, I thought as I looked into the woman's mind and felt all the rules and more rules that she had floating about in there. She had rules governing dress and deportment, names of rank and people, lots of information that means nothing to us today. Everything that was in the woman's head was very proper, which made me smile rather smugly.

But then I again sensed that fear. The woman was afraid of something but I had no idea what.

I had every intention of leaving her mind. Honest, I did. But one second I was myself even though — if this can be imagined — I was inside the head of another woman, and the next second the woman had retreated. She was still there, I could feel her, but now I was in the forefront. It was as though the captain of the ship had stepped aside and allowed the first mate to pilot the boat.

"No!" I managed to say, the word coming out of the woman's mouth, then I closed "her" eyes as I did my best to will myself out of her mind. I called to Milly with my mind, but she wasn't there. I had no more idea how to get out than I did about how I got in in the first place.

All I knew for sure was that I was in trouble.

When I opened my eyes I was standing in front of a mirror wearing a peach-colored dress so covered with froufrou it looked as though it had lost a duel between drunken cake decorators.

And instantly, I knew what had killed Lady de Grey. There was such a pain in my midsection that I could not breathe. With my eyes rolling back into my head, I grabbed my stomach and felt my knees give way under me.

"My lady!" I heard someone gasp just before everything went black before my eyes.

They woke me by putting under my nose a tiny bottle of some acrid stuff that could only be smelling salts. Now, I thought, if I were a true heroine I'd leap up and give everyone a lecture on the advances in modern medicine. But then, just what would a Harvard-educated 1994 doctor do to revive a lady who had just fainted from a too-tight corset? Biopsy something?

Anyway, I woke up, but due to the middle of me being squeezed until I had a waist that an ant would envy, I didn't leap up and disclaim anyone. In fact, well, it was rather nice having the two women and the avuncular gray-haired man hovering over me. Living alone as I do, when I'm ill all the TLC I get is from the delivery boy at the local grocery when he brings me a bag filled with oranges and tissues. So this solicitude was rather nice.

"There now," the man said in a tone that only a doctor could get away with. There are some things that even a century can't change. "I think you'll be all right now. You ladies do like to tighten your stays." He turned to the maid. "Next time see that you leave room for her to breathe."

The maid murmured a "Yes, sir," but I could see it was only to pacify him. And to think that men think there was a time when women did actually obey them.

"Are you all right?" the young girl on my other side asked as she leaned over me, holding my hand and looking at me as though concerned I might die.

"A little disoriented," I managed to say, then tried to sit up from where I was lounging on a brocade-covered fainting couch — and it seemed the piece was appropriately named.

"I think you'll be fine," the doctor said while he patted my hand as though I were a four-year-old. "Perhaps there's another reason for this fainting," he said, his eyes twinkling knowingly.

I didn't think he meant time travel so I just gave him what I hoped was a ladylike smile. The *last* thing I wanted to find out about Edwardian times was how a gynecological exam was carried out.

My smile must have satisfied him because he stood up, began rummaging in his monogrammed doctor's bag, then gave me the obligatory advice about rest and careful diet before leaving the room. Just like my doctor, I thought, except I would have to go to his office and he'd charge more.

Through all of this the maid was trying to look busy, fussing with clothes in a wardrobe, re-straightening silver-backed brushes on a dressing table, but I could see she was dying to find out why I had fainted. At least this told me Lady de Grey didn't faint often. Which to me meant that she was tough enough to have learned how to breathe while locked into an iron maiden.

Again, I tried to sit up, but it wasn't easy for this thing that was on under my clothes encased me from just below my breasts to my hips, and it was about as flexible as one of those old diving suits from a Jules Verne book.

"Leave us," the girl said to the maid, and there was authority in her voice.

Instantly, I was alone in the room with the girl, who was looking at me intently. Okay, Hayden, I thought, Now what?

"What has happened?" the girl asked. "You are different."

"Am I?" I asked, lying back and closing my

eyes so the girl couldn't see into them. I needed time alone to orient myself. Surreptitiously, I was trying to look about the sumptuous room. Perfectly polished silver ornaments winked from every surface in the room. Jeweled Fabergé trinkets filled a tall corner cabinet and I could see the little green jade monkey pictured in the book.

With a wince, I thought of my bedroom in New York with powder all over the top of my dressing table, Horchow Home catalogs falling off the dresser, a box of clothes I'd been meaning to send my sister in one corner.

"Catherine?" the girl said. "Are you all right?"

Turning, I gave the girl what I hoped was a wan smile. I'd better get this over with. As soon as I spoke, she was going to know I was an imposter. "I'm not feeling well," I said and for the first time actually *heard* myself. I had an English accent. To test myself I said, "Castle, tomato, and bath." They came out as "Cahstle, tomahto, and bahth." I don't want to go into it, but when I first came to New York, I had an editor say to me, "I just saw a movie about your life." "Oh? And what was that?" I asked. *"Coal Miner's Daughter."*

I can tell you that now I was thrilled to hear myself sounding like Princess Diana.

The girl sat down on the edge of the chaise and glared at me. "If you're concocting another of your stories, I'll not help you this time. My brother is very angry with me."

Before I thought, I said, "Who is your brother?"

but even as I said it, I *knew*. This girl was my sister-in-law, she was sixteen years old, and she desperately, frantically wanted a husband.

The girl gave a grimace. "I know *you* hate him, but I don't. If you'd just give him a chance, he —"

"Chance!" I heard myself say. "Your brother deserves no more chances. I have done everything to make my marriage work but what can I do when he refuses to . . . Refuses to . . ."

Refuses to what? I thought then felt a distinct pain in my temples as I tried to read the thoughts inside my head. But then this head wasn't mine, it belonged to someone else. Does that make sense to anyone besides me?

"Catherine," the girl said impatiently, "what is wrong with you?"

I would have loved to take a deep breath but my "loosened" stays still allowed my waist to be only about twenty inches in diameter. "I don't remember."

"Don't remember what?"

"I don't remember what I don't remember," I said, smiling.

"One of your riddles! Oh, Catherine, can't you *ever* be serious?"

I frowned at that. I hadn't expected to travel a hundred years into the past and hear the same complaints about my character I'd heard all my life.

The girl got up and began to pace about the room. "You don't know how serious this is. Tavey is really angry at you this time." She turned to glare at me. "He's planning to *divorce* you!"

At that statement I knew that the woman cowering inside me did know that her husband planned to divorce her. Was that what she was afraid of? Scandal? Come on, wasn't she — I — made of sterner stuff than that? "Why?"

The girl put her face in her hands and began to cry.

With difficulty, since the middle of me did not flex, I got up and went to the child. "Ellen," I said softly when the name came to me. "Everything has changed now. There will be no divorce. Your brother . . . Tavey and I will make up and everything will be fine." I tried not to be too smug when I smiled. Ellen had no way of knowing that she was not talking to an innocent Edwardian lady, sheltered and protected all her life, but to a thirty-nine-year-old woman who'd seen some of life. And, also, I knew so much more than Lady de Grey did. I knew that this man, my husband, was my soul mate, the one person who was most perfect for me on all the earth. Lady de Grey had never known that.

Ellen pushed me away. "Not this time. This time you've gone too far. Tavey knows about . . . about *him*."

At that my eyes widened and I tried to get the spirit of Lady de Grey who was cowering inside my own mind to own up to what she had done, but I couldn't get a peep out of her. "It will be all right," I said, trying to reassure the girl.

"It *must* be all right. It *has* to be! You promised."

Instantly, I knew that I had sworn to get Ellen a husband. "I will keep my promise." Heaven only knows how, I thought. Buy one? Three Fabergé eggs for one husband?

"You know how Tavey hates marriage. He says I'm better off unmarried. But I must, must, must get married!!"

At that I took Ellen's hand in my own. "Are you . . . in the family way?" I asked softly.

She was aghast. "Do you mean, am I going to have a baby? You know I'm not married, so how could I be going to have a baby?"

I did not laugh at that. I wasn't going to allow myself to laugh at Ellen's innocence. When I was a kid I thought that going to Mr. Lloyd's drugstore on Sunday morning was how you made a baby. Looking back on it, it made perfect sense. Every Sunday, my mother came home from church and said, "George, if that oldest Bales girl doesn't stop going to Mr. Lloyd's drugstore on Sunday morning instead of attending church, she's going to get into trouble." Then one day came the big, big scandal when it was found out that the oldest Bales girl was going to have a baby but she had no husband. I put two and two together and realized that "getting into trouble" meant "having a baby without having a husband." And this came about by going to Mr. Lloyd's drugstore on Sunday morning. The bad time came when my mother stopped at the drugstore after church and asked me to go in and pick up her prescription. I was paralyzed with fear.

In the end, though, my fear of my mother won over my terror of what happened in Mr. Lloyd's drugstore on Sunday mornings.

So now I wasn't about to laugh at Ellen, but she sensed that something was wrong, or at least that something was different about me. She grabbed my arm, showing an extraordinary amount of strength for one so young. But then I remembered that upper-class Edwardian girls often spent their lives on horses, so maybe her strength wasn't unusual.

She stared into my eyes. "If you betray me, I'll . . . I'll . . . I don't know what I'll do to you but you must not break your promise."

Maybe it was this cowardly other self inside me, but there was a little thrill of fear that ran through me at her words. I reminded myself that Lady de Grey had "disappeared" off the face of the earth and her remains had never been found. Someone had not wished her well. Could it be her little sister-in-law who thought a promise was going to be broken?

All I could think of was that I wanted to see Jamie. I needed to tell him that I loved him, that I didn't hate him and that we belonged together. I wanted to warn him; I wanted to —

"Where is my husband?" I asked Ellen. "And do we have any guests?" Visions of Jennie Churchill and the Duchess of Devonshire danced through my head. What about Consuelo Vander-bilt? How about the *king?*

From Ellen's sharp intake of breath, I took it there were no guests. She looked shocked. Story of my life, I thought. I'm always shocking some-one.

"No one will come here after what has hap-pened."

I wanted to ask her what had happened but at the look in her eyes, I held back. Or maybe it was Catherine keeping me from asking. There was more to this Ellen than I thought. Why was *I* to procure her a husband? Wasn't that her brother's job? But then from what I'd read, Lady de Grey could have chosen a husband for her based on who was the best in bed, since she seemed to have gone to bed with all of the men.

I put my hand to my forehead and did my best about-to-die act. "I am sorry, Ellen, but I seem to have forgotten so much lately. And you know how angry Tavey has been at me. If you'll just tell me where he is, I'll talk to him about your husband."

Ellen squinted her eyes at me. "He is where he always is at this time of day. You know where he is."

"Yes, of course I do. I'll just go and see him."

With a great deal of effort, I managed to get off the chaise and head for the door, but Ellen's horror stopped me. "You do not mean to wear that, do you?"

"Whatever was I thinking of?" I asked as lightly

as I could. "Where are my jeans and sweats?"

Ellen did not laugh; in fact she didn't seem to laugh about much of anything.

"I will call your maid," she said as she left the room and I was glad for that because I had no idea what the maid's name was.

The maid came in, didn't ask me a single question about what I was to put on, then began to undress and dress me without a word exchanged between us. I could get used to this, I thought as I extended my arm and let her put me into a scrumptious little dress of pale green cotton.

Being relieved of the necessity of dressing myself, I had time to think about my objective. I had no idea how long I would be here. After all it wasn't as though I were actually here; I was just temporarily visiting this woman's body. I could be pulled back by Milly's chauvinistic hypnotist at any second. What I needed to do was make contact with my soul mate, erase centuries of hate, then go home and find the real Jamie.

If I didn't accomplish this feat, I'd spend all of my life alone and the next and the next and not find Jamie until the next.

After I was dressed I went in search of the bathroom, hoping this wasn't one of those houses with enameled pots under the bed, but I found a nice little room with a modern flush toilet, then spent some minutes trying to rearrange my clothing, which was no easy task considering how much there was of it.

All in all it was some time before I was on my way and by this time all I could think of was food. Having stayed in country house hotels in England I knew that meals were at set times, and if you missed them, you were out of luck.

I spent an hour exploring that house. It was huge and complicated and there were rich treasures beyond belief. On the walls: Renoir, Rubens, Gainsborough, lots of John Singer Sargent. Rugs the perfect size for each room, so no doubt they had commissioned someone in India to make them. Each piece of furniture was a work of art.

What I liked about the house was that it was used. This was no museum. Invitations had been stuck into the frame of a fifteenth-century portrait. New silk brocade upholstery was next to a chair with the leather falling off it. Boots and coats and walking sticks were flung about in a jumble that would have taken six decorators days to duplicate. This is what Ralph Lauren is trying to achieve, I thought, yet never quite makes it.

By the time I left the house to see the garden I was weak with hunger, as I'd had nothing to eat for hours and that corset was cutting off the blood going to my feet. No wonder Edwardian women didn't run marathons, I thought as I began the slow process of walking through the gardens.

They were divine, manicured to look as though they just happened to grow the way they were. In the house I caught sight of servants, but they vanished as soon as they saw me coming, but in the garden it was different. Here there were several men with wheelbarrows and huge clipping shears. They wore heavy trousers and shirts rolled up to their elbows to show off their strong fore-arms.

I love blue-collar men. I know that shows my origins, and I know that now that I'm a writer and therefore an "intellectual" (except to the re-viewers of course) I'm supposed to like men wear-ing suits. But maybe I'm paranoid or maybe it's just my rich fantasy life, but I keep thinking, If I were stranded on a desert island would I want to be there with the world's best lawyer or with a building contractor? I like men who are *useful.*

And, well, okay, I also like muscles. Not those stringy muscles of the long-distance runner or the artificial ones made in a gym. I like a man with heavy forearms created from using a screw-driver most of his life. Seeing a man drive twenty-penny nails with one whack can make me weak-kneed. A shirtless man with a fifty-pound bag of cement over one shoulder climbing a ladder can make me so dizzy with desire I have to sit down.

In the house the servants had acted as though I had a contagious disease, but from the way these well-built men in the garden were smiling at me and pulling their forelocks as I walked by made me think I knew how Lady de Grey got her bad reputation. I hope I — she — didn't have an affair with a gardener. Daria would be very disappointed in me. Everyone knows that the hero *must* be titled. If all the dukes in romances had actually lived, we would all be titled. Barbara Cartland alone could populate a small country with her dukes.

But I couldn't help looking at these men as they went about their work in the garden. Not one of them was handsome, but several of them filled out their rough clothes rather well. As I walked, I began to like having a waist that felt as though it could not possibly be more than four inches in diameter. And Lady de Grey did have a nice bosom. All in all, she was a bit scrawny and no wonder, since she didn't seem to eat, but her figure appeared to be rather fashionable.

I hoped that these thoughts might bring her out of hiding so I could find out some information about her life, but she stayed down very small and I could feel her fear.

The garden was glorious, acres of plants, all of them seeming to be in bloom. I walked along the paths, moving from long grassy avenues with riots of flowers on either side, to quiet glades, to ponds with lily pads growing in them. There were statues and hedges and trees and flowering shrubs. As I walked I was beginning to think of stories I wanted to set in this garden. A poor but titled heroine who married an old man to save her unappreciative family from poverty, then in this garden she met a man, a beautiful man, but they couldn't marry because —

I broke off because coming toward me was the most gorgeous man I'd ever seen. Not that

114

sunken-cheeked overly perfect look of an American model, but a look of repressed passion. Looking at him was like standing at the foot of an active volcano: You know what it's capable of doing but will it do it *now?* As you walk up to the side of the volcano, your heart pounds faster the farther you get from safety.

That's what this man did to me the closer he got: made my heart pound harder with each step he took. He hadn't seen me, or if he had, he wasn't interested, as he kept his eyes on the wheelbarrow he pushed in front of him.

He was dark: black hair, skin dark by birth and not just the sun, thick black lashes. His strong jaws and squared chin were dark with whiskers under the skin. Muscles moved under his clothes in a way that made me feel quite warm.

As always, business was on my mind and I thought, This is the man I want on the cover of my next book. No, actually, this is the man I want on the cover of my next *life.*

As I took a step toward him, inside me I could hear Lady de Grey saying, "No, no." Maybe gardeners were off-limits to a lady. But I'm from a more egalitarian century and country.

"Hello," I said, smiling sweetly at him.

He walked past me without so much as a glance. Weren't gardeners of old supposed to be thrilled to be spoken to by the lady of the manor?

"Hello," I said again, only this time louder. Inside me, Catherine was frantic. "No!" she was screaming, and I knew she was afraid of this man.

She'd disappeared, maybe been killed, so was this man a candidate to be her murderer?

I did my best to control my burgeoning lust and turned away to look back at the garden. After all, I did have my pride. If he wasn't interested in me, I cared nothing about him. I —

"Ow!" I yelled as a sharp pain hit the back of my legs, then I turned around to see the back of the man, the full wheelbarrow before him, muscles straining as he wheeled it down the path away from me. He had on a dirty white shirt, a wide leather belt and heavy wool trousers. From the back he looked like Laurence Olivier at thirty-three, when he played Heathcliff.

As he passed me, he'd hit the back of my calves with the wheelbarrow, making a black mark on my pretty and undoubtedly expensive dress as well as hurting me.

Forgive my stupidity but I think that when a person hits you he should apologize, but this man just kept going. When he stopped about three yards from me, I walked over to him. "Excuse me, but did you know that you hit me with that?" I was being very polite but he didn't so much as look at me as he lifted the handles of the wheelbarrow.

I leaned over the barrow and got closer to his face, never mind that my heart was pounding. Just because he was gorgeous gave him no right to cause me pain. On the other hand, maybe he was deaf. Whatever, I was ready to forgive him. "Excuse me," I said much louder.

116

He didn't respond in any way, didn't look at me, didn't react to the sound of my voice. At this close range, I could see that he wasn't one hundred percent English. It was my guess that he was from somewhere in the Mediterranean, for his skin was dark and his eyes dark and he had a mop of black hair. Maybe he didn't speak English.

"Excuse me, but you —" When he still didn't look at me, I said, "Oh, the hell with it" and turned around to walk off. What did I care if he did or did not speak English? I had more important things to do than pant over the gardener.

But as I turned away from him, he then . . . I can hardly believe this even now. He dumped the contents of his wheelbarrow on my feet. On my feet, on the bottom of my pretty dress, up the front of my dress.

I just stood there and looked down at the mess that was me. Of course there was no question of what was in the wheelbarrow. Manure. What else? Only it wasn't good American manure that you buy at the nursery in plastic bags. This manure hadn't been baked to take bugs as well as the smell out of it. This manure had been hauled out of the stables, thrown in a heap, and allowed to "ripen" for a few years. It was now "ripening" around *me*.

"Look what you have done to me," I managed to say. "Look at my dress."

That man just stood there and looked at me.

I could see that he wasn't deaf, and if he didn't speak English it didn't matter because manure is manure in any language. His black eyes were twinkling and he had the tiniest bit of a smile playing on his mouth.

He had done it on purpose! I knew it as well as I knew . . . Well, better not go into that, since lately I didn't seem to be too sure of much of anything. Contact through hostility, I thought. He's some redneck foreigner, fresh off the boat, who has no idea that I am the lady of the house and should be treated with respect. From the look of him he might be from a country where the men think any woman out of the harem is worthy of a man's abuse. Wherever his origins he seemed to think that his looks allowed him to get away with anything.

When he just stood there looking at me, saying nothing, I decided to forgo my manners. Forget that this was Edwardian England and I was called Lady Something or other. After a quick glance about to see that no one else was within hearing distance, I let him have it. I told him what I thought of him. I used langnage I'd only heard on cable TV comedy routines and never said out loud before.

From the light that left his eyes, I was sure he spoke English, and I don't think he knew all the words that I did. I was willing to bet that no woman had ever said anything to him but the word "yes."

When I felt that I'd told him what I thought

of his manners and his ancestors, I finished with a little lesson in democracy. "You're in England now and this country is almost as free as America. You cannot treat a woman any way you want." Even to myself this sounded wimpy but I was weak from hunger and fatigue.

To tell the truth, I felt like crying. I was hungry and I was alone, not only in a foreign country but in a foreign time period and I wanted to go home. Where was Jamie? Where was my beautiful Jamie I had written about and had loved for centuries? Why wasn't he here to rescue me? All my paper heroes were there to rescue the heroine when she needed him.

To my utter horror, I could feel tears prickling behind my eyes. The smell of horse manure wafted around me and this dreadful man was still staring at me in silence. Another second and my tears would be running down my cheeks.

"I'm going to tell my husband about you," I managed to whisper, knowing I sounded like a child. With my chin held high, I turned away and started to leave.

I'd gone about two and a half steps when the man's voice stopped me.

"I, madam, am your husband."

For the second time in one day, I fainted.

10

What happened next was something I don't want to remember. The horrible, silent man who said he was my husband tossed me over his shoulder and carried me up the stairs. I couldn't help remembering that Scarlett got carried in Rhett's arms and he made love to her later. I was up for that. This man was a throwback to a Neanderthal but he was rather sexy. And he was my husband and he was Jamie — I think.

But he tossed me on the bed, left the room, locking the door behind him, and minutes later the gray-haired doctor appeared again and I got to see what an Edwardian gynecological exam was like. I wanted to hobnob with the king but instead I get a historic pap smear.

Let's just say that it was done under the covers with as much politeness as such a thing can be done, with as little embarrassment as possible. I knew what the problem was. Fainting twice in one day probably meant that Lady de Grey was pregnant. *Now* I knew why she'd disappeared.

I somehow didn't think she and her dark, hostile husband spent lazy afternoons in bed, so if this Catherine was pregnant, it was by another man.

When the doctor, with his hands involved in the examination, gave me a startled look, I knew I was on the mark. No doubt everyone knew of Lady de Grey's approaching divorce and here she was pregnant with another man's child.

I'm sure I turned red with embarrassment but the doctor said nothing as he closed his bag and left the room.

My maid came to me, took off my corset (thank you, Lord), and put me in a lush dressing gown. Then she brushed my hair down my back and left me to wait, no doubt for *him.*

So what was I to say to a man who had just been told that his wife who hadn't slept with him in heaven knows how long was pregnant?

By the time he came to my room I am ashamed to say that I was very nervous. I don't like promiscuity. I always believe in one man at a time, both in my books and in my life. Maybe what happened to me in this life is what taught me that lesson.

"You have made me the laughingstock of England. Why?" he asked, his dark eyes glaring at me for a moment before he turned away to stare out the window.

I must say that he did funny little things to the inside of me. I always believe in keeping control with men. With Steven I made certain that I analyzed everything; I wanted to do what was good for me. But this man made me feel emotion. That's the best way I can describe his effect on me: emotion. Now if I could just figure out what that emotion was, I'd feel a great deal calmer.

I swallowed. "I take it you mean all the men. I was . . . I was lonely. You're always in the garden and —"

He whirled around to glare at me with his piercing eyes. "I mean there have been *no* men — as you know."

It took me a moment to understand that one, and when I did understand, I could hardly believe it. There was only one way he could know that there had been *no* men. "You mean I'm a —" I smiled. "I'm a virgin?" At that thought I couldn't help but laugh. A thirty-nine-year-old American woman transported back in time into the twenty-seven-year-old body of a virgin!

"This is a matter of jest to you?" he asked with anger.

"Just sort of," I answered, then looked up at him. "If I'm a virgin, why do you want to divorce me?"

"As you well know, I am going to marry Fiona."

How very modern, I thought, with more anger than I should have felt. Should I invite the harlot to tea?

While I was digesting this disgusting bit of news, Catherine spoke up, using what I had come to regard as my mouth. "But a divorce will make me an outcast. No man will want me if you divorce me."

"Then you should have thought of that before you made all of England laugh at me."

"And how did I do that?" I asked, growing more angry by the second. *He* had already chosen his next bride, his wife was a virgin and *I* was the one to be punished.

"With your lascivious letters!" was his enraged answer. "By telling the world you'd slept with every man in England from the king down. I will *not* be a cuckold."

"A cuckold! Are you crazy? I *didn't* sleep with any other men. You heard the doctor say I'm a virgin. You could tell everyone the letters weren't true. Tell them you have proof that I've never slept with *any* man."

His eyes seemed to grow blacker. "Tell the world that my *wife* is a virgin? My *wife?!*"

I couldn't believe what he was saying. "You'll divorce me, make me a pariah, set me aside, knowing I am innocent?"

The look in his eyes answered that. Yes he would.

During this exchange Catherine had been hovering around, letting me know how devastating a divorce would be to her. It would ruin her life, but it wouldn't affect him; he had the money and the title. The unfairness of it all made me very angry. I looked up at him with a smirk. "*Why* haven't you taken her . . . I mean, my virginity? You can't do it so you don't want anyone to know, is that it? Have you told your lovely Fiona you're only half a man?"

I'd never before provoked a man to sexual rage. Were I a character in a novel by some romance authors of a decade before I would have found myself on the bed with my skirts over my head, but I've always fought against the device of rape in romance novels. When I turned in my second novel, my editor (*not* Daria) said, "I'm afraid we can't publish this because the hero doesn't rape the heroine, so the reader won't believe he's virile." I burst into tears and said, "Then I'll have to find another publishing house because if the hero commits rape, then he's not a hero." This seems logical now but back then it was revolutionary. The editor did publish it but she warned me it wouldn't sell. It did, of course, sell very well, and that editor now edits for a porn publisher.

However, this was real and I didn't have complete control here. I put my hand to my throat and backed away from him. There was murder in his eyes and I knew in my heart he wanted to show me he could do what he hadn't done before.

But I saw he wasn't going to do anything. He had too much honor to hit a woman and something was keeping him from the rape I could see that he wanted to enact. Sometimes there's a devil in me. A little forked-tailed red-skinned devil that sits on my right shoulder and makes me do awful things. I could feel poor virginal Catherine cowering inside me, terrified of this man, and I felt all the injustice of what-men-do-to-women.

I stood up straight and glared at him. *"Can't,* can you?" I taunted. "If you divorce me and marry Fiona how will that help you? If you can't with me, you can't with her."

I knew right away that that was the wrong thing to say. His face turned into a rage that was frightening. Where did Edwardian men stand on the wife-beating question?

He didn't make any attempt at physical violence, I'm happy to say. He just turned his back to me but I could see he was shaking with his anger. "You go too far," he whispered and from that I knew he had a "problem."

I think the media in America has made us all feel too guilty if we don't care about everyone's problems, so even if this man was scum, I felt sorry for him. Impotence is a very big deal to men, in any time period.

I went to stand by him. "Look, sometimes these things can have a cause, you know, a physical cause or maybe it's psychological. Maybe if you talk about it, maybe we could find the reason for your . . . your inability to perform and finding the cause would solve the problem. In the meantime I'm sure this doesn't mean you're less of a man just because you can't —"

His laughter stopped me from going on. I really hate being laughed at. And I especially hated the smug, condescending way he was laughing at me.

"What a child you are," he said. "What an innocent child you are."

Smug doesn't begin to describe his attitude.

"I don't think I'm quite as innocent as you think," I said, beginning to get angry all over again. You should have seen the way he was looking at me! He looked like a painting on a romance novel cover — and who should know better than I what that looked like? Impeccably dressed (I *hate* that term!), snowy white cravat (ditto), broad shouldered, slim hipped, elegant, long-fingered hands on his hips. His gorgeous head tipped back and looking down his long, aristocratic nose at me. So smug. So arrogant. So sure he, big macho male, knew everything and little micro-waisted me knew nothing.

"Are you not so innocent, Catherine?" he said as he advanced on me, moving toward me with the unshakability of a tidal wave in slow motion. "Are you not?"

I could see that he meant to kiss me. I wanted to stop him, because part of me echoed Catherine's fear of him. But I couldn't have moved myself any more than I could have moved the house a few inches to one side.

Just before his lips touched mine I remembered that Nora had said, "If you were to kiss him you would feel a merging of spirits." I don't remember what question I had asked to get this answer, but I do remember that response.

When his lips touched mine, I don't know if it was a merging of spirits or not, but I'd never felt the way he made me feel while kissing any other man. It wasn't as though the kiss were confined to just our lips; it was as though our

126

bodies were trying to merge into one. I wanted to sink into him, to become him, to blend with him in a way that was not physical so much as . . . as . . .

Oh, who cared about trying to describe it? All I can say is that when he kissed me I lost myself. I wasn't me or Catherine or anyone else; I was just part of him.

I think my body collapsed; my legs gave way under me and we went flowing back onto the bed. I say flowing because by that time I felt more like the consistency of mercury than I did of something supported by bone. He went with me, falling down on top of me, his mouth fastened onto mine, his heavy body moving on top of me.

I had felt lust many times in my life. There were many men who'd inspired me to . . . well, to do things in bed that are no one's business but my own, but they were nothing compared to this man. Desire such as I'd never known existed flooded me, filled me so there was no room for thoughts or other feelings. I was just aware of him and nothing else.

I *had* to have him. I wanted him as close to me as nature could achieve, and at that moment I thought that sex was not exactly what I wanted from this man. I wanted all of this man inside me; I wanted all of me inside him.

There are no words to describe what I felt for him. Maybe he felt the same about me because he was kissing my neck as though he'd die if he didn't kiss me. I leaned my head back and the only word I fully understood was, yes. Yes, whatever he wanted. Yes, whatever I could give him or do for him. Yes to anything and everything.

His hand was on my breast; my hands were on his back, his chest, in his hair, everywhere that I could reach of him. Never in my life had I wanted anything as much as I wanted this man.

But it was then that I put my hand between his legs, and there I felt nothing. Oh, he had all the correct equipment all right, but, at the moment, it wasn't working. At least it wasn't working at the touch of *me*.

The instant I touched him, he rolled away from me and put his hand over his eyes so I couldn't see the anguish in them. My body was vibrating all over and I felt bereft at the absence of him. Maybe I should have cared about him, but all I could think about was me.

"Is it just me?" I whispered. "Only with me?"

"Yes." The word came from somewhere deep inside him and I knew that admission caused him pain.

Turning my head, I looked at him, and even with what I had felt, I couldn't make myself believe that he "couldn't" or that we should stop. I wanted to touch him. Actually, I wanted to remove his clothes with my teeth and lick all the color off him.

"Tavey," I said and rolled toward him, placing my mouth on his chest where his shirt had come unfastened. Under my lips I could feel his heart beating; I could feel his warm, dark skin; I could feel —

He pushed me away, then looked at me with mocking eyes. "Can you not see that I do not want you? I have never wanted you. You are undesirable to me."

I have mentioned that I have a lot of pride, and at those words my pride was hurt, but it did not rear up and protect me. I was quivering with how much I wanted him. My body felt as hot as though I were running a fever, yet no matter that he was saying horrible things to me, had he held out his hand for me, I would have taken it.

"We can try," I said, my body longing for his as I lifted my hand toward him. "Perhaps we can —"

He got off the bed then stood over me, his eyes laughing, ridiculing me. "Catherine, I married you for your money and I have used that money to put a roof on my house and horses in my stable. Now I should like to put sons in the nursery and I will never get them from you. I will speak to my attorneys tomorrow and begin to dissolve this farce of a marriage."

He gave me one last look of contempt. "And do not try such as this again. It will not work. Such behavior only debases you."

With that he left the room, closing the door behind him.

For a few moments I was too stunned to speak. Recovering from my encounter with him was rather like recovering from a two-week bout of flu. I felt weak and helpless and tired, and inside me, I could feel Lady de Grey shouting, "I told you so. I told you so."

Maybe she had warned me and maybe I should have listened to her, but I was feeling the beginnings of unfairness. I had done *nothing* wrong. I — I mean, Catherine — had done nothing but write some hot little letters and if I knew myself I — she — had written them in an attempt to get his attention. Was she as attracted to him as I was? At that thought I felt a weakening of her spirit. She loved him very, very much. Worse than that, so did I. I knew without a doubt that if he walked back into the room, I'd lean back on the bed and open my arms to him.

"But I hate him, too," I whispered, for who could not hate a man who was going to ruin a woman's life by divorcing her because he could not perform with her? Hate him for the horrible things he had said to me.

Nora's words echoed in my head. "Love. Hate. It's the same thing."

"I love him and I hate him," I said, and I could feel Catherine agreeing with me. "*Real* hatred," Nora had said, "is the other side of the coin from love. Hate lasts centuries, just as love does." Now, at last, I understood what she meant, and I sure as hell wish I'd never found out.

11

I must have fallen asleep and when I awoke I knew that I had been crying. Crying for what I had lost and for what would never be. Why hadn't I just left well enough alone and married good, safe Steven?

Hunger drove me out of bed and out of the room. Whatever happened to maids who brought the mistress meals on a tray? In fact, what happened to my efficient, silent maid altogether? From what I knew of Edwardian history, I was aware that I was off schedule and therefore would probably not be fed.

I started to dress in something other than a frilly robe, but there was no way I could get into one of Lady de Grey's dresses without that iron maiden lashed about my middle, and I wasn't masochistic enough to put it on when I didn't have to. The room was dark and one glance at the drawn curtains at the windows told me it was night.

When I opened the door, out of the dim hallway

sprang a woman holding a candle, which she promptly shoved into my face, so close that I feared I might be burned.

"He is mine," she said. "You cannot have him. You will never own him." With that she turned and ran down the hallway, her long dark skirts swishing after her.

Had she been younger I would have thought she was the fertile Fiona, but she was about my mother's age, with that unlined, perfect skin that the moist English climate produces. When she was younger she must have been quite pretty, but now her features had twisted in malevolence when she saw me.

"I am living in a Gothic novel," I muttered aloud and wished very much that I could go home. At that thought Lady de Grey piped up and said, "I want to go with you," which made me laugh.

I followed my nose to find food. In a beautiful dining room, aglow with candlelight, sat my loved/hated husband with a feast before him and he was chowing down as though there were no tomorrow.

Oh yeah, I thought, soul mates. Any stress sends me to the kitchen.

"Do you mind?" I asked, and at his gesture, I took a seat to his right and filled a plate higher than his. He didn't so much as raise an eyebrow. Let's see Lady de Grey get back into her corset after *I* had finished with her body, I thought.

"Tell me about the letters," I said, mouth full.

"Why should I tell you about your own letters?"

was his unhelpful reply.

"I have lost my memory. I'm from the future and my spirit has taken over your wife's body so I'm actually someone else. Take your pick."

"Ah, Catherine, I shall miss your stories."

I didn't even make a smart reply.

"All right," he said, "I will play along with your little game. I do not think you meant for them to be delivered. I can see that now." With that he gave me a look up and down. Maybe it had been a jolt for him to find out that I was a virgin. "Where did you learn all the things that you wrote about . . . about love?"

"Sex, you mean?"

At that he raised one eyebrow. I don't think Catherine had ever said that word, or maybe even knew it. "I'm good at research," I said. "Very good. Any information I want to know I can find out. So I wrote some hot little letters to whom?"

"Half the men in England, it would seem. Some of your letters found their way to the newspaper office. The king has declared that he does not know us. He fears more scandal."

"I see. Do you have any idea who sent them to the men and to the newspaper office?"

He gave a shrug that seemed to mean that he didn't know or care.

"Is it possible that I wrote them only to make you jealous? That I meant for you to see them and no one else?" This is what I would have had one of my heroines do if she needed to get

133

the hero's attention. But of course I had never had a hero who had the "problem" that this one did. And all my heroes were rampantly virile and paid enormous amounts of attention to the heroine.

"It does not matter why you wrote them or who sent them. It matters only that it has been done. It is a point of honor to me that I must now divorce you."

I kept eating. I wish I could describe how I felt in his presence. I thought that what he was doing was about the lowest, rottenest thing I had ever heard of. None of my heroes would ever do what he was doing. Of course with *my* heroes, after years of marriage the heroine would have three children and another one on the way. I detested him, but at the same time I wanted to be with him. There was something about his very presence that fulfilled something inside me. It wasn't that he made me happy, far from it. But when I was near him I felt, This is where I should be. How could he send me away?

"I have never loved anyone but you," I heard myself saying softly. "Not in any life have I ever loved anyone but you."

"Yes," he said, "I know that."

"Then how could you do this to me?" I was *not* going to cry. I was not!

"We are not good for each other," he said. "There is something wrong between us."

"You didn't marry me just for my money, did you?"

"Of course not!" he said angrily, as though I had made that up.

"But you said —"

"*You* said that you'd been to bed with every man in England! How could you have done that to me, Catherine? How could you? We had agreed that it was better that we divorce quietly, but you had to write those letters. Lord! But why doesn't someone take your pen away from you? I have never seen anyone lie as you do when you have a pen in your hand."

"Perhaps I should write novels."

"Always making a jest, aren't you? Well, I have had enough of it. You have gone too far this time. Tomorrow is the sixth and I must go to London on the tenth. Then I will —"

That jolted me. Why hadn't I thought of looking at a calendar to see what today's date was? "The sixth of what?" I asked.

"June of course. Do you want to know the year also?" he asked archly.

"You will not go to London," I said softly. "On the eighth of June you and I will die together. At least I think I die. My body will never be found."

For a moment he just stared at me, then he threw back his head and laughed. "Catherine, I will indeed miss you and your stories. I shall miss them very much. You have been most entertaining during these years."

My first impulse was to plead with him to listen to me but inside of me Lady de Grey was telling

135

me that she'd tried everything to make him listen to her, but he'd refused. Having written letters saying I'd had sex with most of London, while in truth I was a virgin, didn't make me a candidate for Most Honest Person.

While I was thinking of this, he put his elbows on the table and looked at me. "All right, tell me," he said. "You know that I can never resist your stories."

I perked up at that. A man who couldn't resist my stories. Steven used to listen politely but he never really, truly *liked* hearing about knights on horses rushing to save the heroine — or the other way around, as it often was in my stories.

I told him. I told him that we were soul mates, and explained what that was. I told him that I was a spirit from the future trapped in his wife's body and that I needed to change the hatred and anger that was between us, so that I could be happy in my life in 1994.

He listened as though he'd had a lot of practice in listening to my stories, and when I finished, he lifted an eyebrow at me.

"I must say that that is one of your best. You really should write them down. Perhaps there is an audience for them. Now, if you will excuse me, I must get to bed."

I was on my feet instantly and grabbed his arm. "What I have told you is true. Someone will kill us three days from now."

"Oh? And who wants to kill us?"

"I . . . I don't know. Your sister desperately

wants a husband and there is an awful old woman skulking about the corridors saying that you belong to her."

His mouth hardened into a tight line. "My little sister is a murderess? And I take it you mean Aya, my old nanny, is also a killer? She does not like the lies you have told about me. You cannot blame her for that."

"You must listen to me. We must —"

"Yes? We must what? Live together as man and wife?" He jerked his arm from me. "You have seen that that is impossible."

I glared at him. "Yes, I have seen that I am to suffer the consequences of *your* inadequacies."

From the look he gave me I knew that I had again overstepped myself. Were our deaths a murder/suicide? Did he kill me then himself? If that were so, then what happened to Lady de Grey's body?

Turning away from me, he left the room.

When he was gone, all I could think of was that I wanted to go home, home to my safe apartment, home to a world that I understood. With heavy feet, I went upstairs and went to bed.

When I awoke the next morning, I had only one thought on my mind: I must return to my own time period. Nora had been absolutely, totally right, and I should never have done this. I had made things worse rather than better. Knowledge did not conquer emotion. Knowing that this man and I should be together didn't help anything at all.

When writing my books, I was always willing to toss out novels that didn't work. As far as I was concerned, this was a story that wasn't working and I needed to cut my losses and get out of here.

But how? How did I go back? There was a chance that in two days, when Lady de Grey and her angry, impotent husband were killed, my spirit would be sent back to the present, but I didn't want to risk it. I wanted to go back now.

I found out when and where breakfast was and managed to show up for it. There I met Hubert de Grey, Tavistock's uncle, a sweet man, who kept looking at me in great sadness.

"If there were anything I could do to prevent this," he said, "I would." I assumed he meant the divorce.

Ellen was there and I asked her about him. "He arranged the marriage between you. How could you have forgotten, Catherine? He loves both of you."

After breakfast I walked in the garden, actually, I paced, as was my habit when I was trying to figure out some problem. An old man named Jack, a great lump growing on one shoulder, gave me a small bouquet of flowers and whispered, "I am sorry for all that has happened to you, my lady," then disappeared.

Nora had said that people remembered things from past lives, and sometimes I got little shivers when I looked at these people. That woman Aya hated me and she seemed to be everywhere, look-ing at me as though she wished to wipe me off the face of the earth. I could sense that Catherine was very afraid of her. If there was ever an un-happy spirit, this old nanny that Tavistock seemed to think was harmless, was it. I couldn't help but think that it had taken more than one gen-eration for her hatred for me to grow. Yet, some-where inside of me, I kept feeling that I very much wanted her to love me. Which of course was ridiculous.

What I really, truly wanted was to stop trying to figure out people's motives and to go *home*.

12

JAMAL, the headline blazed, THE WORLD'S GREATEST MESMERIST, WILL BE APPEARING IN BURY ST EDMONDS ON THE SIXTH OF JUNE AT EIGHT O'CLOCK. ONE NIGHT ONLY.

Reading the ad on the back of the newspaper my silent husband had placed between us over lunch made me nearly choke on my overcooked vegetables.

"Are you all right?" Ellen asked, but my husband — the love of all my lives — said nothing. If I did choke it would no doubt save him a great deal of time and expense. And clear the way for his precious Fiona, I thought. Maybe *she* was the killer.

"I am fine," I answered. My impulse was to demand that I be "allowed" to go to see this mesmerist, but I decided to be quiet and find a way to get to him. If I had been hypnotized to get here, maybe I could be hypnotized to get out of here.

During the meal, I could hardly sit still as I

was dying to get Ellen aside and ask her, among other things, where Bury St Edmonds was. As far as I was concerned the town was in Chaucer and that was a long way from the time of Edward VII.

An hour later, in whispers, I told Ellen what I wanted.

She gave me an odd look. "You are not a prisoner, Catherine. You may go where you wish, and Bury is not far, as you well know."

"Yes, of course," I said aloud, straightening from my spy position. "Do you think we could go tonight? I mean if you don't mind, that is." I didn't want to go alone because there was no telling where I'd end up. In theory, I spoke English, but there were some men in the garden who spoke a variety of English that could have been Arabic as far as I could understand it, so I had to have someone with me.

"Tavey will be away tonight so we may go where we wish," Ellen said.

Still feeling quite foolish, we made arrangements for what time to leave. It seemed that Catherine was always interested in things like mesmerists and palm readers, as well as gorgeous Fabergé ornaments, so my wanting to see the great Jamal was no surprise to her.

Have you ever tried to explain past lives to an Edwardian man? I think I could have easier explained what a CD ROM was. For all that the man called himself "Jamal" and tried to make

141

himself look old enough to have some wisdom, I could see that he was just a young man from the English equivalent of Brooklyn. The stain he'd used to darken his skin during his performance had furrows from his sweat.

"You have lived other lives?" he asked, and I recognized a kindred soul; he was thinking how he could use this information in his next act. It wasn't that the concept of past lives was not known in Edwardian times, it was just that this man had never heard of it. I doubt if he'd ever read much and there were no TV specials to inform him, so he had missed this bit of knowledge. For a moment I thought of how much information we absorbed in the modern world thanks to mass media.

"And you want me to send you back to one of these lives?" He looked me up and down in a timeless way. "Shame to lose all that."

"Listen, kid," I said, feeling all of my thirty-nine years, "keep your hands off the merchandise. I just want one kind of service from you, not anything else."

He smiled at me. "All right, but it'll be ten pounds for a private performance, so to speak."

Poor little Ellen had been hovering in the background, torn between horror at being backstage at such a low place as a theater, and being thrilled within an inch of her perfect little life. Now I held out my hand for her to give me money, since I had none.

It was fifteen minutes later, after Ellen had scurried outside and borrowed some money from the driver of the Tavistock coach, that I was stretched out on a table and the young man had started putting me in a trance.

"All you have to do is want to go under," Nora had told me, and I did indeed want to go under. Very much. I envisioned my apartment with the white linens on my bed. I thought of my computer and Daria and Milly and of movies. I tried to see all that my life in New York held for me.

Instead, what I kept seeing and feeling was Tavistock. His eyes. His hands. I remembered the way he made me feel when he kissed me. I remembered how fascinated with him I had been, how I'd wanted to follow him wherever he went. I thought of how I felt when I was near him, as though I were *supposed* to be with him. I hated him; he was despicable, dishonorable, and all-round rotten, but there was a feeling inside me that he was *mine*. How could some other woman have him? I think I might kill him myself rather than allow another woman to have him.

"You will go back to where it all began," the man was saying and I was already feeling dreamy.

"You will go back to the beginning."

Yes, I thought. Back to the beginning. I began in New York.

I could feel my spirit detaching from Lady de Grey's body, and as I again felt that floating sensation, I smiled. Back to . . . What was that name I'd seemed to remember when Milly's hypnotist had put me under? Tally. Yes, that was it. Back to Tally.

Suddenly, I knew that what I was doing was wrong. There seemed to be a voice inside my head — was it Nora's? — that said that something was wrong. No, I thought, I don't want to go back to the beginning. I want to go back to 1994. Not the beginning. I opened my mouth to protest, but now it seemed that I was no longer attached to a body. I tried to will myself back into Lady de Grey's body, but I couldn't seem to move.

Slowly, I began to feel . . . What was it I was feeling? I was feeling as though I were trapped and I had to get out. Had to, had to, had to. I was going to die if I didn't get *out*.

In the next second I had the freakish realization that I was a baby about to be born.

Part Two

13

England

1571

"There, madam, is a *son,*" John Hadley said to his heavily pregnant wife. He didn't so much say the words as spat them. In nineteen years of marriage he had had much practice in saying these same words to her. As a man of little imagination and no complexity, his one goal in life had been to have a son as tall, broad shouldered and as handsome as he was himself.

His beautiful blonde wife, Alida, her hand on her enormous belly, sat by him, her eyes glittering with blue fire. She knew better than to answer him or to make any comment; it was better to let him rage.

"Look you at what you have given me," he said, not bothering to keep his voice down, but truthfully no one could have heard him if he'd shouted. The old stone castle that had been in his wife's family for a couple of hundred years was now filled with half-drunken guests at the wedding of the first of John's eight daughters. The girl was eighteen, late to be marrying, but it had taken years of begging her father to find her a husband before she was allowed to marry. John's reluctance to allow a daughter to marry was caused by the fact that he cared only for the expense of such a marriage. He had hated the idea of giving the girl a dowry of one of his castles. It did not matter to him that this and all of the property he owned had come to him through his unexpected marriage to the rich Alida Le Clerc so many years ago.

As always, John's anger toward his wife came not only from the eight daughters she had borne him but from the two sons, whom he despised. Rarely did he see all of his ten children together because they expended great effort in staying away from their father, for he never considered keeping his hostility secret. The girls begged their mother to persuade their father to get husbands for them — any husbands. There were no complaints if their father suggested marriage to a man thrice their ages, a man with blackened teeth and foul breath. The girls were in accord in their single goal to get out from under the constant fiery furnace of their father's enmity.

Now, one of the girls was escaping and her seven sisters looked on with envy. Never mind that the man she was marrying was so thin his bones nearly showed through his clothes and that his manners were worse than any stable lad's. What mattered was that tomorrow this daughter would be able to escape their father's house.

As for John he tried his best to forget that

his life was plagued with eight daughters and two worthless sons. He spent every waking moment badgering the peasants in the fields, trying to squeeze yet more money and work out of them, and killing any creature that had the misfortune to walk or fly across his lands.

"Look you at them," John repeated to his wife. "I must bribe some poor man to marry them, eight of them. Do you know what that will cost me?"

Alida wanted to say that it would cost him about half of what her father had given him to marry her, but she did not dare. Brains did not stand up against muscle and obstinacy.

It wasn't that her husband was stupid. In fact, he was clever in his own way. He was very good with the everyday aspects of life, such as hounding the peasants into producing more food than any other farmers in the county. He knew where every grain of wheat went and no one ever cheated him, as he always found them out. And when he did, his punishments were swift. He was a big, good-looking man, with as flat a stomach today as he had when they were married nineteen years ago.

But John had no understanding of anything that didn't involve producing more coin, food, or power. Music bored him. "It does not feed me," he said. He thought education was a waste of time; he thought any entertainment except getting drunk now and then was for fools. Once when he caught his wife reading a book, he grabbed it from her and threw it out the window. "*This is why you give me daughters,*" he bellowed at her. "I put sons into your belly and you change them into worthless females with your fairy stories."

Now, John was in his worst mood because he could see all eight of his daughters and his two young sons. Four years ago when Alida had at last given birth to the much-coveted son, she had wept with joy. And through her tears she had seen her husband come running to her. As he grabbed her into his arms, heedless of the fact that she had just given birth, Alida did not care, for there was such happiness on his face. For a moment her heart filled with all the hope and joy she'd felt before she married him. Dreams of a happy life filled her as John held her, kissing her face and neck, telling her she was the most wonderful of wives.

"Let me see him," John had demanded, and in an instant Alida's happiness had fled her, for she saw the faces of her maids and knew instantly that something was very wrong.

"No," she whispered, trying to prolong the moment of truth when that sublime joy would leave her husband's face when he saw whatever was wrong with the child.

Alida could see that the maids were trying to conceal the problem, so they presented the boy in swaddling clothes, bound tightly to prevent his limbs from growing crooked. But John wanted to see for himself that the child was a boy and bade the maids unwrap him.

With her breath held, Alida watched her husband and when he saw the boy's perfect body, his face seemed to melt in tenderness as he cradled it in his arms. John had never touched one of their daughters, never done anything but ask its sex then wave it away. But now he cradled his son as though it were what he had lived his life for — as it was.

"He is beautiful," John said and Alida's eyes overflowed with tears. Her husband had never seen beauty in a flower or a sunset or even a woman, but he thought that this son she had given him was beautiful.

With her maid's help, Alida had sat up straighter in the bed to look with her adoring husband at the child and, innocently, she had started to move the swaddling cloth back from the child's feet. But the quick intake of breath from her maid had made her draw her hand back as though the cloth were on fire.

John, not usually aware of subtlety, had caught the movement and tossed the blanket back from the child. One of its feet was deformed. The boy would never be able to walk properly.

What had a moment ago been love and joy in John's eyes was replaced with hatred. "How could I have thought that you, madam, would give me what I want?" he spat at her as he opened his arms and let the child fall. Had not the nurse caught the baby it would have hit the stone floor. In another moment John had left the room and thereafter he did not try to conceal the disgust he felt for his wife.

The next year she presented him with another son but by then John had grown cynical. He did not go to see the boy when he was told it was born. "What is wrong with it?" he asked, and when the maid hesitated, he bellowed, "What is wrong with it? I do not believe that that wife of mine would give me a perfect son." John had three choices in life: He could believe that God was the cause of his having only daughters and a deformed son, he could believe that he was the cause, or he could blame it all on his wife. He chose to blame his wife.

"The child is not well," the maid managed to whisper.

At that John began to laugh. "I will not hope that it will die. Nor will I dare hope that that cursed wife of mine will die in childbirth and free me to marry a woman who knows how to breed proper sons." He grabbed a tankard of wine from a table. "It will live," he said with fatalism. "As all my children live so will this one. It will cost me to feed and clothe it and never give me pleasure. Go! Leave me."

John's prophecy was right and the child did live, but the boy was always sickly, with a disease of the lungs that made him cough continually.

Two years later Alida gave birth to a healthy baby girl, but John did not even look at it; he did not so much as ask after it. He noticed that his wife had once again been relieved of a child, but he threatened never to visit her bed again. What use was it? The surrounding villages supplied him with women to appease his lust. He refused to notice that whenever a girl was brought to bed with a child that he had reason to believe was his, it was *always* a girl. John merely denied that these children were his. No matter that the baby girl had his blue eyes or the set of his chin. John's policy was that if the child was a female then he did not father it. It was well known that if any woman, no matter what her background, could give John Hadley a son, then he would take her into his home and she would live a life of luxury. Although several had tried (one woman three times) no one had yet succeeded in giving him his perfect son.

"Look you at him," John demanded of his wife, nodding toward a man on the far side of the room. "Why is it that his wives can beget sons and you cannot? It is said that his wives give him sons so large that the women die from the birthing of them."

Trying to look dutiful, as though she wanted to learn something, Alida turned toward the man John was pointing to. But her heart, indeed her entire body, was filled with rage. Was this another point against her, that she had not died in giving birth to a child the size of a calf? Were children to be judged solely upon weight, as though they would be sent to the butcher's? Her husband did not look at the fact that the daughters she had given him were intelligent and comely; the oldest were even pretty. Their two sons were sweet natured and the oldest could already read. It did not matter to her that one of the boys limped and the other coughed as though each day would be his last.

With a cold heart, Alida looked at the man her husband was pointing to. Gilbert Rasher was a brute of a man, the size of a bear, unwashed, bad-tempered, uneducated, but, in his day, he had been a great jouster, unseating any man who took him on. Some said that too many lances hitting his helmet had scrambled his brain and made him stupid. But then how did one account for his calculating eyes that saw everyone and everything and always managed to get every bit he could get out of them?

Gilbert had had three wives, each presenting him with a hulk of a son in the image of the father, then dying from the birth. Gilbert liked to brag that his virility killed his wives, but most women agreed that the women died to get away from his filthy body and his filthier mind.

Now Gilbert was burying his face in the over-generous bosom of one of the kitchen maids, a girl Alida vowed to get rid of on the morrow, while his sons were, as always, causing trouble in the noisy chaos of the wedding festivities. One son, about eight years old, but looking at least twelve, was terrorizing a couple of dogs with a little whip and laughing delightedly. His younger brother was making two of Alida's daughters cry in fear. There was a third great lout of a son somewhere else, but Alida didn't want to know where he was or what he was doing.

Is *this* what her husband wanted in a son? she thought. She had given him two boys who were good and gentle, intelligent and thoughtful, loving children. John had never so much as addressed an encouraging word to his sons, but here he was drooling over these despicable churls whose only pleasure was in terrifying something smaller than themselves.

Around them, no one listened to John. His ranting had gone on so long that everyone considered John's complaints a great joke. His neighbors held up their own sons and offered to show him how it was done. When John had no sense of humor about this matter, they laughed harder and teased more.

But her husband's rage was no laughing matter to Alida. Her knees were raw, bloody, from kneeling for the last nine months as she prayed to God to give her a healthy son. She was 35 years old now and she knew that she would not get many more chances to produce the perfect male child her husband wanted. If only . . . she thought. If only she could produce that child. Night and day she was haunted by the look she'd seen on her husband's face when he had thought she had borne him a perfect son. A woman could live on looks like that, she thought. A woman would not need heaven if she had a husband who looked at her like that.

This time when she knew she was with child

she began to pray. She spent most of the night and day on her knees, begging God, beseeching Him to give her this son.

She did not like to remember what else she had done. There had been a furtive, secret trip to another village to a horrid, dirty woman who said she could foresee if her ladyship was carrying a boy. When the old woman had said that the child growing in her belly was another girl, Alida had become hysterical and said she'd see the woman burned for witchcraft. But the woman was gone the next day, fled from her tiny house to travel the roads. Better to die of hunger, she thought, than to be killed by fire.

Alida had found another woman who said the sex of the child could be changed by concentrating on masculine things. Even now, Alida's face blushed when she thought of the pictures and the tiny statue the woman had given her to concentrate on. All of them male. In these nine months Alida had read no books, as her husband said reading was a feminine pursuit. She had done as little as possible that was considered women's work, trying to point her every moment toward men and think only of them.

But more than anything, she had prayed to God, staying so long at her altar that her maids had entreated her to come away, saying such long kneeling was not good for the babe. "I would rather that it were born dead if it is not a healthy boy," she said as the maids hauled her upright. They did not tell her not to think this way because each of them silently agreed with her.

But her husband saw none of this. To him she showed a face with as little emotion as possible. She would not throw herself on him and beg him to forgive her for not giving him a son. She would keep her pride, if nothing else.

Because of her memories, she did not hear the first of what her husband was saying.

"It must be a boy if it is killing the girl," he was saying. "Now she lies above and I have seen her. Her belly is larger than she is. It's said she has not been able to walk for a month. It will be another boy for Gilbert."

This startled Alida. "There is a woman in my house who is giving birth?" Why had no one told her of this? She would skin her maids when she got them alone. If someone were indeed giving birth to a child while in her house, there were things that must be done.

Clumsily, heavily, Alida started to get up. "I must go to her."

As she stood, the first pain came to her belly and she knew that her own time had started. No, no, she thought, it is too soon. She was not big enough. She had prayed for a boy that was huge, something that would impress her husband. If she gave birth now, with a stomach only this big, the child would be small.

Grabbing the back of the chair, she tried to keep her face from contorting as another pain took her, but she did not succeed. John, looking away from her, his attention on some jugglers, would not have noticed if she'd given birth in the straw on the floor at his feet. But their guests were not so callous.

"John!" someone yelled. "It looks as though you are to be a father again."

"And what day does he *not* become a father?" someone else shouted, making everyone laugh.

John didn't join in their laughter. Fatherhood had long ago ceased to be of any interest to him. Airily, he waved his hand. "Leave me," he said.

"It is good of you to give me your permission to leave," Alida said with as much bitterness as she dared.

Gilbert Rasher removed his face from the bosom of the maid long enough to yell to John, "You should put your wife next to the girl I married. Mayhaps she can teach that woman of yours something."

Alida did not know that she could despise the filthy creature more than she already did. Her husband and this man were alike: to them women were only bodies, put on earth to give them children. And if those children killed the mother in the birthing, what did it matter? There were more women about. To them women had no souls, no thoughts, no wants; they had only bodies.

With the next pain, Alida's maid Penella came to her, putting her arm under her elbow, and helped her mistress upstairs to her chamber where all was ready for the birth. As they neared the door, Alida halted. "Take me to Rasher's wife. I will give birth with her." And mayhap some

158

of what Rasher has will come into my unborn child, she thought.

Penella, who loved her mistress well, looked at her in concern.

"Yes, yes, what is it?" she snapped. "I do not have long."

"The girl is dying," Penella whispered. "The priest has already come to her. She will not live more than a few hours. It would not be good for you or your unborn babe to be so near death. That is why I did not tell you of her presence."

"But what of her child?" Alida gasped as another pain overtook her. "What of *it?*"

"It has not come. The midwife thinks it will die with her. It is too big for her." Penella took a breath. "Oh, milady," she whispered, near to tears. "You should see her. She is a foreign thing, so tiny, not a word can be got out of her. And she is dying from this babe inside her. She has been in labor for two days now."

Alida's mind was working. If the woman was dying from having a boy and the boy was about to die, perhaps at the moment of death the boy's spirit would enter her child and change it into a male. Someone had told her once that the sex of a child was not determined until the actual moment of birth. Before that the child was neither male nor female. Perhaps this was true.

"Take me to her!" Alida demanded, leaving no room for the maid to disagree.

Alida was led to a small, dirty room where a flea-infested straw-filled mattress was tossed onto the floor. On it lay a girl, her face streaked with dirt and tears. She had bitten her lip through and there was smeared blood on her chin. Black hair straggled about her face in limp, dirty strands, entangling under her arms, and around her neck as though it meant to strangle her.

Under the dirt, Alida could see that the girl had once been pretty. Her olive skin showed that she was from a country that had been kissed by the sun. Looking at her, imagining what she must have been once, a person could see sunlight and flowers, could hear birds and the tinkle of her laughter. She was young, no more than sixteen, if that, and under the pallor of death was the bloom of youth in her pretty face and skin.

But now Alida could see that the girl was very near death. It was as though this girl had given up the will to live and now all that was left was the slight movement of her chest above the great lump that was her dying child.

"Help me," Alida said, motioning for her maids to help her lie beside the dying girl.

Penella, ever protective, protested that she, the lady of the house, could not lie on such filth, but Alida gave her a fierce look, forcing her obedience. The bed was narrow and with the bulk of the two women, the contact between them was intimate.

There had been a time in Alida's life when she would have felt sympathy for this poor, dying girl lying so close beside her. But that time was long gone. Now all she could think of was giving her husband a strong son.

Berta, the midwife, came trundling up the stairs. She was a fat, lazy creature who was needed so often by Lady Alida that she had permanent residence, living somewhere in the top of the old stone castle. Yesterday she had pronounced that the foreign girl was dying and nothing could be done to save her or the baby. Berta was not about to exert any effort on the wife of a man like Rasher, who she knew would never pay her. Never mind that she worked only a few hours every nine months, she thought she was nearly a lady herself since she delivered her ladyship's babies.

When Alida raised her legs to the very familiar position of birth, the old woman's hands were so slick with pig grease from the wedding feast, she did not need a lubricant to check the progress of the coming babe.

"It will be here soon," Berta said with authority, then glanced at the closed eyes and the deathly pallor of the girl close beside Alida. "That one's done for. I told you so yesterday," she said as though the girl's persistence at holding on to life was an affront to Berta herself. She was thinking only of the dinner she'd had to leave behind to attend to her ladyship and she wanted to make sure that everyone knew it was not her duty to look after dirty, dark-skinned foreigners as well.

As Alida's contractions came with closer frequency, she twined her arm about the girl's, feeling her cold skin next to her own. Her fingers slipped about the girl's nearly lifeless ones. She did this not for comfort or even for relief of pain, for the truth was, Alida often felt that she could have continued her embroidery during birth.

The reason she held the girl's hand was to encourage the spirit of that child to enter her child. Alida began to pray, turning her head toward the girl so she was close to her ear. "God, grant that this child may come unto me," she whispered, for what felt like hours.

The girl had shown little sign of life for quite a while, but just lay there unmoving, her huge belly swollen. It was as though the child inside her had given up hope of trying to get out and had resigned itself to its approaching death.

When the girl seemed to be drawing her last breath, Alida turned the limp head toward her so they were nose to nose. With all the life Alida had in her, she prayed and begged God to give her child the spirit of this woman's son.

When she felt Alida's breath on her face, the girl's eyelids flickered and after several tries, she managed to open them slightly. When she looked at Alida, with her eyes closed in fervent prayer, the girl seemed to rally some.

To Alida's astonishment, for she thought the girl past any sensibility, the girl's fingers tightened around her own. The girl's grasp was as weak as a kitten's, but Alida could feel life lingering in the frail body.

When the girl spoke it was so quietly that only Alida could hear her. The rest of the women in the room were bustling about, trying to look busy so no one else noticed the faint whispers of a dying girl.

> *"My child shall be your child;*
> *Your child shall be mine.*
> *They will be one spirit in two bodies.*
> *They will live together; they will die*
>   *together."*

Her English was broken, and in ordinary circumstances Alida would have had difficulty understanding her. But it was as though the experience they were now sharing, this giving of life, made the girl's words crystal clear. Alida heard her and knew without a doubt that what the girl had said would be emblazoned on her heart forever.

"Take my child," the girl whispered.

Even Alida blanched at the words. To take the child would mean ripping the girl open, leaving her to die an even more agonizing death than she was now experiencing.

"What's the gypsy girl saying?" Berta asked. To her anyone who did not have the white skin of an Englishman was a "gypsy."

"Take my child," the girl said louder.

When Alida hesitated, the dying girl gripped Alida's hand with all her strength.

"Take my child!" the girl said, her face so close to Alida's that her breath went into Alida's lungs.

"Yes," Alida said and gripped the girl's hand in response. She knew what it felt to be a mother.

"Take the child," Alida commanded, and when the four maids in the room and the midwife did nothing but stand there and look at her as though she weren't aware of what she was saying, she half shouted at them. "Take the girl's child, I tell you. Take it!"

The midwife responded first. "I will need a knife," she said to a stupefied maid behind her. "A large knife and sharp," she repeated, shoving the maid toward the stairs.

Alida had no more time to think as three contractions came together quickly and she knew that her own child was near to being born. She started to pray again, no longer trying to lower her voice, but making sure the girl could hear her. "Let our children blend," she prayed. "Let them be one. Give me this girl's son. Let me have it for my own child."

Suddenly, everything seemed to happen at once. The terrified maid returned with a kitchen knife, and Alida's child began to shoot down the birth canal just as the midwife ripped the belly of the girl open to free the suffocating child from inside her.

Blood was everywhere. It was astounding that so tiny a girl could have so much blood — and there seemed to be something wrong with Alida too, so that for a while no one could tell whose blood belonged to whom.

In the turmoil of seeing to the mothers, the

babies were nearly forgotten. Still attached to their mothers, who at the moment both seemed in danger of dying, the babies were dumped on top of each other, like newborn puppies, lying between their pain-crazed mothers.

One of the children was a boy, an enormous boy, with lots of black hair and black eyes, his skin the color of pale honey. The other child was a girl, as pink and white as a dew drop. The downy hair on her head was golden and her skin was like cream.

Both babies, stunned after the birth, seemed to wrap themselves around each other, clinging to each other as though seeking comfort for what they had just been through. Since no one was holding them aloft and smacking various parts of their bodies, they seemed to feel no need to cry.

Into this chaos of screams for more cloths and more straw to sop up the blood, into the confusion caused by the midwife, who knew that now was the time she had to prove that all the food she'd eaten over the last year was worth it, came the wet nurse.

Meg Watkins was a large woman, perhaps fat, but many said that it was Meg's huge heart that made her so big. She was now nearly thirty years old, an old woman by the standards of the farmers who were her neighbors, and she had taken loving care of hundreds of other people's children.

Nine months ago Meg had become pregnant and nearly everyone in the village had rejoiced for her. They teased her "old" husband, Will, mercilessly, and he, in his quiet way, had blushed. But everyone could see that he was as pleased as Meg was.

But just four days ago Meg had given birth to a set of twins who had lived only long enough to be blessed by the priest. Neither she nor her husband had cried or shown any grief when the babies had died. Meg had gone about her business as though her life had not ended, and her husband had buried the sweet little bodies in the church-yard.

Within minutes of Alida's leaving her daughter's marriage feast, the entire village knew what was about to happen, and they knew that a wet nurse would be wanted. As a body, they went to Meg and her husband and when they met with re-luctance, with Meg saying she wanted to take care of no more children, her husband "per-suaded" her by picking her up and shoving her into the back of a wagon, which took off running, not allowing Meg a chance to change her mind.

So now, Meg found herself entering the chaotic room, with women running hither and thither. Meg took one look at the two women on the bed, saw that one, her belly ripped open, was already dead, while her ladyship looked pale enough to be near death. Meg dismissed the women, for her love of children was such that she cared little for the mothers. Meg's only con-cern was for the two children entwined about each other, nestled between the women.

For all that Meg was sweet tempered, she knew how to get things done and she had known Berta since they were girls together. She knew that Berta was a bully and if allowed, would cause as much confusion as possible and do as little work as she could get away with — all while trying to look enormously important.

While Berta had the young, gullible maids enthralled as she gave an incomprehensible lecture on the state of Alida's afterbirth, Meg took the knife that had been used on his mother and, after tying it off, cut the cord of the boy. In spite of his size, the boy looked as though he needed attention first as there was a quietness about him that made Meg fear for his life. Had she the time, she would have reduced the midwife to tears for her neglect of the babies, but instead, Meg's big, strong arms went out to pick up the slippery boy.

But the minute she touched him, the children's arms and legs tightened about each other, renewing their grip on one another. When Meg gave a gentle tug, they clung tighter. Putting one hand on the girl's chest, and one on the boy's, she pulled, but they held fast to each other. They did not cry; they clung.

Removing her hands, Meg looked down at the children in wonder. In her experience, newborn babies cried or slept after birth. Sometimes they were born hungry and sometimes not. But she had never seen children who were as wide-awake as these two, staring into each other's eyes, their bodies entangled with each other's. If their skin had not been different colors you would not have been able to see where one began and the other ended. The boy, so much larger than the girl, but at the moment so much weaker, was held by the girl in a grip that could only be described as protective.

"So you want to be together, do you?" Meg whispered as she cut the other cord, then scooped up both children into her ample arms.

The two children felt good to her; they felt right. She was still quite shaken by the loss of her own two children and now her arms were at last filled with babies.

The babies did not trust her. They seemed to think that she would again try to separate them, so they held each other fiercely, defiantly, as though they dared anyone to try to separate them.

"It's all right," she cooed to them. "I won't let you be taken from one another. I will protect you. I won't let anyone harm you."

As though the children understood her, they relaxed their fierce grip and softened in Meg's arms.

14

"Let me see my son," Alida said, beginning to recover from her near swoon after the birth. She could not understand her reaction to what had happened. This birth was no different than any of her others, in fact it was less difficult since the child had been rather small. But when the midwife's knife had touched the girl beside her, she had felt the pain, felt every inch of flesh that the callous woman had cut into. Somehow, Alida knew that the girl had been alive until the birth of her child, until she knew that the child did indeed live, and only then had she died. Alida also knew that the girl had died happily, knowing that her child would live and be cared for.

Alida did not like to think of it now but after the girl died, it was as though Alida could feel the girl's spirit hovering above the scene, looking down at them, watching everything, taking a moment to look at her child. The girl was at peace, no longer in the body that had been split nearly in half; she felt no pain.

It was Alida who felt the pain. Her body felt as though it had been the one cut open. She, who prided herself on her easy births, she who had great contempt for women who screamed and ranted over such a small thing as giving birth, realized that she was screaming with all her might. She was incoherent with pain, her hands on her belly, making sure that it was still in one piece. It did not feel as though it were in a single piece but felt torn and bleeding, ripped, slashed. The pain was intolerable and she screamed hysterically while the midwife and her maids searched frantically for the cause of her pain. In the turmoil of the search, the children were temporarily forgotten.

Now, with utter confidence, Alida asked to see her son, for of course she had given birth to a son. No woman could go through what she had and not be given what she wanted. Alida had never done anything to God to cause Him to be so cruel as to give her another daughter.

Alida's words effectively managed to hush the room as all eyes except Meg's were upon her. Meg was interested only in wrapping a clean cloth about the children so they wouldn't get cold.

"Well!" Alida said with as much strength as she could manage, for she was weak from pain. "Where is my son?"

None of Alida's maids wanted the blast of her wrath when she was told that she had had yet another daughter.

Meg felt no such qualms. She knew, of course, about her ladyship's prayers for a son, but Meg thought they were ridiculous. What did it matter whether a child was a girl or a boy? A child was a Gift from God and should be treated as such.

"You have a beautiful daughter," Meg said, moving forward in the sudden stillness of the room to smilingly present the children to Alida.

At first Alida refused to hear what was being said. She could *not,* could *not* have had yet another girl.

"There now, isn't she pretty?" Meg was saying as she bent over Alida and showed her the two children in her arms. Meg pulled back the soft cloth covering them. "See how white her skin is, how fine her hair. And such pretty eyes! She will be the most beautiful of your daughters, I can tell."

Alida, dazed from pain, stunned with disappointment, could not yet believe her misfortune. Now all she could see was the big, golden-skinned boy next to the insignificant blonde girl.

"Let me see my son. Let me see him," Alida said frantically, her hands reaching out to take the boy, ignoring the girl.

When Meg realized what she was about to do, she drew back. "No!" she said sharply. "The children want to be together."

There was an intake of breath in the room. Alida's fierce, quick temper was renowned. The anger her husband took out on her, she took

171

out on those around her, and now they feared her wrath.

But there was something about Meg's common sense, her lack of fear, that brought Alida back to reality. "I want the boy," she whispered. "He should have been mine." Quickly, she began to look about the room, seeing who was there, calculating if she could terrorize these women into silence and secrecy.

She meant to have this boy for her own. Hadn't the girl given him to her? Wasn't he by rights hers? And who's to say that in the confusion the children weren't switched and this boy was hers and the girl belonged to that dead foreigner? Never mind that all her daughters had been blonde and this boy had a thick crop of black hair.

Could she do it? she wondered.

Only Meg, who did not live daily with Alida and therefore did not see firsthand what she had suffered from her husband over the years, did not know what her ladyship was thinking. And had she known it would not have mattered to her, as long as both children were cared for.

Penella, who had been with Alida since her marriage, was the first to speak. There were tears in her eyes, for she loved her mistress and had, over the years, seen her change from a happy, laughing girl into the virago she now was. "That one," she whispered, pointing to the dead body of the boy's mother, "had an old servant woman here. The instant the boy was born, she went to tell the father."

For a moment Alida's head reeled with anger, anger at herself, anger at everyone for not having earlier thought of switching the babies. She could have made the suggestion to her maid and she could have cleared the room except for the midwife and herself. The switch would have been easy then. No one would have dared dispute that the son was hers and not this dead girl's.

And if she'd told John that the boy was his he would have killed that odious Gilbert Rasher if he dared contradict the statement. But most important, her husband would *love* her. Truly love her.

"I will try to catch her," Penella whispered as she opened the door to run after the herald.

But John was standing outside the door and behind him, drunk, his dirty face red, was Gilbert Rasher.

In spite of all he could do to keep the hope from his voice and from his face, there was anticipation on John's face. "There has been a son born," he said, trying to sound as though he did not believe this could be true, but he was not a good actor.

Pushing her way through the two men standing in the doorway was a tiny, monkeylike creature, an old woman with black eyes and hands like a bird's claws. "*My* lady has given birth to a son," she half yelled in heavily accented words. "They killed her to take the babe. He belongs to me. He is *mine!*"

173

At that Gilbert Rasher pushed his way into the room and smacked the little woman across the face, sending her reeling. "Out!" he commanded. "I don't have to stand that ugly face of yours any longer."

He lumbered his way into the room, pretending to be drunker than he was, pretending to be oblivious to what was going on in the room, but the truth was, he was a very, very shrewd man. In order to make a decent living a lazy man had to find ways other than actual work to keep furs on his back and beef on his table.

For the last two days he had chosen the plainest-faced maids and pretended great lust at the mere sight of them. They were so pleased by his attentions that they each went to bed with him and when he asked to hear all the gossip of the castle, they were more than willing to tell it. He now knew in detail how much John wanted a son and how his wife had paid much gold to an old witch woman to try to help her to get that son.

Gilbert had paid the hideous little creature that his wife had brought with her from her foreign country to stay in the room, silent and unseen, and bring him news immediately when his son was born. Unlike Alida, who acted out of desperation, Gilbert planned things, and he correctly guessed that if Lady Alida's time came during his wife's, she would think of switching the children, for surely Hadley's next child would also be a daughter.

It wasn't that Gilbert especially wanted another son. The three he had ate enough for half an army and it cost to clothe them. He did not bother with education and was therefore spared that expense, but unfortunately that meant he was burdened with sons who knew no more than he did.

Now he knew that if he played his cards right he might be able to get John to pay him while still bearing the cost of raising a son who was not his.

"Let me see my son," Gilbert said, his voice as full of love as he could make it sound as he went toward Meg, the babies cuddled in her arms. He meant to take the child, to display it like something won in a tournament, but he didn't like babies at best and this one was covered with blood and grease and was unnaturally clinging to the tiny white girl. Right away, some sixth sense of self-preservation — the trait that was honed to its keenest edge in Gilbert — told him that there was something unusual about this child and he'd do best to get rid of it — with a profit of course. He should never have married that silent, big-eyed foreign girl that was the child's mother. Even thinking of her, he had to resist the urge to cross himself.

John was still standing in the doorway, staring at his wife, and the hatred in his eyes was enough to set the room on fire. It was a while before he could find his voice. It didn't matter to him that the words he said he'd said a thousand times before. With each daughter his rage was fresh.

"How can this worm of a girl breed a son and you cannot?" John asked, glaring at his wife. Gilbert Rasher's tiny wife had now been covered with a blanket so the wound that split her body in half could not be seen, but her lifeless form barely made the blanket rise. Beside her, Alida was big and healthy, her skin glowing with life in spite of what she had just been through.

For several minutes John told his wife what he thought of her, humiliating her in front of her maids and Rasher, whose eyes gleamed with delight at the altercation.

Through all of this Meg clasped the children to her and they had not uttered a sound, still awake, still alert and looking into each other's eyes.

For the first time John seemed to be fully aware of the children, or rather, the boy. With one stride, he went to stand in front of Meg and look down at the two babies she held. John was not a superstitious man and he did not have the cunning of Gilbert. When he saw the two children clinging to each other, no feelings of oddity occurred to him. Nor did any thoughts of fastidiousness cloud his mind. All he saw was a large, perfect son, a son such as he had always wanted.

With one great wrench, before Meg could protest, he pulled the two children apart and clasped the boy to him.

Never had such a howl been set up as when the children were pulled apart. If there had been any thought that the boy was weak from the birth, it was dispelled the moment he opened his mouth and began to bellow — as did the girl. The sheer volume of the cacophony was startling. It was as though a hundred banshees had been loosened into the old stone room and the sound reverberated off the walls.

The eyes of everyone in the room widened, one maid put her hands over her ears, Meg looked frantically at the boy squirming in John's arms, while Gilbert, seated near his dead wife's body, thought that by having to stay near this he had to work too hard for a living. Only John seemed oblivious to the noise.

"*This* is a son, madam," he shouted to his wife. "*This* is what you should have given me. No twisted feet. No weak lungs. Do you not know how to make sons in that belly of yours?"

Gilbert saw that John was going to keep on in this way for some time and might never arrive at the bargain he had in mind so he took the initiative. "Oh, my beloved wife," he wailed and had to raise his voice to the level that he used on the tournament field. What with those damned brats squalling and John's bellowing, he could hardly hear himself.

"My beloved wife!" Gilbert yelled. "You of all the women did I love. And now I must try to raise yet another son alone, with no mother. I can hardly afford to feed those I have. How will I feed this one? And what about teaching him? When will I find time to teach him what a boy needs to know? Who will ride with him?

Hunt with him? Who will celebrate with him when he brings down his first boar?"

John had at last stopped his tirade against his wife and was looking at Gilbert, blinking as, slowly, thoughts came to him.

"Give the brat to the woman to feed," Gilbert said crossly. Was the man unnatural that he could not hear that din?

When John realized that he might be starving the precious child in his arms, he acted as though a fire had been lit under him. In one step he was across the room to Meg and tenderly handed her the baby. As soon as the boy and the girl were again touching each other, the crying stopped.

With satisfaction John watched as Meg pulled her rough gown open and revealed a pair of splendid, full breasts and within seconds both children had latched onto them and were hungrily sucking.

This bit of diversion had given John time to consider what he had heard — and in case he did not fully understand Gilbert's meaning, the man started again.

"Oh Lord," Gilbert loudly prayed, "give me strength in this my hour of need. You know that I am a poor man. I have been blessed with connections to the throne through the Stuart line but I have not been blessed with money. I do not know how I will afford to clothe this son as befits his rank. I do not —"

"You may leave us now," Alida said coldly,

knowing full well what Gilbert was trying to accomplish.

John was thinking so hard about what he wanted and the seed that Gilbert had planted in his head that for once he did not rage at his wife. He merely held up his hand to her for silence. It did not enter his head that Gilbert Rasher *wanted* to give his son away; to give away something as valuable as this was tantamount to giving away a mountain of gold. Hadn't he worked for this all his life? But to Gilbert sons were easily made; gold was much more valuable.

"I . . . ," John said softly, praying he wouldn't offend Gilbert, "I will undertake the care of your son. I will feed him, train him."

Gilbert looked as though this were a startling idea. "You could not do such a kind thing for me," he said. "No man is capable of such generosity." As though weighed down by grief, Gilbert lumbered to his feet and started toward his hungrily nursing son.

John blocked his way. "I must do something to help a man in need." Frantically, he searched his mind for something he "owed" Gilbert. "Your wife died in my house. It is the fault of the midwife who works for me. To repay you I will toss her out and pay for the care of your son."

At that Berta began to protest, but a look from Alida shut her up. Alida wanted to stop what she could see was going to happen but she knew of no way. She had given her husband many daughters and two sons but all that pain was now being thrown away. It would have been all right if she could have switched the children without the knowledge of her husband. He would have loved her for giving him a son. But now he would know that she had failed and he would hate her. And what is more, he would give everything — all land and property — to this child who was not his.

"No, no," Gilbert said with a great sigh. "You cannot throw your midwife onto the streets. I'm sure she is good. It was not her fault, it was mine. I breed sons of such great size that the women cannot bear them. Had I any consideration I would give my women small, golden girls as you do."

"The horse you admired yesterday," John said. "It is yours."

Gilbert looked offended. "You think I would trade my *son* for a horse?" he said righteously.

"No, no, of course not." All the horses in the world would not have made John part with a large, strong, healthy son.

Slowly, to give John time to come up with a richer offer for the boy, Gilbert sauntered over to where Meg held the babies. When John could think of nothing else to say, Gilbert helped. "I cannot take a nursing child from its milk. I must wait." With another dramatic sigh, he said, "I wish I could leave the boy with you."

At that John's eyes widened.

"If there were only a connection between our

families. Perhaps a marriage bond. I need a new wife."

"Take your choice of my daughters," John said quickly. "You may have any of them you want. For yourself, for your sons. Whatever you want. They are yours."

"I will take that red-haired one," Gilbert said instantly.

At that Alida gasped, for her daughter Joanna was only ten years old. "You cannot." She looked imploringly at her husband.

John did not so much as look at his wife. "She is yours."

"And what of her dowry?" Now that the bargaining was under way, Gilbert was dropping his guise of grief.

"Peniman Manor," John said quickly.

Alida's hands tightened into knots at her side. Peniman Manor was *hers,* given to her in her own right by her father. It was where she went whenever she had a chance, a place where she could have a beautiful garden that she knew was not going to be trampled by the hooves of men's horses. It was a place where no man was welcome and it was where anything that she had ever owned or made that was beautiful was stored. Her husband hated the place, with its tapestries and books and great bowls of scented herbs on the polished tables.

When Alida opened her mouth to protest, John turned a face black with rage toward her. "You have taken from me what was mine by right and

181

now I will take what is yours." He looked back at Gilbert. "Peniman Manor is yours, as is the girl. And I will keep the boy." He was at last beginning to realize that getting the boy was only a matter of money.

"I do not know if I should leave the boy. He is a fine lad, is he not? Look how strong he is. Already the girl has stopped sucking but the boy continues. I guarantee that he will grow into a fine, strong man."

With his heart beating in his throat, John tried to make himself think of this as bargaining for a horse. Except that he had never wanted a horse as much as he wanted this boy.

"Children die," John said with a shrug that fooled no one. "I am not sure I should agree to keep the boy. What do I get from raising your overlarge son? He will no doubt eat me out of house and home."

"It would be an honor for you to raise a boy who is connected to the throne," Gilbert said as though affronted.

"Ha! I will raise him, educate him and then you will take him away and marry him to some puny girl who is nothing to me."

Gilbert did so love negotiating. It made his blood course through his body. "Mmmm," he said, rubbing his chin. "You are right, of course." He always liked to flatter the other dealer. Gilbert's head came up. "We will betroth those two. What say you to that?"

John wanted to jump up and touch the sky

in joy but he didn't say anything at first. "I spend a lifetime feeding him, clothing him, educating him, then he marries my daughter and goes to live in the house I must provide them. I can get husbands for my daughters and I do not have to raise them."

It took Gilbert a few moments to figure out what John was after. "You want an heir," he said softly and he was astonished. John was a fool if he trusted anyone, especially to leave all his property to a boy who was not his blood relative. For a moment Gilbert looked John up and down. John was nearly forty years old, and for all that Gilbert had led a life of debauchery that made his look much older, he was only twenty-eight. If John made this boy his heir, after his death Gilbert could come in, claim the boy and take everything.

"Do not do it!" Alida shouted at her husband, for she read Rasher's thoughts as though he had spoken aloud. "Do you not see what he is after? He has found a way to steal all that you have. If you die he will take all."

John turned a furious face on her. "If I die, what do I care what happens to my property afterward? Should I work all my life and leave it to a woman who gives me only daughters? Should I give it to those two worthless boys you gave me? One can hardly walk and the other is too weak to live." He glared at her. "All of you can live on a dung heap for all I care."

He turned back to Gilbert. "Give me the boy,

183

we will draw up contracts, and I will betroth him to a daughter — I have enough of those — and I will make him my heir. While I am alive, he will be mine."

While I am alive, Gilbert thought. If John died before the boy reached age, Gilbert would have control of him. Truthfully, Gilbert would have control no matter how old the boy was when John died. Gilbert had always thought so but today had proved that John's heart was too soft. He gave away everything for something that could never truly be his. Blood was everything; contracts on paper meant nothing. When the boy was a few years older, Gilbert could say that he was lonely and meant to take the boy back unless John paid him more money.

"What can console me now, this moment, for the loss of the son of this woman I loved so much?" Gilbert asked.

For a moment John was at a loss. What more could he give than everything he owned?

"There is a horse . . . ," Gilbert prompted. "And a few gold goblets. I need something to drink out of. But, alas, I have no wine in that old castle of mine. Perhaps a new roof might keep the rain out."

With hatred boiling inside her, Alida listened for nearly an hour as her husband "bargained." It could not rightfully be called bargaining, since John gave that contemptible man everything he asked for. He gave him wine and cattle and lead for his roof, as well as craftsmen to install the roof. He gave away the six gold goblets that Alida had brought to him upon their marriage. They were beautiful things, set with rubies, chased with designs of the lives of the saints, and her family had used them for generations. She had meant to give them to her eldest son's family, but now they were going to this dirty man who she had no doubt would melt them down within hours of receiving them.

After a while she stopped looking at her husband and turned her attention to the sleeping children the wet nurse held. *Here* was the cause of all her problems.

Perhaps it was the years of misery, of the constant, ceaseless belittling from her husband. Maybe it was nineteen years of praying and not receiving what she begged for, but in that moment something inside Alida broke.

Alida could no longer believe she would ever win her husband's favor. She had been a good wife to him, running his estates cleanly and efficiently. He never had any idea how things inside his houses got done, how food was properly cooked and put on the table. He left all of that to his wife, and Alida had done a brilliant job of it. She had managed servants while nearly constantly pregnant. When there were problems, and there were many, she took care of everything and her husband was never disturbed.

Now, after nineteen years of being an excellent wife to him, he was giving away everything that had been her family's for centuries to a child who was of no relation to him. He was ignoring his own children, children who were intelligent as well as handsome, to bestow everything on that creature.

She looked at the black-haired child cradled in the fat arms of the wet nurse and a hatred such as she'd never before known existed came over her. And every fiber of her hatred was directed at the baby still sucking life from that farm woman. Already today the child had killed his mother and now he might as well have killed her too. He had robbed an entire family of its rightful inheritance, of its future.

15

"I will name the boy," John said and there was a new light in his eyes, a light that his wife had never seen before.

It was a full day since she had given birth and out of exhaustion she had been able to sleep, but not so John. He had insisted that a lawyer be brought to him straightaway and that documents be drawn up between him and Gilbert Rasher. He was afraid Gilbert would change his mind about the child and take him away.

After the papers were signed, John had gone to the wedding guests below and announced that he had been delivered of a son. For being able to give this lie without contradiction, he had agreed to pay Rasher three fields of grain every year for as long as the boy lived. This in addition to all the other riches he'd promised him.

There was much rejoicing when John told his news. To show off his new son, John snatched the boy away from the wet nurse and again the boy, as well as the girl, began to scream so loudly even the riotous laughter of the guests could not cover the noise.

Quietly, Meg went to John and handed him his daughter into the other arm and instantly the crying of both children stopped. For a moment John could not think what to do. He was terrified that the people would guess that the boy was not his and know that this girl was what his cursed wife had given him.

Gilbert, seeing the rage creeping up John's neck, stepped forward and announced that since the children were born on the same day, they would be betrothed to each other.

At that there was more cheering and more drinking.

John glanced with disgust at the girl he held, looking as though he might drop her as he would any distasteful object.

"Hold my daughter up," Gilbert said. "Let the people see how beautiful she is. None of you knew I could breed such beauty, did you?" Raucously, he winked at the crowd and they howled with laughter. Maybe Gilbert Rasher could have been a handsome man, but he'd had a father who beat his nose flat and he'd been thrown from horses and hit with lances, and from the time he was ten, he'd fought every male and some females he came across. His face was now too distorted to know what he should have looked like.

"What are their names?" someone in the crowd called out.

"Yes, yes," John answered, still annoyed at finding himself holding two children instead of the one he wanted.

"I will name him . . ." John looked up at the crowd and smiled. "I will name him after my father." He smiled broader. "And myself, of course. I give you John Talis Hadley." For a moment he was too overcome with emotion to speak but when he did, his voice trembled. "My son."

The applause was thunderous as people were genuinely glad for him. Only one or two suspected the truth, but they were smart enough to keep their mouths shut.

"And, Gilbert," someone yelled, "what of your daughter? What is her name?"

Since Gilbert had never in his life given a thought to something as mundane as naming his children, he was at a loss. For a moment he stood with his mouth opening and closing.

Greatly daring, Meg spoke up. "Callasandra," she said loudly. "Do you not remember, my lord? You named the child Callasandra." It was a name she had heard years before from some traveling players and she'd thought it was beautiful, almost as beautiful as the little girl.

The people around them toyed with this name for a while then a woman said, "How very pretty," and nodded her head in approval. Soon John was agreeing, as well as Gilbert, that this was the child's name.

"Let me take them," Meg said, slipping both

the children from John. She could not bear to have them out of her arms for much longer.

While Meg sat in a corner and nursed the children, John announced that Gilbert was to marry John's ten-year-old daughter and after a moment this news was greeted with great grumbling. Gilbert was not liked by anyone, but because of his connection to the court he was tolerated. But now that most of the people were drunk they had fewer inhibitions in showing their disgust at this man's lechery of this innocent child.

Gilbert had to control his anger at John's stupidity for making such an announcement. He would have liked to marry the girl in private and taken her away for his own amusement with no one knowing it.

"Have no fear," Gilbert said loudly, trying to make a jest. "I will not take her to bed until her womanhood is upon her."

"And may God rest her soul," a woman muttered and too many people laughed.

John cared for nothing or no one but the boy who was nursing so eagerly. He would never let the boy out of his sight. Never let anyone or anything harm him. He would give him the best of everything. He would give him *all*.

16

Only Alida's maid, Penella, knew the extent of how affected her mistress had been by the last few days. Because of John's deal with Gilbert she knew there would be no more chances for her to give her husband a son. Her husband would never again visit her bed, and besides, it had taken her months to conceive this child. Her time of childbearing was at an end.

On the day John Hadley claimed that black-haired boy as his son, his wife gave up hope.

For nineteen years Alida had somehow sustained hope. She had believed that if she gave her husband what he wanted, someday he would turn to her in love. She knew now that it would not be. Just as he had given away Peniman Manor, he would not hesitate to take away anything that had meaning to her.

"All I have now are my children," she whispered as she stood before the arrow slit window of the old stone keep. "*My* children. Not the child of another man and his . . ." She could not think how to describe the child-woman who had held her hand during the birth and said such strange things to her.

> *"My child shall be your child;*
> *Your child shall be mine.*
> *They will be one spirit in two bodies.*
> *They will live together; they will die*
>   *together."*

That's what the girl had said. The words were emblazoned on her brain.

"Come to bed, my lady," Penella said softly, her hands on her mistress's shoulders, trying to make her rest. She had never seen her like this and she was frightened. Alida had always been a beautiful woman, and age and years of child-bearing had only barely dimmed her beauty, but the events of this week had changed her overnight into what Penella saw now.

Alida's hair straggled about her face, each day showing more gray. It had been two days since the birth of the children and with each passing hour Alida looked worse. She refused to eat. She slept only after she'd paced the floor for many hours, then she fell into a fretful sleep in which she talked nonsense. Penella had shooed everyone else out of the room and was now taking care of her mistress alone. She did not want anyone else to see her like this.

It was on the night of the third day that Alida's sleeping rambles made sense to Penella. At first she did not believe what she was hearing. There was something about, "They will die together," then over and over again, "They must die together. They must die together."

Penella put down her knitting and sat very still. She didn't want to think that her mistress had lost her reason.

"Fire will cleanse them," Alida said. "Fire will make them both die together."

Penella had no idea what she was going to do, but she got up and went to the door. Catching a passing maid, she told her she was to remain outside her ladyship's door and if she allowed anyone to enter, she would be punished severely. Since all the maids knew of Alida's punishments, she obeyed.

Raising her skirts, slipping through the night, Penella made her way to the far tower. This is where John had ensconced "his" son along with the daughter he cared nothing about. There was a guard outside the door but he was asleep so Penella had no trouble slipping past him.

Inside the dark room there was only moonlight to show her the big bed where the wet nurse slept, a sleeping baby cuddled on each side of her.

"Wake up," Penella said softly so the guard wouldn't hear.

She nearly jumped out of her skin when she felt a man's hand on her shoulder. Turning, she saw a short, stout, pleasant-looking man, his face weathered by years of sun and wind.

"Who are you?" she gasped.

"Will. Meg's husband. What is amiss?"

She could see that he was a man of great sensibility. "I am afraid," she said and instantly felt guilty, as though she were betraying her mistress. Thinking that perhaps she was wrong to have come, she turned to leave, but Will kept his hand firmly on her shoulder.

"What is it? You must tell me."

There was something so sweet natured about this man, something so reliable, that she found herself pouring out everything to him in a voice barely above a whisper. "It has been too much for my mistress. I think she means to harm the boy. I think —" She put her hands over her face.

"How?" Will asked.

"F . . . fire," she answered. "She speaks of fire."

Will had had no formal education but he had handled many emergencies in his life on a farm and he knew how to act quickly. "We must get the children and Meg out of here."

"There is probably no danger. I'm sure my mistress was only rambling. I'm sure —"

"Yes, of course she was," Will said soothingly. "Mayhap she was talking in her sleep. She has just had a baby. Sometimes women say odd things at times like that. I'm sure it is nothing, so you must go back to her and see that she is well cared for."

"Yes, you are right," Penella said gratefully,

so glad for this man's calm strength.

"Go on now. Go to bed. Everything will look all right in the morning."

After she left, Will lost no time in waking Meg. He knew he had to get all of them out of there as quickly as possible. Since Meg had told him of the switch of the children, he had expected something like this to happen. Of course Alida would kill this boy who now threatened her own children.

Meg, good, sweet Meg, did not ask questions when her husband woke her and told her she was to sneak the children past the guard and get out of the castle grounds as fast as possible. She sensed that the children were in danger and that was enough for her.

Will went outside and distracted the guard with an exceedingly vulgar story while Meg held the sleeping children close to her and ran down the old stone steps. Once outside she pulled her shawl over her head and kept walking briskly toward the village. She thanked heaven that in these modern times there was no raising and lowering of the drawbridge. The truth of why John Hadley still lived in a castle was that he was too cheap to build a comfortable house. The thick stone walls were no longer needed for protection.

Once Will was sure there had been enough time for Meg to get away, he tried very hard to think. If there were a fire and babies were to have been burned, tiny bodies would be expected to be found. If bodies were not found, a search would be made and, alive, the boy would always be in danger.

It took Will only a moment to decide what he had to do. He did not like it and he thought that perhaps performing such a hideous deed would guarantee that he would not be allowed into heaven. But when it came to Meg and those children she already loved so much, he didn't mind giving up heaven.

Leaving the castle, he went running toward the churchyard where the bodies of his twin sons had been laid to rest days before. If there were a fire, there would be the bodies of two babies found in the rubble.

Just before dawn a fire broke out in the old castle. The ancient oak floor joists went up like paper, making a blaze so hot the lead roof melted and rained down on the people of the courtyard. There was an attempt to put the fire out, but it was too hot too soon.

In the middle of it John Hadley stood and screamed, "My son, my son," over and over again. He would have flung himself into the flames to rescue the child but for half a dozen men holding him back. They could see there was no use, as the first room to go had been the top of the tower where the children were kept.

It was two days before the ashes cooled enough to go through the rubble and in it were found the bodies of two babies. There wasn't much left of the old castle and everyone whose lives depended on the running of the estate waited in anxiety to see what John was going to do. By now the rumors of what had happened after the birth of the two babies had reached epic proportions. Some said that John's wife had given birth to a monster. Some said that the boy was the result of Alida selling her soul to the devil in return for a son. Most people agreed that it was better that both children had died in the cleansing flames.

Some guessed at the truth but the ones who knew were wise enough to keep their own counsel.

What everyone feared was what would happen when John came out of the room where he had barred himself.

When he did emerge a week later, he was a changed man. His hair, once solid black, was now the color of steel. There were deep runnels down the sides of his mouth and there was a hard, cold, dead look in his eyes.

He rode into the courtyard on a violent horse, one that John had previously said was good only to feed the dogs, and its mouth dripped blood from the saw-toothed bridle he was using.

"What are you doing lying about?" he bellowed at people in the courtyard, and even his voice seemed to have changed. "There is work to be done," he yelled. "I am going to build a house. A fine house. A house to honor my queen. Now get off your backsides and *work!*"

From that day forward there was no mention of the son who had died in the fire and John

Hadley was a changed man. Before, he had been a man of simplicity, a man of great passion, of great loves and great hates, but now he seemed to have nothing inside him. He hated no one, loved no one. His only concern was in building a stone house, a beautiful stone house filled with beautiful things. It was as though he'd come to the decision that if he could not leave behind children who suited him, he would leave behind a house of great significance.

As for his wife, she too had changed, but for the better. Now her husband did not curse her or revile her. He no longer visited her bed but for that she was glad. In truth, John came to look at her as he would another man, and when he found out she knew something about gardens, he began asking her opinion.

As the years went by, their marriage was replaced with friendship and little by little, Alida's hope began to come back to her. Some women would have hated their husbands to look at them with no warmth, but for Alida, the absence of hate in her husband's eyes was almost love.

Never did she for a minute regret what she had done in setting the fire and killing the boy, and her own daughter as well. She felt that the two of them had died so her many other children could live now and in the future. Now there was no more talk of giving Gilbert Rasher all of her children's property. In fact the man had shown up after the fire and said that John "owed" him even though the boy was dead. It was not his fault the boy had died. John had spit on the contract and walked away. Gilbert rode away and did not bother the Hadley family again, not even to claim the ten-year-old girl who was to have been his bride.

Nearly fifty miles away, Will and Meg Watkins bought a farm and settled down to raise "their" two children. Will never told his wife that on the night they left, he had stolen a bag containing six exquisite gold cups out from under the very arm of a heavily sleeping Gilbert Rasher. The cups were now hidden under the floor of the farmhouse, quite safe, one missing a ruby he'd used to pay for the farm, but otherwise intact. When the children were older he planned to give the cups to them.

He didn't tell Meg the truth about the fire, about the burned bodies of the infants found in the rubble. He didn't want her to think her precious babies were in danger or he feared she might never let them out the door.

He told her John had given him money to buy the farm and had wanted them to move away from the village where they'd both grown up because there had been cases of plague reported there. Will said that John and his wife were building a fine new house and many, many years from now he would want Meg to bring the children to him. Until then she and Will were to give them a safe, country upbringing.

All Meg cared about was that the children were

hers. She was glad she wouldn't have to take them to the castle and turn them over to someone else as soon as they were weaned. But just in case, she nursed them until they were two years old.

And after they were weaned and no one came for them, Meg seemed to forget that the children were not hers.

But Will never forgot and never for an instant did he stop his vigilance in watching any strangers who appeared on the horizon.

17

Eight Years Later

1579

"Horses!" Callie said in disgust. "You always want horses. Have you no imagination?"

"As much as you have," Talis said, defending himself, but he knew it wasn't true. Callie was the one with the stories in her head.

He was walking in the dusty road behind the slow-moving wagon as they returned from taking their produce to the village market. Will was, as usual, sitting on the wagon seat sound asleep, letting the ancient old horse find its own way home. Callie was sitting on the back of the wagon, swinging her insect-bitten bare legs, her hands tucked under her legs as she leaned forward and watched Talis brandishing his wooden sword.

They were very different-looking children. Talis was as dark as Callie was fair, and he was as big and sturdily built as she was delicately made; he was as handsome as she was plain. He was quite large for his age, being only eight, but he looked at least twelve years old, while Callie had a sweet, innocent expression that made her seem much younger than her years. Talis often demonstrated that he could pick her up and swing her around. But then Callie retaliated by slipping through tiny places that he could not get his big body through. She took delight in reminding him of the time he got stuck in the iron bars across a window in the cellar of an old house.

"Can't you think of something better than horses?" she asked with great disdain in her voice.

Talis made a fierce jab at an imaginary foe with his sword. "*Your* job is to think of things."

"Oh? If I am to think, what good are you?"

"Men are to protect women, to be brave and honest. Men are made for honor and good deeds; men are —"

"Ha, ha!" Callie mocked. "What do you know of brave deeds? Your last fight was getting that big turnip out of the ground. Unless you count the cow stepping on your foot."

She didn't bother him at all as he kept on thrusting with his sword. "All right, then, dragons," he said after a while.

Callie gave a mock groan. "It's always either dragons or horses."

He ran a couple of steps, then leaped onto the tail of the wagon to sit beside her. "Someday you might be grateful that I know so much about dragons when I come to rescue you."

"I can rescue myself."

"Ha!" he said. "How can you defend yourself from a dragon? By talking him to death?"

Callie considered the question. "Why yes. I will

tell him such a wonderful story that he'll stop and listen."

Holding out his sword, Talis narrowed his eyes. "Then while he is listening to you —"

"Listening so hard he cannot move," she added.

"Turned to stone, he will be. While he's listening, I'll creep up on him and —"

Callie's eyes lit up in a way that Talis loved: It meant she was about to tell a story. "You will climb up his back. He won't feel you because you will have on magic shoes, shoes that were given to you by a witch who wanted you to kill the dragon, and —"

"Why?"

He didn't have to explain his "why" because she knew what he meant. "You saved the witch's baby and —"

"Witches don't have babies!" he said in disgust.

Annoyed, she said, "All right then, it's a baby she loves because it's so beautiful. Everyone loves the baby, even the dragon. *He* loves it so much he wants to *eat* it. That way the baby will be with him forever."

Talis's eyes rounded at that.

Secure in her audience now, Callie dithered a bit. She was clever enough to have no vanity about her looks, but when it came to her storytelling, she had a great deal of vanity. For the rest of the way home she kept him enthralled with her story of magic shoes that made him weightless so he could climb the dragon's back and pierce its heart. As it lay dying its only request was to hear the end of Callie's story.

When she had finished, Talis was unsmiling. "I'm glad I killed him, Callie. Maybe he would have wanted to eat you so he'd have all your stories inside him."

"Would you be sad if a dragon ate me?"

"Sure," he said. "If you died, who would tell me stories?" At that remark, he jumped off the wagon and started running the few feet to the house while Will, awake now (the horse knew just when to jerk the reins to wake him), drove into the yard.

"I'll get you for that," Callie yelled, jumping off and running after him.

Talis ran toward Meg, standing in the doorway and watching for them, as she always was when they returned. Will said she sensed when they were going to return, but the truth was that she was always so terrified that the three of them would disappear that she spent most of market day standing in the doorway and waiting.

Talis, nearly as tall as Meg, grabbed her thick waist and dodged Callie as she tried to hit him.

"Now, now, what's this?" Meg asked. "Have you two been quarreling again?" She was trying to be stern, since Will was always telling her that she spoiled the children outrageously, but she didn't fool them. They knew Meg would give them anything it was in her power to give.

As for the children quarreling, it wasn't so much that they got angry but they teased each other mercilessly. They competed with each other constantly. There was no feeling that Talis could do something because he was a boy or that Callie did things because she was a girl. They challenged each other to see who could climb the highest in a tree, and to Meg's horror, Callie would follow the much stronger Talis *anywhere.*

Meg would never forget the time two years ago when Will had taken Talis with him to the market for the first time. Neither of the adults thought much of it at the time. Will needed help and Talis was big enough to give him help, while Callie, being so tiny and a girl, would just be in the way.

Talis had been so excited about getting to go to the village, he'd talked about it for days. Callie had realized from the first that she wasn't going to go but she'd said nothing. On the morning he was to go, Meg hadn't had to wake Talis, and that was unusual since he was a sleepyhead. He got dressed quickly, wolfed his breakfast and when Meg told him to get on the wagon, he ran to the door. Then, abruptly, he halted and turning back, frowning, he said impatiently, "Come on, Callie, it's time to go!"

It was Will who told him that Callie was too little to go with them.

Meg would never forget the look on Talis's handsome face. He was stunned; it had never occurred to him that Callie would not go with them. She doubted if he'd ever contemplated doing anything without Callie. They slept in the same bed and spent every minute of every day together. As far as she knew, they had never been apart for more than minutes since they were born.

Silently, with what Meg knew was a false show of bravery, Talis followed Will out the door and got on the wagon seat beside him. He didn't once look back at Callie, standing in front of the house, staring after him with big, lonely eyes.

Meg and Will had talked about this and decided it would be "good" for the children to be apart now and then. It would prepare them for what life had in store.

But what could prepare the adults for the devastation of two children who they loved so very much?

All that day Meg had tried to interest Callie in what she was doing. But Callie just sat down on the grass in front of the house and stared at the road. Usually, Callie was very conscientious about her animals, as taking care of the rabbits was her job, but that day she paid no attention when Meg told her the rabbits were hungry.

Meg tried to get some response from her, but there was nothing. Callie just sat there, her knees drawn up, her arms wrapped around them, and stared at the empty road. Meg even tried to get her to come inside to help her cook something special for Talis, but even that got no response.

After a while Meg couldn't stand it anymore so she picked the tiny child up, planning to take her inside the house. Never in her life had Meg seen anyone fight as Callie fought. Callie was usually the sweetest child, but when Meg touched her that day she turned into a raging animal. She stiffened her little body and her hands began to scratch and claw; her feet kicked painfully.

Quickly, Meg put her back down to allow her to continue her silent vigil. By midmorning, Meg gave up trying to interest Callie in anything, so she moved her chair outside and shelled beans while watching the little girl, her heart aching at the emptiness she saw on the child's face.

Then, in the early afternoon, abruptly, Callie's head came up, her ears perking up as though she were a dog listening for something. Meg looked up and down the road that ran before the old farmhouse but saw nothing. Callie sat up straighter, listened more, then, with an agile movement, she was on her feet and running.

Meg tossed down the beans and ran after her but wasn't able to keep up with the eight-year-old child. She was worried that in the state Callie was in she would run in front of a wagon and be hurt.

Meg reached the crossroads and there was tiny Callie standing in the dusty road, turning about, round and round, as though she were demented. Meg went to her, knelt down and tried to hold her in her arms. "Callie, love, Talis will be back soon. You'll see. He'll be back very soon and he'll be all right."

There was a wild look in Callie's eyes. "He can't find me. He can't find me. He's looking for me. He can't find me. He's looking for me.

He can't find me. He can't —"

Clasping the child to her bosom was the only way to stop her frantic cries, to keep her arms from flailing about in a crazy way. Meg's first thought was to get the girl home and into bed. She wanted to reassure her that Talis was safe with Will and he couldn't be lost, but then Meg's heart lurched as she thought, What if Callie is right? What if Talis ran off from Will in the village and had tried to get home? For all that Talis looked half-grown, he was only eight years old and he'd never been to the village before. And if he were anything like Callie was now, he wouldn't have his senses about him to find his way back home.

Right now they were standing at a crossroads of six lanes. It was confusing to an adult, much more so to a child who was frantically trying to get home.

Meg stood up and took Callie's shoulders in her hands. "Listen to me, Callie. You must pay attention. I want you to go down that road there and shout with all your might for Talis. Don't go too far. I don't want to lose you too. Do you understand?"

When the girl's eyes continued to have a glazed look, as though fear was overcoming her reason, Meg gave her a little shake. "Yes," Callie said.

"If you see anyone on the road, tell them what Talis looks like and ask if they have seen him. Ask —"

"Like a magic prince," Callie whispered. "He

208

looks like a magic prince."

"Yes, well, perhaps you'd better tell them he is so high and has black hair and is wearing a green leather jerkin and no doubt has that dreadful sword with him. Can you do that?"

Callie nodded and Meg was sure Callie could and would do *anything* for her beloved Talis.

They shouted and described Talis to people for two hours, then Will came tearing down the road from the village, whipping the old horse into a lather. Will's face was ashen. "He disappeared," he told Meg, not in the least surprised that she and Callie were standing in the middle of the crossroads a mile and a half from their house.

Callie's eyes were so big with fear they threatened to consume her face. She had eaten nothing all day and she was shaking with fatigue, but she would not so much as touch the water Meg tried to get her to drink. "Talis is thirsty," was all the child would say.

After another hour of searching, with the two adults afraid to get out of sight of her, Callie sat down by the side of the road and said in a very adult voice, "I am going to call him to me."

"Yes, of course. You must keep calling. Maybe he will yet hear you," Meg said, trying her best to keep panic from her voice and from her mind. Will had taken the wagon and traveled all six roads for at least a mile, then returned to report that he had seen nothing, nor had anyone he talked to seen a boy like Talis.

Callie sat in the grass by the side of the road under some trees, pulled her knees up, wrapped her arms around them, and put her head on her arms.

"She is resting," Will said to his wife. "Good."

But Meg knew that Callie would not rest as long as Talis was lost so she went to the child and knelt by her, listening. Softly, barely audible, Callie was saying, "Come to me. I am here. You must come to me. Follow my voice. Listen to me. Come to me. Come to me. Come to me."

When Meg stood up she could feel the hairs on the back of her neck standing on end. "She is praying," she said to Will when he looked at her in question, but Meg knew that Callie wasn't praying. Meg had no doubt whatever that Callie was "talking" to Talis — and what is more, she was sure that Talis would "hear" her.

With absolute certainty that she was doing the right thing, Meg quit running down the roads and shouting. She sat a few feet behind Callie, nearly hidden under the trees so as not to disturb her, and waited. Will said something about continuing to look for Talis, but Meg waved him on. She wanted to be here when Talis came back to Callie.

It seemed like forever but it was actually less than an hour, just before sunset, when there was a sound in the bushes on the far side of the road.

Callie's head came up but Meg knew it couldn't be Talis or Callie would be running to him. Callie just sat there, looking at the sound with unblinking intensity. To Meg's surprise, within a moment Talis appeared.

Meg wanted to run to him, to snatch him into her arms and hold him tight enough to crack his ribs, but she forced herself to stay where she was. Never before had she realized how much these children belonged to no adult; they belonged to each other alone.

Slowly, as though she were an adult, Callie lowered her legs and held out her arms to Talis as he came limping across the dirt road. He was filthy, with dried blood on his face from a bloody nose, his trousers torn at the knee, and Meg could see that he'd scraped his knee rather badly. He was missing a shoe and it looked as though his foot were cut. There were streaks of long-dried tears running down his dirty cheeks. Whatever he had been through today had been an ordeal.

Slowly, obviously in pain from his foot and his knee, he limped toward Callie, not even seeing Meg sitting in the shade of the trees. When he reached Callie he collapsed onto her, his arms going around her neck, his body falling against her. He weighed quite a bit more than Callie did, but the girl's little body was as solid as a rock as she supported him with surprising strength.

In as adult a way as could be, Callie maneuvered Talis until his head was in her lap, then she crossed his arms about his chest and held both his hands in hers, her other hand stroking his dirty hair.

Softly, Talis began to cry. "I couldn't find you. You were lost to me. I looked everywhere."

"Yes," Callie whispered.

"I kept hearing you call me."

"I wouldn't let you get lost. You are mine. You are me."

"Yes," Talis whispered, the tears still flowing down his cheeks, his chest heaving while Callie clung to his hands, her fingers intertwining with his, caressing his fingertips with her own.

There were tears running down Meg's cheeks too. Talis was a very, very proud boy and nothing on earth could make him cry. Will had given him three lashes with a belt a few months ago when he'd left the henhouse door open and a fox had eaten four chickens, but Talis hadn't shed a tear at the pain. When he was four he had fallen out of a tree and twisted his arm badly but he hadn't cried then. Even when he was just a year old and he'd been chased by a dog bigger than he was, he hadn't cried. As soon as he was old enough to talk, he'd said, "Boys do not cry."

But now he was lying in Callie's lap and crying until Meg thought her heart would break.

Callie reached behind her head and pulled her fat blonde braid to the front and unfastened the leather thong that tied the bottom of it. Callie was not what one would call pretty. She was plain, with no outstanding features, with her pale eyes and pale lashes, her pale pink lips. Next to Talis's nearly flamboyant good looks she was insignificant. But Callie did have one exceptional feature:

She had beautiful hair. It wasn't thin like most blonde hair but thick and gorgeous, the color of honey, with great streaks of lighter and darker hair running through it. Nearly everyone who saw Callie, not able to comment on her looks, mentioned her hair.

Now, Callie unfastened her braid, ran her hands through her hair to spread it into one luxurious blanket of softness, then began to wipe away Talis's tears, to stroke his face with the richness of her hair.

As Meg watched them, she was embarrassed. She should not be seeing this; no one should be seeing such an intimate thing between two people. At this moment she could not think of these people as children, could not think of them as only eight years old. What Callie was doing was as ancient as love itself, and if Meg had known the word, she would have called it erotic. For that's what Callie's actions were, as erotic as what any woman had ever done for any man.

While Callie stroked his face with her hair, she began to talk to him very, very softly, and as always, Meg wondered what Callie was saying. She had many times speculated about what Callie talked to Talis about, but the children kept their secrets and never let anyone know what went on between them. She had seen Talis stretch out under a tree and listen, without moving, to Callie talk for an hour at a time. But no matter how often Meg asked, they would never tell her what they were talking about. She'd tried to get Will to find out, as Meg knew that Callie talked to Talis on their trips back from the market, but Will had no curiosity. "They talk of all things that children do: ghosts and witches and dragons. What matter is it to me?"

But Meg knew there was more that passed between them than what went on between ordinary children. Sometimes she thought Will forgot that the children were the product of lords and ladies. Sometimes she thought he cared only about getting the work done on the farm. It never occurred to her that the safety of the children might someday depend on their being "ordinary" and looking like a farmer's children.

That day, Meg leaned forward to try to hear what Callie was saying because it seemed to soothe Talis until his body began to relax, but just as she was beginning to hear a word or two, Will burst upon them with a great shout of anger.

"I have been tearing the country apart looking for you, boy. You should not have run away from me!" Will shouted. "Callie, get your hair out of his face so he can hear me. Talis! Do you know how much trouble you have caused all of us?"

Meg knew her husband well, and she could feel how frightened he was at the possibility of losing the boy he'd come to love so much. She knew he planned to punish Talis for running away, but she was not going to allow it.

Coming out of the darkness of the trees, Meg stepped forward. "Will," she said sternly, her back to the children. "I think Talis has had

214

enough for one day. He is hurt and we are all hungry." Her eyes said more than her words. She was a good wife and a mild-mannered woman. She agreed with Will when he said he had to punish Talis when he left the henhouse door open, but he could see that she was going to fight him over this.

When Meg put her back up, she was stronger than anyone, a fact that Will did not like to look into too closely. He was too relieved at seeing Talis safe to want more trouble. Best to put this day behind them.

"Yes," he said, "I can see that the boy needs care." He said no more but bent and swooped the big boy into his arms, and when Talis protested, saying in his best grown-up voice that he could walk, Will ignored him and carried him to the wagon.

Once the children and she were in the back of the wagon, Meg sat to one side and in a moment it was as though they turned back into children. Blinking as though they had awakened from a dream, they fell upon her, burying their dirty faces in her soft bosom, both wanting her motherly comfort.

Neither Meg nor Will ever discussed what had happened that day, but never again did they try to separate the children.

18

"Meg!" Will said for the fourth time, snapping her out of her reverie. "Is there any supper for a hungry man?"

"Yes, of course," she answered, stepping away from the children's laughing and clutching. "Come inside and tell me of your day. Was the market good today? What did you see?"

Later, after supper, when she and Will were in bed together, as she often did, Meg asked him what the children had been talking about while he drove home. Will said he had no idea and turned away to get some sleep. But Meg kept pestering him. "When we're near it's Talis who talks. He's not got a shy bone in his body; never met a stranger. But Callie rarely says a word."

"At least *one* woman knows how to keep her mouth shut," he muttered, glancing at her over his shoulder.

Meg didn't take the hint. "But when the children are alone together, it's Callie who talks and Talis who listens. She'll talk for hours at a time and he'll never say a word. When I arrive, she stops talking."

Will could hear the hurt in Meg's voice and knew how it upset her that there could be anything going on with "her" children that she was not a part of. Reaching behind him, he squeezed her hand. "You'll find out. I've no doubt that you will find out soon."

"I mean to," she said and turned over, snuggling her backside into the comfortable and very familiar position against him.

It had been raining for three days now and Will hadn't been able to get much work done. It was winter so he didn't mind. He said that a man worked all summer and needed to rest in the winter, which for him meant sitting before the fire, harness in his lap so he looked as though he were working, and sleeping.

Meg sat across from him, her knitting in her lap; the children were sitting on the floor, staring into the flames and saying nothing. Meg, industrious as ever, noticed that Talis was whispering to Callie, but she kept shaking her head and glancing meaningfully over her shoulder at Meg.

Curious, Meg thought perhaps there was a way for her to find out what the children talked about. Slowly, so she wouldn't look too suspicious, she let her knitting fall slack in her lap and her eyelids gradually close.

Within minutes, she was rewarded with a loud

whisper from Talis. "She *is* asleep. Go on, look at her."

Meg could hear Callie tiptoe across the brick floor, her soft leather shoes making a shushing noise. When she was very close, Meg let her knitting drop to the floor, her head fall back and her mouth open as she emitted a short, loud snore. She was rewarded for her acting with a giggle from Callie.

"See," Talis said in a normal voice. "I told you she was asleep. And you know how nothing can wake them once they're asleep. We've proven that often enough."

Meg almost opened her eyes and asked him just what he had done to "prove" that she and Will could not be wakened once they were asleep. But now she was after bigger fish. Opening her eyes just the tiniest crack, she could see the children in the bright light of the fire.

"I shall give you something hard," Talis said, his face screwed up in a way that made him look about thirty years old.

Callie's eyes sparkled. "Yes, please," she said. "Make it very hard."

Talis's eyes lit up with his idea. "Make him a yellow butterfly."

"And her?"

"Ugly and mean. Long thin face. Long, thin body. And she has a horrible character."

Meg almost laughed aloud at that. The children had been bickering all day because Talis had said his chores were much more difficult than hers, so Callie had offered to trade with him. Talis had an inflated opinion of what he did and he was so very sure of himself that he never exerted his full effort. But Callie had a plain girl's knowledge that she was always going to have to work for what she had, so she'd scurried around and done all Talis's chores in half the time it took him to do them. So now his reference to "long, thin body" and "horrible character" had to refer to the way Callie had taunted him after she'd beaten him in the chores.

"And what else?" Callie asked, smiling knowingly at him.

"Mmmm. Three wishes. I like the three wishes and . . . And I want fighting. Not so much kissing this time."

Callie looked into the fire for a moment then began to give a slow, secret smile. After a glance at Meg to make sure she was still asleep, she began to tell a story about a mean little boy who had been turned into a yellow butterfly after he insulted a wicked witch. His quest was to find a girl who liked him for himself. This was difficult, since he'd never said a kind word to anyone and actually didn't even know *how* to be nice.

It took Meg some time to realize what Callie was doing, that she was making up this fascinating story. It wasn't something the child had heard in the village — Meg had never heard such a story — but she was creating it as she went along. At some point Meg opened her eyes and leaned forward to hear the story, no longer pretending she was asleep, and began to listen.

When Callie saw that Meg was awake and listening, she stopped her story. Her stories were for Talis and him alone; no one else had ever heard them or knew anything about them. They were a secret between the two of them, and she thought that he liked her stories because, well, because he loved her. Surely no one else would want to hear her stories. Surely other people had their own stories running through their heads as stories constantly ran through Callie's head.

But when she stopped, Talis nudged her crossly in the ribs, motioning for her to go on. Also, Meg was frowning, as though she too wanted to hear the rest of what Callie was telling.

Tentatively at first, but growing stronger by the minute, Callie kept on with her story, and she found that an audience of one was nice, but an audience of more than one was even better.

After the story was finished, Meg didn't say a word. She just picked up her knitting from the floor and told the children it was time for bed.

Callie was very disappointed that Meg said nothing about her story. Did she like it or not? Maybe it was too silly for her, what with yellow butterflies who were actually boys.

All the next day Callie moped about, poking at her food, feeding her rabbits, feeding the chickens, but not enjoying the animals as she usually did. The only thing she showed any enthusiasm for was making lots of hints to Meg to give her compliments about her story.

But Meg, usually so smart where the children were concerned, didn't seem to understand what Callie was hinting at. She just did her daily chores as usual and said nothing about the night before.

That night as they sat around the fire, Talis nudged Callie. "Go on," he said. "It's all right."

"No," Callie said sullenly, by now truly hurt by Meg for all day saying absolutely nothing about her story.

A few minutes later, when Will was beginning to nod off, the never-to-be-repaired harness in his lap, Meg said so loudly, he nearly fell out of his chair, "I should like a horse, a white horse that . . . that flies."

Will looked at her as though she'd lost her mind. "You're going daft, old woman," he said. "Horses can't fly. And if one was for sale I couldn't afford it."

Meg, her hands full of clothing to be mended, was pretending to look down but, actually, all her attention was on Callie. It had been half-humorous, half-heartbreaking to watch her sulk all day. And Meg had quite vainly enjoyed the way the child had practically begged her for praise.

While Will was still looking at his wife, waiting for her to explain what she'd meant by horses that fly, Talis jumped up, his arms extended. "Yes, a white horse that flies and a boy who leaps on him and rides to the stars."

Will's eyes and mouth were agape.

"You like that, Callie?" Talis said encouragingly.

Callie was sitting with her knees drawn up, hugging them to her body, a smile of great satisfaction on her face. She now understood that Meg had been teasing her all day, just as Talis teased her. Actually, Meg had liked her story very, very much. She had given Callie the highest compliment a storyteller could be given: She was asking for more.

"No," Callie said softly. "The horse hates boys. Hates them very much. A boy hurt her once."

Will stopped trying to figure out what was going on. Both Meg and Talis were dead silent, leaning toward Callie and waiting. He did the same.

"Before the boy can ride he must win her trust, for she is a filly, a filly with a beautiful, long, golden mane."

When Callie paused, Talis knew that was his cue to ask a question. "How does he win her trust?"

Everyone listened as Callie began to spin a story of mischief and magic.

19

"Why do *I* have to pick berries?" Talis whined. "That's women's work. I'm a man."

Before Meg could speak, Callie gave a snort of laughter. "You're no more a man than I am," she laughed. "You're a vain rooster of a boy and you are good for nothing but picking berries."

Her words were harsh, but over the winter Talis had grown at least three inches while the only thing that seemed to grow on Callie was her hair. It annoyed her that in the village he sometimes ran off with boys twice his age and left her alone for as long as an hour at a time. She would have loved to run off with girls her own age, but — she would have died before admitting it to Talis — the girls bored her. So she ended up staying with Will while Talis ran around the village.

But yesterday Talis had stepped on two honeybees and today his foot was so swollen he couldn't do his chores, the chores that, in spite of what Callie had done to prove otherwise, he considered something only a "man" could do. But Meg said Talis was well enough to hobble up the hill with her and Callie to fill buckets with fat, juicy berries. So Talis was protesting this great imposition, saying it was too unmanly for him to do.

But Callie knew the truth. Talis liked to pretend that he was very tough, that he was fierce and strong, but she knew what not even Meg did, that Talis had very, very delicate skin. Stinging nettles hurt him so much that at night, silently, tears ran down his face. It wasn't that he couldn't stand pain; he hadn't been nearly as hurt by the blows from Will's belt that Talis had felt more than once for his carelessness. But anything that affected only his skin hurt him terribly. He hated that his skin blistered easily; the chafing of a leather jerkin could raise a great welt on him, so in secret Callie often sewed patches over rough places on his clothing.

Now, today, because of his bee-stung foot he was going to have to hobble up the hill and traipse through nettle-laden berry vines that would sting his sensitive skin.

Usually Callie would have cared about him but she was angry that he had been stung yesterday while running with some village louts and leaving her behind. When Will teased Talis, saying he could later bake the berries into pies, Callie laughed extraordinarily loudly, making Talis look at her with narrowed eyes that said he'd pay her back later.

There is nothing as inept as a male doing something he doesn't want to do, Meg thought as she watched Talis picking a berry an hour. Also, he had no qualms about complaining incessantly about everything he could think to complain about. Mostly he complained that Callie wasn't doing her "duty" in telling him a story to pass the time while he was laboring under such duress.

After putting up with Talis for about two hours, just when Meg was about to give him what he wanted, which was to be sent home, out of the trees came a dark streak. It was a horse, a great, fierce beast of a thing running straight toward the brambles and Meg, Talis, and Callie. When it reached them, it reared on its hind legs, towering over the three of them like some giant bear out of a legend.

For the first time in her life, Meg swooned, the blood leaving her head, her knees buckling under her as she started to go down. Even as she started for the ground her one thought was for the children: They would be terrified by this giant animal rearing over their heads. She *must* stay alert so she could protect them — at the risk of her own life if need be.

As she was falling, trying her best to bring herself out of her faint, she saw that the children were staring up at the underbelly of the horse with wide eyes. She had to save them!

Minutes later, when Meg opened her eyes, she was on the ground but the children and the horse were nowhere to be seen. Instead, lying in a heap at the foot of a tree, was a boy.

Shaking her head to clear it, Meg pulled herself up and went to the child, but when she looked down at him she hesitated. He was richly dressed, clothed such as she'd never before seen anyone dressed. There were jewels on his cloak; the little knife at his belt was a work of silver wire and emeralds. By his head was a velvet cap that had rubies as big as walnuts about the brim.

"Sir," Meg said hesitantly, reaching out her hand to touch the child, but not daring. Was he a great nobleman's son? He had to be.

A groan came from the child as he moved to sit up and Meg held out her hand to give him support.

Abruptly, he opened his eyes and glared at her, his thin nostrils flaring as he looked her up and down. "Do not touch me, old woman," he said in an accent that only education and illustrious ancestors could bestow.

Immediately, Meg drew back, watching as he struggled to his feet. He was a thin boy and Meg guessed he was a bit older than Talis, even though he would have been a shadow next to Talis's blooming health.

She watched as the boy, almost staggering, held on to the tree and raised himself. There was a great lump forming on the side of his head.

"What have you done with my horse?" he asked, looking at her as though she had the animal hidden in her skirts.

"I . . . ," Meg began, then, suddenly, her senses came back to her. Where *was* that animal and, more important, where were the children?

Fear ran through Meg as she envisioned her dear, innocent children being trampled by that monster, that Satan's demon she had seen rearing over them. What did her dear little children know about unruly horses with steel-shod hooves that could split a man's skull? Her children had been raised on a farm with gentle beasts of the field. The only horse they had seen had probably pulled a cart for Moses when he crossed the Red Sea.

After a quick bob at the boy holding on to the tree for support, Meg grabbed her skirts and started running up the steep hill that overlooked the berry patch. Had it been a normal day, she would have had to struggle to climb that hill but when the safety of her children was involved, she had wings on her feet.

Still, at the top of the hill, she paused, her heart pounding so hard her chest was about to burst, so it took a moment for her eyes to clear. Even when she could see, she didn't believe what was before her.

At the bottom of the hill, on a flat piece of land that was common grazing, was that hideous horse the boy had been riding, its nostrils flared, its hooves half on the ground, half off. On top of the animal's back was Talis, sitting in the saddle as straight as a knight's lance, looking for all the world as though he had been born in that saddle. He was controlling the big horse easily, pulling on the reins, not near to losing his seat when the animal's front hooves came off the ground.

Meg couldn't move; she was frozen in place. Somewhere along the way she had forgotten that Talis was not a farmer's son. Here was a young gentleman. In spite of his rough clothes, Talis was as elegant as the rich boy who owned the horse.

"Me!" Meg heard Callie shout as she pulled at Talis's leg. "Let me."

It took Meg a few moments to realize what Callie was saying, that she wanted to ride the horse too. Meg's heart, just now beginning to calm down, leaped once again to her throat as she started to run down the hill. Talis will take care of her, she told herself, not allowing herself to ask who would take care of Talis. He will not allow anything to happen to her, Meg reassured herself.

Once again shock made Meg stand still as she saw Talis dismount then pick Callie up so she could climb onto the saddle of that angry beast. Alone. He had put tiny Callie on that huge, angry horse alone. Meg couldn't breathe. She couldn't breathe, couldn't think, and definitely couldn't make a protest.

It would be hard to describe what she felt as she saw that wee girl, her hair having come loose from its braid so it looked as though there was more hair than girl, sitting alone atop an animal the size of a small building. Meg was sure that in the next second she'd see the child crushed and bleeding beneath the great hooves.

But what she saw was Callie pulling on the

reins, her laughter ringing out across the fields when the horse's front hooves came off the ground.

"Hold him!" Talis shouted at her. "Keep him under control."

How, Meg wondered, could a tiny girl control such an animal? And more so, how did Talis know about controlling such an animal?

Meg sat down on the ground hard. She was seeing something that she did not want to remember. These children were *not* hers. Had they been hers and Will's, they would have been afraid of an animal such as this. They would be doing what Meg had done with the boy who owned the horse: bobbed a curtsy and called him sir. Never, never would farm children have felt they had a right to take turns riding the richly draped horse of some bejeweled lord.

"Do you want a turn?" Talis shouted at Meg when he saw her sitting on the ground halfway down the hill. "It's much fun."

Meg could only shake her head and look on. It was as though she had entered one of Callie's fairy stories. When Talis ran to the front of the horse and it reared back on its hind legs, Meg's heart hardly fluttered. She knew that Talis knew what he was doing. She didn't know how he knew, since she was sure he'd never seen a horse such as this one before, but she had almost as much confidence in his abilities as he seemed to have in himself.

Leaping to catch the bridle, Talis pulled the

horse's head down to his own. At first the animal gave him a wild-eyed look but within seconds, Talis managed to calm it with his hands and his voice, whispering secret things that the creature seemed to understand.

"Oh, you've tamed him," Callie said, disappointment in her voice as she sat straight in the saddle. "I could have made him fly."

"Fly! Ha! What do you know of flying horses or any horses, for that matter?"

"I know as much as you do. Let him loose and I shall gallop over the fields."

"Not alone, you won't," Talis answered as he easily vaulted into the saddle in front of her. He seemed to have forgotten his injured foot that less than an hour ago he had declared was killing him. "Hold on to me," he called to her before the great horse reared once more then took off as though it had been hit with a whip.

Meg sat where she was, still not believing what she had seen.

What brought Meg to her senses was the yelp of the young lord as he came limping down the hill, just in time to see his horse with its two riders galloping away. For a moment Meg's mind raced. Within the flash of an eye she envisioned Talis and Callie strung from a gibbet, hanged by the neck, their little bodies lifeless. Hanged for stealing this boy's horse.

Meg's first thought was to kill the child. Better she should hang for murder than her precious children should be touched.

If Meg was dumbfounded, she was not more so than the boy. This morning he had stolen his father's horse, trying his best to prove to his father that he was indeed a man and could ride the brute. But the horse had run away with him the moment his seat touched the saddle. It had run for so many miles and for so long that now Edward had no idea where he was. And what is worse, two peasant children had just stolen the horse. Under no circumstances was he going to admit that the children were riding the horse with more ease than he had ever managed.

With a glance at the fat old woman who was obviously nothing more than a farmer's wife, Edward saw that she was looking at him with murder in her eyes. She might as well kill him, he thought, it would save his father the trouble.

But what put the steel back in his spine was that the children sitting atop his father's horse came back into sight. God's teeth but that boy could ride! *Where* could he have learned to ride like that? Who was his teacher? He could only be ten years old, twelve at the most, yet he rode as though his mother had been a mare.

Edward looked at the children, laughing, the girl with the extraordinary hair flying out behind them, sometimes wrapping about both her and the boy, and he was eaten with jealousy. If he could ride like that his father would take him everywhere. Edward doubted if this boy had ever fallen off a horse in his life.

One minute Edward was watching them, that malevolent woman glaring at him, advancing stealthily on him as though she meant to do him harm, and the next he was tearing down the hill.

"Get down!" he shouted. "How dare you steal my horse! I will see you hanged for this."

Meg came running down the hill, her hands outstretched, going for the child's throat.

"Stealing?" Talis said, laughing. "We kept him from running off. Had we not been here you would have lost your horse." He cocked his head to one side, looking down at the boy from his lofty height from atop the horse. "Or is it *your* horse? If it was yours then you should have been able to ride him."

Meg wanted to weep. She should have known Talis wouldn't consider apologizing to this young lord. No doubt her whole family was now on its way to the gallows.

"I'll have your ears for that," the boy said, seething. How dare this lout of a peasant speak to him like that? His accents were of the coarsest nature, the talk of a boy meant for nothing but pulling a plow. He would be dead of overwork by the time he was twenty-five.

"Oh, will you?" Talis said easily and slid off the horse to stand before the boy. For all his great height, Meg knew that Talis wasn't quite nine years old yet, while she suspected this boy was eleven or twelve.

Immediately, Meg stepped between the two

boys, or as she was beginning to think of them, between the two young gentlemen. "There's no harm done, sir. You have your horse back. The children were only bringing it back to you. No harm done at all."

Neither of the boys seemed to notice she was there. With each passing moment, Edward was getting angrier. It was the arrogant stance of this dark-haired, dark-eyed boy, and it was the way that girl on the horse looked down at him. She was just a child, but with that hair swirling about her and with those eyes that looked so old, she bothered him. He didn't like that she was looking at the peasant boy as though he were capable of anything, while he, Edward, was worth nothing. And how could that be possible? He was the one wearing the velvet and the jewels, not this coarse lad.

Edward struck the first blow — a blow that Talis easily parried, stepping aside to miss the boy's fist coming at his face. But Edward's next blow caught Talis on the shoulder, then, by accident, he stepped on Talis's bee-stung foot and pain shot up his body. Talis leaped on the older boy and they fell to the ground, fists and feet flying.

Meg thought she might faint again. They were going to be hanged for sure.

"What's this!"

Never in her life had Meg been so glad to see anyone as she was to see Will.

"I thought you were picking berries," Will said,

more annoyed than anything else. "Can I not trust any of you?"

Will was not concerned with matters of class and whether one of the boys in the tangle of arms and legs at his feet was a gentleman and the other not. All he saw were two boys fighting and so he broke them up. Grabbing the collar of each one, he pulled them apart, holding them at arms' length while they fought to tear each other to bits.

"Behave yourselves!" he said, giving them each a curt shake.

"Unhand me, you . . . you . . . farmer!" Edward shouted at him, trying to recover his dignity.

"Aye, I am that," Will said, unperturbed. "Now, what's this about?" he asked as he set the boys to the ground.

"They stole my horse," Edward said, pulling down his doublet, dusting himself off.

"*This* horse?" Will asked. "They stole this horse that's standing here? You mean they took it away from you?"

"No, I . . . . There was a mishap. It was not my fault but I landed on the ground."

"So they stole it after it tossed you off and ran away? And where did they take the horse after they stole it? To London? Shall we send the sheriff to pursue them?"

Meg knew she had never loved Will so much as she loved him at that moment. He was so very sensible. He treated boys as boys, no matter what their status.

When the young gentleman looked confused by this, Will slipped his arm around the boy's shoulders as easily as he did with Talis. "Now, where do you live?"

When Meg saw quick tears come to the boy's eyes, she knew that he was lost.

"Meg!" Will said sharply. "Is there more of that beef pie left? And what of a berry tart? Callie, get down off that animal and bring it home. All of us are hungry."

What was nearly a disaster, and would have been had it been left to Meg, she guiltily thought, turned into a lovely day. After the initial hostility between the boys passed, they found they were interested in each other. Both of them were very proud and hated to ask each other questions, but at Will's urging, they soon warmed up, with Talis showing Edward his wooden sword. Edward laughed when Talis punched the air with it and was soon giving lessons on how a real knight correctly held a sword.

Will instructed Meg to try to keep the boys interested in each other while he made some inquiries and tried to find out the direction of the boy's home. As far as he could tell the boy was at least twenty miles from his home. Finding this place was not going to be easy, since the villagers considered any man who had traveled more than six miles from his birthplace a world traveler. Meg had no doubt at all that Will would find where the boy lived. After this morning she knew that Will could do *anything*.

After Will left, Meg watched Talis's concentration, seeing that Talis studied the boy, studied his clothing, his walk, even a couple of times mimicking his way of talking.

What was sad was Callie's face, the way she watched the two boys, feeling left out and alone. It was Talis who invited her into their world as they sat under a shade tree and drank Meg's sweet cider. "Tell us a story, Callie," Talis said.

Smiling, feeling confident, Callie started one of her best stories, a story she had been working on for days about a dragon, a horse, and a witch with green hair. But she was hardly into the story before Edward yawned and said, "I've read much better than that. Isn't your father going to come back? I wanted to . . . to say farewell before I left." He wasn't about to admit that he wanted to ask a farmer how to get home. Not that he thought a peasant would know where a house as rich as his father's was, but perhaps he might know something.

Because he was thinking of his own problems, Edward did not see the look of shock on the faces of Callie and Talis. He wouldn't have known what caused it had he seen it.

Read a story, Callie thought. Only the village priest could read. He said it wasn't good for any but men of God to read. Reading took great thought, so the priest would read the Bible and tell the villagers what it all meant. Ordinary people, people not chosen by God, could not read.

"What do you read?" Callie whispered, her

236

knees drawn into her chest. "The Bible?"

Edward looked at her out of the corner of his eye. He was at the stage where he wasn't sure whether girls were good or bad. And he was especially unsure about this girl. She wasn't pretty and never would be no matter how old she got; her face was too pale, too colorless, the features too plain. Her hair, however, was glorious, now pulled back into a fat braid hanging down her back. What was odd about her was the way she followed this boy about, this black-haired Talis who dressed and spoke like a peasant but carried himself as though he were a king's son.

The girl followed him about as though she were his shadow and he never seemed to be aware of her — except when she so much as took her eyes off of him, then he would whip around and frown at her. Talis seemed to know exactly when her attention was on something other than him, even if his back was to her.

It was very strange to Edward, since in his house, boys and girls were kept separate from one another. They wanted to be. Who wanted a stupid girl hanging about all the time? And why was this girl so silent? The girls Edward knew chattered all the time. The only time this Callie had opened her mouth was to start some boring story about flying animals and witches. He had tired of those stories years ago. Now he liked real stories, stories of knights and kings and wars — something this peasant girl could know nothing about.

Edward opened his mouth to tell her this when Will reappeared, and moments later, he was being sent on his way. He didn't know how to say good-bye. He couldn't very well say thank you to peasants, could he? What would his father do in this situation?

Edward mounted his horse and looked down at the four of them. Now that he saw them all together, they were a curious-looking lot. The two adults had the sun-weathered looks of farmers, but the children were . . . Well, dress them richly and they would fit into the queen's court. Especially that boy (Edward could afford to be generous, now that he had found out he was four whole years older than Talis). If Talis were dressed in velvet instead of leather, he would be a very handsome lad.

Suddenly, Edward didn't care what his father would say or do. His father was going to kill him as soon as he got home anyway so what did it matter what his last act alive was?

Gallantly, he swept off his hat, placed it on his heart and gave a bow to the four of them. "Thank you one and all for a splendid afternoon." On impulse, he opened the leather bag attached to the back of the saddle and withdrew a leather-bound book of tales of the knights of the Round Table — a book that belonged to his father. "For you, my lady," he said to Callie as though he were a courtier at Queen Elizabeth's court, then tossed the book down to her eager hands before dramatically reining his father's horse to the left then speeding away down the road — in the direction Will had said his father's house was.

After the boy was gone, three of the people left standing in the front yard felt as though something had changed in their lives. Will just thought of the chores that had gone undone while he'd been chasing about trying to find where some lost boy lived. But Meg knew that never again would she see "her" children in the same way. For all that she and Will had raised them to this age, they were not like Meg and Will. She had felt less than that rich boy, but Callie and Talis had known from the start that they were equal with him.

As for Talis he had seen a world that he somehow knew he belonged with. He had told Callie that the reason he spent so little time with the village boys was that he felt sorry for her being alone (he loved to make her feel guilty; she was nicer to him when she felt he had done something just for her). But the truth was that the village boys bored him.

But today! Ah, today, he had not been bored. This Edward was a fearful snob, of course, but he knew things that Talis would like to know. He knew about horses and swords and about how a knight obtained his spurs. He even knew gossip about the queen's court, had even once seen the Great Leicester, a man many said should be king.

As for Callie, she clutched the book to her flat, child's bosom and dreamed of every word the boy had said. Read, she thought. He had *read* stories like hers. Stories *better* than hers.

There was part of her that was defensive. Everyone liked her stories. Meg and Will loved them. Talis thought they were divine. So who was this boy to say that her stories weren't as good as others' stories?

Callie didn't know the word *competition,* but it's what she knew was missing. There were no stories to compare hers with. She'd never heard of a traveling storyteller, those men who walked about the country, going from rich castle to an even richer house to tell stories for food and a bit of gold when they could get it. Those men compared their stories with one another's, and their audiences certainly compared their stories to ones they had heard before.

For the rest of the day the three of them were silent. Will didn't want to admit it but their silence bothered him. He was a quiet man himself but there was nothing he liked more than the happy chatter of his family. Now the three of them sat at the supper table looking at their food in thoughtful silence.

After supper they sat in front of the empty fireplace, Meg with her mending in her lap, the children staring into space. "Come, Callie-girl," Will said, "tell us one of your stories."

With a frown of concentration, she turned to Talis. As always, she looked to him to make decisions. "What would you like a story about?" she asked tentatively. Her self-confidence had been bruised by that boy today.

"No magic," Talis whispered, then, slowly, he turned to look at her. "I want a story with no magic in it."

Callie could only blink at him as her mind raced with thousands of thoughts. How could a story have no magic? How could a boy kill a dragon without magic? Dragons were big; boys were little.

When Talis saw the wide-eyed expression on Callie's face, he began to perk up. All his life he had been trying to stump Callie on a story. It annoyed him that she was so very clever. No matter what he gave her to make a story out of, she easily did so. Now, he smiled with more assurance. "No magic, no dragons, no witches, no horses that fly. No anything that isn't real."

Callie had the very oddest expression on her face. It was as though her mind had flown away to some distant land. Her eyes were seeing nothing; they weren't focusing. "I must think of this," she whispered after a while, then made no further response. She didn't even react when Talis began to dance about in glee. He wasn't subtle in his delight that he had finally, at last, confounded her.

For two days Callie said not a word. She ate only when Meg put her in front of food. She did her chores only because her body seemed to remember how to do them, but her mind was somewhere else. Meg would have been very worried had it not been for the smug, overweening, self-satisfied, superior attitude of Talis. He was so pleased with himself for having stumped Callie that Meg felt a longing to shake him. She began to root for Callie just to take that young man down a peg or two — or four.

On the afternoon of the third day, Callie came out of her trance. She came out suddenly. One second her mind was not there and the next she had come back to them. She opened her eyes, blinked at all of them sitting at the table as though she'd just awakened, then she looked at Talis, gave a smile that was mostly smirk and said, "No magic."

For the rest of the day she went about her chores with a spring in her step, ignoring all of Talis's hints to tell him what she was planning. It wasn't often that either of them kept a secret from the other for even seconds, but Callie kept her story secret for that whole afternoon.

By the time night rolled around, all three of them were anxious to get supper over so they could hear Callie's story. Will pretended he didn't like all the fuss and didn't care one way or another, but Meg noticed that he didn't eat his usual third helping before taking his seat before the empty fireplace. There was a soft rain coming down on the roof, and when Callie began to tell her story, there were three people listening with great anticipation.

Slowly, Callie began to tell a story about two children who loved each other very much, but he was very handsome and came from a family connected to the queen, while she was plain-faced and only one of many, many daughters of a man who wanted to get rid of all his daughters.

At this statement, Meg and Will looked at each other over the children's heads. It had to be coincidence that Callie's story was so close to the truth.

Her story was of politics and marriages made for money, not for love. While the children were still very young, just barely adults, the girl is told she must give up the boy for his own future happiness. If he marries another woman he could become king, and thereby become wealthy beyond all comprehension. If he marries the girl he loves, his father and hers will disown them both and they will be cast out with no money.

At first the young people agree to this because it is a very sensible thing to do and because they want to please their parents. But on his wedding day the young man runs away, goes to the girl he loves, and carries her away with him.

Since they have no money, he becomes a woodcutter, as there are no jobs for an almost-prince. They live in a tiny house deep in the woods. The winter is hard for them because they have little food, but the people of the village know their story so they help this poor young couple who gave up everything for love.

Sometimes when the young couple wake up in the morning, there are scraps of meat on their doorstep. Or maybe a handful of beans. But when the spring comes, everyone in the village is hungry and the young man knows he cannot support his bride. She is very thin because she gives all her food to him so he can have the strength to chop wood.

After thinking about it a long time, the young man decides it is better to die now than to watch his beloved starve. He plans to kill her in her sleep then walk with her body into the river and die with her in his arms.

That night, he tells her how very much he loves her then he gives her something to drink that will make her sleep, as he does not want to hurt or frighten her. When she is asleep, he kisses her and arranges her hair prettily.

As he raises his axe to bring it down on her, tears are streaming down his cheeks. He knows that when she dies, his soul will die with her.

But hark! What is this? He hears a horse coming at a gallop. He puts down his axe to go to the horseman. It is a messenger coming to say that his father and elder brother have died and the young man now owns everything.

After he hears this, the young man gives thanks to God, not because his father and brother are dead, but because now his beloved can live and have enough to eat.

With great happiness in his heart, he wakes her, takes her onto the messenger's horse, and rides to the castle with her.

Once he is lord of the manor, he repays all the villagers for their many kindnesses by giving a great feast. And he sends many bad men who worked for his father away and in their place hires good men from the village. And for the rest of his life he shares all the crops and no one in his village ever goes hungry again.

And the young man and his bride have many children and live happily ever after.

When Callie finished this story Meg and Will wiped away tears, but Callie only glanced at them. Her true interest was in what Talis thought.

For some time Talis sat still, not looking at her, but very aware that she was watching him, her breath held. After a long while, he turned to her and said softly, "I like no magic better."

"Yes," she said quietly. "No magic is better."

Meg knew that when the children thought no one was looking, they were very affectionate toward one another. They held hands, Talis often putting his head on Callie's lap, and whenever no one was near, they sat as close as possible to each other. But in the presence of others, they never so much as touched. Meg was sure this was Talis's wish, for she felt that if Callie had her way, she might chain herself to his side, but Talis liked to pretend that he didn't need Callie.

But now, on this night, after this extraordinary story, Talis stood up, then held out his hand to Callie. In front of the two adults, he openly held her hand and led her off to bed. It was Talis's highest compliment: public praise.

20

Meg's feet hurt. For that matter, her entire body ached. She had been walking for two days now and she wasn't used to walking.

When a cart full of cabbages came rumbling by, she stepped to one side into the dust and muck at the edge of the road, then leaned against a tree for a moment's rest. For the thousandth time she wondered how Will and the children were faring without her. When she returned, would Will be very angry with her? Or would he have been so worried about her that he'd put his arms around her and welcome her home? Or would he not speak to her for days — or maybe not for years?

Since Meg had never heard of a wife who'd run away and returned, she didn't know what a husband would do. She'd once heard of a woman who'd run away with another man, but she'd never known anyone to run away to get a teacher — as she was doing.

Looking up at the sun, she saw that she had

another couple of hours before sundown and would spend another cold night sleeping on the ground, so she heaved herself away from the tree and started walking again.

It had been almost a month since the event that Meg knew had changed the lives of her family. A month ago the boy Edward had come into their lives and nothing had been the same since. At least not for her and the children, that is. Will was exactly the same, and when Meg tried to talk to him about the changes in their family, Will got almost angry. He refused to speak of what Meg had seen, that Callie and Talis were actually little ladies and gentlemen.

"Better that they are a farmer's children!" Will had snapped in such a way that all of them looked at him with startled eyes. Will only got angry when there was reason, and now they could see no reason for his anger. "Forget this boy!" he shouted. "How I wish he had never come here."

As the days passed, the children did not forget Edward's visit. Meg was right — he had changed something in them. Callie looked at her book until Meg thought the pretty squiggles would disappear. And Talis tried to play with his sword in the way Edward had showed him.

But after a month of this, suddenly Callie stopped looking at her book and Talis put his sword down and didn't pick it up again.

"What is wrong?" Meg asked them, for they were long-faced and silent.

"It is no use," Talis said, "I have no need

for a sword. I should learn blacksmithing."

She was used to Talis's gloomy words; he was always predicting that misery was just around the corner. But what was unusual was that Callie didn't ridicule him, didn't tell him how silly he was. Meg had never before realized it but they all assumed that part of Callie's "job" was to cheer Talis up, to make him see the bright side of things. When Talis hinted that he couldn't do something, Callie stepped in and told him he could do anything in the whole, wide world. Meg knew that Talis thought he could move mountains because Callie believed that he could.

But Callie said nothing when Talis put away his sword. When Callie put aside her precious book, Meg asked her why.

"I cannot read," she said. "I will never be able to read. I am good only for feeding rabbits."

Meg had never heard Callie say a negative thing in her life. And Meg had never heard Callie say that she wanted anything. All Callie seemed to want was to be with Talis. Talis did things while Callie followed along behind him and told him he *could* do them. They were a perfect pair: his pessimism and self-confidence combined with her shyness and belief in magic and beauty. But, most of all, her unshakable belief in Talis.

When Meg heard Callie complain that she couldn't read, Meg had to sit down. She had to face it: Things had changed and they weren't going to return to the way they were.

It took Meg a couple of days to figure out

what she was going to do. She was going to go to John Hadley's wife and demand that she be given money to hire a teacher for the children.

Meg liked to leave things up to her husband to take care of, following him almost as blindly as Callie followed Talis, but Meg wasn't stupid. She had an idea why John Hadley had not come to claim his precious adopted son. In the ensuing years, his wife had either given birth to a healthy son, or she had somehow persuaded her husband to forget the boy. Meg wouldn't be surprised if the woman had lied to her husband and told him Talis was dead.

But Meg knew that Lady Alida knew the truth. Will had bought this excellent farm with money given him by her ladyship; he'd told her that, changing his original story. So if John thought the children were dead, Meg knew that Lady Alida knew they were alive somewhere. And if her ladyship cared nothing for another woman's son, she must care for her own daughter, and she would not allow her to grow up uneducated. What would be said about her lack of education when Callie was at last accepted back into her father's rich house?

Meg didn't like to think that far ahead, to a time when she wouldn't have the children. She envisioned the time of parting as a long, long way away, maybe when the children were adults.

And when they were adults they were going to need to know all the things other ladies and gentlemen knew. If Talis wanted to learn to be a knight then he was going to have to learn whatever a knight needed to know. And if Callie wanted to learn to read — heaven only knew why she wanted such a thing when she made up stories better than could possibly be in any book — then Meg was going to help her to learn to read. When Meg went to heaven she planned to be able to tell the Lord that she'd done everything in her power to help her children get the best that life had to offer.

It took Meg nearly a week to walk the fifty miles to John Hadley's house. She got lost a couple of times and spent one evening plucking chickens in return for her dinner, but she at last reached the place, then nearly wept with exhaustion and frustration to see that the old keep was a burned-out shell. Was this why John Hadley had never come for his children? Had he and all his family been killed in a fire?

She didn't like the idea of sleeping near the ruins, as they had a ghostly, eerie feeling. How long after she and Will left had the castle burned down? That night nine years ago Will had told her that plague had broken out in the castle and the village so they must flee at once. She hadn't listened to all of what he said before she started running with the children. And she hadn't said a word over the next days while Will went to moneylenders and traded something (she never knew what) for money, then bought a wagon and drove them far away from the village where they'd both grown up. He'd bought a beautiful farm for her and the children and she'd never looked back.

Had it not been for the arrival of the boy Edward, she wouldn't have returned to her home village now. As she stretched out on the cold ground near the ruined castle to sleep, she smiled, thinking of all the people in the village she'd like to see before she went back to Will and the children.

In the morning, in spite of her lack of a bed, she felt better. Today she'd find out what had happened to John Hadley and his family and if it was possible, she'd see her ladyship and get her to give her the money to hire a teacher for the children. During the last days Meg had had some time to think of what she'd do and say when she saw her ladyship. Before she'd spent years with Callie and Talis, she'd always thought of herself as clever enough, probably as smart as the next person, but nine years in the presence of those two rascals had taught her a thing or two.

They were as clever and as wily as snakes, teasing her, tricking her, using their minds, which moved like lightning, to dupe her into participating in anything they wanted. Talis was by far the worst. He loved to play jokes on her then laugh outrageously when she fell for the same trick again and again.

Sometimes Will got annoyed with her. "Meg," he'd say, "you mustn't always think good of everyone. You must understand that people are not always what they seem. They sometimes tell lies in order to get what they want."

"What does it matter?" she would say. "Talis means no harm when he puts a tiny frog in my shoe or empties out an eggshell and fills it with mud."

"True," Will said, "but sometimes people *do* mean harm, yet you believe everyone has a good heart."

"I think there is more good in the world than bad," she said indignantly, making Will throw up his hands in despair. Truthfully, she had no idea what he was talking about. It was just more pleasant to be good, wasn't it?

Now, she tried to remember what Will had told her. Today she needed to be clever. She wasn't as naive as Will seemed to think; she had seen those many years ago that there was evil lurking about in that castle that now was blackened stone. At the time of the children's birth, she had still been grieving because her own babies had died. When God had given her two more babies to care for, she hadn't looked much past the two of them. But she had been vaguely aware of the anger and turmoil of the people around her.

Because of these things she was going to see Lady Alida alone. She would talk to her of her pretty little daughter (to Meg, Callie was as beautiful as a princess in one of Callie's stories) and hardly mention Talis, since that was bound to be a painful memory to her ladyship. Then, after their talk, Meg planned to take the money for the teacher and leave — forever. She would swear never to bother her ladyship again. Actually, she wouldn't be bothering her now if this teacher weren't so important.

Meg thought this bargain would be perfect, since it was what both women wanted. Lady Alida would get to hear that her daughter was well cared for and happy, and Meg would get the money for a teacher. Afterward, the two women would probably never see each other again and that would suit them both — and her ladyship would be reassured that her husband would never hear about his adopted son, if that was her wish.

Meg had thought of going to Lord John first, but that idea had not appealed to her. By now John Hadley had obviously forgotten the black-haired boy — or perhaps he thought he was dead — so Meg did not want to remind him that Talis was alive and living with her and Will. John might want to take Talis away. But Meg did not plan to tell Lady Alida that she didn't want Lord John to know where Talis was. In fact, if her ladyship gave her any problems, Meg planned to . . . well, perhaps threaten was too harsh a word. Maybe she might just mention the possibility of telling his lordship about the children if the money was not forthcoming immediately.

Yes, Meg thought, and was very pleased with herself. Will would be very proud of her. For once she was being very clever indeed.

21

The maid was whispering so frantically to Alida
that at first her ladyship did not hear what the
woman was saying. Sometimes Penella took too
much upon herself; sometimes the woman reminded Alida of the horrible time before the fire,
that time Alida now wanted to forget had ever
happened.

Looking at Alida now no one would guess she
was the same woman she had been nine years
ago. Then she had been beautiful. She had worked
at her beauty, trying her best to entice her husband to her bed, always trying to win his love,
which she was sure he'd give her as soon as she
gave him a healthy son.

But after the night of the fire — Alida refused
to think of anything else of that night, refused
to remember that she had been the one to start
the fire that had killed several people, including
her own newborn daughter — she had changed.
When she saw that her husband was willing to
give her, if not love then companionship, she

began to will herself to not remind him of the time when he had desired her body. Almost overnight she had aged twenty years: her hair had grayed, her waist thickened, her skin dulled. When they were together now, she and her husband were friends, old friends who worked together and enjoyed each other's company. Now when her husband looked at another woman, Alida smiled fondly and thought how pleasant it was to no longer have such passions raging through her old bones.

The greatest pleasure she had in her life was her children. She saw to their education, to their religious training, to all aspects of their lives. Somehow, she had been able to persuade John that his sons were indeed worth something. James, the elder one, had a club foot, true, but he could ride a horse, so she pointed this out to her husband. And for all that Philip, the younger son, had very weak lungs and tired easily, he was willing to try anything his father asked of him.

Of course John never knew that it was his wife's willpower that made his sons do whatever they did. James could not sit a horse easily, not so much because of any physical deformity but because his inclination was toward his studies rather than learning to handle a sword nearly as large as he was. Had his father been different, had James not been the eldest, the boy would have been sent into the church or to law where he could spend his life with his nose in a book.

As for Philip, at night, in secret, Alida often

went to him and talked to him about how important it was that he spend all day in a saddle chasing some wild-eyed boar through the forest. When the boy's weak body was ravaged with pain and exhaustion, she administered herbs and, if need be, threats and punishments, to get him to face his father without tears and pleas to be excused. Philip had to choose which parent's wrath to provoke, and of the two, he knew his father to be the more lenient.

As for Alida, try and deny it as much as she could, she was haunted by that time when her husband had come so close to giving away everything he owned, as well as what she owned, to a boy who was of no blood relation to him.

Now, with Penella buzzing in her ear like a mosquito, Alida was, for an instant, transported back to a time she had worked hard to forget. She remembered all too well that night when the insanity had overtaken her. She had not been herself that night; what she had done had not been her doing. The devil had overtaken her soul that night; he had possessed her — and her husband. The devil had maddened all of them on that night.

After much annoying buzzing, Alida realized that the woman who had been the wet nurse on that night-in-hell was here. Now. Was waiting to see her.

"Who has she seen?" Alida asked sharply, all her senses alert, when she and her maid were alone.

"No one," Penella answered, proud of herself, hoping that this deed would put her back in her lady's favor. A short time after the night of the fire, Lady Alida's attitude toward her maid had changed, but Penella did not know why. Whereas once they had been almost friends, abruptly, Alida's attitude had become one of coolness and distance. Whereas once Penella and Penella alone had been privy to her ladyship's thoughts, suddenly Alida confided in no one, and there were times when Penella caught her mistress looking at her with what was almost hatred.

Since the coolness began, Penella had done everything she could imagine to ingratiate herself to her mistress, had worked long hours for her, done anything she wanted, thought of whatever she could want before she named it. She had made herself as valuable, as indispensable as possible to her mistress. Lady Alida had taken all her work but no longer were there any confidences, no longer time when they talked about children or the future. After a lifetime of the borders between mistress and maid being blurred, now the boundaries were very clear-cut.

Had Penella been less adoring and more astute, she might have figured out what had caused her ladyship's withdrawal. A few months after the fire, an old man who lived alone in a derelict hut in the woods, eking his living out of a bit of ground and tending to injured falcons brought to him by John's men, saw her ladyship limping along the path after her horse had thrown her.

Trying only to make conversation and distract the lady from her pain, he mentioned that it was a blessing that young Meg (everyone was young to him) had escaped the fire with those two babies. Upon questioning, he told Alida that Meg and Will had come running through the woods. Since they were some distance from his hut he wouldn't have seen them if he hadn't been, er, unable to sleep. At the look of rage on her ladyship's face the old man was sure that she'd guessed that he had been poaching, as he did every night.

After her ladyship left, the old man knew his days were numbered. He had been found out and he knew that if he didn't leave of his own accord, a hangman's noose would take him. When Alida's man came stealing through the woods that night with murder in his mind, there was no sign of the old poacher.

The old man would never know what went through her ladyship's mind when she was told he had disappeared. She couldn't have cared less that he was poaching. What were a lot of rabbits to her? For months she had felt safe that the boy her husband wanted to put in the place of her children was dead. Now she had found out that he was not dead. Somewhere, he was still living. More than anything in the world she wanted to start a search for the boy, find him and kill him. She could never be safe until the boy was dead — by her own hand if need be.

But there was no way she could start a search without her husband finding out. And if there was a search, he was bound to discover the reason for it and know that the boy was still alive. Then, no doubt, *he* would start a search.

All Alida could do was sit still and hope that no one else had seen the wet nurse and her husband fleeing with the newborn children through the woods in the dead of night. After many long hours of thinking about this, Alida began to wonder how they had known there was any danger. The only answer could be that they had been warned. And only Penella could have warned them.

At that moment Alida began to hate her maid — and she knew best how to punish her. Penella's great pride was that she was close to her ladyship, sometimes so close that she thought she *was* the lady. Many times Alida had caught her maid giving orders in a manner that she had no right to use. Previously, it had been amusing to Alida. Amusing until the night when her maid had overstepped herself — and in the process may have ruined Alida's life.

Alida punished her maid by withdrawing her favor from her. She shared no more secrets with her; treated her as one of many instead of as special. Burning her at the stake would have been kinder to Penella than such treatment, and Alida well knew this. It was the perfect revenge.

Now, Penella should have been suspicious when she told her mistress that the old woman who had been hired to be a wet nurse to her daughter and that boy was asking to speak to her, and Alida showed no surprise. But Penella was so pleased to have something private to share with her mistress, that she noticed nothing extraordinary. Her mind was fully occupied with dreams of getting back into her mistress's favor, of having her old privileges, her old *power* back.

"Who else knows of this?" Alida asked sharply.

"No one. She was walking about the courtyard with a shawl over her face and when she saw me she ran to me. You may imagine my distaste, my lady, when such as she dared to speak to *me*."

Alida had to control herself to keep from reminding the woman that she was merely a maid and no more important than this fat farm wife. But in the last few moments, Penella had slipped back into the close relationship she had once enjoyed with her mistress; it was as though the past nine years had never been.

"She spoke to no one else? You are sure?"

"Most certainly. She made a point of saying such. She said she has been waiting outside for two days, hoping to see you or me. She knows that I am close to you, that to tell me something is to tell you, so she spoke only to me."

What had once pleased Alida now disgusted her. How had she stood this woman's presumption? When she'd been so alone that she'd had no husband, no friend, nothing but hatred in her heart, she had clung to this woman's cloying ways.

"Bring her to me," Alida said. "Let no one

see her. Give her a basket of herbs to carry so no one will suspect that she has anything to say to me but of her wares."

"Yes, my lady," Penella said, joy racing through her heart. Some part of her knew that her ladyship's anger had been caused by what had happened the night of the fire. Over the years Penella had come to regret warning those peasants of what her ladyship intended. What did they, or those babies, matter to her? If her ladyship wanted them dead, who was she to question that? But if the truth were told, she did not fully understand what she had done that night to anger her ladyship. Everything had turned out well since then, hadn't it? So what had she done that was so wrong? Didn't she do *everything* for her ladyship's own good?

"Yes," Penella said, "I will get her then you and I will talk to her."

"No!" Alida said sharply. "I will talk to her alone."

Penella opened her mouth to protest but closed it. "Yes, my lady," she said, allowing as much anger in her voice as she dared.

When her maid was gone — Alida thought that she *must* get rid of her — she tried to calm herself. Calm herself and think. She had to find out where this woman lived, where the boy was being kept. She *had* to make her talk.

What Alida saw when Meg shuffled into the room was a very ordinary-looking woman, her face lined with ceaseless toil. She was fat and walked slowly, carrying her basket of herbs as though it were very heavy.

What Alida also saw was the woman's guileless blue eyes, as open and as innocent as a kitten's. This was a woman who had not been tormented and hated all her married life as Alida had been. Alida would have died before she admitted it, but what she was feeling was jealousy. This fat old farm woman had not been born with beauty or wealth; her only children, born late in her life, had died. But, as though she were blessed by God, she had been given two strong, healthy children to replace them. No doubt her husband loved her, protected her, wanted nothing more than her happiness. While she, Alida, lived in this great, fine house John was still building and had a husband who, if told his wife had died, would do little more than shrug his shoulders.

Alida smiled at Meg as though she were an emissary from the queen. "Do sit down. You must be tired from your journey. May I pour you a glass of wine?"

Meg, prepared for coldness, was disconcerted by such warmth. Only three times before in her life had she had wine to drink, and then it had been heavily watered. And it had never been poured into a silver goblet by the white hand of a lady.

Tentatively, Meg took the wine — and it went straight to her head. There was not a drop of water diluting this wine.

Spreading her gown of dark red velvet about her, Alida took a seat across from Meg and watched until the wine was finished and the sweetmeats eaten. When Meg hesitated to take a second glass, Alida entreated her to do so, saying she would be hurt if Meg did not. "After all," she said, "I owe you a great deal. You have been caring for my daughter these many years. Have you not?"

"Yes," Meg said, feeling wonderful and relaxed, then she had the sacrilegious thought of understanding why men liked drink so much. And why they did not want women to drink. Feeling like this, it's no telling what a woman would do. For herself, Meg was feeling quite confident; she could do *anything*.

"Tell me about my daughter," Alida said in the sweetest possible tones. "That is, if you wish to do so. I fear that now she is more yours than mine."

"Oh no, none of it," Meg said, knowing she was lying, for both the children *were* hers. But the fuzzy feeling the drink gave her made her feel that this lie was all right.

"Then you don't mind talking about them?" Alida said, subtly hinting that she wanted to know about *both* children. Then, frowning, she took the goblet from Meg. Another moment and the old woman was going to be asleep.

There was nothing on earth that Meg wanted to do more than talk about her children. Sometimes she got very annoyed with Will when he wanted to think about his farm and not their children. Once he'd said, very sternly, "Do not get so attached to what is not yours." She'd laughed at that because there was no one as attached to the children as he was. Sometimes Meg thought that Will's love for the two of them was even stronger than hers, so strong that he *could not* talk about them.

"They are strange children," Meg said softly, her mind going back to the farm. For all that, by comparison with this rich house, the farm was a poor place, she would not trade one rose from her cottage for all of this wealth. In the two days she had been waiting to see her ladyship there had been a feeling of, well, of something unhealthy about this place. Now all she wanted to do was perform her task and go home.

Happily, her mind went back to the farm, to the simplicity of Will and their children. "The children are as alike as though they were two halves of a whole. When one is hungry, the other is hungry. What makes one ill makes the other ill. They like the same colors, the same foods. They have the same temperament, both loving . . ." She hesitated, searching for the right word.

"They both love being players, like in the village," she said at last.

Concentrating, Alida tried to understand what she was hearing. Drama, she thought. Flamboyance. The children loved all the emotion that she had learned to suppress.

Meg continued. "Sometimes the children will

264

not talk to each other for hours — they will be working at their chores — but you can ask what they are thinking and it will be the same."

Meg's eyes took on a dreamy quality. There was nothing in life she loved more than her children. She was sure she would never get into heaven for this thought, but sometimes she was almost glad her own children had died so she'd been able to spend these years with Talis and Callie. Her own children would not have been as entertaining as these two were; they would never have jumped on a great black horse and gone running off across the countryside. Her own daughter would not have told stories at night as they sat about the fire.

Meg's head came up, maybe a little too suddenly, since she felt dizzy at the movement. How could she have thought that this woman had evil intentions? She must be heartbroken that she had been denied the company of her delightful, adorable daughter. Of course she wanted to hear all about her. It did not occur to Meg that while she was telling Alida all about her own daughter, she was telling an equal amount about a boy Alida possibly hated.

"The children learn at the same speed, and they are interested in the same things," Meg said, thinking how clever she was to casually mention learning. By the time she finished, Lady Alida would be begging to hire a teacher for her daughter.

22

Once Meg had started, she couldn't stop talking about the children. Nine years of living with them, loving them, and telling no one about them, had built up inside her. She had never been able to tell her neighbors because her children were so different from theirs. At every village festival — the ones Will allowed them to attend — Callie and Talis stood out from the other children. Instinctively, everyone knew they were separate and distinct.

Now, Meg was free to talk to her heart's content. And talk she did. She told of Talis's arrogance, how he sometimes hurt Callie's feelings. Talis would never think of apologizing when he did something to hurt Callie, but at night he would put the best pieces of meat onto her plate. Then Callie would serve him the best of the bread.

"You'll both starve from giving the other the best," Will had said to them more than once. The children would deny this, then Talis would lapse into a long speech of how he and Callie couldn't abide each other. Callie would nod her head in agreement, both of them too proud to admit what they were each to the other.

"They can *not* be separated," Meg continued. "They won't sleep if they aren't in the same room, preferably in the same bed. And they . . ." She hesitated as she cocked her head to one side, thinking. "They talk to each other through their minds." Embarrassed, she looked up at Lady Alida, whose face showed interest but also some revulsion. Meg decided it was better not to talk about the mind-talk. "When one cuts his finger, the other feels it. If you were to strike one, the other would feel it." Neither of the children had ever said this, but she remembered too well the way Callie had sat down quite gingerly after the times Will had taken a belt to Talis.

As Alida listened, she became more angry with each sentence. Here was proof that her prayer to God had been answered. He had not answered her many prayers she'd offered Him for the nine months of her last pregnancy that she had spent on her knees. No, He had not granted her wish for a son. Instead, she had prayed that her child share the soul of that foreign woman's baby and *that* prayer had been answered. Why, *why* could not He have answered her request for a boy? A boy of her own, one to inherit? A son who was healthy in mind and body?

Now this fawning old woman was saying how sweet the children were, how kind and loving, how they liked to do things for other people.

Alida knew she had to stop her before she became nauseated.

"Come, come," Alida said, "they must have at least one weakness. Or are they not human?"

Meg's back stiffened at the very thought that her children were not what was best in the world. "Yes, of course they have weaknesses. They . . ." She hesitated, but then she remembered that this woman was Callie's mother so she could confide in her. "They are jealous," she said softly. "They are both very jealous."

Alida gave a little smile. "That does not seem such a bad weakness. We are all jealous. Here, have some more wine. If you do not tell me what their flaws are, I will not believe their virtues."

That made sense to Meg, and, besides, wasn't it her own vanity that was keeping her from telling this woman all the truth about her own child?

"Their jealousy is stronger than most people's. It is not normal. Talis is the worst. He cannot bear Callie to give her attention to anything but him. There was a boy who came for one day and he gave Callie a book. Talis has several times become angry at Callie when she looks at that boy's book. He wants all of her attention all of the time."

"And what of the girl?" Alida could not bring herself to call her her daughter.

"She . . ." Again, Meg hesitated. How to state Callie's biggest sin? "Callie worships him," she said at last.

For a moment, all Alida could do was blink.

"Worships him?" She paled. Perhaps this boy *was* from the devil.

"No," Meg said quickly, correctly reading the lady's horror. "I do not mean she goes against God. She —" How could she explain? Right now she wished she had Callie's gift for words. "Talis has a great sense of honor. Yes, that is the word. Honor. He talks all the time about the honor of a man and that a man can*not* lie."

"Ah, then the girl is a liar," Alida said, understanding the need to lie.

"No," Meg said sharply. "Callie doesn't lie. She is very honest, but she cares very, very much for Talis. She cares *only* for him." Meg's voice lowered to a whisper. "I sometimes think Callie would sell her soul to protect him from a bee sting."

Meg shook her head to clear it, trying to explain what she meant. "They are only children, you understand. It is nothing serious. Callie will steal tarts for him but Talis would die before he stole for any reason on earth. My Callie is a good girl, honest, God-fearing — except when it comes to him, then she's the devil's own."

Meg was finishing the glass of wine and beginning to laugh. Even when she told the worst of the children, it wasn't very bad. "Will and I have to watch Callie, for she will take the blame for anything wrong. Whether Talis has left the barn door open, broken something with his wooden sword, or anything else, Callie will say she did it."

"And the boy allows her to be punished for his crimes?" Alida asked, smiling. Here at last was evidence that he was indeed Gilbert Rasher's son.

"No, no, of course not," Meg said. "Talis is angry when he hears that she has taken the blame for his misdeeds. He will ask her how she can lie, then tell her that lying is a sin."

Meg smiled. "Callie won't lie otherwise, just for him. And he never *asks* her to lie for him. It's just that she says she can't bear to see him in pain. She says he's seen enough pain."

"What pain has the boy experienced?" Alida asked sharply. At the moment she felt that only she knew of pain.

"I do not know, my lady. I am only telling you what your daughter says. She says that Talis has experienced enough pain and he needs no more. Perhaps she means about his mother dying." Meg was unsuccessful at keeping the hurt from her voice when she said this. Perhaps the children thought she, Meg, was not good enough to be their real mother and that is why Callie referred to Talis's birth mother.

"Then you have told them the truth of their birth?"

"Oh no! Will said it was better that the children did not know — until it was time, that is."

At that statement, Alida was sure the old woman's husband knew more than he was telling his naive wife, but, whatever the reason for the secrecy, she was very glad that the children knew nothing of their birth. If these two old people were killed, and if, by chance, the children were left alive, they could not come to her and demand sustenance — or recognition. They would not know to come to her and, more important, to John.

Meg took advantage of the momentary silence, and of her completely relaxed state, to explain the reason for her long journey, the reason for risking the wrath of her husband. "I need money to hire a teacher for them," she said all in one breath.

Alida understood at once. So this is why the woman was here. Of course it was inconceivable that Alida would pay to educate that boy. If he did somehow escape the death she had planned for him, she would not want to give him the advantages of an education. Besides, she did not want to part with money for even an instant. Nearly losing everything had made her very careful of her money.

Meg knew what Alida was at, knew why she was stalling. She didn't want her husband reminded of Talis. So now, Meg thought, was her time to be clever.

Meg began to talk, saying what she'd thought of over the days of her long walk. "It's not right for the children to be left uneducated," Meg said with determination. She had resolved to be utterly firm on this matter. "They must have a tutor, someone to educate them to their station in life."

When Meg saw her ladyship hesitate, she

plunged a knife in. "It is all my husband and I can do to feed young Talis. He grows so fast we can't keep him in clothes. Did I tell you that he is near as tall as me and he is only nine? I am sure the master would be delighted to see him."

Alida stalled for time while she thought. In the past she had had no time for planning. On the night of the fire she had made mistakes, but this time she wanted to make things right. "You want to educate the boy," she said graciously, doing all she could to keep the hatred from her voice. She now understood that this horrid woman was trying to *blackmail* her, to threaten her that if she was not given the money for a tutor, she would present this healthy boy to John.

"Oh no!" Meg said. "They must *both* go to school. You cannot give one something and not give it to the other. They could not bear to be separated."

"Oh? And what would happen if they were separated?" Alida said, smiling, but thinking how much she disliked this old woman.

"It would destroy them," Meg said simply and with utter honesty. "Have you not understood? They are not two people. They are only one person. They are two halves of a whole. They do not exist one without the other."

Again, Alida felt the hairs on her neck rise as she remembered her prayer nine years ago. Two halves of a whole. One spirit divided into half.

"Yes, yes, come tomorrow and I will give you the money," Alida said hastily. Yes, she thought, come tomorrow and I will have everything arranged. I will find out where you live and I will have all of you annihilated.

Understanding that she was being dismissed, Meg started to leave, but when she stood, she was unsteady on her feet. She did not want to come back tomorrow. Maybe it was because her senses were different because of the drink or because of something else, but suddenly, she wished very much that she hadn't made this trip. She wished she had talked to Will about all of this. Maybe Will could have found a way to afford a teacher for the children. Maybe Will could have —

Meg didn't think anymore because all hell broke loose in the house as the maid Penella came running into the room to tell her ladyship that one of her daughters had just caught herself on fire.

"Wait for me here," Alida said, then gathered her skirts and ran from the room.

For a moment, Meg sat where she was, not moving, too sleepy and heavy to move. Wearily, she rested her head against the back of the chair and for just a few seconds she dozed.

She was dreaming and she knew she was dreaming but it didn't make any difference. There seemed to be something she had to remember, but couldn't. She and Will and the children were running, running through the woods at night, allowing no one to see them. In the dream, Meg was in a daze, the two babies clasped to her in a sling Will had rigged for her. He wanted to carry one child while she carried the other, but the babies screamed so when they were apart.

"Come, Meg, we must go," he whispered to her after one very short rest. "She will come after us soon."

With a start, Meg awoke and she was as clear-headed as she could be, considering the amount of wine she had consumed. *She,* Will had said. "She will come after us soon." Quite suddenly, Meg understood everything. It was Lady Alida who had set the fire that night, trying to kill the boy who threatened her own children's futures.

Suddenly, things that Meg had not remembered for years began to come back to her, things that had been said that night when she'd first come to the children. Now she understood why Will had insisted on secrecy all these years. Meg remembered all the times she had argued with him, saying it wouldn't hurt the children to go into the village now and then. Will rarely allowed them to go into the village except on market day and then only because he needed the help. Talis was great at selling produce, while Callie had a talent for displaying the wares so everyone wanted to buy from them.

Now Meg understood. She understood why no one had come for the children, why no one was ever going to come for them. These people thought she and the children had died that night in the fire. And Lady Alida had set the fire.

Maybe it was the wine, or maybe it was a mother's instinctive protection that made rage run through her body. In that moment, Meg learned how to hate. This woman, this . . . this *lady* had tried to kill one innocent child and had not cared that her own daughter would be killed in the process.

Standing, Meg knew that she must get out of this place and get home. And what is more, she was convinced that Lady Alida owed the children for what she had done to them.

Without another thought, not even for her immortal soul, Meg took a short, heavy silver candlestick off the mantelpiece and secreted it inside her skirt.

The next moment she was running down the stairs, her face red with fear, her heart pounding. She had not gone three steps when a woman came running up to meet her with orders from her ladyship that she was to stay the night.

What would Callie say to this? Meg thought. If she had Callie's clever brain what would one of her story princesses say to get herself out of this mess?

"Stay the night?" Meg gasped. "Have you not heard? This house is on fire."

"No, Lady Joanna fell against a log and her skirt caught on fire."

"I was there. I heard Lady Alida say that is what people are to be told. She is worried that everyone will run away and there will be no one

275

to help put out the fire. But I do not want to risk being burned to death. Let me pass!"

Within ten minutes the whole household was in chaos and, easily, Meg escaped through the shouting people. Twice she saw men looking about as though they were searching for her, but she had an advantage in that she looked like every other village woman.

Meg traveled all that night, moving in the opposite direction of home. If she were caught, she did not want her captors to have any idea of the direction of the farm.

On the second day she was walking past a stables when she heard two men wearing the arms of John Hadley asking for a woman of her description, accusing her of thievery. There was a reward offered for her that was at least twice the value of the silver candlestick. To hear the men tell it, Meg had stolen half of all that his lordship possessed. Meg knew that her time alive was limited — if she did not do something. No one could turn aside from the huge reward offered.

What would Callie's princesses do? she thought since that had worked before. She would disguise herself, was the immediate answer.

Two hours later, Meg was gone and in her place was a crippled old woman with only one arm, with blackened teeth and a limp that made walking very slow. To keep people from coming too close to her, she filled her pockets with fish so old the cats wouldn't touch them. Wherever she walked she cleared a wide path; children threw clumps of mud at her and told her to get away from them.

She tried her best to stay off the roads, but it was hard going traveling across fields and through woods with heavy underbrush. At the end of the first week two Hadley knights stopped her and started to ask her questions, but Meg's fear was so real and her supplications for mercy were so exaggerated that they could get nothing out of her. Her hysteria combined with her smell was enough to make them sick. They left her to her walking, muttering that she was crazy.

Being so vile that people would not get near her made getting food difficult, so Meg spent the last three days of her journey without food.

When, at long, long last, after close to a month's absence, she arrived home, at the sight of her beloved farm, she collapsed on the doorway.

Will was the first to see her. He came running from the barn, swooped her into his arms and carried her into the house.

"You will hurt your back," Meg managed to murmur.

"You're as light as the day I married you," he said, his voice thick with tears he was trying not to shed.

"I stink," she whispered.

"You smell of roses and nothing more," he said as he carefully laid her on the bed.

No one in her family asked where Meg had been. They were all too glad for her to be back to ask any questions. Talis made Callie tell a story that had Meg captured by gypsies, but due to her heroic nature and her superior wisdom, she had escaped and come back to her family.

Although Meg never told anyone the truth, after that day she was a changed woman. In a way she listened to Will less, but she also listened to him more, listened to what he was *not* saying. She now knew that he was aware that the children's lives were in danger, and instead of being the naive little wife who knew nothing, she worked with him in protecting them.

But Meg also knew that the future of the children was very important. She was *not* going to allow that evil woman to deprive the children of what was their birthright. When she told Will she was going to hire a teacher for the children, he started to argue with her, but he took one look at her face and gave in. "I will find someone," he said and she knew he would.

Will always kept his word. He found Nigel Cabot in a ditch beside the road. When Nigel got drunk he stood in the front of the town and gave pretty speeches to try to earn more drinks. His clothes, despite the fact that they were worn ragged and filthy, were the clothes of a gentleman; his speech was like the boy Edward's. One of the things he bragged about was that he had been a tutor in several noble households.

When the town got tired of his cadging drinks, tired of his arrogant ways, they threw him out. Picking him up by the scruff of the neck, Will lifted him from a gutter filled with mud and various animal manures.

"Can you read?" Will asked and had to shake the man to get him to answer.

"Of course I can read. I'm no country lout who uses paper only to wipe his —"

"I don't care about the country folk. I want you to teach my son and daughter to read."

Nigel's eyes opened wide. He had a keen sense of humor and to see this stolid country farmer asking him — *him!* — to teach his stupid, ignorant children their *ABC*'s made him forget the muck on his face. Hauling himself up to his full height, making a valiant effort not to reel about on his feet, he said, "And shall I teach them to count too?" At that he thumped his foot on the ground as though he were a horse that had been taught tricks, implying that Will's children were of the same intelligence as a horse.

Will, for all his country background, was intimidated by no man, be he king or scholar. "I will make a bargain with you," he said. "If my children are clever enough to learn all that you can teach them, as fast as you can teach them, then you will give up the drink."

After a moment's stupefaction, Nigel put his head back and roared with laughter. The reason he had lost so many good positions and had not been able to secure references for other positions was that he told the parents the truth about how utterly stupid their sons were. He'd once told a duke that a monkey could more easily be taught to read than his son.

So now here was this farmer offering him a challenge of learning. Nigel had no hope of finding intelligence in a farmhouse, but he did hope for a few free meals. He accepted Will's challenge and after he met Callie and Talis, he never took another drink. He was too busy to drink, for those two children's hunger for knowledge was inexhaustible.

23

Sixteen Years After Birth

1587

"What do *you* know of babies?" Talis asked haughtily.

"The same as you know of knights and great deeds," Callie said, then looked away from him. Lately, she seemed always to be thinking of babies and marriages and a home of her own. She and Talis had always laughed at such things, thinking that courting couples were a ridiculous sight, but in the last few months it was as though everything about her was different.

Today they had escaped Will's never-ending chores, and Nigel had escaped his always-questioning pupils, so she and Talis had gone to their favorite place on the side of a hill under a huge, spreading copper beech. The branches of the tree hung so close to the ground they almost formed a room, a place where she and Talis could be alone.

Now, she was standing with her back to the tree, watching him as he thrust about with the rusty old sword Nigel had found for him. Over the years the physical disparity between them had grown. Talis was only sixteen years old but he looked twenty. Already he was six feet tall, broad shouldered, and was developing more muscle with each day. Nearly a year ago, his voice had abruptly changed. No months of cracking, squeaking tones for him. He just woke up one morning and had a deep, and quite gorgeous, voice — the voice of a man.

Talis had not been humble about the good fortune of his maturity. He lorded it over Callie at every opportunity, for adulthood seemed to have passed her by. For all that she was also sixteen years old, she had no curves of a woman. Talis was taller than most adults; Callie was inches shorter than girls her own age.

Her height was not Callie's only worry, for there were no other signs of maturity on her. She told Meg that bread could be kneaded on her chest, since it was as flat as a bread board. And Will could use her body for a straight edge to build the new chicken coop. One night at supper Callie said that her stomach was so flat that if she swallowed a cherry pit it would show. She said that other girls had red lips and pink cheeks but her face was so pale that if she closed her eyes no one would be able to see her. When Will was planing a narrow, flat board of pale new oak for a bench, Callie said, "I think she's my twin sister."

Meg tried her best not to laugh whenever Callie made one of her self-deprecating remarks, but the men howled. Even Will couldn't keep from laughing when she made one of her disparaging remarks. At least Nigel and Will had the courtesy to make no replies to her woeful comments. But not so Talis. He was a monster; never passed up an opportunity to remind Callie of her little-girl looks.

Handing Callie a mushroom one day, he said she could use it to shield her from the rain. Pea pods were boats. On market day, he once persuaded (he could persuade anybody to do anything) a six-year-old boy to kiss Callie on the cheek and ask her to marry him. Once Talis was arguing with Nigel (a common occurrence), talking about a toy boat Nigel was making. Talis said the bottom of it wasn't straight but Nigel said it was. In the heat of the argument, Talis held the boat against Callie's chest. "There, I told you," Talis said. "Measured against an absolutely flat surface, you can see that it's not level."

Will got angry once when a wagon load of gypsies stopped in the village on market day. Talis was astonished when a lushly endowed girl started flirting with him. For a moment he stood gulping in air, his eyes as big as horseshoes as the girl came to stand very close to him, her breasts almost touching his chest.

When she saw them, Callie went into a blind rage, ran at the corner post of Will's produce stall and with amazing, even unbelievable, strength, knocked the entire booth down on top of Talis. Ignobly, he went sprawling to the ground in the midst of a load of cabbages and tomatoes. To Talis's mortification, the whole village, and especially the gypsy girl, had a long laugh as he sprawled amid the ruined vegetables.

Talis, hating the laughter at his pride's expense, took after Callie with murder in his eyes. She further humiliated him by escaping each of his attempts to catch her, finally seeking safety behind Will, who was furious at what had been done to his stall. When Talis demanded that Callie be severely punished (not that he'd actually allow anyone to hurt her, but at that moment he thought that's what he wanted), Will further angered Talis by taking Callie's side. "If you'd been tending to business instead of panting after girls twice your age, none of this would have happened."

Both Callie and Talis were shocked by this statement, but the truth was, Will was worried about Talis's adult looks. His body was near to being a man's but his mind was still that of a boy. That was not a good combination. And in spite of his laughter, Will felt sorry for poor Callie with her thin, straight body. In his opinion, the children were the same age and they should look the same age.

The villagers thought the whole episode was enormously entertaining and thereafter teased Talis so often about his gypsy "girlfriend" that he began to be nicknamed "gypsy." It started out to be a derogatory name given him by the jealous boys, but, much to their dismay, the girls of the village thought the nickname suited Talis's dark good looks, so they kept calling him that.

Now, Callie and Talis had run off to their favorite place under an enormous copper beech tree; it was where they could be alone, away from others. Here they could be themselves; here they were equal. It didn't matter that their bodies were so different, for when they were alone, they were the same.

"What's going to happen to us?" Callie asked seriously. Lately everything seemed serious to her.

"I don't know. Maybe I can apprentice to a knight and become like Lancelot."

"Pssph!" Callie said. She hated it when Talis mentioned stories not created by her. Many of her stories were quite as good as that thing about a man who had fallen in love with another man's wife. She was glad the illicit lovers had both been punished. Talis, however, thought the story was grand. What *really* bothered Callie about the story was that Lancelot got his strength from remaining a virgin, from never marrying anyone.

Callie glanced down at her flat chest, not so much as a ripple showing in her clothes. Every morning she looked at her body, hoping it had changed into a woman's body during the night, but it hadn't. In the village there were girls her age who were married. More important, there were girls in the village older than she who openly said they wanted to marry Talis.

She saw the way he looked at them, watching them as they sauntered by him on market day, their hips twitching, their heads turned away as though they weren't aware of him. But Callie knew that their sole purpose in life was to get Talis's attention.

She tried to make jokes about her lack of feminine curves, because she made jokes about everything that hurt her. The truth was, she was worried. What if Talis fell in love with one of them?

She'd tried to talk to Talis about this, but he would just look at her blankly then start talking about knights and armor and swords. She tried to talk to Meg about girls her age who were married, but Meg wanted Talis and Callie to remain children, so she wouldn't answer Callie's questions. She was terrified that the two of them would leave her. Talis joked that if it were left up to Meg she'd still be spoon feeding them.

Will was the most understanding of Callie's "problem." He'd smiled at her and said, "You and Talis are mixed up. In here," he said, tapping her forehead, "you're a woman, but nowhere else." He was too polite to look down at her shapeless body. "Talis is the opposite. He looks like a man but he still thinks like a boy." When Callie looked sad at this, Will smiled at her. "It's often this way. Don't worry, your body will catch up with you and when it does, Talis's mind will be ready." He tweaked her under the chin. "One day he will look at you and he will trip over his tongue."

Callie giggled at this thought and it had sustained her for days. But nothing satisfied her for very long. She always seemed to feel restless. If she was sitting, she wanted to stand, if she was standing, she wanted to walk, if walking, she felt desperate to run. Nothing pleased her. Sometimes she wanted to climb onto Meg's lap; sometimes she wanted to push Meg away from her.

The worst of everything was the way she had come to look at Talis. He had always been Talis, the person who was always with her. She could not imagine a day without him. They always seemed to want to do the same things at the same time, go the same places. Sometimes she'd be feeding her rabbits and she'd hear Talis "call" her. Within seconds she'd start running and be able to find him wherever he was, whether it was on the banks of the river or even hiding in a tree.

But in the last months it was as though she could only *look* at him. He was so very, very beautiful. She looked at the way he moved, the way his hair curled. Sometimes when she looked at him, she could feel her blood rush hotly through her body. It was as though she had too much blood for her body to contain.

Talis still wanted to chase her and play as they had always done, but sometimes when he caught her and whirled her about in his strong arms, her heart started pounding. This feeling would make her angry, so she'd jump away from him, sometimes afraid even for him to hold her hand.

Now, everything seemed to have changed. Even

sleeping. She and Talis had two separate chicken feather mattresses on the floor of the attic and that's where they had slept since they were old enough to climb the ladder. But nearly every night, Callie had left her bed and gone to sleep with Talis. He slept so easily and she always felt better cuddled near him.

When Nigel arrived seven years ago, their sleeping together had stopped. Nigel had insisted that curtains be put between the two of them, with his mattress at the foot of the two beds.

Nigel's arrival had changed a great deal in the Watkins' household. Meg loved his fine manners and was a bit intimidated by him. But Will treated Nigel as though he were on probation and as though at any moment he could turn into a demon.

From the first moment of his arrival, Nigel said he thought Callie and Talis were odd. Neither Talis nor Callie liked that. No one had ever before said they thought they were strange. The village children accepted them but they saw them only on market days, and the only thing they seemed to think was odd was that Callie and Talis were not brother and sister. Whenever anyone called Callie his sister, Talis adamantly set them straight. And the same was true for Callie.

When they were ten years old, it had been Meg who had insisted that Will tell the children some of the truth of their births. When Talis was ten a prosperous farmer had made an offer of marriage for him with his only child, a daughter. He wanted Talis to come and live with him and to inherit half the farm upon marriage and the other half at his death. Since all the village assumed Callie and Talis were brother and sister, on the face of it this sounded like a good arrangement. Callie's husband could inherit Will's farm.

Meg could not bear the thought of the children being separated, nor could she bear for them to leave her and Will. With her mind set, Meg told Will he *must* tell the children that they were not brother and sister and that they were meant to stay on the farm (that being as close as she could come to saying that they were to marry). At this news, Talis merely nodded, but Callie had laughed outright. Talis never thought of a future that included marriage to anyone, but Callie thought of it often and the idea that she might have to live with anyone other than Talis had worried her.

When Nigel arrived, he changed things. He said that Callie and Talis were not as other children and he wanted to separate them. At first he wanted to give lessons only to Talis but Will wouldn't allow that. When Nigel had pointed out that a female could not learn as well as a man, Will had laughed at him and said he was younger and dumber than he looked. After the first month with Callie as his pupil, Nigel never again mentioned dull-brained females.

Teaching them both did not keep Nigel from wanting to separate the children in other ways.

He didn't want them to sleep together, or run off for many hours alone together. "You do not know what they can get up to," Nigel had said pompously to Meg and Will. There was a hint of mystery in his voice, as though only he knew what could happen when two healthy young people of the opposite sex were alone together.

Will didn't tolerate Nigel's arrogance. "Aye, lad, we bumpkins in the country know nothing as to what a lad and lassie can get up to alone all day. We cannot read books so we know nothing."

Blushing, Nigel had shut up for the moment, but that hadn't kept him from continuing trying to separate the children, for he seemed to see sin at every turn. At one point Will said it was like the Garden of Eden, there was no sin until Adam and Eve were told there was. "You should tell them, lad," Will said, "what could happen when they are alone together. I don't think they know." To Meg, Will said, "I think that boy did some things he is ashamed of when he was younger."

Meg hesitated. "You don't think he's right, do you?"

Will shook his head. "What if he is? Would you mind a hasty wedding and grandbabies to rock?"

At that Meg perked up, and since then she had amused Will greatly by shooing the "children" out of the house at every opportunity. Like Will, she knew that Talis's body was ready and

Callie's mind was. Someday soon, the two were going to catch up with each other.

But what to Meg and Will was amusing, was to Callie infuriating. She had no idea what she was feeling, what was plaguing her night and day. At night, Talis whispered to her to come get in bed with him, saying that he was cold. Callie refused to go to him because she knew that he wanted her with him because he *was* cold.

Now, under the spreading tree, she was frowning ferociously at Talis. He had been playing with that blasted rusty sword — or another one — for as long as she could remember. In the village all he wanted to do was talk to the other boys about any men on horses who had ridden through the village. He wanted to know what they wore, what they said, whether they laughed or frowned. He had an extensive repertoire of knightly knowledge, saying a knight says this and a knight says that. He pestered Nigel about knights until the man was screaming with impatience.

"What's wrong with you?" Talis asked suddenly, giving a mighty thrust at the air near her head.

"I don't know," she said petulantly. "It's something. I feel strange inside. Angry. Sad. Happy. I don't know." She was leaning against the tree, her head to one side, looking away from him.

Talis didn't show much concern at her words, but it annoyed him when she didn't want to play. In the village, because he was so large, he had to pretend to the other boys that he was a man, with a man's knowledge. But with Callie he didn't have to pretend. Sometimes she made believe she was a lady held by a dragon and he would rescue her. But the last time they'd played that, at the end she'd acted very strange, talking about how they must now get married and make babies. It was very confusing to him and since then they hadn't played that game or any other.

Now he was trying to interest her in what he was doing. Thrusting hard, he jammed the sword into the tree by her ear. "Now you are my prisoner, princess."

She knocked the sword away. "You're such a baby," she said with great contempt.

"Me?" He was incredulous. "*You're* no bigger than a baby," he said, starting to grab her.

This physical teasing was normal for both of them, something they had always done. In public they kept their hands off each other but in private they loved to touch. When they escaped Nigel's watchfulness, they did their lessons, studied their Greek and Latin, their astronomy and mathematics, while sitting close together, one whole side of their bodies touching.

But today Callie angrily moved away from him. Having never before experienced her not wanting to touch him, Talis didn't have any idea that she was serious. He grabbed her again and even when she started twisting away from him, he still thought she was teasing.

When Talis did at last understand that she was

genuinely fighting him, he thought she was afraid of something. This pleased him, as he liked to think of himself as a great, strong knight. "There's nothing to be afraid of," he said in his deepest voice. "I will protect you."

"And who will protect me from *you?*" she snapped back at him with great sarcasm.

"From me?" Talis was shocked. How could she think that *he* would hurt her? She had done horrible things to him, such as embarrass him in front of the entire village, yet he had never harmed her in any way. "I would never hurt you," he said softly, then turned away from her. Callie had hurt his pride at times, but she had never insinuated that his honor was such that he could think of hurting something as small and weak as she was. Is this what she thought of him?

Right away Callie knew how much she had injured his pride. She always knew just how far she could go in her teasing of him. But now she had done something to bruise that ridiculous sense of honor that was so important to him. And she knew that he'd starve rather than betray what he thought was his honor.

She ran to him, moving to stand in front of him, her hands on his forearms, gripping him hard. For all that he bent she could have been holding on to a piece of rock. His back was rigid, his head held high above hers, his eyes looking over her head.

"Talis, I'm sorry. So sorry. Of course you wouldn't hurt me."

All her feelings of restlessness were gone, all her sense of pride. She could bear most anything in life except that Talis was unhappy with her. It didn't happen very often, but when it did, it was the most miserable feeling in the world.

Standing on tiptoes, then having to lean against him for support, she started to kiss his face, all of it that she could reach.

"Tally?" she said, whispering. "Tally, honey, my love, I'm sorry." He didn't respond in any way so she tried harder, kissing him more and more, putting her arms around his neck, then, because he was so rigid, she lifted herself off the ground, her full weight suspended by her arms around him.

"You would never harm me, I know that. I know I've been awful lately and you've been a saint to me, and I apologize. I really don't know what's wrong with me."

After several minutes of groveling, she pulled back and looked at him. He was still standing rigid, still looking at something far away from her, but she knew that his hurt was gone. So why wasn't he doing what he usually did when he forgave her? Usually he took full advantage of her contrition to get her to play some game where she was a helpless female rescued by the big, strong male.

But now he was still standing there, his arms at his side. And he wasn't pushing her away and telling her to stop getting his face wet, as he usually did on the rare occasions when she kissed him.

With her toes barely touching the ground, her arms tight around his neck, her body pressed full against his, she looked at him. Had his eyes *always* been this dark? she wondered. Had his hair always been this black, his skin this exquisite color? Her heart was pounding in her throat. This was Talis, a boy she had shared her whole life with. He was as familiar to her as the sun, as the air, but at this moment he seemed to be the most glorious, the most *un*familiar thing on earth.

"You missed a spot," Talis said, and Callie could feel his voice against her chest.

"Missed?" she said, her voice catching in her throat. She had no idea what he was talking about.

"You did not kiss *all* of my face," he said quite seriously, then bent his head so she could kiss him more.

A moment ago her kisses had been quick, the way she had always kissed him, little girl kisses that she'd given him when he'd killed a spider for her, or once when he'd hit a big boy who was teasing her in a nasty way. Then, in happiness, she'd kissed his cheek several times. Then the only indication Talis had given that he was even aware she was kissing him was that he had bent just slightly so she could reach his cheek.

He had never kissed her, even after Callie had done very nice things for him, such as doing his chores because he'd fallen asleep under a tree. Talis said that knights didn't kiss girls. "What *do* they kiss? Their horses?" she'd asked mockingly. At that retort, Meg, in one of her rare witticisms, had said, "Knights kiss their mothers," then had lowered her cheek to receive Talis's kiss. Talis had left the house whistling in triumph.

So now Talis was almost asking Callie to kiss him. And kiss him she did. Never in her life had she wanted to do something as much as she wanted to kiss Talis this moment. It was as though the whole world had disappeared; nothing else existed but the two of them under this tree.

She kissed his chin, long, slow, lingering kisses, then moved upward, and as she did so, he lowered his head just slightly.

When Callie placed her lips on his, it was not the hard, puckered kiss of a child, but her lips were soft and a tiny bit parted. For weeks now Talis's lips had fascinated her. They were full and soft-looking and she liked the way they moved when he talked. In fact, lately she had not been able to hear him for watching his lips curl about the words. Sometimes she had angered him by looking away when he was telling her something, but she had needed to break the connection between her eyes and his mouth.

Now she felt his intake of breath when her lips touched his, felt his body soften, then his strong arms tighten around her. He was always showing off his newly discovered strength and picking her up and twirling her around. He delighted even in turning her upside down, or tossing her in the air. So feeling Talis's arms around her, feeling his body close to hers was nothing new, but today this was somehow different. Today she could feel his strength, feel his big body, feel the power of him in a way she'd never felt before.

Callie wondered at his touch, wondered at the feel of her lips on his. Her inexperience, her awe, made her hesitant, but Talis did not seem to be hesitant about what to do.

For just a second, at first, he pulled away from her, looked at her, his eyes wide, then, with great assurance, he put his hand to the back of her head, turned her head to one side (she'd always puzzled over what to do with the noses in a kiss, but obviously the question had not plagued Talis. He just, somehow, *knew* what went where), and kissed her hard.

She was awfully glad for his strength because her knees gave way under her and Talis had to support her body fully against his. He did so easily, without seeming to notice that she had melted into the consistency of butter left in the sun.

For just a second, Callie's eyes opened wide as he somehow managed to support her weight with his upper arms, leaving both his hands free to roam unobstructed and firmly over all of her body that he could reach. Callie had nearly despaired because she had not curves in the front of her body, but it had never occurred to her that her backside was *very* curvaceous and that that curve had caused no little interest in most of the boys in the village. She didn't know that Talis had once shoved a boy three years older

297

than himself into the mud for making a remark as Callie bent over a barrel of pickled turnips.

Now Talis cupped her buttocks as he kissed her sweet mouth in a way that made Callie nearly faint. She felt some timidity, but he didn't. He had always been the aggressor between them, the one who walked into a cave without any thought of caution. He was the brave one, is what Meg said. And now, he was the adventurous one when it came to kissing.

He thrust his tongue into her mouth, hard and firm.

Startled, Callie pulled away from him, looked at him in surprise. Had he done something like this a few months ago, she would have thought it was disgusting, but now . . . now, she liked it.

One minute they were standing in the open air and the next Talis had shoved her against the tree, and it seemed that he was taking her clothes off. Callie could not think. It seemed that everything in her mind had fled and she was just one mass of feeling. She wasn't sure what she wanted from Talis and she didn't know if he knew what he wanted from her, but she was certain that she wanted to find out.

She was never to find out what would have happened because suddenly the cacophony surrounding them was deafening. Men thundered by on horses; men were shouting; armor clanking; chaos; confusion.

Talis was the first to hear it. Horses and men,

with or without armor, were of no interest to Callie. Her one and only interest in life was Talis.

But not so him. Pulling himself away from her, his hand still on her bare thigh as it rested on his hip, he cocked his head to one side and listened.

Callie, impatient, tried to pull his face back to hers. They were safe and secret under the tree; no one would see them, no matter what they were doing.

"Something has happened," Talis said.

"Yes," she answered, meaning something totally different. In the last moments everything in her life had changed: The way she looked and thought about life had changed.

As though what was going on between them was no longer of interest to him, he dropped her leg, then took off running toward the house. After allowing herself a brief luxury of cursing him, she began running after him. How could what had just happened between them affect him so little that he could just leave her like that?

But by now her brain had recovered enough to think that perhaps something horrible had happened to Meg or Will. It did not occur to her that, horrible as that may be to her and Talis, the mishaps of two peasant farmers was hardly cause for an alarm raised that involved shouting knights on horseback.

Lifting her skirts, she took off running, as close to Talis's heels as she could manage.

24

There was no way that Callie's legs could keep up with Talis's long legs as the two of them ran back to the farmhouse. She half ran out of one shoe, and her hair came untied from its neat braid as she leaped over hedges, dodged three bleating sheep, and tried to follow Talis.

What she saw when she arrived made her halt. The yard was full of big men, richly dressed, their horses' great hooves trampling Meg's flowers. The men were all staring down at a man on the ground; Callie could only see his legs, but from the stillness of them, he looked to be dead. Standing to one side, Meg and Will clung to each other and there was fear on Meg's face.

Callie may have hesitated to run into the midst of the dozen or so men standing about, but not so Talis. He plunged into the midst of them, and in spite of his rough clothes, he looked as though he were one of the noblemen.

Callie didn't think of hesitating when it came to following Talis. Within a breath, she was behind him, taking advantage of the space he made for himself between the silent, staring men.

Peeping out around him, Callie saw a man on the ground, a handsome man with steel gray hair, but now his once handsome face was blue from lack of air. On the lower half of his face, around his mouth and down his throat, were bloody scratches from where he and others had clawed at him. It didn't take a great deal of intelligence to figure out what had happened, since a half-eaten apple lay near the man's head. He had taken too big a bite, a piece of apple had lodged in his throat and he had choked to death. All attempts to save him had failed, and now all the stunned people could do was look down at this man as he lay dead.

Talis didn't even look to see if Callie had caught up with him; he knew she was there. "Tildy," he said, and immediately, Callie knew what he had in mind.

At first no one noticed the tall young man with the pale girl peering around him. But Talis's quick movements drew their attention.

Before anyone could recover from shock, Talis lifted Callie by the waist, her legs extended straight out, picked her up over his head, then dropped her — straight onto the stomach of the dead man.

Shouts erupted in anger over this hideous disrespect of the dead man. But even as the men started to shout at Talis and tried to grab the girl the boy was protecting with his body, others saw that the mouth of the "dead" man opened and out flew a huge, unchewed piece of apple.

"Quiet!" bellowed a man who obviously had some authority and they all turned to look down at the man on the ground.

Talis had more of an idea of what was going to happen than the others did, so he shoved his way through the hovering men, Callie in front of him, and looked down to see the eyelashes of the man flutter.

Seconds later, with the help of his men, the man was coughing and sitting upright.

Quietly, Talis ushered Callie away from the crowd that was now reviving the almost-dead man.

"How?" was all that Nigel could say, and in his eyes was his renewed suspicion that Talis and Callie were strange people.

"Magic," Talis said, as always, enjoying Nigel's skeptical looks.

"Magic, ha!" Callie said. "Once he fell out of a tree right onto Tildy," she said, referring to one of the milk cows. "He hit her so hard, her cud went flying across the field. We just did the same thing to that man."

Nigel was impressed that Talis had been able to apply such knowledge to the present emergency, but he did not say so. In his opinion, Talis was already too proud of himself and didn't need more praise.

It was Callie who noticed that Meg and Will were still standing to one side, their arms wrapped about each other, their faces pale. Callie could understand why they had been so frightened. She had heard of the anger of some lords of the manor being used against poor farmers. What would have happened if this rich man had died on their land? Would his relatives have blamed them for his death?

But why were Meg and Will still upset now that they knew the man was not going to die? Talis had saved the man's life. Perhaps now there would be a reward.

As she was looking at Meg and Will, Talis was asking questions of Nigel about the men who were overrunning the small yard.

"They stopped here to buy cider," Nigel was saying. "This year's apple crop failed for the man and he was told that Will had good cider, so he thought to buy some. He wanted to taste an apple. It was all so simple. Will handed him an apple, he took a bite, then Meg came out of the house and the man looked as though he had seen a ghost."

Nigel frowned. "The man was still on his horse and when he saw Meg, he seemed to suck in air, the horse reared and the next moment he was choking to death. There were many attempts to save him but the apple piece was lodged deep in his throat. By the time the men could get him off his horse he was already . . . dead." As he said this he looked askance at Talis, as though he were a witch who had brought a dead man back to life.

"He was not dead, as you can hear," Talis said, unconcerned with Nigel's suspicious looks. To their left, they could hear the coughing and hacking of the man. Since he was surrounded by guarding knights, they could not see him, but they could hear him well enough.

"Who is he?" Callie asked, still watching Meg and Will. There were silent tears running down Meg's cheeks and Will was doing his best to comfort her, but he too looked shaken. Callie wanted to go to them, but she had an idea that they would tell her nothing. She had long been aware that Meg and Will had secrets that they told no one. One of the requirements of being a storyteller was watching people and looking for answers to questions. Callie had already found out that all people have secrets.

"I have not heard of him," Nigel said. "His name is Lord John Hadley, the third son of an earl. I believe his title is one of courtesy. He married well," Nigel informed them, letting them know that Lord John was not of the highest rank in the aristocracy. "The men say he has never traveled this way before." He gave an odd look at Callie. "They say he had a dream that told him to travel this way."

Before Callie could say a word, the men near them parted, making an opening to Lord John, who was now standing with the support of two men.

"His lordship wants to see you," said a handsome man dressed in a long velvet robe, his hair hanging to his shoulders. Part of his manner said he wanted nothing to do with these peasant brats, but a part of him seemed to say that he was grateful. Still lingering behind his eyes was grief at what he'd almost lost, for Hugh Kellon genuinely loved his master.

John Hadley had no such ambiguity. There was no doubt in his mind that he had been dead. He had been able to look down on his own dead body, see the bloody marks on his neck where he had clawed his own throat. He had seen his men bent over him. And as he was floating away, John had felt only relief to at last leave a world that had given him no happiness. He had never been given what he most wanted in life and his many days on earth had been full of a sense of loss.

Seeing that woman today is what had made him so acutely aware of his loss. It was as though he had been transported back into time to the day that had been the happiest of his life. That night he had at last obtained the healthy son he so much wanted.

But it had all been taken away from him within the blink of an eye. He had received and lost all within the space of hours. Over the ensuing years he had been able to block out the pain of the loss of those days. He had concentrated on building and on trying to make something of the two worthless sons he did have. Although nothing had been able to give him life again, he had managed to survive.

Then today he had seen that woman and she had reminded him of that night. She had been there. He knew that. She had been there.

The pain had been too much for him. At that moment, he'd wanted to stop living. Better death than the pain of remembering that night.

And so he had chosen to die. He did not fight the lack of air that was causing him to die. He gave up.

But as he was hovering over his own body, two angels came to him. One was a tall boy, as handsome as an angel, with black hair and eyes, lightly tanned skin, as straight and strong as a knight from a fairy tale. The girl was as white and pale as something from the netherworld. All the features of her face were without color, her brows, her lashes, her lips even, were the same pale ivory. Only her eyes, which were an extraordinary blue-violet, added color to her face. Around this ivory face tumbled a great mass of golden hair, falling to her waist, wrapping about her arms, looking nearly as heavy as all of her body combined.

Looking down at them, John hesitated before leaving the earth altogether. There was something about these young people that drew his attention.

He knew now that that moment's hesitation was the reason he was still alive. The boy dropped the girl on his bloated belly, the apple piece went flying from where it was lodged in his throat, and the next moment, John was back in his body and breathing again.

Now, weakly standing, supported on both sides by his men, something was haunting him. There was a name that had rung in his head as the boy was dropping the girl onto his lifeless body. It had taken him a while to remember the name, but when he did, his coughing increased.

Gilbert, he thought. Gilbert Rasher.

The men around John parted and allowed their master to see the boy who had saved his life.

Talis stood straight and strong, staring levelly into this man's eyes. Even though he had been raised on a farm, there was no subservience in his manner. Talis had the unshakable self-confidence that only youth and intelligence could give. He believed he belonged, therefore he did.

Slowly, John looked the boy up and down. But he could hardly be called a boy, for he was taller than most men. His body had not yet filled out, so his hands and feet were too large, his shoulders awkwardly broad above his thin waist, but in a few more years he was going to be a giant of a man.

"What is your name?" John rasped out of his raw throat.

With his shoulders back, he said, "Talis." He did not give Will's last name of Watkins as his own, for Talis had known for a long time that his true name was something else. But he knew that Talis belonged to him and to no one else.

John nearly swooned on his feet at the sound of that name. It was his father's name, an old name, an unusual name. He didn't know how and, honestly, didn't care how the boy had survived the fire. All he knew for sure was that this was the boy given to him sixteen years ago. This was *his* son.

With all the strength he could muster, John pushed the men around him from his side. Then, standing unsteadily on his own feet, he opened his arms wide. "Come," he said, emotion choking him, "give your father a kiss."

Talis did not hesitate before walking into John Hadley's strong arms. Always, since his first day of awareness, Talis knew that something like this was destined to happen to him. It was what he had "trained" for. At least trained as best he could, by learning all he could about being a knight. When his real father came to him, he did not want to disappoint him. Years ago, when Meg had returned from that awful time when she had disappeared and later said she had gone to find a teacher, Talis had not been surprised. A knight needed to be taught, and he needed to learn all he could to prepare himself for this day.

Talis could feel the man's tears on his neck, but Talis did not feel close to tears. Now it will begin, was all he could think. Now his true purpose in life would start.

John pulled away from Talis to look at him, to put his hands on the sides of his face, to touch the unblemished young skin, to feel the clean curls of his hair. And as John touched the boy, life seemed to flow back into him. For years now, sixteen years to be precise, he had been willing himself to die. He had not had a reason to live. But now, touching this beautiful boy, he once again had a reason to live.

Talis smiled happily as John ran his hands over him, feeling him as though he were a horse he'd just bought. Grinning, Talis looked at the men around them, some of them frowning, some half-smiling, some looking on in bewilderment.

Suddenly, John straightened. "We must ride. We will not get home before dark as it is. Hugh! Give my son your horse."

Through all of this, Callie, Meg, Will, and Nigel had stood in silence. With each word that was spoken, Meg clung more heavily to Will's arm. Will, trying to be strong, was weak at the thought of losing Talis. Until this moment he had not known how very much he loved the boy. Talis, with his teasing sense of humor, his moods, and his demands for attention, even the sheer long-legged size of him, was everything to all of them.

Nigel would have died before he admitted it, because he was careful to make the farm family think that he was of a different class than they were, but the truth was, he was better fed and better treated here than he had ever been in his life. And in spite of his reservations about his pupils, their life spirit was infectious. They were the two most likable people he had ever met. And now he saw it all ending.

Callie was too stunned by what was happening to so much as move. She was happy for Talis.

Yes, yes, yes, she told herself. She was very, very happy for him. This is what he wanted; what he deserved. Maybe someday she would get to see him in his armor. Maybe someday he would stop by the poor farmhouse and allow all of them to see him.

At this thought, she imagined herself in rags, having little to eat, having to take the barn down beam by beam to use the wood to stay warm in winter. She imagined Talis returning to say that his life had been miserable without her, rich but miserable, and would they all please come to live with him?

It was Talis who stepped away from the man who said he was his father. "No, sir," he said as politely as possible. "I cannot leave my family alone."

No one could speak after Talis said that. Some older men smiled at the idealism of youth. Idealism was not much good in the cold of winter, and, of course, the boy did not know what he was turning down when he refused his lordship's offer of protection.

Although Talis looked as though he made a daily habit of turning down offers of life with a nobleman, Callie knew all too well what he was feeling. He was scared and uncertain. Now his honor, what he knew to be right and what he wanted so very, very much, were warring inside him.

Silently, she went to stand behind him. She did not touch him but she knew her close presence would give him strength. They were stronger together than apart.

With her mind, she willed him to be calm, to be still. Meg had said a thousand times, "Talis is strong because Callie believes he is strong."

For a moment John looked puzzled; he couldn't understand what was being said to him. No doubt his confusion was caused by his recent brush with death, but his mind seemed dazed. He had found his son, but his son was refusing him.

Hugh Kellon had been with John for many years now, since just after the night he had heard so much about, the night John had at last been given a son and that son had been taken from him in a fire. There were many whispers about that night, about what it had done to both master and mistress, and Hugh knew that John was not what he once was.

Was this boy John's son, the boy who was supposed to have died in the fire? Had this fat farm couple stolen him away in the night? Why had they not brought the boy back to John when the danger was over? And who was this waif of a girl standing so close behind the handsome boy? She looked like a blonde shadow, almost as though she were part of him.

Behind him, Hugh could hear the rumbles of the other men. What had been a simple outing had almost become a tragedy and at best it was turning into a mystery. Best to get everyone at a supper table, he thought. A little wine and a good joint would go a long way toward calming people.

With one long stride, Hugh stepped forward and put his arm around Talis's shoulder. "This lad is a son to be proud of. Of course he will come with us, my lord. And the girl, too." He started to pull her to the forefront but she eluded him, stepping to one side to hide under the boy's arm.

"Ahem," Hugh said, shaking his head to clear it. It was going to take a hogshead of wine to help him make sense of this day. "And the others. They shall go too. Is that not right, my lord?"

"Yes, of course," John Hadley said. "Take all of them. What do I care of peasants?"

"By the look of her, that girl is no peasant," whispered one of the men behind John.

"Do you think she is the boy's doxy?" asked another man.

"If she is, he *is* John's son," the first man answered, chuckling.

John was beginning to recover himself. Death and life, all in the space of an hour, had rattled his brains. To the world he had said that his wife had given birth to a son, but he knew that she had not. This pale girl standing so close to "his" boy was almost surely his daughter.

"Come to me, child," John said, holding out his hand to her.

Callie hesitated, then looked up at Talis. When he nodded that it was all right, she stepped forward.

Yes, John thought, she had the look of his wife when she'd been younger. Although this one

312

was no beauty, that was for sure. She was too colorless for beauty. Standing beside this great, beautiful boy who towered over her, she was insignificant.

"Yes," he whispered, more to himself than to anyone else, "you are my daughter."

No one was prepared for the violence of Callie's reaction to this very generous statement. "No!" Callie screamed at him. "I am *not* your daughter! I am *not*. Do you hear me? I am not!" For all that she looked meek and mild, anyone who knew Callie for long knew of her temper — which was only roused when it had something to do with Talis.

"The whole family is mad," one of the men said. First the boy had refused to acknowledge his rich father and now this simple-minded girl was screaming that she was not his daughter.

The screams of her beloved child brought Meg out of her fear. She knew that Callie's problem was not whether she was or was not Hadley's daughter, but whether she was Talis's sister. Brother and sister could not marry.

"My lord," Meg said loudly, moving forward. "Do you not remember that this child is the other man's daughter?"

There was silence for a moment until one of the men who had been there that night remembered. "She is old Gilbert Rasher's daughter, my lord. Although it is hard to believe that he could father something as delicate as this child. I'd think a horse like Rasher more likely to father sons

313

like that boy of yours," he said, nodding toward Talis.

The man had no idea why John turned a face of black hatred toward him. He had merely made a comment on the girl's looks. Actually, he felt sorry for her if she was to have to live with Rasher and that animal brood of boys of his. They were a cunning, crude, and filthy lot of curs and the girl would not last long.

After a moment, John turned back. "Yes, she is Rasher's daughter." What did he care? He had enough daughters to open a convent; he needed no more. "Bring the girl," he said to Talis. "Bring the whole damned village for all I care." All he wanted was this boy as his son.

Through all of this Talis had stood straight and silent, saying not a word. Judging by his face, one would not have guessed how much he wanted to ride away with these men, to wear clothes such as theirs, to sit atop a glorious horse. But his family knew.

Also, looking at him, Talis seemed an adult. He stood as tall as an adult, had the bearing of an adult, but inside he was still as innocent as a boy. When John gave him what he wanted and Talis knew that he could have his honor *and* a horse, he turned to the person who meant everything to him: Callie. With an easy, practiced gesture, he picked her up by the waist as she crossed her arms over her chest, locked her ankles together, then he tossed her high into the air where she went twirling around and around. It was something they had once seen traveling players do and they had practiced it for months — with Talis never once failing to catch her.

Seeing Talis tossing Callie about was a familiar sight to the people they lived with, but not to the fifteen or so men standing in the farmyard. With mouths agape, the men stood and watched the girl go spinning through the air, hair whipping out about her like a windmill. More than one man held his breath that Talis was going to catch her.

He did, with ease and expertise, then, oblivious to everyone else, he grabbed Callie's hand and they went running into the house.

25

The first sight Callie and Talis had of Hadley Hall struck them dumb. For two days they had been riding together, Callie in front as they made their way back to what was to be their home. For them it had been days of trying to settle themselves to the prospect of their new life. Callie had cried for some time at leaving Meg and Will, who had refused John's offer to go with them.

"Our place is here," Will had said. "We will be here if you need us."

Meg had been too upset to say a word.

Talis had done his best not to show the wrench he was feeling at leaving his home. Part of him wanted this great adventure and part of him despaired at leaving Will, who had taught him so much and whose quiet wisdom had always been there for him.

However, neither Talis nor Callie had shed tears at leaving Nigel behind. Lord John had given him a couple of gold coins and he'd gone on his way.

While riding on the horse toward Hadley Hall Talis had talked to Callie at length, softly telling her that she was going to be separated from him and that she must be strong. "I will not always be there to take care of you," he said. "You must learn to do without me every minute of every day."

Swallowing, Callie had nodded. "Will you miss me?"

"Yes, of course, but we are not children any longer. We must be adults. Promise me you will behave. You will obey my father?"

Callie nodded. She would try. She would make Talis proud of her and would be very adult and grown up about their new lives. No more sleeping just a few feet apart. No more — No more anything, she thought, remembering the days when they had belonged to just each other.

"When will we see each other?" she asked.

"As soon as I can arrange it. I will have to impress my father first. I will have to make him care for me before I ask him things about . . . About us."

She was not sure what Talis meant by those words, but she hoped — prayed — that he meant marriage. If they were not married they would not be allowed to stay together as they had at the farm. She knew that just from what she had seen of the members of the upper class who had ridden through the village.

She snuggled her head back into Talis's shoulder. She did not know how she was going to

317

live without touching him every day. It was painful to her when Nigel made them sit apart during lessons. Neither Meg nor Will minded when she and Talis ate with their ankles entwined at the table.

As always, Talis knew what she was thinking and he put one of his hands over both of hers on the saddle. "Soon," he whispered. "Soon. I promise you. I will do what must be done as soon as possible. It will be more difficult if we have caused trouble. Do you understand?"

"Yes," she answered, and she did understand. Angry adults did not give younger people permission to do what they wanted. If it meant she could have Talis all to herself in the end, she would stay away from him for a year. She would, of course, die a little bit each day, but she would do what must be done.

For the days of travel toward his home, John Hadley had done little except stare at his son, his head reeling with all the things they would now do together. At last his life would hold some meaning; he'd have someone to leave all his worldly goods to. He discounted those two weakling boys his wife had given him. At nineteen and twenty, his sons weren't as big or as healthy as this handsome, dark boy who hovered so protectively over the pale girl.

In his silent watching, John was thrilled to find out that the boy was as likable as he was beautiful. Last night at the inn, he had not been shy. If the truth were told, John had feared that being raised by peasants would have made him into a peasant, but this boy was a prince even though his hands were stained and hardened from manual labor. No matter that his clothes were rough and crude, discolored by the barnyard, he carried himself as though he were destined for the throne of England.

Silver tongue. That's what one of his men had said that Talis had: a silver tongue. He talked and joked and laughed with men twice his age last night, and when they said he was too young for the beer they were drinking, Talis showed them all by drinking twice as much as they did and still being able to walk up the stairs. He said that Will's beer was stronger than the innkeeper's; Will didn't water his beer.

Oh yes, John thought, the boy was a wonder: good to look at, personable, talented, strong (he had beaten three men in arm wrestling, then made them all laugh when Talis had accused them of soft living). Talis was a son any man could be proud of.

The only oddity about him was the way he kept the girl near him, that pale shadow of a girl who watched everything. John had ordered her to bed, but Talis, without so much as turning, had said, "Callie may stay."

Just like that. For a moment, John's temper had started to rise. He did not allow *anyone* to talk to him in that tone. No one countered *his* orders. But some part of him knew that if he told Talis he could not have the girl near him, the boy would leave them. In a flash he would walk out of the inn and no offer in the world would bring him back.

With great interest, his men watched him, and John knew he needed to establish his authority, but the outcome could be too serious. After a while, he laughed. "I defer to my son," he said, then saw the way Talis looked at him in puzzlement. The boy had not known that, in countermanding John's orders, he had issued a challenge. It was just that no one had ever before suggested that Callie be taken away from him, not Will, not Meg, no one. Nigel had mentioned the idea, but no one had listened to him. To Talis, Callie was his, and she belonged with him and she was going to stay near him as long as possible.

John looked at the girl with distaste, and for the first time in his life, he felt jealousy. Until now, there had never been anything he'd ever wanted to possess so completely that he wanted to share it with no one else. But he wanted this boy. He wanted Talis as he'd never wanted anything else. And he wanted him for his own. John did not like it when Talis spoke so often of that farmer, Will Watkins, as though he were a man of great standing in the world. John didn't like it when Talis mentioned Will; nor did he like the way the girl followed Talis everywhere.

Without a thought of what he was doing, John

decided that he would separate them as soon as possible.

Callie and Talis looked up at the house, their mouths open in awe. "Have you ever seen such?" Callie whispered.

"Never. I did not know a house could be so large."

John had spent the last sixteen years in a frenzy of building. John put every bit of his energy into this house. This house had become his family, his very reason for living. In spite of all the children he had produced, to him, his life was barren. He dismissed the daughters, despaired of his weak sons, so he had done the best he could to leave something behind.

The stone house spread out over a long L shape that from the outside looked solid but actually hid several beautiful and useful little courtyards. There was a courtyard for the retainers, one for the kitchen, one for private family use, and another off the large hall court.

Not far from the house were many smaller buildings in a matching gray stone, and everywhere people were moving about, men with scythes on their shoulders, women carrying skeins of wool, all looking prosperous and busy.

Following John's example, Callie and Talis dismounted and gave the horse's reins to the boys who were waiting to take them. Curiously, the servants looked at the newcomers, not dressed as nobles but riding a horse meant for a nobleman.

If nothing else, the rare smile on John Hadley's face was enough to make them step back in wonder.

"Come on," John said fondly to Talis when he and Callie walked slowly through the courtyard, looking up at the three stories of the house around them. Glass windows winked at them in the sunlight, and curious faces appeared now and then to look down on them.

They entered a huge hall with a stunning hammer-beam ceiling that rose majestically overhead. The plaster walls were covered with every manner of arms and armor, ready to be used in case of trouble.

Tables were set up, covered with huge platters of food, richly dressed people laughing and talking as they ate. At one end was a raised dais, two ornate chairs set in the middle. In the smaller of the two chairs sat a once-pretty woman who was now soft and past her youth. In the larger of the two chairs sat a boy, maybe older than Talis, but not much. He was tall, thin faced, underdeveloped, and when he saw his father, what pleasure there was on his face disappeared.

It did not take much to bring the diners to a halt. John Hadley was not known for his generosity. He wanted people to eat and get back to work. When he was away, the household was much more relaxed and everything was easier.

Now, they could not believe the happiness on his face. With long strides, he went straight toward the head table where his wife sat, one of her sons on either side of her. John did not so much as offer a greeting to his two sons, who looked at their father as though begging for approval. The people saw Lady Alida's hand go out to touch the sleeve of her eldest son. For all that John cared nothing for his imperfect sons, his wife loved them very, very much.

"Behold, wife," John said, as though he were a performer at a fair announcing the magician's coming act. "I have found our true son."

With a great flourish, he stepped back so everyone could see Talis and Callie standing in the middle of the room.

In England, the classes were divided in every way: clothing, houses, even in food. People who could afford it ate the most expensive food, which was meat and sugar. Upper classes separated themselves from lower classes by never eating vegetables if they could help it: Peasants and animals ate vegetables. Eating fruit raw showed that you could not afford a cook to stew the fruit in a sugar sauce. Brown bread with the bran still in it showed you could afford only the cheapest grain.

The Hadley house was rich, with the inhabitants living on meat, white flour, and sugared pastries. As a result, they suffered from what the continentals called the English Disease of blackened, loose, rotting teeth. No amount of cleaning could compensate for the sugar-laden diet.

Callie and Talis had been raised by farmers on a diet of vegetables, little meat, fruit eaten raw from the trees, and sugar eaten so seldom they hardly knew the taste of it. Added to their diet was a lifetime of physical activity — running, climbing over fences, chasing chickens.

The result of all this was two people of dazzling good health: strong bones, lithe muscles, glistening white teeth, hair that shone from good health and sunshine. They stood straight and strong, their limbs supple and glowing.

Talis with his dark handsomeness, Callie with her blue-violet eyes and hair to her waist, looked like a couple from a fairy story: the knight and his maiden fair.

All eyes were drawn to Talis. He looked like every man's dream of a son: healthy, strong, tall, broad, his dark eyes gleaming with intelligence. What he did *not* look like was John Hadley's son. John was a tall man, broad shouldered, but his was not a body that carried much weight. In his youth, his hair had been red and his skin white; sun burned him, it did not tan him. There was no doubt that his sons now flanking his wife at the table belonged to him: They were slighter versions of John. But now, this young giant standing next to John looked like a bear beside a golden-haired deer.

But, of course, no one dared say such out loud.

Alida tried her best to remain calm. Even though she was seeing the end of her life, the end of her children's lives standing before her, she tried to remain calm. But the emotion was too much for her.

She tried to rise, to offer her hand in welcome to this boy who was laying claim to what belonged to *her* children, but she could not. The moment she stood, the blood left her head and she fainted.

She had no idea that Talis, ever quick in an emergency, leaped across the table and picked her up into his strong young arms before she hit the floor.

Speechless, the audience looked at him as he held Lady Alida, her arms hanging limply at her side.

"Sir?" Talis asked, looking at John, wanting to know where he was to take the woman he held.

Had there been any part of John's heart that did not already belong to Talis, this incident would have claimed it. "Come, son," he said. "I will show you where to take her."

Pandemonium. That's what broke forth in the Great Hall when Alida fainted after the announcement of her son's return from the grave. People began talking at once, everyone speculating on what had happened and what was going to happen. Anyone who knew, or thought he knew, anything about the events of sixteen years before was in great demand as a speaker and considered a font of knowledge.

As Talis carried her up the stairs, Alida awoke from her stupor long enough to say to her oldest unmarried daughter, "Keep her busy." Then, with one more look at the dark young man carrying her up the stairs, she lapsed back into her swoon.

It took Edith, the eldest, a while to understand who her mother meant when she said, "her." If there was anything less interesting than yet another unmarried woman in the Hadley household, one would be hard pressed to discover it.

After Edith did figure out who her mother meant, it took her a while to find the girl. She was so close to the young man who was their new brother that Edith couldn't at first see her.

Dorothy, the youngest of the unmarried daughters, standing behind Edith, looked at Talis hanging over their mother's bed and gave a great sigh. "*Why* does he have to be our *brother?*" she said, tears of exasperation in her voice.

"Be quiet! He's too young for you anyway," Edith, ever practical, said.

At that Dorothy gave a nasty little laugh that said what all the daughters thought: She'd take any man she could get; none of them were too young or too old, too anything.

Edith didn't allow herself to think about what was going on around them, nor did she look at her new brother. Edith took her responsibilities *very* seriously. "Come along," she said to Callie, and when Callie started to protest, Edith took her firmly by the arm and began to pull her from the room.

As Callie was being forcibly led from the room, she looked back at the crowd of people around Talis. Immediately, his head came up as he frowned at her, not wanting her to leave. But before he could say anything, Alida gave a groan that sounded as though she were dying.

"My son," Alida said. "My son. It is a miracle." With amazing strength for one so weak, she pulled Talis's head down toward her own. "Let me look at you."

By the time Talis could pull away from her, Callie was gone.

Callie was frantic. She hadn't seen Talis in two days now. Two days of doing the most inconsequential, most boring, most useless nonsense she'd ever not known existed. There were lute lessons, and dress fittings and scheduled walks in the garden, during which there was a lot of talk about what went on at Queen Elizabeth's court. There was endless talk about who was getting married and who wasn't. The oldest of the unmarried sisters still left at home constantly made declarations that she wouldn't have so and so man if he were offered to her on a platter.

The youngest sister (who Callie rather liked) said Edith would take a man if he had one eye, one arm, and no legs.

"And you?" Callie asked.

"Mmmm," Dorothy said, thinking. "I'd really like for him to have at least one leg."

Callie laughed, which made Edith stop walking and reprimand them for being frivolous.

Once, Callie heard the clanking of swords and immediately started in the direction of the sounds, but Edith, with an astonishing burst of speed, caught her. "Ladies do not consort with men without chaperons."

"We could all go?" Callie asked tentatively, making Dorothy giggle.

By the third day, Callie felt as though she would explode. Of course the steel corset the daughters had laced her into didn't help her feel settled. At the first feeling of those hooks being closed around her ribs, she nearly fainted. Catching herself against a windowsill, she managed to whisper, "Why?"

Dorothy didn't have difficulty figuring out what she meant. Why bother with a corset when Callie had nothing on top to tame, was what she meant. "All of us are like that," Dorothy said. "At sixteen I had nothing, then within three months, everything popped out." With a delighted smile, she glanced down at her own plump bosom. "Don't worry. You'll be just like us."

Callie started to point out that there was no reason to compare her to these women because she wasn't their sister. She was the daughter of some man named Gilbert Rasher, a man no one wanted to speak of. But when she looked at the five unmarried daughters of John Hadley, she knew that they *were* like her. They were thin and blonde just as she was. Even the two boys she had glimpsed briefly the first day were like her. Talis, who was supposed to be their brother, when compared to them, looked like some great black bull let loose in a sheep pen.

"Why? Why? Why?" Dorothy was saying as she leaned out the window, staring down at the courtyard. Dorothy was eighteen and never married. Neither were her four older sisters because their father refused to part with money for a dowry. And none of the five were pretty enough to make a man take them without a dowry.

Beside Dorothy was Joanna, twenty-six, the plainest of the sisters, and threatening to run away with one of the gardeners if her father didn't find her a husband. In one bold moment, she had said this to her father. John had merely looked at her and said, "Just so it's not the head gardener's boy. I need him." Joanna had gone running from the room in tears.

"He is the most beautiful creature I have ever seen. Is incest *truly* a mortal sin?"

"Joanna!" Dorothy said, trying to act as though she were aghast, but actually working hard not to smile.

Callie went to the window to look out. Below them she saw Talis, a gleaming sword in his hands as he rammed it toward a man twice his age and half again his size. Talis was struggling with all his might to down the man while John sat on a horse and looked on, a faint frown on his face.

"I don't think Father is so pleased with him," Edith said, coming to look out the window. "I heard that for all his size, he isn't very strong. Philip unseated him yesterday." She was speaking of her weak-lunged younger brother.

At just the sight of Talis, Callie's legs nearly folded under her. Some part of her seemed to fly out the window to be with him. Two days seemed like twenty years. She did not just miss him, she felt as though someone had cut her body in half and taken away the half containing her heart.

As though he knew she was watching him — which he did — Talis turned and looked up at Callie. For all that Callie had recently been told all sorts of idiotic things about the proper conduct of ladies, she dismissed everything she'd heard as she leaned so far out the window, she nearly fell. "I am here," she shouted, waving her arm at him. "I am here."

Callie's unladylike shouting almost brought the people of Hadley Hall to a halt. No one had hardly heard the girl speak since she'd arrived; it was easy to forget she was there.

Below, John was especially annoyed that his precious son should be so distracted by the pale girl, and he thought of reprimanding her that night. But John was not prepared for the change that took over Talis when he heard Callie's voice.

When Talis turned to look up at Callie, Hugh Kellon, the seasoned knight he had been struggling with (the man was having no trouble beating Talis's awkward, weak, untutored thrusts), started toward his back. He meant to show the young whelp that girls should not distract a man from the important business of life.

But Talis knew that Callie was watching him,

and when the man came at his back, Talis whirled in one brilliant flash and attacked the man, driving him backward. Within seconds, the man was on his back in the sand, Talis's sword at his throat.

Ever the showman, Talis put his foot on the man's chest and raised one arm toward the sky as he looked up at Callie, who immediately began applauding him.

It would be difficult to know who was more surprised: John or Hugh Kellon, the man who now had Talis's foot on his chest. For a moment, rage went through Hugh, rage at his humiliation, rage at the arrogance of this young pup for his foot and his bravado. But then Hugh saw the humor of it all. It had been a long time since *he* had performed great feats to impress a girl.

Removing his foot, Talis turned to give a bow to Callie and to the two other young women who were politely applauding him.

Edith pulled the three of them away from the window. "Have you no shame! Really! You're acting like harlots. And with your own brother, too!"

"He's not *my* brother," Callie said, as always letting everyone know that she and Talis were not blood relatives.

Edith looked at Callie standing between her sisters Dorothy and Joanna and she could see the very strong family resemblance. But she turned away, not wanting to acknowledge what she saw. Her parents had told her that the young man was her brother and this hoyden Callie was not related to her. That was good enough for her.

"Come, all of you. There is a music lesson in the solar."

Callie followed Edith and the other two, but she knew that her heart was in the courtyard below.

26

"What ails you, son?" John Hadley asked Talis as the boy toyed with the food on his plate. John rarely allowed the boy out of his sight, which was why he had him eating in his private chambers instead of with the others in the Great Hall. At the first meal they had shared, Talis had asked that his brothers be allowed to sit with them. Talis had thought it odd that a father would choose one son over another, and, besides, he liked the company of Philip and James.

"How do you expect to grow if you do not eat?" John asked.

"Has he not grown enough?" Philip said, half teasing, half in jealousy at the way his father treated this new "brother." "All the horses scream in fear at the very sight of him."

At that statement, John drew back his hand, ready to cuff his son for his insolence, but Talis laughed and reached for another roll of white bread. He missed Meg's cooking, her table laden with simple food, undisguised. In this house he sometimes had trouble figuring out what food was, as even cheese was sometimes formed to look like beef. "And shall we saddle a grasshopper for you, little brother?" Talis asked. "Or a garden snake so your feet will not drag the ground?"

Startled, John dropped his hand.

"And what of you, brother?" Talis said, looking at Philip, whose hands shook from the exertion of the day.

"Me?" Philip asked, never wanting attention focused on him at best, and never around his father.

For a moment, Talis studied Philip, looked at his shaking hands, at the circles under his eyes. The three of them slept in a bed together and he knew all too well how much Philip coughed during the night. "Tomorrow we shall compete," Talis said. "I will take both of you on. If either of you unseats me, both of you shall spend the day on your backs under a tree. If neither of you can unseat me, then I will nap under the tree while you train."

The two young men looked at Talis as though he'd lost his mind. Their father would *never* allow such laziness.

"Come now, don't look so glum. I will not snore too loudly as the two of you train in the sun. Hugh will leave you all in the dirt. Tomorrow I shall be ready to spend the night dancing and you will be too tired to stand."

John chuckled at this, as Talis reminded him of himself at that age, so cocky and sure of himself.

It was Philip who understood what Talis was doing and for a moment the beginnings of love filled his eyes. He had done what he could to make their father understand that James could not train every day, that he needed rest. Philip knew that tomorrow, early, Talis was going to be landing in the dirt and James would "win" the competition and therefore spend his day resting under a shade tree.

"You!" Philip said. "You have the finesse of a butcher. You could never unseat someone with my training. Tell me, Talis, on this farm of yours, did you by chance ride cows?"

"I'll —" John began, but Talis cut him off.

"I was as good a farmer as I will be a knight," Talis bragged. "I raised chickens so big that I rode *them*. Of course I had a problem when I jumped fences with them as their feathers got into my mouth. But I solved that problem by selling the feathers to be used for logs for building boats. Chicken feathers float, you know."

At that, even John laughed, and for the rest of the meal, he ate in silence, listening to his sons taunt each other. It seemed that with each day that passed the gloom was lifting from the house. John had always believed that his happiness lay in having his own true son, and this beautiful, strong, intelligent boy was proving him right.

But it was by the evening of the fifth day that John began to notice that something was wrong with his precious son. At first his exuberance had known no bounds. He had teased and laughed

335

and pushed himself to show his strength with a weapon. He was untrained but he was extremely talented.

Off the field, his teachers had raved about his knowledge of the arts as well as the sciences. They said that only James had been a better pupil. John dismissed this; what did it matter what his weak son learned? He would be dead in a short time so John refused to give the boy any part of his heart.

But Talis was another matter. Here was a boy worthy of love.

So what was wrong with him? John wondered. It was as though something was draining him. When John had expressed a concern that perhaps the boy was tired, Hugh had snorted. "How can a sixteen-year-old be tired? At his age did you not train all day and wench all night? I know I did not sleep at his age."

"Then what is wrong with him?"

Hugh had no idea. They had been given a clue to Talis's problem when Talis easily knocked Hugh to the ground and insolently placed his foot on his chest. In that moment, Talis had certainly not lacked energy. They had, of course, noticed that young Talis wanted to impress the girls hanging from the window, but all boys wanted that so they'd paid no attention to it.

Tomorrow would be nearly a week that Talis had been with them, and during that time John had made sure that every moment of the boy's time was taken up. Talis had not been left alone for a breath. John wasn't sure what he was frightened of, but he seemed to fear that Talis would disappear if he were not supervised and guarded at every second.

Now, after dinner, John started to walk the boys upstairs to their chamber, Hugh close behind them.

It was on the stairs that John came close to finding out what was plaguing Talis. Coming down the stairs were a gaggle of his daughters — he did not bother himself to tell one from another; they were all alike to him.

Suddenly, as though a spell had been cast upon him and he could not move, Talis halted on the stairs, his eyes wide, as though he were seeing something not quite of this world. Across from him, against the wall, one of the girls also stopped, her face a mirror of his.

At first the two of them, the girl and Talis, did not touch, but the way they looked at each other was something that John had never seen before. No, it was more than something one could see; it was something that could only be *felt*. When the two of them looked at each other, they seemed to fill the air with a charge, like on a summer's day before a lightning storm.

None of the people on the stair could move or speak as they felt the vibration of the atmosphere around these two people. It surrounded them, making the very air quiver.

As for Callie and Talis, they were trembling with such force that no words could pass between them. It had been days and days and days since they had seen each other. Never in their lives had they been apart for an entire day; separation was not something either of them had fully known the meaning of. So long ago when Talis had gone to the market without Callie, the two of them had nearly died getting back to each other.

Now, to say they "missed" each other meant nothing. They were like plants that had had no water or sunshine for days on end. They were like rain barrels with staves missing; slowly all their contents were draining out.

Very, very slowly, Talis put up his hand toward Callie, his fingertips extended, as she brought her fingers to his. Then, with the others watching, as unable to move as though they had been turned to stone, Callie and Talis touched fingertips.

To a person, everyone on the stairs felt the thrill of that touch. The strength of their reunion overflowed from their strong, young, yearning bodies to the people around them. It was as though the stones and the air shivered with the connection of these two people.

Neither Callie nor Talis was aware of the others on the stairs or of the sensation they were causing. For days now they had both tried to be good, tried to be brave and strong, tried to be what they thought of as "adult." Talis especially had tried to keep Callie from his thoughts. He was a man, wasn't he? He did not need a pesky girl to follow him about as she had on the farm. He knew that here he would be laughed at if she were near him as she had been all his life. These people were not Will and Meg, whose whole lives revolved around their children. These people believed that children should conform to their ways.

No one knew how long Talis and Callie stood there in silence, their hands outstretched, the tips of their fingers touching, drawing life and strength from each other. Had it not been for some other diners wanting to get up the stairs they might have stayed there all night.

John was the first to recover. "Here, boy, let us pass," he said, giving Talis a little shove, thereby bringing him back to reality.

Abruptly, everyone came to their senses, and, like a dog shaking off water, each person shook himself, not wanting to remember what he had just felt.

"Come along, Callasandra," Edith said, pushing Callie and her sisters down the stairs in front of her. She would do most anything to keep from experiencing her father's wrath.

Callie turned away, not looking back at Talis as he started up the stairs. Her heart was beating faster and her legs were weak with wanting to touch him, to talk to him, to do nothing but look at him, but she made herself go down the stairs.

Behind her, Dorothy whispered to Joanna. "Is that what it feels like to be in love?"

"No," Joanna said. "I do not think those two love each other."

Dorothy, ever a romantic, looked at her sister

in horror. More than anything in the world she wanted to be in love. "Not in love?"

"I think what is between them is something different from love. I do not know if it is of the devil or of God, but I am sure it is not natural."

Frowning, disappointed, Dorothy followed her sister down the stairs.

Quietly, so as not to disturb the two girls in bed with her, Callie got out of bed, tossed her clothes over her arm, and made her way to the garderobe. In this stone-seated toilet, she was able to dress without being heard. Then, silently, she left the room and started down the wooden stairs to the back of the house, toward the doors that led out to the kitchen.

She had been waiting in bed for a long time, until the others went to sleep. Waiting and knowing that Talis was going to meet her.

When he stepped from behind a tree, his body no more than a dark shadow, she did not so much as hesitate. Picking up her heavy skirts, she ran toward him, wanting to throw her body on his.

But Talis did not hold out his arms to her. Instead, he caught her hand in his and began running, Callie working hard to keep up with him as he ran around buildings and equipment, around trees and through garden paths. She didn't know where he was leading and she didn't care. She truly hoped he was leading her to the edge of the world where they'd both jump off — or if it was a circle, maybe they'd run round and round the earth and never stop. Just so they were never separated again, she didn't care what happened.

He took her to a place she did not know existed: an old, burned-out castle that had two towers still standing, its walls blackened from a fire, timbers tumbled to the ground. There was evidence that the villagers were taking stones from the castle to build new homes for themselves.

Talis, holding firmly onto Callie's hand, ran with her up ancient, worn, slippery steps. Once when her feet went flying from under her, he caught her, then pushed her against the wall, his big body pinning hers to the stones.

He was different tonight, she thought. Different than he had ever been. The last time they had been alone, they had kissed each other and his hand had traveled up under her skirt. Now, as he pressed her against the wall, for a long, long moment, his breath was on her face, his black eyes boring into hers; she could feel his heart pounding against her breast.

Callie could feel her body growing limp as she leaned against him, her lips moving toward his. But then his laugh rang out and he grabbed her hand and began to pull her up the stairs, coming at last to an ancient oak door that was sealed with a rusty lock.

Turning, he saw the disappointment on her face, then, with one powerful kick, Talis broke the weathered and rotting oak of the door. When the old door went crashing to the floor, Callie laughed in triumph as Talis swept her into his arms.

On the parapets, the old walk where the sentries guarded at night, he held her and whirled her around and around, while Callie threw back her head and laughed in delight.

Talis began to laugh too as he set her on her feet and snatched the headdress off her head. Then as she shook her head to free her hair, he ran his fingers through it, pulling it out to surround her body. A gust of wind made her hair wrap around both of them, enclosing them even further in the silent moonlight.

Easily, naturally, he slipped his arms about her and kissed her softly and sweetly, and when he pulled away, there was wonder on his face.

Moving onto her tiptoes, Callie started to kiss him again, but he spun her around. "What is this you wear?" he asked, feeling the corset under her dress.

"Steel," she said, knowing that at this moment she was happier than she had ever been before.

Talis didn't take two minutes unlacing the back of her dress, those laces that had caused her great trouble in the dark garderobe. He smoothly slipped the dress from her shoulders, then unlatched the corset from her ribs.

Holding the thing at arm's length, he started to toss it over the side of the walls to the old, dried-up moat far below, but Callie squealed in protest. "No! Edith will kill me if I lose that."

Talis only laughed and in the next second it went sailing over the battlements to the ground below. Running to the wall, Callie watched it fall, then over her head, he sent her headdress sailing. "You idiot," she said. "I will get into trouble for this."

When he didn't say anything, she turned to look at him. She would have thought she'd seen every expression Talis could put on his face, but she'd never seen *this* expression before. His dark eyes were black in the moonlight, glittering in a way she'd never seen any man's eyes glitter. For a split second she was almost afraid of him. He looked so very old, so very adult standing there. He wasn't the boy who'd chased her through brambles, but a man who was looking at her as he would look at a woman.

Callie's fear lasted only a breath, a breath that caught in her throat and stayed there. With a leap, she was on him, her mouth hitting exactly on the target of his, clinging to him. Her dress was about her waist, hanging on to her slender hips, nearly off of her, while above she wore only her thin linen nightdress.

Whether her attack on him knocked him to the ground or it was his own overwhelming emotion, but the two of them went tumbling to the floor of the worn stones, their hands and mouths exploring each other. Hungry, eager, excited . . . ravenous.

Callie had no thoughts of stopping what was starting to happen between them. She had been restless for months now; she had been watching parts of Talis's body that had held no interest for her in years past. She looked at his thighs as he walked, at the hard muscle of his buttocks as he strained to help Will get a wagon out of the mud. When he stripped to the waist to wash sweat from his back and shoulders, Callie nearly swooned with the beauty of him.

Now she was touching all the parts of him that she had seen. She had no shyness, no inhibitions, no sense that she should not do what she wanted to do. Talis was hers, more than her own body was hers, and now she needed him more than she needed all the food and drink in the world.

When her hand went between his legs and there was a groan from him, Callie felt it in her soul. It wasn't just that her heart was pounding; her entire body was throbbing. She wanted to feel his skin next to her skin and she began to claw at his clothes.

"No," he said. "Callie, no."

Callie paid no attention to him as she pushed her hands under his shirt and ran them up his bare, warm skin, her mouth seeking his.

"No!" he shouted, and in one quick, strong move, he was away from her, standing with his back to the stone battlements, his chest heaving with emotion. Even in the moonlight she could see that he was flushed.

As for Callie, she could not properly breathe, much less think as she sat still on the stones and looked up at him. "Tally," she whispered, holding out her hands to him.

He would not be able to deny her if she kept looking at him in that way. Turning his back to her, he looked out over the landscape, but his heart and mind were with her. He could feel her wanting him, her willingness. For a long time he stood there looking into the dark night, willing his body to calm down, willing her to stop beseeching him. His honor and what he wanted so very much waned within him.

In the last weeks so many things had changed. Everything had changed. On the farm he had yearned for what he had intuited was his birthright. And now that he had it all, all he seemed to want was Callie. Even to himself he did not want to admit how he had felt in this last week without her. Empty, drained, weak. How could he be a knight if she were not there beside him?

And now that he was a son of this rich house, how could he have her without the sanction of his father? How could he provide for her? Give her a home?

For a moment he was tempted to take her hand and run with her back to Meg and Will. Sometimes he thought that having been found by John Hadley was the worst thing that had ever happened to him. But that was absurd. Now he had a chance to give Callie everything. He could give her a home. He did not want to see her work weary and worn-out by the time she was thirty. He wanted her to have the best of everything, the best the world had to offer.

Turning back to her, he smiled, but saw that she seemed to be on the verge of tears. Knowing her, she probably thought he did not *want* to touch her. If only she knew how much he wanted her. Until this week he had not realized that she was everything to him. He wanted to be a knight so she could be proud of him; wanted riches so she could have the best life had to offer. Everything was for her.

But he was not going to take what was not by right his to have. He knew that Callie didn't care what happened between them. If he warned her that continuing what they had started could lead to disgrace because of her carrying his child, he knew she would not care. He also knew that Callie would look to *him* to solve the problem. He knew she would live in a hovel with him; money meant nothing to her. But he also knew that he would die rather than see her working as he'd seen village women work, old before she had time to live.

He *had* to tend to legalities and practical things before he took what he wanted so much. Otherwise, he had no right to what she offered; no right to the reward if he had not done the work. His honor would not allow him to take what he had not earned.

"Do not look at me so," he said. He meant to sound lighthearted, but his voice was pleading, full of what he felt for her. She had no idea how beautiful she was in the moonlight, her eyes

346

big and filled with longing, the silver of the moon making them liquid.

"You are hurting me," he gasped out.

Callie heard the pain in his voice and, for the thousandth time in her life, damned his sense of honor. No doubt he thought that what they were doing was wrong. How could anything they did together be wrong?

Extending his hands, he held them out to her, offering to help her up but keeping her at arm's length.

With a sigh, Callie accepted his offer, then betrayed him by trying to kiss his mouth. Laughing, Talis pulled away from her.

"Look at my hair. Has it turned gray tonight? You are aging me. Have you no sense of decency? Girls are supposed to hold themselves away from men. They shouldn't jump on men and knock them to the floor."

Callie laughed as he turned her around and began fastening her dress. It didn't fit as well without the corset underneath, but it certainly felt better. "Odd that you are strong enough to break down the door but not strong enough to hold *me* up. Unless you think *I* am stronger than an oak and iron door."

He could not keep from kissing her neck as he pulled her back laces together. "*You* are stronger than all the oak in the world."

"Oh? Am I?" When she started to turn toward him, he pulled her laces so tight she gasped, her hands to her stomach.

"Callie, you must behave yourself. I am only a man."

She laughed at his tone of weakness. "And I am glad you have at last seen that I am a woman," she said softly.

"Yes," he said, his voice heavy with regret. There were almost tears in his voice, as though he were in great pain. "Yes, I have seen that you are a woman."

With his hands on her shoulders, he turned her toward him and looked into her eyes. He did not have to say that things had now changed between them. It wasn't just that they had moved away from the farm, but tonight they had continued what had started that day they had met John Hadley. And this week they had learned how separation affected both of them.

"Come and sit with me," he said as he climbed onto the battlements, his back to one crenelation, his long legs extending to the opposite one and past it. Holding out his arms, he welcomed her to sit on his lap, her legs on his, her back against his chest.

Callie didn't hesitate as she climbed onto him and leaned back against him.

"Be still!" Talis commanded in a way that made Callie giggle.

"Tell me everything," he said when she was still. "Tell me everything big and small that you have done and seen and thought since I saw you last. Have you made up any stories and told them to someone else?"

With her head leaning back against his shoulder, she delighted in the jealousy in his voice. Maybe she should taunt him, tell him she had been so happy without him, but she couldn't do it. On the other hand, she didn't want him to think she was miserable. That would worry him.

"You are sad," he said, sensing what she was feeling.

"No, no, of course not. It is all wonderful. It's so nice to have such lovely women around me. They are like sisters, so kind, teaching me many things."

Talis buried his nose in her hair, smelling it. In the past he had often thought that Callie's hair was a nuisance. If she didn't keep it braided, it caught on tree branches, in briars, even on his hands. When had it become so beautiful? "You are lying," he said easily. "Tell me the truth."

She was silent.

"Come now, have you forgotten me?" he said coaxingly. "Do you know that you cannot lie to me?"

When she spoke there were tears in her voice. "*You* have forgotten *me*."

He moved away from her to look at her profile. "How can you say this to me? There has not been a moment when I have not thought of you. Everything I looked at, every person I talked to made me think of you. I was —"

He cut himself off, not wanting to tell her more. After all, he had to preserve his manliness. It wasn't good to tell her all of the truth.

Callie was smiling. He didn't have to tell her more. "You were miserable without me and you wanted to impress me."

"Ha!" he said. "Impress you! Impressing you takes nothing. Look at you. You are so tiny I could break you." With that he clasped his arms around her waist and squeezed until she couldn't breathe, then he relaxed his grasp.

Laughing, she leaned back against him.

After a while he said, tentatively, "I should like you to be proud of me. I'd like to show you my skill with a sword."

Never would she tell him that she would have loved him whether he had any skill with a sword or a horse, or no skills at all for that matter. She just loved him. She loved him with or without skills, even, as Dorothy said, with or without arms and legs.

"Have you learned much?" she asked, not because she cared but because it was important to him and *he* was all to her.

When he was silent she knew that something was bothering him. But then she had known that for some time. She just had to find out what it was and mend it. It didn't matter that she was bored out of her mind living with a bunch of blond women who had nothing in their heads. What mattered to her was whether Talis was happy or not.

"What is wrong?" she asked.

Talis hated to admit weakness, hated to admit

that he needed her. But with each passing moment of every day, he knew he needed her more than he had ever thought possible. A triumph meant nothing, a thing learned meant nothing if she was not there to share it with him. No, more than share. If she was not there to do it *for*. Why bother to train to be a knight if Callie was not there to tie her sleeve about his armor?

But none of the other men seemed to need pretty girls in order to want to do anything. Other men seemed content to accomplish deeds for themselves. True, they liked having a girl watch them, but they didn't seem to *need* one as Talis needed Callie.

In the past Will was sometimes annoyed at them for incomplete chores he'd assigned them separately. "You are each only half a person. It takes both of you to make one complete person," he'd once said in exasperation.

Is that what was wrong with him? He was only half a person and Callie was the other half? Even to him it sounded ludicrous. Such a thing was not possible.

"Tell me," she said. "Tell me what is wrong."

But he couldn't bring himself to say what he thought. He wanted Callie to think he was the strongest, bravest person on earth. *She* must lean on *him*, not the other way around. "You must tell me the truth about those girls. Are you happy with them?"

She knew his pride was keeping him from telling her what was wrong. "They are hardly girls. They are old women who want a man." *My* man, she almost said.

"Oh? Perhaps I should —"

She hit him sharply in the ribs before he could finish that sentence, making him laugh.

"You do not like them," he said.

"They do not like me."

He laughed at this. "How could they not?" he asked, saying what, to him, was absolutely honest. To him, Callie was funny and smart and entertaining; she was the best company in the world, knowing when to be quiet, when to talk.

Thinking about her while holding her made him kiss her neck, her ear, but within seconds he realized he had to stop that. Trying to return to the innocence of their childhood, he began to tickle her. But her squirming on his lap did things to his body that even the kissing could not. "Callasandra . . . ," he whispered in anguish.

Callie was starting to tell him about the Hadley sisters. "Actually, it is not that they do not like me; they don't like or dislike me. Oh, Tally, they are so very, very *boring*."

Talis was still absorbed with her body on his and was not listening to her, but now Callie had formed a plan. But, as always, she knew that she had to make him believe that the idea was *his*.

"It is *your* fault," she said, and that declaration got his full attention. Like every man, he'd take responsibility for his errors only if there was no other possible path.

"Mine? What have I done to cause those women to dislike you? Callie, really, it must be something that you have done to make them think ill of you."

"They say I have a man's education."

At that Talis snorted in laughter. "You? A *man's* education. Do you know how to wield a sword or dagger? You are so weak you could not even lift the armor you would need to wear."

Callie persisted. "And having your company for all these years has ruined me for being around a gaggle of girls. They talk of the most nonsensical things, such as clothing and gossip. I am used to your talk of politics and philosophy and all the really important things of life."

For a moment Callie wasn't sure if he was going to believe her on this. Talis just might laugh at this and point out they had never talked of politics or philosophy, more than anything else they had talked of clothing and speculated at what was going on at the queen's court.

But right now honesty between them would ruin everything. She wanted him to take her away from the women. She wanted them to be *together,* and if Talis thought he was doing this because she needed it, then he'd move heaven to keep them together. If she told him the truth, that she felt as though she were dying without him, he might tell her that this was frivolous and that it would be good "discipline" for her to go back to the women.

"I am learning nothing," she whispered. Without you, there is nothing I want to learn, is what she thought.

For a moment, Talis said nothing, but sat there frowning, thinking of this matter. At first he didn't know what to do, then he saw a way out. If he helped Callie, he wouldn't have to admit that he was dying without her, that his energy, his very will to live was lessening every day without her near. "You will come to me," he said firmly. "You will stay with me. A person must learn in life."

"I cannot," she said gloomily. "They will not allow it." She knew that the best way to get Talis to do something was to tell him that he could not. "You do not know how these people are. Woman are here and men are there. They are separate. They get together to make babies and that is all."

"Oh?" he said, an eyebrow raised. "And what do you know of making babies?"

She was silent, but she was smiling in the darkness, liking this teasing. "Not much. Would you tell me all there is to know?" When she asked this, she wiggled a bit on his lap.

But Talis's reaction was not as she'd hoped. For some reason, when he spoke, there was anger in his voice. "What has happened to make you talk of making babies? What man has spoken of this to you?"

"No one," she said truthfully. For the last week she had lived with women and women alone. "There was a boy who said I was pretty, but that is all. Do *you* think I am pretty?" It was not Callie's intention to make him jealous (not that she wouldn't have if she'd thought of it) but right now all she wanted was to coax him into giving her a compliment.

"Who is this boy?" Talis asked fiercely, his arms tightening about her waist.

"No one," Callie answered, exasperated, but still determined to get a compliment out of him. "He said I had nice hair. Beautiful hair. Do *you* think so?"

"Why did you not have on that thing that covers your hair? How could he *see* your hair?"

Callie was smiling. She now realized that they were at cross-purposes and she was going to get no compliment from him. But then, perhaps his jealousy was a compliment. His jealousy was quite odd; it erupted when Callie least expected it, and she could never predict it. The times when she had tried to make him jealous, she had failed miserably.

"It was at night and —"

"At night!" he half shouted in her ear.

Abruptly, Callie put her hands over her face. "Oh, Tally," she said, "it is horrible. All the boys and most of the men are in love with me. They talk of nothing but kissing my beautiful slender feet, my delicate hands. They fight to give me the most exquisite of presents. They write poems about my hair and the heavenly color of my eyes. One man said my eyes are like the sky just before a storm. And my hair! I blush to repeat what they say about it. They —"

She could feel the tension leave his body with each word she spoke, and finally, he squeezed her until she stopped talking. "You have had your fun with me. Now be still and look at the moon."

Leaning back against him, her arms holding his, she looked up at the moon and wished the night would never end. A large part of her wished they had never left Meg and Will. "Do you think Meg and Will think of us?"

"As often as we think of them," he answered, and she knew that part of him also wished they'd not left home. There were things happening at Hadley Hall that neither of them understood. How could a man dislike his own children as John Hadley did? The sons said they loved their mother, but Philip once said they were fearful of her.

"I am afraid," Callie said. "I am afraid of what goes on here. It does not feel good."

He knew what she meant and he often felt the same fear, but Talis wanted to reassure her. "It is just different here. They are rich."

"It is more than that. It is something else. I am afraid for us."

"For us? What could happen to us? Do you worry that beautiful women will fall in love with me and carry me off?"

"Ha! You would run after them; no woman would have to carry you."

Talis knew that he never looked — well, maybe *looked* at other women — but none but Callie

356

interested him, but it was nice for her to believe that he was so desirable. In his eyes, of the two of them, Callie was the beauty. She was the most gorgeous, most splendid creature on earth. "What do you worry about?"

"I don't know. Does it not concern you that no one questions our existence? Or, rather, your existence. According to the story, after we were born, a fire burned us. I heard that the bodies of two babies were found in the fire. If we were burned, how are we alive? And what happened to my mother? Dorothy said she was small and dark, with black hair and eyes. If that is so, then why do I have brows and lashes like a rabbit's?"

"I am not a storyteller like you. Perhaps there are things those women do not know. They were babies themselves then — I think. They are not old enough to remember then, are they?"

"No," she said tentatively. "It is all a puzzlement. But, whatever the truth, there is a feeling here that frightens me."

"What do you fear will happen?"

She turned in his arms, her face to his. "I am afraid of losing you. I would die if I lost you. I do not want to live without you."

Talis thought it was unmanly to say the same things to her, but he felt them. Holding her tightly, he said against her lips, "No one can take us away from each other. We are one, do you not know that? Do you not sense it?"

"Yes," she whispered. "Yes, oh yes, but I am

afraid. I am afraid people will not allow us to stay together."

"Callie, my love, *why* would anyone want to separate us? Do either of us have great estates? Are either of us the child of a king and stand to inherit a country?"

"No," she said, smiling. "We are not important."

"True," he said, holding her close to him. "We are not important at all and tomorrow I shall tell this man my father that you will stay with me always. If he tells me you cannot be with me, then we will go back to the farm." Sometimes Talis had trouble thinking of John as his father; Will Watkins was his father and always would be.

For a moment Callie held her breath because she knew that Talis would keep this promise, and she knew what he would be giving up if he left this rich house for her. Talis *hated* farming. He did his chores but he had no interest in growing the best turnips in the county as Will hoped to do. Market days bored him. Talis was born to ride a horse and wear armor and *he had always known that is what he was meant to do.*

She could not, *could not,* allow him to give up what he was meant to do on earth. She had no doubt that, given the chance, Talis would become the greatest knight who ever lived.

"Why do you look at me like that?" he asked, his voice husky.

He didn't wait for an answer; if she didn't quit

looking at him that way, they'd be on the stone floor in another minute. His head knew they should get back to Hadley Hall, but there were a few more hours until daylight and he couldn't bear to leave her. It had been so very, very, very long since he had last seen her.

"Act as though you have some manners and turn round," he said firmly, and when she was facing away from him, he said, "Tell me a story. I have not heard one of your silly old stories in a long time."

"If they are silly, I will not bother."

"All right then." He didn't say anything for a moment. "Did you know that there is a man who lives here who does nothing but tell stories? I have been told that he is very good. Very interesting stories."

Immediately, Callie began to talk. "There was once a princess with five very jealous sisters. They were all very ugly but the princess was so beautiful. She had long golden hair, glorious golden hair. The most beautiful hair ever put on a human being."

"And the most vanity," Talis added.

"No, no, she was good and pure. Only others saw her beauty. She thought of herself as plain."

"Hmph."

"And there was a prince," Callie said.

"A handsome prince?"

"Oh no, not at all. Ugly as a toad."

At that Talis started to get up.

"All right," she said, "perhaps he was a little

handsome." For a moment she put her cheek against his chest, held his arms close to her body. "He had black, glossy curls, thick black lashes, and a mouth as soft as a baby's. But his nose was too long and thin."

"I am sure he had a perfect nose."

"Perhaps. One day the princess —"

"No," Talis said, "tell me more of what this divinely handsome prince looked like. Was he tall and strong?"

Callie's first impulse was to tease him but then she smiled and picked up his hand and said, "He had beautiful hands, long fingers, very strong hands . . ."

27

"Sir," Talis said, his shoulders back, his head up. "I should like your permission to marry Callasandra."

John was taken off guard at this. His son was just a boy. Why, just yesterday he had been in swaddling cloths. How could he think to *marry?*

Slowly, he turned from the table where he was inspecting the accounts his chamberlain had left with him. When a boy married, it changed him, made him put his energies into something other than what was at hand.

Never in his life would John have admitted to himself that he was jealous. He had just found his son; he did not yet want to share him with anyone. But at the same time he did not want to disappoint the boy. There was an independence about Talis that frightened John. His other children belonged to him, belonged to him body and soul. He could demand what he wanted of them, dismiss them or congratulate them as he felt and he knew they would be near him the next day.

But this Talis was something that John had not experienced before. He did not feel gratitude coming from the boy for having saved him from a life of poverty. John often felt Talis's delight in his new life, but never gratitude. John wasn't sure, but he thought that if Talis did not like what his father did, the boy might well take the girl and leave Hadley Hall forever.

"Yes, yes, of course," John said, not wanting to directly tell the boy no. "I must of course speak to your mother first."

"Yes, sir," Talis said, his face breaking into a radiant grin, his happiness fairly lighting up the room. Then, trying to calm himself, he left the room, running down the stairs. In his exuberance, he practically knocked the prim, proper Edith to the floor, but, easily, he caught her in his arms, and kept her from falling. Then, to her disbelief, he kissed her hard on the mouth. A kiss, to him, of brother to sister, but to Edith a kiss such as she'd never had from a man.

Talis continued his run down the stairs, making one leap to hit the bottom of a tapestry hanging above the stairwell, then running out the door.

On the stairs, Edith's sisters Dorothy and Joanna were openmouthed in their astonishment at the way Edith was staring after Talis. Edith considered herself above any man. According to her, the reason she was twenty-nine years old and not married was that she had never found a man to her liking. But now, judging by the look on her face, she certainly did like Talis!

When Joanna gave way to a giggle, Edith pulled herself to her full height and started up the stairs, trying her best to regain her dignity. But at the top of the stairs, she could not keep herself from looking out the window to see that glorious creature run across the courtyard.

Turning back, she tried to keep her face straight. "Come, there is work to do."

"Yes, Edith," Joanna said, and behind her back, she exuberantly kissed the back of her hand, then mocked Edith's straitlaced walk down the corridor.

"Of course he should marry your daughter," Alida said to her husband. It took all her willpower to remain calm. She must not allow her husband to see that her heart was pounding in her throat, that her breath was wanting to come rapid and harsh.

"My *son*," John said sternly, his brows knitted together, emphasizing the point that Talis was his.

Alida knew that she had to tread carefully, but she also knew that she could not be a coward. If ever she had to think quickly, this was the time. It did not matter about her, but her children's future depended upon what she did in the next few minutes. Her first instinct was to laugh at her husband. What an old fool he was to think he could pass off that dark boy as *his* son. He was a thin man, she was a thin woman and together they had produced eleven thin, pale children. Who did he think was going to believe that in the midst of these blonds he had produced an olive-skinned, black-haired, black-eyed giant?

As rapidly as possible, Alida tried to think. There were many reasons that she could not allow this marriage to go through. A marriage would insure that John would leave everything to this boy who was not his son, and she could not bear to see her own sons disinherited.

There was something else that only she knew: She had at most two years more to live. Months ago she had begun coughing blood, just rusty smudges, but enough to alarm her. She had not allowed any of her maids to see this but had instead gone to an ancient old woman who had looked into Alida's eyes, then looked into a bowl of grease-stained water and told her of the future. She had foretold Alida's death within two years and she had predicted that someone not of her blood would gain all that belonged to her sons. But the old woman had explained to Alida that predictions were what *could* happen. What *did* happen was based on what people did to alter the future. In other words, if Alida did nothing, when she died, everything would go to a boy who was not of her blood.

And now, armed with this information, Alida meant to change the future. She was not going to see all that her family had worked for, all that her husband had built, given to a boy who was of no relation to her.

"Come, husband," she said sweetly, "you and

I know the truth and you must look at the facts. The boy looks like Gilbert Rasher. Put the boy amid that dreadful man's sons and you would not be able to tell them apart."

"Then it is good he is to marry *my* daughter," John said, anger rising in his throat. "Do you mind, woman, that I can send you from this house, that I can —"

Alida knew she must not betray her fear. "Yes, you can, but do you not see that I want the same as you do? *I* want the boy to marry our daughter also. He is good stock. I am sure he will give the girl many fat, healthy sons." She nearly gagged at these words, at pretending that she was as obsessed with sons as her husband was. She had given him two boys who were intelligent and sweet natured. That they could not lift the back half of a building did not seem to her to be a detriment.

"My concern is Gilbert Rasher," she said loudly, making herself heard over the anger that was closing his ears. "Do you not worry that that man will come forward and claim his son? He was never paid for the boy, remember? After the . . . the fire, you refused to give him the payment you had promised him. He wanted a daughter for a wife as well as land." She had to pause as she remembered that John had promised the odious man Peniman Manor — her manor.

Alida could see that John was listening to her now and she went on rapidly. "If Rasher were to come forward and claim the boy and he were married to your daughter, he could cause great trouble. He could demand an enormous dowry from you for the girl. He could petition the queen about the way you have said the boy is yours and it is easy to see that the boy is not."

At this John's hands gripped the arms of the chair. He did not like her insinuation that he could *not* have produced a son like Talis. It was, of course, her fault that he had not. Had he married a stronger woman, a more robust woman, she might have given him the son he needed. Conveniently, he forgot that Talis's mother had been small.

Alida went to him, knelt by his chair, and put her hand on his. She wasn't as pretty as she had once been, but she still had pretty ways and she knew how to look up at a man as though he were the bravest, strongest, et cetera, man on earth.

"You must make sure it is safe before you marry the boy to your daughter. You must have something in writing, a document sworn to in secrecy. You must *pay* Rasher for the boy, make amends to him for what happened so many years ago. You know, don't you, that Rasher has lost two of his sons to accidents?"

Over the years she had kept up with Gilbert Rasher and his brood of foul-mouthed dirty sons. They had tempers and strong bodies, and, with their father's admiration, the boys bullied and berated everyone. Twice, people had grown sick

366

of the "boys" and killed them. After the eldest had been found with his throat slit, Gilbert had demanded an investigation. Every person who had even the slightest reason to hate his son was to be brought before him.

It was said that the queen's laughter had echoed off the palace walls when she was told how one hundred and twelve people had been brought before Gilbert Rasher, all of them having valid reasons for wanting to see his son dead — and that was just the people who had not been able to flee the countryside when his death was announced. Gilbert had been enraged when, later, the queen had ordered that no one was to be hanged for the crime (Gilbert had decreed that seventeen men and three women were to be hanged for the killing). The queen said that any man who had made that many enemies had not been murdered but justifiably executed.

Alida did not tell her husband that she had been told that, when he was drunk, Gilbert sometimes blamed John Hadley for all his misfortunes. He said that all his "bad luck" had started that night when the babies had been born and later died in the fire. According to him, if he'd received all that John owed him — he never said what John owed him for — he would have been able to make himself into a rich man. As it was, his crops had failed, not because he taxed his peasants to the point of hunger, but because he had never received payment from the rich John Hadley.

No, she did not want to tell John any of this.

If her husband's obsession with having a son made him blind to all else on earth, so be it.

"If he is married to" — John swallowed, not wanting to admit that Talis was not his son — "to my daughter, then he will be tied to me." Forget money, forget about inheritance, he thought, the truth was, he *liked* the boy. In the short time he'd been there, the boy was already changing things in the house. Several times in the last two weeks Talis had made John laugh, had made his other sons laugh. John knew well enough what the boy was doing when he pretended to have "contests" so he could lose and thereby give the weak-lunged Philip a rest. John knew what Talis was doing when he talked at length of James's great learning, talking of how he, Talis, was not so good in lessons as his brother.

But even though John knew everything, it only made him feel better that Talis cared about others so much. And what was more, John was beginning to look at his sons differently. Perhaps James's head was worth something. He'd asked the boy to look over the accounts, something that had always bored John, and the boy had found many errors.

"Talis is a good boy," John said, even liking to say his name.

"Of course he is. He is the best. All your sons are good; they have a good father." For a moment Alida held her breath, wondering if he was going to believe this.

But then John said, "Yes, they are. In their

368

own way, they are all good."

At that Alida almost burst into tears. At last, she thought, all her work was coming to fruition. For many years now she had done all that she could to show her husband that his sons were clever and well worth his effort. But now, just when she was making him believe that, here was this boy taking all that she had done away from her sons. This boy, with his glorious physique, with his sparkling eyes, his easy laughter, was overshadowing her own sons. Soon all that she had worked for would be eclipsed by that boy. Soon he would take all from her sons.

It did not occur to Alida, nor would she have believed it if she'd been told, that Talis, with his laughter and good nature, had done more in two short weeks to make John like his sons than Alida had managed in twenty years of bullying. Alida was always trying to make her sons into what John wanted them to be. Talis pointed out to John what they actually were and that their talents were quite useful.

"Now," Alida said sternly, "you must plan for the future. You want the boy and so do I. He is intelligent and he is strong. He will do well at managing the estates when we are gone." Gilbert Rasher's estates, she thought. She had not had any contact with the boy herself, not since the day when he had arrived and carried her to her bedchamber, but Edith kept her informed of what was going on. Edith said he was cocky, too sure of himself, but . . . Here, Edith had put her head down and blushed. Even cold-blooded Edith had been won over by the boy.

It annoyed Alida that the boy was liked by one and all, as that made everything harder. It was not that she wished the boy harm, it was just that she wanted him out of *her* family. From what she knew of Gilbert Rasher, he had need of a boy like Talis, a boy with at least a shred of decency about him who could put those bankrupt estates of his in order. Yes, actually, getting rid of the boy would benefit all of them.

"Do you think the boy should spend so much time with Callasandra?" Alida asked.

John turned a blank face toward her, having no idea who she was talking about.

"Your daughter. The one this boy wants to marry." John still looked a bit blank, and he obviously did not have any idea why she was mentioning this girl. "Yesterday Edith reported to me that Callasandra had defied her most impertinently. I was going to speak to you about it. I have given Edith the care of this girl, as she has the most unsuitable education I have ever encountered. She can neither sew nor play any music."

Alida did not bother telling her husband of Callie's knowledge of Latin and Greek, as well as of mathematics, not that she wanted to hide such a thing, but because she knew her husband would not be interested in this.

"It seems that two nights ago Callasandra slipped out of bed and stayed away all night."

She raised her eyebrows at her husband to let him know what she thought their daughter was doing. "She did not return until morning and her corset and hood were missing. Later one of the gardeners found both of them in a field near the old castle."

John did not like this at all. "Can you not control your daughters, madam? Do you mean to make whores of them?"

Alida stiffened. "I have not had the care of *this* daughter these many years." She managed to sound hurt that she had been deprived of this daughter for so long, as well as hint that had she had such care, the girl would be the epitome of virtue.

When John raised one eyebrow at her, she did not understand his meaning. The truth was, John found his stiff daughters, with their pious ways and their perfect manners, to be quite boring. Only the saucy Joanna interested him on the rare times when she challenged him.

Alida continued. "The corset and hood belonged to Callasandra and since that night she has not been more than inches away from the side of that young man, that Talis."

John sat there blinking at her. All day yesterday and today Talis had been with him. They had been training in the courtyard and Talis had been especially good, alert and strong, twice knocking Hugh to the ground until Hugh was complaining about being too old for the games. In the afternoon they had all walked about the gardens, with John showing Talis where everything was, telling him what he planned to do. Since finding Talis, John acted as though he might die tomorrow, and he wanted his son to know everything.

"You are mistaken," he said. "There has been no girl near my son."

It took Alida a moment to still the sarcasm that came to her lips. Well did she know that a purple dragon with flaming nostrils could stand next to that boy John claimed as his son, and John would not notice it. Unless, of course, the dragon threatened Talis's life, then John would no doubt put himself between the fire and his beloved son.

She smiled at him. "You are too busy with weighty matters to notice a pale girl near him, but she is there. She has been near him constantly these last few days. You must send her away."

"What does she matter?" John asked, not wanting to thwart his son. "If the boy wants her, what do I care? If it makes him happy to have the girl admiring him, what does it matter to me?"

With her hands balled into fists, Alida tried to control her temper. Mere minutes ago her husband had come to her, long faced, miserable because he was eaten with jealousy, afraid he was going to lose the adoration of his precious son if the boy married. John had tried to conceal his misery, but it had been easy to guess that he wanted his wife to give him a reason *not* to allow Talis to marry. Why else would he have come to his wife? Had John wanted Talis to marry he would have said yes and never considered consulting his wife.

But now that Alida had done her wifely duty and played the villain, John was tying her hands by refusing to physically separate the children. Their daily proximity was going to be crying nine months from now.

"It is not seemly," Alida said weakly, knowing this argument was going to have no sway on her husband. No doubt if the boy wanted a gaggle of whores near him, John would allow it.

Tired of all this talk, John heaved himself up and started to leave the room. He had now dumped most of the problem on his wife; he had accomplished what he wanted. "I will speak to Rasher," he said. "This must be done." He would rather have hot irons placed on his body than go to that man and beg.

On impulse, Alida said, "May I go in your place?"

John looked at her.

"May I go to him and speak for you? I have heard that Gilbert Rasher has not felt kindly toward you over these years."

At this John laughed, letting her know he knew more than she had assumed he did.

Encouraged, she smiled at him. "Perhaps a woman's softness might get more from him. I hear he is now between wives and we have a few unmarried daughters."

John smiled broader. "Rasher's taste gets younger the older he gets. Although, what he *needs* is Edith."

At that jest, at the thought of the prim, bossy Edith with a drunken wastrel like Gilbert Rasher, both of them laughed heartily. For the first time in years, they shared some of the intimacy they had known at the beginning of their marriage, before John gave up the idea of getting a son from her.

"Yes," he said, his hand on the door. "Perhaps you could bargain with him." There was gratitude in his voice. As he opened the door, on impulse, he turned back to her and kissed her sweetly on the mouth. A kiss of friendship, of years shared, a kiss hinting that there might perhaps be more later.

"I will do my best," she said, then, after he left, she leaned on the door and closed her eyes.

For a moment, Alida leaned back against the door. This was her fault, she thought. She was the one to have caused all of this. If only on that night so many years ago she had not demanded that she be carried to the chamber where that poor girl was dying. If Alida had not interfered, that boy John loved so much would not have been born.

Stepping away from the door, Alida knew that it was too late for regrets. All she could do now was try to right her wrongs.

First of all, she could not allow that charismatic young man, Talis, to stay at Hadley Hall. Whether he stayed as John's son or as John's daughter's husband, was immaterial. If Talis remained near John, John would give him everything: land as well as all his love and attention. All the children Alida had given him would receive nothing. John would ignore his daughters more than he already did; they would never get husbands. John would as soon toss his sons away as look at them again.

No, Alida had to get rid of Talis. But how? She well knew that if Talis continued asking to marry Callie, John would soon overlook his jealousy and allow the boy to marry.

Alida's head came up. The solution was to prevent Talis from asking. The solution lay in making the children stop wanting to marry each other. What did they know about love and marriage, anyway? They were children and they had never even seen other people who might be worthy of their affections.

She *had* to separate them, both physically and within their own minds. If she could plant a seed of doubt within the minds of the children, make them doubt their love for each other, in time they'd no longer want to marry each other.

Yes, she thought, her mind racing with the beginnings of a plan. If everything worked out the way she planned, in the end, the only person who would be hurt would be John. And at that thought Alida's heart soared. She *wanted* to hurt him.

As for the others, she would have to be quite unkind to her own daughter at first, but she'd make it up to Callie later. Later she would find Callie a husband of the best sort, a man who would love and take care of her. Talis would go to court, find favor with the queen, and marry some beautiful heiress. Her own sons would inherit what was rightfully theirs. If John were not "saving" all his money to give to Talis, Alida would be able to persuade him to dower his daughters for husbands.

Yes, Alida thought, smiling. She would be able to go to her grave knowing that she had straightened the horror of what she had done so long ago. Now, with death so very near her, she knew she had to make amends. When she saw Talis's mother in heaven, she wanted to be able to tell her that she had taken care of that poor girl's son.

Opening the door, Alida called to a passing maid. "Where is Penella?" she asked.

The girl was young and new. "Penella?"

"In the kitchens, ma'am," said a woman peeping around a corner. "You sent her to the kitchens years ago."

"Send her to me. Instantly." Knowing that her time on earth was limited made Alida want to make amends for the bad that she had done in her life. Penella had been a good maid, a loyal one, but she had betrayed that loyalty once and Alida had not been able to forgive her. But now Alida felt that perhaps Penella had learned her lesson, and besides, Alida needed someone she could fully trust.

"Can I trust you?" Alida said, her voice cold as she looked at her former maid, standing as close to the fire as she dared. In the years Penella had been in the kitchens, she had aged centuries. Alida would not have recognized her: emaciated, grizzled hair, raw hands, deep lines in her face, stooped shoulders.

When Penella looked into her mistress's eyes, Alida saw begging, no pride at all. She had been well punished for what she had done that night so long ago when she had warned the peasant man that he was about to be set afire. There had not been a day of her life that she had not regretted what she had done.

"You may trust me to the giving of my life," Penella said with feeling in her voice, meaning every word she said. For a comfortable bed, for warmth, she'd now kill the peasants herself.

"Sit," Alida said warmly. "Eat all you want." When Penella was seated, her trembling hands reaching for the food on the table before the fire, Alida said, "I want you to tell me everything you overheard from the old woman who came here that night. She told me about this Talis and my daughter. I want to know what you remember. Every word."

For a moment Penella thought she should protest that she had obeyed her mistress and left them in privacy, but one look at Alida's face told her that now was not the time for pretense. She had eavesdropped on every conversation her mistress had ever had.

It wasn't easy to clear her head enough to remember all of it, but with each delicious bite of proper food — whole food, not the leavings of others — she knew that the continuation of such food depended on what she remembered.

"She said they are two halves of a whole. If something hurt one it hurt the other. They want what is best for the other, will sacrifice personal wants for the other's good. They cannot be separated; separation will destroy them. They are very jealous, especially the boy. He cannot bear for the girl to give her attention to anything but himself. The girl worships him, lies for him, would steal, and possibly even kill, for him. But he has a sense of honor and will commit no foul deeds for anyone."

At this Penella could not resist thinking that a few years in John Hadley's kitchens would knock the honor out of anyone. It was honor that had made her warn that peasant; she'd thought that what was being done to the innocent children was not "right." It was amazing what an empty belly could do to a sense of honor. Now she'd no doubt set the fire herself if it meant a few days without hunger.

"Good," Alida said and poured her maid some wine. Over the years she had almost forgotten Penella's remarkable memory. "I need your help. I need your complete discretion, but I need to be sure that I can trust you to be loyal to me and me alone."

For a moment Penella looked up from the food, her eyes glittering. "I will do whatever you desire of me," she said, and the words came from inside her soul.

"I want to get rid of the boy," Alida said.

Penella put down her plate of food. "I will kill him."

"No!" Alida said sharply. "I want to send him back to his real father. I do not want him connected to this house." She lowered her voice. "And I have a secret that must be kept. I am dying. I have two years at the most."

Penella did not so much as glance up from her plate at that, and Alida knew what she had lost. At one time Penella would have done anything for her mistress out of love, but now her only love was in survival. But Alida had no time for sentiment. She had to save her family, and, like Penella, she would do *anything* to accomplish that purpose.

28

"Yes, yes, Edith," Alida said irritably. "I know the girl is pliable, that she gives you few problems. And I know you are doing the best you can with her and I am pleased with, you, but I wanted to know what you thought of her as a *person*."

Edith looked blank at this, not knowing what her mother was talking about. She liked reporting accounts to her mother, liked making lists. "She chases after that boy. I mean," she said, lowering her head and blushing, "our brother."

"Oh, Edith, you are a mother's dream of a daughter."

Edith's head came up at this. She wasn't sure she'd ever before received a compliment from her mother. At least not like this. If she turned in account charts and managed the servants perfectly, with no flaw at all, her mother might utter a "good," but that was all. It was a great deal more than her father, who Edith wasn't sure knew who she was. "Thank you," was all Edith could manage to say to this fulsome praise.

"Here your father has set down in your midst a girl like that and you have taken her under your wing and given her the best of treatment. You act as though she were your . . . your equal."

Edith could make no reply to this, as she'd thought the girl *was* her equal.

"I can see that you are so good-hearted that you don't even see the differences. Does it not bother you that her talk is that of a farmer's? She has learned nothing of importance in her life — unless one counts growing beans as important. Perhaps she would be good at tilling the soil, since she has no hands for the lute. Did you ever see such hands! They are as wide as a plowshare. And her feet! Do you think she has ever had on a pair of shoes before now?"

Alida smiled at her wide-eyed daughter. "Look at you! I can tell you never even saw these things. You are a good daughter, Edith, the best."

Alida walked to the window. "Edith, my dear, dear daughter, may I trust you?"

"Yes," she said, then her voice broke. She'd never seen her mother like this, so open and kind, so needy. Edith felt tears prickle at the back of her eyes to think that she'd sometimes thought that her mother cared nothing about her, that, mayhap her mother didn't even *like* her. "Yes, you may trust me."

"This boy, this Talis. Do you not think he is handsome?"

"He is my brother. I cannot judge a brother as handsome or not. It is my duty to —"

"Yes, yes, of course," Alida said, as always annoyed with her daughter's lack of passion. She sat on a chair opposite her and took her hands in hers. "The night he was born I was in pain. You cannot yet know what the pain of childbirth is, but during it a woman sometimes does not know all that is going on."

Edith had no idea what was going on now.

"The night the boy was born I was confined with another woman, a dark woman, with dark skin and hair and eyes." She looked deep into her daughter's eyes. "Eyes like the boy's."

It took Edith a long time to figure out what her mother was saying. "You think the children were switched?"

At that, Alida put her hand over Edith's mouth and looked about the empty room as though for people hiding. "You cannot say such aloud. It is something that has worried me all these years. I was too much in pain to see what baby I was delivered of. That dark girl's child was born at the same moment. It was all so confusing."

"But that would mean . . . ," Edith whispered.

Alida leaned toward her daughter and also whispered. "Yes, that would mean that Talis is *not* your brother. It would mean that Callasandra is your sister. She does look a bit like she could be one of my daughters, does she not?"

"Dorothy said she did, but I —" Edith decided it was better not to tell her mother how she had ridiculed her sister for saying such a stupid thing.

"Oh, Edith, what am I going to do? You can

see how your father worships that boy. How could I go to him and tell him that I think there is a possibility Talis might not be his son, that he has only one more daughter, this one even less satisfactory than the others?" For a moment she buried her face in her hands. "And I have no one on earth I can truly trust with this knowledge."

"You may trust me, Mother," Edith said softly, feeling more privileged than she ever had before in her life.

"Can I, Edith? Can I truly trust you?" Before her daughter could answer, Alida said, "I hope I can because I have been told of a widower who is looking for a wife. He is thirty years old and has two young sons, such sweet boys who desperately need a mother. And I have been told that his wife was a pig of a housewife, so the man would be grateful for a wife who could keep his estates in order and tend to his children."

Edith squeezed her mother's hands so hard she hurt her. "I will do *anything* for you, Mother. Anything at all."

"What a very good daughter you are. Now, shall we discuss some arrangements? I think this boy, this Talis, should be given a few lessons. In dancing, and manners, playing a lute, courtly etiquette for a woman, that sort of thing. Do you think Joanna and Dorothy would like to help him with these lessons?"

Edith had to control herself to keep from laughing aloud. Each of her sisters would sell her soul to so much as touch the beautiful Talis. She wondered if Joanna's heart could stand it if he lifted her onto a horse. "Yes, I think I can persuade them to help. Although they are very busy." She didn't want to sound *too* eager, lest her mother think her daughters did nothing useful.

"Yes, I am sure they are," Alida said, knowing that there was not a square inch of fabric within the counry that had not been embroidered by her "busy" daughters.

"And, Edith," Alida said innocently, "do you think Callasandra should be allowed to spend so much time near the boy? Do you not think you could find enough tasks to keep her occupied? Perhaps she could manage a garden somewhere, since that is her background." Her head came up as though she'd just had an idea. "Father Keris needs help caring for the medicine herbs."

At this Edith caught her breath. The medicine garden was full of poisonous herbs: wolfsbane, belladonna, hemlock, foxglove, all the herbs used to produce sleep and alleviate pain, or, if improperly used, to kill. They were grown in a separate garden so they wouldn't be confused with the kitchen herbs. The Poison Garden — as it was called — was on the top of a hill about a mile from the house in a place where no one else went.

Of a sudden, there were a thousand questions that ran through Edith's orderly mind. "If Callie is our sister, should she be sent to the Poison Garden? It is very lonely there; something dreadful could happen to her; it is not a job for a lady. And if the world thinks Talis is our brother, how will it look to have my sisters tittering at his touch, as I know they will? And if — ?"

"Edith," her mother said sternly, "I am treating you, not as a child, but as the adult you are, and I am trusting you with this great secret. I leave it to you to keep my secret, to honor my trust. And I leave it to you to follow your own judgment as to what you do or do not do. I would never ask you to do something that you feel is against your morals." She leaned forward. "But whatever you do, you must *never* hint to your father or your sisters that you think there is some doubt as to the paternity of that boy. Do you understand?"

When Edith hesitated, Alida smiled and said, "The widower's name is Alan. He is taller than your father and very handsome. He will not go long without a wife. I must soon travel to the home of Gilbert Rasher. Perhaps I can stop there and tell him of what a good, faithful, dutiful, obedient daughter you are. Of how useful you are and how you help me when I most need you, that you are trustworthy to the ultimate degree."

She stroked Edith's cheek. "And I will tell him how very pretty you are. By the time I stop talking I will have his name on a marriage contract. I am sure of it." She gave a little laugh. "Think of it, Edith, by this time next year, you could be heavy with your own child. Would you like that?"

Her mother's words took Edith's breath away, and for a moment her hands trembled at the thought. Her own house to manage! Her own husband, her own *child*. "I will keep the secret. I will see that this boy receives lessons and . . ." She could not call the girl by her name or she'd remember that the girl was probably her sister. "I will see that she manages the Poison Garden."

"Ah, good," Alida said and kissed her daughter's cheek. "I am glad we agree. You may go now," she said abruptly. She was finished with Edith for now; she'd got what she wanted from her: blind obedience.

Later, when Alida was alone with Penella, who had been eating steadily for four days now, she said, "Remind me to look for a husband for Edith. Although it will be difficult to find one for her. She is as dried up as a two-year-old apple."

"Mmmmm," was all Penella said, her mouth too full to speak.

29

"You are indeed handsome," Alida said to Talis, looking up at him. She had taken extra care with her dress this morning, knowing that she was going to see this boy privately for the first time since he'd come to Hadley Hall. For just a moment, she had a feeling of envy that that tiny dark girl could have produced a beautiful boy like this when her own sons were so delicate and frail. And *how* did Gilbert Rasher father such as him?

Looking at Talis, it was almost as though sunlight radiated from him. She would have known even if she hadn't been told that this boy would rather die than betray what he believed in. He was like something out of an ancient story of great deeds and men too good for the world. For just a moment she shivered as she remembered that all those beautiful young men died very young.

"You are not well," Talis said softly, then put a strong young arm under hers and led her to a chair. When she was seated, he knelt by her and looked deep into her eyes. He looked at her as none of her own family had ever looked at her.

In the next moment he had placed a robe about her knees and had stoked the fire, and when he turned back to her she knew that he knew she was dying. Again, it ran through her that she wished this boy was hers.

She did the best she could to straighten herself. She must not give way to self-pity. In just months she was to meet her Maker, and she had a great deal to atone for. She could not go to God knowing that she had left her children's lives dependent upon someone who was not her blood relation.

"Come, my son," she said weakly, "you must sit by me. Let me look at you."

Instantly, he sat at her feet and she held his face to the light. Perfect skin, perfect teeth, open, honest dark eyes.

She took her hands away from him. "You have asked to marry Callasandra."

"Yes," he said. "It is what I most want in the world. Callie is —" He hesitated and blushed, then looked at the fire.

"She is very young," Alida said sternly.

"Not too young," he said, smiling.

She could feel his conviction, his feeling that this was something he *must* have.

"You are the son I always wanted and never had," she said softly.

Talis frowned at that. "Philip and James are —"

"Yes," she said quickly. "They are good and kind but no matter how many children a woman has, to lose one leaves a hole in her heart. Do you know that my hair turned white after I thought I had lost you in the fire? Do you know that all of us were demented over the loss? Your father never fully recovered."

"I had heard," Talis said softly.

She stroked his hair, so soft, the curls twining about her fingers. There was a time in her life when she was capable of great love. If she had been able to bear her husband a son like this from the first, her life would have been very different.

"And now you wish to leave me so soon after I have found you? To marry and leave me?"

"We will remain here if that is your wish."

She smiled at him. "If you marry you will give me none of your time. Young men think only of the young wife waiting at home in bed for them."

At that Talis gave a soft laugh and looked back at the fire. She could see that his mind was full of touching his sweetheart, kissing her, and, seeing this, Alida's heart was further hardened. Once she had thought of the same things as this boy, but look how her life had turned on her! Kisses did not last; property did.

They were silent a moment, alone in the room, Talis sitting on the floor, Alida leaning back in the chair. The only light in the room was from the fireplace, its glow enclosing them.

"Do you know that I am dying?" she asked softly.

"Yes," he answered, not looking up at her.

"How do you know?"

"You forget that I did not grow up in this rich place. I have lived on a farm. You learn to look into the eyes of an animal and see when it is in pain."

"Only three people know: you, my maid, and a soothsayer I consulted. She says I have at the most two years."

When she said no more, Talis's hand crept upward and took her small one in his large, dark one.

"Will you help me?" she asked, her voice pleading.

"I will do whatever I can."

"I have missed all of your life. I missed holding you as a baby, watching you take your first steps. I have been able to spend no time with you as I have with my other children." She clasped his hand in both of hers. "Oh, Talis, I love my children so much that I am very selfish with all of them. I cannot bear for my daughters to marry and leave me."

She paused to see if he was going to believe this and he did. Obviously he was not used to deceit. As far as Talis was concerned, people told the truth.

"I . . . I know," she said hesitantly, sounding as though pain ran through her breast. "I know that you love this girl very much but I want to ask a favor of you. Let me get to know you. Let your brothers and sisters get to know you before you pledge yourself to another. Before you have children of your own who take all your time. If you marry now and have children, we, my husband, my children, we will not get to spend any time with you."

She paused. "I know it is a lot to ask of you. I have no right. I have not been here to be a mother to you. The night you were born I nearly died in the birthing. You were so very, very large and I am a narrow woman." She laughed and put her hand on his head. "You nearly split me asunder with the size of you."

Talis was frowning, not looking at her, embarrassed by this talk and feeling bad that his entry into life had so hurt his own mother.

"I am not complaining, but I feel I must explain why I was not as attentive to you as I should have been that night you were born. I was nearly insensible with the pain." She lowered her voice. "And the blood. I lost a lot of blood that night. Your birth is the reason I had no more children. I was unable to bear more children after that night."

Talis was feeling heavier and heavier. He owed this woman so much. He had nearly killed her, robbed her of her ability to have children, deprived her of the company of her own child.

"When I heard that, after all I had been through to bring you into the world, you had died in a fire, I nearly lost my mind. I was not well for a long time after your birth."

She stroked his hand and looked into the fire. "I am telling you these things because I want to ask something of you. I want to ask you not to marry until . . . until after I am gone."

"But —" Talis began, but she cut him off.

"I know what I am asking. I know the hot blood of youth, how it rages. I had hoped you could control yourself, but perhaps not."

"I can control myself," Talis said, sounding affronted.

"Yes, of course you can. I did not mean to imply that you could not. Talis, my dear son, it is just that your father and I want to see you."

All Talis could think of was Callie. Holding her, being near her. In the last weeks, since the day he'd first met John Hadley, having her with him had become an obsession. In fact, he was finding that being a knight was not as important to him as was Callie.

"How will you support her?" Alida asked.

"Pardon?"

"How do you mean to support your wife?"

At this Talis's heart sank. He had two choices: farming with Will or relying on his father's generosity. If his father did not want him to marry, then Talis would have to take Callie back to the farm — and see her spend her life wringing the necks of chickens.

Alida tipped Talis's face up to hers. "If you will do this thing I ask, I will leave to you in my will my own estate of Peniman Manor."

While he sat there blinking, she went on to describe the place: a stone house only fifty years old, gardens she had spent years on, with intricate knots of herbs, a rose garden. She talked of the stables, the cottages for the farmworkers. "With your knowledge of farming, think what you could do with the acres of land that go with the house."

She could see the light in his eyes. "Have you thought of the people who raised you? They are not young and it will be hard for them to continue farming, will it not? Peniman Manor is large enough for them to live with you, to see your children."

At that Talis smiled, thinking how much Meg would love to have a dozen grandbabies to dandle on her knees. She could feed them until they were bursting. And Will could still have his vegetable patch.

And Callie could have a fine house, beautiful clothes. She would not be burdened with a life of hard work. Their children would have the finest education, the best horses.

"Is it too much to ask that you wait two years before you marry, when the reward is so great?"

"No," he said. "It is not too much to ask." His mind was reeling with the thought of telling Callie about all of this. They could plan their future, plan what kind of horses to buy — or, knowing Callie, talk endlessly about the names of their children. Just the idea made him smile.

"You must not tell her," Alida said, seeming

393

to read his mind. "You cannot tell Callasandra."

He looked at her sharply.

"You cannot tell her. If you did, then you would have to tell her that . . . about my health, and she must not know. She is no relation to me. I could not bear to have her look at me in pity. And she would. I am sure she has a soft heart."

"Yes," he said, "the softest. But she will not tell. I —"

"Talis! Listen to me. I am relying on you as I am on no one else. Not even my husband knows how ill I am." To emphasize this, she fell into a fit of coughing, and, holding a handkerchief to her mouth, it came away with traces of blood, which she showed to Talis.

When she spoke again, her voice was lowered and harsh. "You must listen to me. You are a man now and you must behave as a man. You cannot be a boy and tell everything that you know. Part of being an adult is that you have and can keep secrets. If you are man enough to get married, then you are man enough to protect that girl you want to marry. Are you that man?"

"Yes," he answered.

"Then you must listen to me. You cannot tell anyone what you know. My family loves me very much, just as you love the woman who raised you. What do you think you would feel at her death?"

Talis could not even think of Meg dying.

Alida continued. "When I die my family will come apart. They will not know how to manage without me. So I must look to you to take care of them for a while. I must place the burden of my death on your head and yours alone. You cannot be so cruel as to give this awful knowledge to the girl you love, could you?"

Talis shook his head.

"And you cannot tell her you have asked to marry her."

"I must tell Callie that," Talis said. "You do not know her. She will think that . . . that I . . ."

"That you don't love her?" Alida asked, her eyes sparkling. "Do you forget that I was a woman before I was a wife and mother? Oh, she will nag you. She will pout and complain, tell you that she thinks she means nothing to you." She chuckled. "Does that sound so bad?"

"No," Talis said, smiling, thinking that it all sounded rather wonderful. Sometimes he thought Callie was too sure of him.

"The truth is, I must persuade my husband to this marriage. You see, Talis, Callasandra's parentage is not as yours. This man who is her father is not someone who is desirable as a father-in-law. When my husband came to me about your marriage, he was against it. He wants to send Callasandra to her father and —" She broke off at Talis's gasp.

"You cannot send Callie away! I will go with her."

"And do what?" she asked sharply. "Become a wood chopper?"

For a moment Talis drew in his breath as he remembered Callie's story of a boy and girl who ran away and nearly starved to death.

"You must trust me," she said. "You *must* trust me. I want what you want and what is best for you. I will persuade my husband; I will leave you rewarded for all your help. But in the next two years you must help me."

"Yes, I will do all that I can."

"I want you to swear to me some things."

At that Talis's eyes widened. Knights made sacred vows. Knights swore oaths to ladies who needed them.

"Hand me the Bible there," she said, raising her arm weakly and pointing to a heavy book bound in ancient ivory. When he had the book in his hands, she said, "You must swear to me that you will tell no one of my approaching death."

"I swear it."

"Now kiss the Bible."

He did so, solemnly and with great reverence.

"Swear that you will not tell Callasandra that you have asked permission to marry her. If she asks, you must tell her that you have not decided who you will marry."

At that Talis hesitated, but at Alida's frown, he swore it and kissed the Bible.

"Swear that you will leave her a virgin until you are married."

Talis's eyes widened.

"You cannot think to take what does not belong

396

to you, can you? What if she were to get with child and then you fell off your horse and broke your neck before you could marry her? What would happen to her and your child? Have you no concern for her? Or are you interested only in your own baser needs? Or have I misjudged you and you are just a boy and not the man I thought you were?"

Talis still hesitated, but after a while he kissed the Bible again and made his third vow.

When he had finished, Alida looked at him, so earnest, obviously taking what he did with utmost seriousness. "You must stay away from her," she said softly. "Already people talk of her. They say she is not of good character, that the two of you have known each other many times."

"That is not true!" he said.

"I know it and you do, but that does not keep people from talking." She looked into his eyes. "They do not talk of you, but of her. You will never be hurt by these malicious words. It is a hateful truth but such words will enhance your status as a man, but the same words will make her look as though she is a woman of less than perfect reputation."

Alida cocked one eyebrow at him. "But then you might not care that people talk of her. Most men would not."

"I am not most men," he said, his back rigid. "I would not want her hurt on my account. I will see that she has no reason to be talked about."

"You are a sweet boy. Now, I find that I am

very tired and must rest."

"Yes," he said quickly and was all concern for her. "I will leave you now."

Moments later, after Talis was gone, Alida told Penella to send Callasandra to her.

30

From the moment Alida saw Callie, she knew that the girl had a spine of steel. This was no Edith who she could entice with empty promises of a husband and her own home; this was no girl who would do whatever someone asked merely because the word *honor* was mentioned. Nor would the word *death* sway her.

On some level, Alida knew that here was the daughter who was closest to herself, but the older woman did not want to acknowledge that. Like any person who was trying to get her own way, anyone who thwarted her was considered obstinate and unreasonable.

Now, looking at Callie, Alida knew that she was going to have a difficult time with this girl. Callie had an inflexible look about her that Alida knew was going to cause trouble.

"Come, sit, eat," Alida said sweetly.

Callie did not sit, did not eat. Yesterday, all in a dither, Edith had gone to her mother, and when she had returned, she had been a different person. Since that time, she had done everything possible to make Callie's life hell. Callie had gone from being one of a group of superfluous females to being picked out for ridicule and harassment. And this morning, with embarrassment she could not conceal, Edith had informed Callie that she was to be in charge of a bunch of poisonous weeds, saying that, since she was a farmer, she was to take care of these plants.

Callie well knew that Edith was too weak to make any decisions on her own. Until now, Callie had felt sorry for the woman, drying up from want of love and companionship, not allowed to have the things that every woman wanted. But after the last two days Callie no longer felt sorry for her.

"What do you want of me?" Callie asked Lady Alida, her eyes hard, her anger barely kept in check. She knew without a doubt that this woman was responsible for every thought Edith had in her empty head.

"My, my, but you sound angry. How can you be angry at one who has treated you as her own daughter?"

This was certainly true, Callie thought, since both John and Alida Hadley treated their daughters as though they were diseased lumps they had to abide with. "What do you want of me?" Callie repeated.

Alida dropped all pretense of being the girl's benefactor. Well she knew that this child was her own daughter, but Alida also knew she had to be sacrificed. Give one daughter up for the good of the others. Besides, what great harm was she doing? All she meant to do was prevent the marriage of these two children. Later, after she got rid of Talis, she'd find this girl a very nice husband.

"You are making a fool of yourself over my son and I'll not have it."

At that Callie gave her a hard look. "Then perhaps I will leave your house forever." As she turned toward the door, she was halted by the words of this woman.

"Then you will go alone. My son will stay here. He cannot be allowed to spend his life with a girl who works on a farm. My son will become a knight; he will marry a *lady*."

At those words, Callie turned back, looked hard at the woman, then quietly sat down on the offered chair. Callie knew that what the woman was saying was true. If she wanted Talis, then she had to remain here, had to do whatever this woman said she must. "What am I to do?" Callie asked softly.

"Stay away from my son," Alida said simply.

Callie paled at those words. How could she stay away from Talis? It would have been easier if the woman had asked her to stop breathing.

"Oh come now, do not look at me as though I am an ogre. I know he is your childhood friend and I have sympathy for what the two of you have been through, living as you did in that hovel. Living with animals, illiterate people such as those —"

401

"Do not!" Callie said. "They were good to us."

There was something in the way the girl spoke that made Alida halt her words. Had she been less intent on her goal, she might have realized that she was looking into a mirror and seeing a younger version of herself. Just as Alida would do anything for people she considered her family, so would Callie.

"What do you want of me?" Callie repeated.

"Not much, just to stay away from my son."

"And to reach this end you have sent me to care for poisonous plants."

"Poisonous plants! How sinister you must think I am. I thought you might enjoy the garden as you have spent your life outdoors."

Callie said nothing. Never in her life would she tell this woman that she *would* enjoy working in the garden. She would love being outdoors all day, away from the rigid rules and ridiculous schedules imposed on the unmarried women in this oppressive house. She would like the freedom to daydream and make up stories in her head.

But most important, she would be free to see Talis whenever possible. Now, she'd tell this woman whatever she wanted to hear, that she'd never see Talis again. If necessary, she'd make sacred vows never to see him again. She'd do whatever it took to appease this woman, then she'd go and do what she wanted to do — which was to see Talis.

Lady Alida began to talk, telling Callie all manner of things about honor and reputation and "saving herself" and whatever else she could think of to try to impress Callie that she must, *must* stay away from Talis. Talis needed to learn to be a knight, needed experience in life, needed . . .

Callie didn't bother listening to much of it. She'd learned to put on her "listening" face, the one she used with Meg when she was saying something Callie found uninteresting. While her face looked as though she were listening, Callie let her mind wander onto a story, fantasizing that Talis would come to her in the garden. Just the two of them, alone, no one else around. Yes, she liked this duty of taking care of the garden and being alone.

It took Callie a moment to realize that her ladyship had paused. And from the way she was looking at Callie, Alida knew her daughter had not been listening.

Alida grabbed Callie's chin in her hand, hurting her. "Do you not know that the way to get a man is to ignore him? If you chase him, he will never want you."

Callie smiled in an ageless way at the woman. "Talis likes what I am and what I do."

"Oh?" Alida said. "Then why is he not asking for your hand in marriage? If he wants you so much, then why is he not demanding to be allowed to marry you? Is it because he sees you for the greensleeves that you are?"

Alida smiled when she saw that she had at last made an impression on the girl. So, Alida thought, it was not what the girl felt for Talis; her concern was what Talis thought of her.

Knowing she had made her point, Alida abruptly dismissed the girl.

When Callie was gone, Alida called Penella to her.

"That girl is a problem," Alida said. "She has no honor."

Penella looked at her mistress quickly, as though to say, Look who's calling the kettle black.

"Something will have to be done with that girl. I'll not have her parading herself before my son. I won't have her sneaking about with him at night as though she's a harlot."

For a moment, Penella paused with a cherry tart halfway to her mouth. Lady Alida was speaking of the boy Talis as though he really were her son — and as though this hardheaded girl belonged to someone else.

"I shall have Abigail Frobisher send her youngest son to me," Alida said.

At that Penella nearly choked. Abigail Frobisher's son was an eighteen-year-old boy whose only goal in life was to cause trouble. He was a very pretty lad, without a moral in his body, and he had been impregnating serving girls since he was fourteen. On his last visit, he had even put his hand on *Edith's* waist!

"Yes," Alida said, "I will have the boy come to stay and I will give him money if he will entice that girl to . . . . to whatever."

Penella finished the tart, making no comment

whatever to these arrangements. Her ladyship did not want Talis and Callie to marry and she was certainly seeing to it that they didn't. The old wet nurse had said that the children were jealous of each other. If anyone could cause jealousy, it was Lady Abigail's youngest son.

But in Penella's opinion, Lady Alida was going to more trouble than was needed to keep the children apart. There was more here than the woman was telling. But it was none of Penella's business — she had learned the hard way to keep her own counsel.

"Go and ready my belongings for the journey to see Gilbert Rasher," Alida said. "We will ride tomorrow. I have business to attend to."

"Yes, my lady," Penella said, slipping the rest of the tarts into her pocket.

31

"It is done," Alida said, her entire body shaking from fatigue as Penella undressed her and put her to bed. Alida's health had greatly deteriorated in the last weeks of traveling. Two weeks ago she had been coughing only rusty bits of blood, but now she often brought up great clots from her lungs.

But it all had been worth it, she thought as she tried to sip the hot liquid Penella handed her. But she brushed the woman away, not wanting to see her, wanting only to be alone with her thoughts and her memories.

She and her small household had ridden hard for days to reach that filthy old castle Gilbert Rasher called home. And she had been greeted by a man eaten with hatred and a lust for revenge. When he had been told that she was John Hadley's wife, it had been difficult to get him to stop raging long enough to make him understand that she wanted the same as he wanted.

Across a dirty table, his breath so heavy with

the fumes of liquor that she felt faint, she finally made him understand that she was trying to *help* him.

After she told him that his son was alive and living at her house, it had taken an hour of shouting to keep him from jumping on a horse and riding to get the boy.

"He is of no use to you," Alida shouted. "He is untutored. He has no social graces, no table manners. He cannot sing or even play a lute."

Gilbert looked at her as though she had lost her mind. "What do these things matter to a *man?*" he bellowed at her. "A *man* needs none of these things."

"A man at court does," she shouted back, sure that he was the stupidest man ever created. He seemed to have made up his mind about life on the day he was born and nothing or no one had ever made him think differently.

"Court?" he asked, as though he'd never heard of the place.

"Listen to me," she said, doing all she could to refrain herself from calling him all the names she wanted to. "Do you forget that you are related to the queen? It is a distant relationship, I know, but it is there." When his witless face registered no hint of understanding, she continued.

"The queen is fifty-four years old. She has yet to name her successor. Do you recall that she has a cousin who has some claim to the throne? Bess of Hardwick's niece, Arabella Stuart. The girl is ten years old now and it is said that Bess keeps her prisoner, always looking for the proper husband for her."

Alida leaned toward the old man with his gray, grizzled whiskers, his greasy hair, his food-stained clothes. "Bess wants her niece to marry a man who could be *king*."

"King?"

Alida was so tired of ignorant men. Could they not see the simplest things? Taking a breath, she tried to calm herself, but she was going to be brutally honest with this man. His mind was not up to subtlety.

"Gilbert Rasher, you breed beautiful sons. Big, intelligent sons, quite gorgeous actually, but then they are exposed to your lack of morals, to your primitive ideas of discipline, to your crude ideas of education, and they become animals like you. You ruin what could be a valuable product."

While she said this, he sat there staring at her with a curled upper lip, looking at her as though she were something to be put on a plate and served to him, his for the taking. But he said nothing, as he was at last beginning to realize that she had a reason for coming to see him.

"*This* son," she continued, "had the good fortune to be taken away from you at birth." She did not say so but she also thought it was good fortune that Talis had been raised away from John also.

Alida gave Gilbert a little smile, knowing she was still a handsome woman, faded perhaps, but not unpleasant looking. "You should see this boy:

tall, proud, excellent at his studies, kind, polite. He is a beauty in every way."

At this Gilbert raised one eyebrow, as always, his mind in the gutter.

"Do not look at me so. *I* am not after the boy. But there is another woman who likes beautiful young men very much."

When Gilbert looked blank at this she silently cursed his ignorance. "The *queen!* Now the Earl of Leicester's stepson, that Robert Devereux, is at court, a young man of only twenty-one and I hear he charms the queen night and day. Talis, your son, is better-looking than Devereux, and more charming. Furthermore, Talis has not a dishonorable bone in his body. I hear that that Devereux is as ambitious as his mother."

There was still no enlightenment shining in Gilbert's drink-dulled eyes, so Alida simplified her explanation. "You and I have the same purposes in mind. I want your son out of my life. I do not want my husband to give everything that he has and that came to him on our marriage to a boy who is not mine."

At that, Gilbert's eyes did light up.

"Do not think he will inherit and then you will take everything from him," she said, accurately guessing what was in his mind. "From the look of you, you will not live the year out, while my husband is the picture of health. You must leave your son with us for two more years, then you must come to take him. By then he will be trained for court; he will please the queen greatly, and you must petition her to make a great marriage for him. If I were you, I would ask for Lady Arabella Stuart. Who knows? With your connections to the throne and his, perhaps when she dies she will leave England to him."

"I will take him now," Gilbert said, starting to rise. "I will make him king now."

"No!" she half shouted. "He is not ready. I told you this. If your purpose is for him to go to court and shoe horses then he is ready." She calmed herself. "Shoeing horses is not what the queen likes. Before he goes to court he must first learn the finer things of life, to play and sing, to dance, to court a woman."

"Is he good on a horse?" Gilbert growled. "Can he hold a lance? That is all he needs."

"All he needs if he is to live with you and spend his life terrorizing the peasants," she spat at him. "If you were to present him as he is now, in his present raw state, the queen would laugh at you . . ." She looked at him. "Again."

Gilbert sat back down. He had never said so, but it had hurt his pride when the queen had laughed at him when so many people had declared that they had wanted his son dead. For all his crudity, in a way, Gilbert loved his sons and he missed the boy. The boy had been a great drinking companion.

"What do you get out of this?" he asked her.

"The happiness of my husband," she said.

At that Gilbert laughed. "If you do not tell me the truth, I will do nothing that you want."

Alida took a moment to breathe deeply and in that time she decided to tell him the truth. "Perhaps I want revenge." She looked at him. Gilbert Rasher was not the person one would have chosen for a confidant, but then perhaps he was the best sort. Nothing on earth, not any motive, would shock him. He understood and indulged himself in any vice he wanted. And Alida knew he would not waste time on sympathy.

"I married my husband for love. Not for money, but because I loved him. I was very young, very naive and I thought he loved me too. He did not. For all of my youth I tried to make him love me, but all he cared about was that I produced a perfect son for him. I did not."

She paused. "Perhaps he never would have loved me, I do not know. I do know that I have lived in hell most of my life because I did once love him. I have watched my daughters go without husbands and turn into fussy old maids because he would not part with the gold needed for a dowry. I have seen him ignore all that was around him in his foolish attempt to get something that he thought was all he wanted in life."

She looked at Gilbert. "Now he has his precious son. He has the boy he has always wanted. You should see this Talis. He is like a dream come true, beautiful, kind, so very, very good. And my husband worships him, truly worships him."

She rose from her chair, taking a few steps across the filthy floor, littered with the remnants of hundreds of past meals. "I am dying. At most

I have two years to live, and on my deathbed I want to hurt my husband as he has hurt me. I want the only thing he has ever loved taken from him, just as the only thing I ever loved was taken from me. After I am dead I want him to hear of that boy he has grown to love so much. I want him to hear all the country talk of Gilbert Rasher's glorious son, *not* John Hadley's son."

She turned back to Gilbert. "Do you understand? I am using you as an instrument of revenge."

Being used did not bother Gilbert; what interested him was what he was going to get out of it. "What money do I get from this?"

"For two years you will receive nothing. But when you come in two years' time, my husband will give you everything in an attempt to keep the boy."

"And the boy will stay with him. I know his kind. He will think Hadley is his father. There is great loyalty from father to son."

Alida smiled, thinking that perhaps Gilbert was not quite as stupid as she'd thought. "I am taking care of that."

"Oh?" Gilbert asked and poured her a flagon of wine. It was cheap wine, nearly undrinkable, and the pewter mug looked as though the dogs had been chewing on it, but, for him, it was extreme generosity. He had not offered her or her servants so much as a crust of bread upon their arrival. "What are you doing to break this loyalty?"

412

"The boy wants to marry one of my daughters. You remember, the one I gave birth to the night Talis was born. They have lived together all these sixteen years with the wet nurse and her husband and they are attached to one another."

"He cannot marry her," Gilbert said. Already he was beginning to think of himself as the father of the King of England. At last his enemies would be his to punish. In essence, *he* would be the next King of England. He would cut off heads at a rate that would flood London.

"No, of course he cannot marry her. It cannot be allowed. And when the time comes, the boy will leave John readily enough."

"And how have you managed that?"

She toyed with the pewter mug, not even seeing the food encrusted on it. "My husband thinks the boy stays because he wants to be a knight, because he likes all the riches my husband has to offer. But the boy stays for the girl. She is his only reason for doing anything. Quite simply, I will take that reason away from him. Already, I am separating them. By the time I get through with them, they will not remember each other."

And that is for the better, she thought. Even if she had no other interest in this, she knew she could not allow her daughter to marry a man she loved. Alida's parents had been too weak and had given in to their daughter when she had cried and begged to be allowed to marry John Hadley. And look where it had gotten her. If she had been married to another man it would not have

413

killed her soul when he turned against her.

"I have separated the children and I am making sure they see other people. I want to surround them with other people. They have spent their lives only with each other and therefore think they love each other. It is only because there has been no one else."

It didn't matter to Gilbert what the woman did to either of them, as long as he came out the winner. "I must be given something while I wait," he said, and Alida could not help but admire his single-mindedness. The man cared only for himself and he never forgot that what he wanted was the only thing of importance.

"We will work out terms," she said, then began making him the lowest offer she could think of. And when he in return asked for the sun and moon and stars, she knew that she would not see a bed that night.

32

Two weeks, Callie thought. Perhaps to others they were merely days, but to her they were a lifetime. Where was he? What was he doing?

But she knew the answer to that. In the last weeks she had repeatedly sneaked down to the house and watched. Always, he was surrounded by a fluttering group of pretty women, jewels winking on their gowns and in their hair. The wind carried the sounds of their giggling, of their little squeals of delight when they tried to teach Talis something.

The first time she had seen him with them, she'd snorted in derision. Talis would hate people hovering over him; he couldn't stand Nigel fluttering about, wanting to see what Talis was doing. And too, she and Talis had taken great pride in their studies, always competing to see who could do the best job.

But the Talis she knew and the handsome young man sitting in the sunlight on the stone bench were not the same man. *This* Talis couldn't do *anything* correctly.

"Show me again how to do that," he'd say, then look up wide-eyed at some fat-chested girl, as though he'd never seen anyone as smart and pretty as she.

In the few minutes Callie stood to one side looking at him, he failed in his attempts to strike the correct strings on a lute, couldn't sing (yet she knew he had a beautiful voice), and expressed amazement at some advice a girl with wide hips gave him on how to dress.

Callie didn't know where all the young women came from. Some were his sisters, some were ladies-in-waiting, but most were strangers to her. It was as though every pretty female in the county had been ordered to surround Talis and tell him he was wonderful.

Callie didn't know that Talis had seen her the moment she turned the corner and that his ineptitude with the hovering women had been solely for her benefit. Truthfully, he had found all — well, almost all — of the women annoying more than anything else. For the first week he had been flattered, but now they were in his way every time he took a step, asking him to help them onto horses, showing him their sewing, wanting to practice French with him, asking him to pick fruit from the highest tree branches because he was so very tall.

Philip and James had nudged him with their elbows, and at first Talis had smiled at them, but in the last few days, he'd turned a furious face to them, making them back away from him in fear.

And Callie, he thought. Callie.

Since he'd talked to Lady Alida he had tried to keep away from Callie. It was better for both of them, was his reasoning, and, besides, he needed to learn to get along without her. He was a grown man, wasn't he? And it would be better for her, too, if she learned to get along with other women.

Yes, he thought, it would be better for both of them if they learned to live without each other's company every minute of every day.

But instead of getting easier with each day, being away from her was becoming more difficult.

And then he had seen her watching him while he was surrounded by all those tittering idiots, and, like a fool, he had tried to make her jealous. Maybe he'd hoped that she would step into the middle of them and use a sword to scatter the girls.

But she hadn't. Instead, she had turned away from him as though she had no desire ever to see him again.

Later he'd wanted to go to her, but his father seemed to keep him busy every minute of the day. For the thousandth time that day he looked up toward the hill behind the house. Edith had told him that Callie had asked to be given a garden to tend, and now she spent her days alone up there.

That had seemed odd to Talis at the time because he knew that Callie, like him, liked animals better than plants. Why had she not asked to care for the birds, the peahens and peacocks?

Just the thought that Callie was doing something he knew nothing about made him ache with longing for her. But this was better, he thought. If he didn't see her, he would be able to keep his vows to Lady Alida and not touch Callie, not hold her in his arms. He wouldn't have to see her eyes when he could not tell her that he was working every day toward the goal of marrying her and giving them and their children a wonderful place to live. She would forgive him for his neglect of her when she saw this Peniman Manor and knew that he had worked to give it to her.

"Why do you not sleep?" Philip asked Talis, annoyed with his brother's tossing and turning. During the day one could see black circles under Talis's eyes and he was becoming weaker by the day in his training. James had said that it was as though the life were draining out of Talis.

"She is crying and her tears hurt my heart," Talis said softly.

Philip had never heard anyone say anything like that. And as any virginal young man, he was curious about the opposite sex. "Do you . . . do you go to bed with her?"

"No!" Talis said then calmed. "It's not like that."

"You just miss her then. I know, I miss James when he is gone."

"No," Talis said and searched for the words to explain how he felt about Callie. "I have loved many people in my life: Meg and Will, and now you and James, our father. Many people. And I miss the people I love when I am away from them. I miss Meg and Will very much, every day even. But with Callie . . ."

He paused. "With Callie it is different. I cannot say that I love her, or that I miss her. There is a deeper feeling than that. When she is not with me, it is as though part of me is missing. It's as though I have been split in half and when she is gone half of me is open and raw. All my blood and muscle, even my brains drain out that open wound. Can you understand that?"

Philip could not, did not, want to understand such a feeling. If this was love, he wanted no part of it. He looked in the dark at Talis's profile, at his staring, sightless eyes and wondered again if this young man really was his brother. Turning away, he went back to sleep. Tomorrow would be full of more of his father's eternal training, and now that Talis was so distracted during the day, Philip got no respite from his father's wrath. If he had his way he'd give this girl Callie to Talis and be done with it. Talis was much, much more pleasant when she was standing in the shadows watching him.

Just before he fell asleep, Philip once again prayed that he'd never fall in love.

"Perhaps I could make you a nice, hot broth,"

Callie said sweetly to the young man lounging under the tree and watching her.

"Mmmm?" he said. "And what shall you put in it?"

"Anything my garden has to offer," she said, batting her lashes at him.

Allen Frobisher laughed in a way that said he knew she didn't mean a word of what she was saying. Why, if she made him something to drink from *her* garden it would have to be poisonous. And of course she didn't mean to do that. Of course she adored him; all women did. How could they not, with his golden hair and his blue eyes and his tall, elegant form? Yet sometimes he almost thought that this girl, this plain-faced girl, did not, well, like him. Which was indeed impossible. Ridiculous even.

"Haven't you someplace you should be?" she asked, a hoe in her hand, chopping at weeds around some purple flowers. "Isn't there some heiress you need to try to wed?"

For an instant, Allen frowned. Sometimes the girl made him sound as though he were a nuisance. All in all, if Lady Alida weren't paying him so much, he would leave this girl and never see her again. "Callie, dear, simple girl that you are, I do not think you fully realize who I am."

Callie opened her mouth to make a retort to that, something along the lines of his being a wastrel, a worth-nothing, when, suddenly, she stood upright and, shielding her eyes from the sun, looked toward the horizon to watch a man making his way toward them.

Following her look, Allen glanced up; his only interest being whether or not the approaching man was that tall boy, that Talis. Two days ago *he* had ridden by, and Callie, who until then hadn't given Allen the time of day, suddenly became the most wanton creature he had ever seen. From under a tight, plain cap, she had unleashed a torrent of the most ravishing blonde hair, spreading it around the two of them as though it were a golden cloak. Then, in a honeyed voice, she'd begun telling him an outrageous story of dragons and mermaids. Allen had never been so fascinated by a woman in his life. Within seconds Callie had changed from a plain-faced girl into a seductive woman.

Allen had been so enraptured with this glorious change that he'd hardly noticed the tall young man sitting rigidly atop the horse, scowling down at the two of them. Allen had been told of the long-lost son John Hadley had found, but, to Allen, Talis didn't look much like the rest of the Hadley family. He was a tall young man, sitting on an unruly horse that looked as though it would have delighted in kicking Allen's head in. In fact, when Talis had looked at Allen, Allen had swallowed hard. If Callie's hair had not caressed his face at that moment, he might have taken off running down the hill. As it was, Talis said not a word but merely looked at Callie then turned his horse away.

As soon as he was once again alone with Callie,

Allen started to pursue her licentious behavior, but when he reached his hands out to touch her, she soundly slapped his face. While he was rubbing his cheek (she was extraordinarily strong for a girl) she twisted all that hair back under her cap and her face changed from radiant back to the dullness he usually saw.

Never in his life had Allen been so intrigued by any female. It was as though there were two Callies: the one he was looking at now, chaste, demure, boring, and the one he'd seen very briefly two days ago, a Callie who was radiant, ardent, and oozed sensuality.

Now, Allen had been waiting for two days for that girl to reappear, but she hadn't and he was beginning to get bored. He had no idea what he had done before to bring out the lust in her but he was a little tired of trying to regain it. He was much too vain to think that her sensuality had been for that dark Talis and not for him.

When the approaching man was close enough that Allen could see that he was nothing more than a peasant farmer, he had no more interest in him. Nor was his interest aroused when Callie threw down her hoe and went running toward the man, her arms outstretched. Lady Alida had hinted that the girl was not a lady, in spite of the belief that she was Gilbert Rasher's daughter. Surely her embracing of this peasant was proof of her common birth.

When Callie returned, arm in arm with the old man, Allen took offense at the way the farmer told him to leave them, but he obeyed the man. For all of his rough clothes, there was an air about Will Watkins that made people obey him. With a great show that said he had meant to leave anyway, Allen mounted his horse and left the hill.

"Now," Will said when he and Callie were comfortably seated under a shade tree, "I want to know everything. All of it."

Will was not surprised when Callie flung her arms around him and began to cry. Never had he seen such unhappiness on Callie's face. And only one thing in the world could make Callie unhappy: the absence of Talis.

"Where is he?" Will asked, not needing to say who "he" was.

"With women!" Callie spat, wiping her eyes. "Talis spends all day with beautiful women, women with bodies that . . . that . . ." She looked down at her own flat chest. "He does nothing but talk to them and sing to them and say sweet words to them. They are all over him. He cares for them, takes them riding, touches them, kisses them. He makes love to them all day and all night. He never stops. He —"

At this point Will smiled at her. "All day and night? Talis? And when does he sleep his twelve hours a day?"

Callie did not smile. "He is not the Talis we have always known. He is . . . He is an animal. He is no longer human. You would hate him if you knew him now."

"Yes, I am sure I would. Tell me who this young man was who was lounging about under the tree and watching you. And what are you doing with these?" He waved his hand at the Poison Garden, his dislike of death plants evident.

"He is no one. Allen Frobisher." Callie waved her hand in dismissal. "Talis lies to the women, tells them he cannot sing when he can. He wants them to hover over him and show him everything. You know how he can do anything that can be done, but when *they* are near, he pretends he can do nothing. He makes me sick. He would —"

"Who is Allen Frobisher?" Will persisted.

"I do not know. He comes here. I think he was sent by that Lady Alida. I do not like that woman. I think she has plans for Talis, and now Talis would not understand if the devil himself were planning to use him. Of course if the devil used a woman, Talis would agree to the plan. He'd sell his soul to get a woman near him. He'd —"

"Callie!" Will said. "Please try to direct your mind to something besides Talis's many women and tell me —"

"Many! He has *thousands* of women! The world cannot contain his women. He wanted to be a knight but now all he does is follow women about. *Dogs* have more morals than he. He is —"

"Has he seen you with this Allen Frobisher?"

"Talis is the lowest snake, the dirtiest —" When she at last heard Will's question, she smiled. "Yes, he saw us." She gave a nasty little laugh. "Allen liked my hair; he liked my story."

At that Will ran his hand over his eyes and shook his head. "Callie," he said softly, "did you know that this Frobisher lad is *very* good-looking?"

Callie looked at Will as though he'd lost his mind. "He has *white* hair," she said, as though Will were blind. "And his eyes are blue. And his skin is the color of unbaked bread. And he has legs as thin as a chicken's." By now she was leaning into Will's face, speaking slowly and deliberately as though Will couldn't understand the simplest of concepts. "Allen Frobisher is *short*."

"You mean that he does not look like Talis, is not as tall as Talis, so therefore he could not possibly be handsome?"

"I did not say that," Callie said with pride. "I'm sure there are many handsome men on earth."

Will's eyes were twinkling. "In these months you must have seen many men. Which of them are handsome?"

"There were a great many of them handsome," she said stiffly. "Many, many of them."

"I am waiting for one name. Just one man you thought was even half as princely as your beloved Talis."

"He is not princely and he is not *mine*," she said, looking away from Will. Then, suddenly, she turned back to him and threw herself onto his wide chest and started to cry. "There is no one on earth as handsome as Talis. No one. He is more beautiful than the sun and the moon together but he has forgotten me. He does not need me or want me. He thinks only of other women."

"Does he sleep at night?"

"No," she said, sniffing. "My crying keeps him awake and I am glad. I want to keep him awake. I hope I never let him sleep. I hope I make him miserable."

Will stroked Callie's back and didn't say a word. She and Talis had grown up in such isolation that they did not know that what they said and thought were quite strange. Callie did not have any idea that other people did not know "in their minds," as she always said, where another person was or what he was doing.

When the children had been little, a few times Talis had not come home at dark. Meg had been frantic, but she and Will soon learned that only if Callie was upset was there reason to be worried. The first time Talis had been "lost" Will had asked Callie to help look for him. "He will be home," she'd said calmly. "I know in my mind that he is all right."

After that, it had been common to ask either of the children what they knew "in their mind" about the other. Now, if Callie said Talis was kept awake at night by her tears then Will knew that it was true.

But what Callie didn't seem to understand was that if the connection between them was so strong that she could keep him awake all night with her tears, then Talis was *not* in danger of falling in love with any other woman.

"Come, Callie, stop crying," Will said, holding her away from him. "I want to know everything that is going on. And do you not want to know about Meg? Have you forgotten Meg? She has sent dried apricots for you and Talis."

"He does not deserve them," Callie said. "I should make him a pie with these." She waved her hand toward the poisonous plants.

At that reminder, Will frowned. "I want to know why you are here. Why have they put a girl in charge of a garden such as this? Why are you here alone with that young man? For all the good that sleeping old man does, you might as well be alone," he said before she could point out Father Keris to him. "You must tell me everything."

It was hours later that Will was able to get the full story out of Callie. For all that Callie was usually an excellent storyteller, when Talis was involved, she was nearly incoherent. She could say no more than a couple of sentences about her life since coming to Hadley Hall before she went off on a tangent about the perfidy of Talis, how he was lusting after every female in the county and how he cared absolutely nothing for her anymore.

Under all the words Will heard the loneliness in her voice, heard the emptiness of her life. If Callie had Talis she was interested in her stories and her animals and in other people, but without

Talis she was interested in nothing. Without Talis she had no one to tell her stories to, no one to make laugh, no one to give to.

"And what does Talis feel about this?" Will interjected into yet another tirade from Callie about his "uncaring ways." "Is he happy here?" They were sharing a beef pie that Callie had been given for dinner. That she was not to come to the house to sit at the table with the others was another indication to Will that something was deeply wrong.

"No," Callie said before she thought, "Talis is not happy."

"Oh? And how could he not be with all those women around him? That would have made me happy when I was his age."

"He is *not* happy," Callie fairly shouted. "He doesn't like them. He wants me. I know he does." She buried her face in her hands and began to cry again. "Why, oh why does he not come to see me? I am here all day and that man, that man he thinks is his father, would allow him *anything,* so why does Talis not come to me? He said that if we could not be together here we would go back to the farm. But he lied. Why?"

"I do not know, sweetheart," Will said, pulling her into his arms, not wanting her to see the shock on his face at hearing that Talis had lied. "But I will try to find out." For a moment he stroked her hair, then, trying to lighten her mood, he said, "What would you have of Talis? Would you like for him to buy you a fine house like

428

that one?" he asked, pointing toward Hadley Hall.

Callie didn't hear the note of envy in Will's voice, envy that another man could give the children what he could not. If it hadn't been for Meg, they wouldn't even have learned to read and write.

"No, I don't want a house. I want . . ." Wiping her eyes with the back of her hand, she said, "I want him not to be ashamed of me."

"Ashamed of you? Callie, how could you say such a thing about Talis? He never wants to be without you."

"Yes, but that was when he had no one else. Now that he has the choice among all these beautiful women, he does not want to see me. His father is this rich John Hadley, while I am the daughter of a dreadful man named Gilbert Rasher. There are horrible stories about him! Talis does not want to be seen with such as me. I am the Poison Girl."

Will did not know what to say to her to calm her. He well knew that Talis was not ashamed of her, but he also knew that something bad was happening if the children were not together. Or perhaps this was just the way it was in rich households; he did not know.

"Come, now," he said coaxingly. "What would you have of Talis?"

"Nothing. I want nothing of him."

"Do not give me your pride. I know what you feel for him. Tell me a story of what you would have of Talis."

When she looked at him, her eyes were serious. "Talis thinks he owns me. He thinks that I am his, yet he has done nothing to win me. Do you understand? He has not fought for me!"

"Yes," Will said, understanding that courtship was so important to a woman. And it was true that Talis had never done anything to court Callie. Sometimes it was as though they had been born married to each other.

"I want Talis to tell everyone that he loves me best," Callie said softly. "I would like for him to . . . to shout it from the rooftops that I am his and he wants no one else."

At that Will had to laugh. The idea of proud Talis sitting on top of a roof like a rooster and crowing that he loved Callie was not something he could imagine. No, Talis's idea of love was to allow Callie to serve him hot gooseberry tarts under a shade tree.

And until now that had been enough for Callie.

"You ask for much," Will said, "but I will see what I can do." There was not much hope in his voice.

33

"Interfering old man," John was muttering, flinging objects on the table about. "I have had him escorted off my land! I have given orders that he is never to be allowed to return. If he comes back I'll have him hanged."

Hugh knew better than to make any comment at this point. John was in a rage because his beloved Talis had nearly fallen to pieces yesterday at the sight of an old, stooped man wearing the rough clothes of a farmer. In the midst of riding at the quintain, Talis had leaped from his horse and run to the man, flinging his arms about him as though he were still three years old.

John, who more than anything else in the world wanted Talis's love, had nearly choked on his jealousy. He had immediately called Talis back to him, meaning to reprimand him, but Talis hadn't so much as heard his call as he repeatedly kissed the old man's cheeks. It was the old man who'd pointed out to Talis that he was being summoned.

To John's further distress, Talis had presented the old man to John as though the man were visiting royalty. John's face had turned purple with outrage and he'd ordered Talis to return to his training.

"But I must to see to my father's welfare," Talis said calmly. "He has come a long way to see me and he is tired and hungry."

"*I* am your father," John shouted.

"Oh, yes sir," Talis said. "I did not mean . . ."

"Go on with your training," Will said. "I will wait."

"No," Talis said firmly, "a knight must take care of those he loves. You will excuse me, sir," he said to John, "while I take my fa— While I see to my visitor." With that Talis had walked away with his arm protectively, lovingly, around the broad, stooped shoulders of the old man.

John had watched them go, his body so full of anger that Hugh had feared for his life. When Talis did not return that afternoon, John went in search of him and found him ensconced in the garden with the old man, their heads together, talking as Talis had never talked with John.

"*I* am his father," John was now raging to Hugh. "Does the boy not know that? Does he not understand that he is to come to me with his problems?"

Hugh peeled an apple with a silver-handled knife. John Hadley was the last man anyone would want to tell an intimate problem to. John had the heavy-handed approach to life that a butcher had with a carcass of beef. "The boy misses the girl," he said at last.

"What girl?" John asked. "Why does everyone talk of Talis and a girl? Perhaps you and my wife see something that no one else does."

At the mention of Lady Alida, Hugh nicked his thumb. He did not like the woman; he found her cold and heartless. Perhaps she had not always been so, but she was now. And he had no doubt that if there was any trouble brewing, she was the cause of it. Also, Hugh could see that John was lying. There was more going on here than people were telling. In fact, lately, the whole house seemed to be full of secrets. Lady Alida riding off at breakneck speed to heaven-only-knows-where; that little nothing, Edith, suddenly acting as though she had a secret that was going to change the world.

And that poor girl Callie sent off to tend a garden of poisonous plants and tolerate that vain rooster, Allen Frobisher.

But the worst of it all was Talis. Hugh thought back to a few months ago when he had first seen Talis, on that day when the boy had saved John's life. On that day when Talis had thrown that girl into the air and caught her, Hugh knew he had never seen anything as perfectly instinctive and genuine as the united movement of those two. The two of them had moved as one person.

On that day Talis had been glorious. Hugh had never seen any young man who stood straighter, had carried himself with as much pride as Talis had. When John had declared the boy as his son, Hugh had wanted to fight him for that honor. Talis was a son any man would want to have.

But now, mere months later, Talis had lost weight, his eyes were dark and hollow from lack of sleep and his energy seemed to have disappeared. He ate little and, according to Philip, he slept less.

Had he been another lad, Hugh would have thought Talis was lovesick, but what was ailing Talis was more than love.

This morning, in a jealous rage, John had sent from his house the old farmer who'd raised Talis. John couldn't bear to see anyone receive the affection of Talis, couldn't bear anyone receiving what he did not. Talis was always respectful of John, but he did not throw his arms around him and repeatedly kiss his cheeks.

It had taken Hugh three hours on horseback to find the old man, driving a heavy farm wagon loaded with bags of grain. Even after finding him, it had taken Hugh quite a while to persuade him that he meant only good for Talis.

The old man, Will Watkins, had said that Talis was very unhappy, that he was unhappy because he could not be with Callie. But Talis would not tell Will *why* he could not be with Callie. "Something to do with 'vows to God,' was what he said." Then Will lowered his voice and his face changed to anger. "More like vows to *her*, if you ask me."

Although Will did not say who "she" was, Hugh knew.

On his way back to Hadley Hall, Hugh wondered why Lady Alida had interfered between young love. What did it matter to her if two sweet children like Talis and Callie got together? Was she so bitter over her own loveless life that she could not bear for others to be happy?

So now Hugh was faced with John's shouting and jealousy that the boy loved the man who'd raised him more than he loved John, who Talis had known for mere weeks.

"I believe," Hugh said nonchalantly, "that the boy is in love. Perhaps you should give him permission to marry the girl." Hugh acted as though he weren't watching John's face, but he was. He had many suspicions about the birth of Callie and Talis.

"I, ah, I cannot . . . I mean, I think he is too young to marry. And that girl is not right for him."

Or, Hugh thought, you are afraid the boy's true father will come to claim him and you fear to have to pay him to keep the boy. No wonder Talis gave kisses to that old farmer and not to John, who couldn't quite decide whether he loved money or a person more.

But Hugh knew one thing he had in common with John: They both hated clever, manipulative women. Hugh had no idea what Lady Alida was up to, or what she was after, but he was sure she was doing something she should not be doing.

"I think someone has told Talis it is dishonorable to so much as speak to this girl Callie. I think he believes he will forfeit his place in your life if he talks to her."

"How could he think that? I do not care if he impregnates the girl. What matter is it to me if he is . . . If he is . . . ."

"Happy?" Hugh asked, knowing that John hated sentimentality and he'd never before concerned himself with the happiness or unhappiness of anyone except himself. But life in this big house seemed to go better when Talis was happy.

"I shall order the girl to sit near him, watch him all day if he wants," John said. All he wanted was his son near him and not to lose any money.

"I think that an angry, sullen girl hissing at him from the sidelines is not the answer."

"She would not dare!" John said. "I will have her head!"

Which will, of course, solve everything, Hugh thought sarcastically. "Someone has been very clever in making Talis believe that he cannot so much as go near the girl, but I think, sir, that you are far more clever."

"Yes, of course," John said then looked expectantly at Hugh. They had been together a long time and he didn't feel like playing guessing games to find out what Hugh had in mind.

"Tell Talis that the girl's beauty's causing havoc among the young men and you need her protected from them and you want Talis to do the job. He is to keep her near him and watch that no other men touch her."

All John could do was blink at Hugh. "Beauty? Why the girl is as pale as a fish's belly. I cannot tell her from half of my other daugh— er, ah, half of the other girls around here."

Hugh forced himself not to smile, for he'd just found out the answers to many of his questions. Talis was *not* John Hadley's son, just as he'd suspected. "Talis does not know the girl is not beautiful. To him she is glorious."

"I would be making a fool of myself if I were to say such to him," John said. "The boy will laugh at me."

"No, the boy will not laugh at you." Hugh's eyes lit up. "I will give you my best charger if I am wrong," he said, speaking of a big roan horse he had bought two years back and John had always coveted.

"You have yourself a wager," John said smugly.

"And what do I get if I am right?" Hugh asked, eyes twinkling, but when John raised one eyebrow, Hugh stepped back. "It is, of course, my privilege to serve you." And with that, he turned away, thinking on why John Hadley did not have the loyalty or love of anyone.

34

"No thank you," Callie said to Talis with all the haughtiness she could muster. "I would rather go with Allen."

The three of them were at a fair in the village, the usually placid streets now alive with merchants and acrobats and the cries of hawkers. People, rich and poor, were everywhere.

"I am to protect you," Talis said, his back so rigid an oak tree was soft by comparison. "Lord John has told me I must protect you."

"From what?" Callie snapped at him. "From unwanted boys like yourself?"

At that Allen perked up, straightening himself to stand taller. He was at least two years older than Talis, and he'd certainly had more experience with women than this young man. "Come, Callasandra," he said, taking her arm.

"Do not call her that," Talis said, pushing Allen's arm away from her. "In fact, do not call her anything at all. Callie, you must come with me."

She glared up at Talis. "I do not have to go with you now or ever. Come, Allen, we must go."

Feeling that he was winning — and surely his extraordinary good looks were doing the job — Allen again took Callie's arm.

"Unhand her!" Talis half shouted, causing some interest in the people near them.

Callie moved so Talis could not touch Allen's arm, but she pulled away from the blond man as she confronted Talis. "You do not own me. You are not my father nor my brother. In fact, you are nothing at all to me. Nothing. You have no rights to tell me to do anything. Now go away and leave us."

With a great sweep of her skirts, Callie clutched Allen's arm and started to walk away from Talis.

For a long moment, Talis stood where he was, staring after them, rage filling him. How dare she! he thought. How could she treat *him* like this? Especially after all he had been through to get them together? He had been doing everything Lady Alida had asked of him, having to put up with a bunch of mindless, giggling girls who wouldn't let him train, wouldn't let him study, but just demanded that he carry things for them. "This needle is awfully heavy," one of them had said, then rolled her eyes at Talis in a way that he was sure was supposed to entice him.

All Talis yearned for were the days when he and Callie were together, the days when he didn't have to be so damned polite all the time. With

Callie he could be quiet if he wanted or talk for hours if he wanted. And, best of all, he didn't have to wait on her, fetch for her, carry things for her, do a lot of really stupid things those overdressed peahens seemed to need from him.

Now, what he ought to do, he thought, was disobey Lord John's orders and leave her here alone. If men made asses of themselves over her because of her . . . of her, well, because she was, in his opinion, by far the most beautiful creature in the world, then it was not his problem. Let that thin, no-shouldered, white-faced boy she was hanging onto take care of her.

But even as Talis thought this, he followed the two of them.

"Oh, Allen, how very clever of you," Callie said, throwing back her head and laughing, her hair catching on her belt.

"Allow me," Allen said, his hands going eagerly to Callie's abundance of hair to untangle it.

But Talis was there first, his dagger drawn as though he meant to hack Allen's hand off if he so much as touched Callie's hair.

But Callie knew what he had in mind. "You touch my hair and you'll be sorry," she snapped at him.

"Why did you have to leave it uncovered? Why did you not shove it under a cap?"

She smiled at him. "Do you mind that other men see my hair?"

He stiffened. "It is only that it catches on everything and is a great nuisance. It is a wonder the birds do not start nesting in it." Talis thought that was a very clever remark, but from the look on Callie's red face, she did not think it was at all clever.

"Allen *likes* my hair," she spat at him. "In fact, *all* the men like my hair. They like it very much."

"I did not say I did not like your hair," he said, blinking in wonder. What was wrong with her? He had teased her all his life. Why was now any different?

"Go away!" she ordered him. "Do you not understand that I do not want you near me? Go find some other woman to bother."

As he watched her walking away from him, Talis could feel anger running through him. He had done everything in the world to be with her, to show her that she was his very existence, but now all she seemed to want was this thin half-man, Frobisher.

Determinedly, he walked behind the two of them, and when they stopped at a booth of fruit pies, he leaned against the stall and looked straight ahead, as though he just happened to be there.

"Oh, yes, Allen," Callie said loud enough to be heard half a mile away, "I would love an apple pie. They are my very favorite. Thank you so much. You are a kind and thoughtful man and you know so very well how to treat a woman."

Allen was flushing with her praise as he held out a copper coin to pay the merchant for the two apple pies.

But Talis's big hand stopped him. "She likes peach pies better. In fact, she thinks apple pies are boring, unless they are coated with a great deal of cinnamon and I can tell by the smell that these are not. If you really want to please her, get her a peach pie, or apricot. But don't get the blackberry as the seeds get into her teeth, and, too, she is a very messy eater so she will get the black juice all over her gown. All in all, you had better get her peach."

"I, ah . . . ah . . ." Allen sputtered.

Callie glared up at Talis, who wouldn't look at her. "I have changed my mind. I don't really want *any* pies. Come, Allen, let us see the acrobats."

"There is a bear here to be baited," Allen said hesitantly. "Perhaps you'd like to see the dogs tear at the bear. It is great sport."

"She would hate that," Talis said, pointedly looking down over Allen's head, showing that he was at least four inches taller than the blond man.

"I would *love* that," Callie said through clenched teeth. "I have changed in the many, many months since I have seen you." She made "you" sound like something that grew in her Poison Garden.

"Oh, is that what's bothering you?" Talis asked. "The fact that I haven't been to visit you? I have been very busy lately. You know, the duties of helping all the ladies with their sewing and whatnot has taken so very much of my time. I do hope you forgive me."

442

"I do not own you," she said, trying to keep anger from her voice. "And you do not own me. Do whatever you want. Right now, I would like for you to leave us. I am with a man who understands that I am a woman."

At that she pulled Allen's arm tightly to her side and looked up at him with what she hoped was a loving expression.

With some effort, Talis managed to put his body between the two of them. "My father has given me the assignment of protecting you and I must obey him. What do you say that we look at the bookstall?"

Allen laughed. "I do say, young Hadley, you know nothing about women." Perhaps he wasn't as tall as Talis, but he was older and more experienced. "Women like excitement, something like bear baiting, not books. Women's minds were made for romance and love, not for what is found in a book. Is that not right, my dear?" he said as he raised Callie's hand toward his lips to kiss it.

"Oh, I do beg your pardon," Talis said as he practically fell onto Allen, nearly knocking him down and preventing the kiss. "Someone pushed me."

"Clumsy bastard," Allen muttered under his breath, dusting himself off from where he had slammed into a man carrying a bag of flour.

"Again I beg your pardon," Talis said sweetly, "but I am not a bastard. My father is Lord John Hadley. Pray, tell me again who *your* father is."

Allen gave Talis a malevolent look, since his own father was not the rank of John Hadley.

"Allen, please," Callie said, "pay him no attention. He is trying to make you angry. Let us enjoy ourselves and pretend that he is not here. Come, look at the cloth merchant."

Behind them, Talis groaned. "Who wants to look at cloth on a day like this? There are men walking a rope over there, and there are many things to eat."

Callie whirled on him so fast her hair spun around and hit Allen in the face. "For your information, other men are not as selfish as you are. Sometimes a man takes a woman out and does what *she* wants to do. Other men are not as selfish as *you* are. Right now Allen would *love* to look at the silks and velvets, would you not, Allen?"

"Well, I, ah . . ."

"There, you see, Mr. Son-of-a-lord Hadley, he wants to look at cloth. If I wanted to stand there all day and do nothing but look at those silks, Allen would love to be with me. Can someone like *you* understand such unselfishness as that?"

Talis had no idea on earth what Callie was talking about. He was beginning to think an evil spirit had overtaken her body. The Callie he knew would rather look at books and rope walkers than piles of cloth. So what was different today?

When Callie saw that Talis had no understanding of what she was saying, her fists tightened and she turned away from him. "Come, Allen, let us go watch the bear baiting."

"But that will make you sick," Talis said from behind her, and there was real concern in his voice. "You hate to see animals hurt."

Again, she whirled on him. "*You* make me sick! You with your ideas that you own me and know everything there is to know about me. You know *nothing* about me. Absolutely nothing. I happen to *like* bear baiting. It is a sport of skill and daring and adventure and Allen knows that I am a woman who likes excitement. I am not the dull, lifeless, prim little virgin you seem to think I am. Now, I want you to get away from me. In fact, I never want to see you again in my life."

Allen couldn't help smiling at that, for this Callie was getting prettier by the minute. When she was angry, her cheeks flushed and her eyes were bright with emotion. When she was like that, she was almost a beauty.

It looked as though at last her words had had some effect on this boy Talis, for when Callie started walking again, he stayed behind. Allen had to run to catch up with her.

Confidently, feeling that he had won a woman in a verbal joust, Allen said, "The bear baiting is that way."

She looked up at him with horror in her eyes. "I have no intention of watching a bear and dogs fight each other. I hate blood sports."

"But you said — You told that boy that — I thought you —"

"Can you never finish a sentence?" she said

445

in an aggressive way. "What is wrong with you and why do you think that a woman has not the intelligence to read a book? Do you think we women waste our lives as you waste yours lounging about under a tree all day watching me hoe a garden? Is that what you think of me?"

"No, I . . . I mean, I —"

"Yes, what *do* you mean? Come on, tell me. Speak up."

Allen took a deep breath. Were it not for all the money Lady Alida was offering him to stay with this girl, he'd walk away now. Let Talis have her, and with his blessing. The two of them deserved each other. "Would you like a cup of wine?" Allen asked, eyebrows raised. "Or perhaps I could buy you a wagon load of intoxicant and you could bathe in it."

To his consternation, Callie burst out laughing. Allen had spent his life trying to win women, so he'd kept his sarcastic remarks to himself. Sweetness won women, not hateful, stinging phrases, so he was shocked when Callie laughed at his spiteful remark.

He had no idea that his remark was exactly like something Talis would have said to her. When she was in a bad mood, he always proposed outrageous things to do to sweeten her up, such as drowning her in honey, or boiling her in sugar syrup. One hot day when they were twelve, she had been too saucy for his taste, so he'd tossed her into a wagon load of peaches, saying she needed the nectar to mellow her temper.

All Allen thought when he made her laugh was that he was indeed a very clever fellow.

Several feet behind them, Talis ground his teeth; his nails cut into his palms as he made a fist. He knew when Callie was really laughing and when she was not. Until now her attention had been on him, on Talis. He knew she did not like this white-haired popinjay. But as soon as they were out of his hearing, she laughed at what he was saying. Really, truly laughed. Laughed in a way that, until now, only he had been able to make her laugh. Not Will or Meg or anyone in the village of the place he still thought of as home had ever made Callie laugh like that. Usually, she stayed close by Talis and looked to him for everything, shared everything with him.

But obviously, now she preferred someone else to him.

The hell with her, Talis thought. If she did not want him, he did not want her.

With every muscle in his body rigid, he turned away from the two of them. Let them have each other, he thought. Let them spend eternity together.

He was so stiff with anger that when he tripped over the obstacle in the path, he nearly fell on his face. He did not have his usual ease of movement, his usual swinging walk; he didn't even have his sense of balance.

"Sorry," Hugh Kellon said, for it was his foot that Talis had tripped on. But his tone implied that he didn't mean the words. "Why are you rushing about? It's a beautiful day, there are lots of pretty girls here, but you look as though you're ready to start a war."

"I must go," Talis said stiffly. "Excuse me."

"No!" Hugh said sharply, then softened. "Stay with me. I need the company."

"I must return," Talis said, each word forced from teeth held tightly together.

"Isn't that your girl?" Hugh asked, nodding toward the figures of Callie and Allen, walking through the crowd, arm in arm.

"She is not mine," Talis said stiffly. "Now, if you will excuse me, I must leave."

"Pride is a very good thing," Hugh said loudly, making Talis turn back. "One should always have much pride. Pride is the backbone of a man."

"Yes," Talis said, glad someone understood. "Pride is very important to a man."

"*Most* important," Hugh agreed heartily. "Pride has always ruled my life and I can swear to the fact that I have *always* kept my pride. Throughout my life I have kept my pride. No matter what happened, I have always retained my pride."

"It is good for a knight to do so," Talis answered, his back stiff, refusing to look after that deceiver, Callasandra.

"Yes," Hugh continued, "when I was your age, I kept my pride no matter what, just as you are doing now. In fact, I was *just* as you are now, even to the fact that there was once a pretty little redhead I was in love with."

At Talis's raised eyebrow, Hugh chuckled. "Oh, I didn't tell her I was in love with her. No, of course not, that would not have been manly. But I loved her; I dreamed of her, couldn't sleep for thinking of her. I watched her even when I couldn't see her. Can you understand a feeling like that?"

"Yes, I can understand such a feeling," Talis said softly, thinking that Callie was incapable of feeling such a thing. Why had he not noticed before that she was fickle and unfaithful? That she could not sustain a love when it was tested?

Hugh continued. "One day when I was on the training field, she came to me, her red hair gleaming, and very haughtily announced that her mother was planning to marry her to another man. She said that if I wanted her I'd better speak up. And she said an odd thing. She said, 'I will fight for you if you will fight for me.' I wanted to tell her that I wanted to marry her more than anything else in the world, but there were a lot of boys around me and I was too proud to say such tender words in front of them, so I told her I didn't have any idea what she was talking about. You see, I knew that if I'd told her I loved her in front of the others, they would laugh at me and my pride could not bear their laughter."

"What did you do?" Talis asked, trying to act as though he were just being polite to an older man's ancient story, but he was somewhat interested. But, truthfully, what could someone as old as Hugh know of love?

"I kept my pride, of course. What else *could* I do? I had no other choice."

Talis thought that was a rather simplistic way of looking at the matter. "You could have told her you loved her. The boys would get over their laughter."

"Ha! What was I to do, fall down in the mud and kiss the hem of her skirt and tell her that I loved her more than life itself? Those boys would have laughed at me forever. They never would have stopped."

Talis was silent for a while, thinking of this. "What happened to her, to your red-haired girl?"

"She married the man her mother chose for her and they now have two boys, and three daughters with red hair like their mother."

"And you have never married?" Talis asked.

"No. I never again loved anyone as I loved her, so how could I marry another? True love comes only once in a lifetime."

"And what happened to those boys who you feared would laugh at you?"

"I have no idea." Hugh chuckled. "But I know they remember that Hugh Kellon was a man of *great* pride." He slapped Talis on the back. "So, see, boy, I am telling you that pride is the most important thing in the world. Let these other timid creatures, like that Allen Frobisher, do without their pride, but let us true men keep ours. Let the boys like that Frobisher walk beside that girl Callasandra and carry her packages. Let him buy her useless gifts. Let him hear her girlish squeals of delight. That is not manly, not prideful. You should continue as you are: aloof, distant, detached, imperious. Yes, you should continue acting as you are. You look like a young lord, too high and proud for anyone. Who cares about a silly girl's laughs, her touches, the way she looks at a man with eyes full of love? You are above such as that, are you not? You are too good, too proud to make an ass of yourself in front of all these people and let the girl know that *she* is more important to you than all the pride in the world. Yes, indeed, you are better than that. You are —"

Talis burst out laughing, at last understanding what Hugh was saying, what the point of his story was. "You think I am being a fool, don't you?"

"I think that pride makes a cold bedfellow. That girl loves you, but you have spent much time with other women of late and she thinks you no longer love *her*." Hugh liked the idea of Talis thinking he was a sage of great wisdom, but he was just telling Talis the problem as Will had told him.

Talis looked through the crowd. Callie was so far away now he could hardly see her. Will had said the same thing that Hugh was now saying, but then Talis had just laughed. Callie was *always* thinking that he, Talis, didn't love her. But in the past, when she had hinted at such nonsense, Talis had usually answered her with physical action rather than with words. The idea that she was anything less than his reason for living was so absurd that at the mention of such a thing, he would pick her up and toss her in a creek or a wagon full of fruit, or even onto a low-hanging tree branch. The first time he had thrown her in the cow pond, when they were about five, Meg had threatened to thrash him. But Callie had stepped between him and the switch and said, "Tally loves me," and she'd not allowed Meg to touch Talis.

"Go on, boy," Hugh said softly. "Don't ask me why, but women love men who make asses of themselves over them. You can knock twenty men off their horses in the joust and the woman you want to impress won't look at you. But slip on an apple skin and fall down a flight of stairs and she will in all probability fall in love with you."

Talis laughed again, knowing that now Hugh was telling the truth.

"And, boy, whatever you do, tell her you *need* her. It is what they most want to hear."

Talis gave him a look that asked, Why? but Hugh only shrugged in puzzlement. "Go on, act as though you are the village idiot. Pride is a lonely friend."

"But Lord John —" Talis began. "The other girls will . . ." He trailed off as he realized that he had been about to do just what Hugh had once done. "Yes," he said, "I can see the problem."

As Talis started to walk away, he turned back to Hugh. "Was there really a red-haired girl?"

"Yes," Hugh said and there was honesty in his voice. "And I didn't fight for her."

35

This is going to be easy, Talis thought, thinking about getting Callie back. Of course she cared nothing for that white-haired braggart she was following around. So maybe Talis hadn't been paying a great deal of attention to Callie lately — for which he had honorable reasons. But then she'd not been spending time with him either — for no reasons at all.

There was some part of him that knew she would have been with him if she could have, but she'd been given the task of working in that odious garden during the day. Talis had visited her a second time, accompanied by four of the women from the household, but Callie had not reacted as he'd hoped she would. She had not shown any of the temper he knew she had; she hadn't fought for him. In fact, she had been downright disdainful of him and his trail of richly dressed women. "Do they dress you? Do they bathe you?" she had said to him. "If I wish it," he'd answered, doing his best to raise her temper.

But her temper had not been raised. Instead, it was Talis who had been angered. "What is wrong with you?" he'd snapped at her.

She gave him an arch look, as though she knew exactly what he was trying to elicit from her. "A woman will die for a man who wants her, but she will do nothing for a coward."

He hadn't understood her meaning, but he had been enraged by her tone. He'd ridden away and stayed away from her, sure that soon she'd come to him and beg his forgiveness for calling him a coward. But Callie had not come to him to beg his forgiveness, and when she didn't, Talis had found that with each day his strength faded. Mere weeks ago he was the strongest man at Hadley Hall, but now he found himself looking at each shadow, wondering if Callie could be hiding there. All day he wondered what she was doing up on that hill with that . . . that person who stayed near her. At night he knew that she cried. If she was so unhappy, why did she not come to him? Why did she not do what the Callie of old did when he flirted with the gypsy girl? Then she had knocked over a food stall onto his head.

Right now, all Talis wanted was to get things back to the way they were. He wanted the strength Callie gave him. That was absurd, of course, since his strength could not possibly depend on her presence, but it seemed to.

What could he do to win her back, he thought. Something quick and simple, something not much trouble.

As he wandered through the fair, he saw a man with some trained monkeys ready to step onto a stage to perform. He and Callie had once sneaked away from Will to watch just such a man who had been traveling through the village. While Will's back was turned, Callie had stolen a bucket full of Will's best vegetables from the stall and taken them to the monkeys. And while she was feeding them, she had laughed in delight at their little pink hands clutching at her fingers. She had said silly things, such as they needed love and she wished she could take all of them home with her. To which Talis had replied that they wouldn't be much use to anyone if she did own them — unless she could train them to milk cows, a chore Talis hated.

Now, standing there and looking at the man and his monkeys, on impulse, Talis said, "I want to buy one of your little apes."

At that the man laughed and said that none of them were for sale, that there wasn't enough gold on earth to make him part with one of his beloved monkeys. Thirty minutes later, Talis had given the man every coin Lord John had given him since he'd arrived at Hadley Hall, and he was also minus some beautiful embroidered gloves Lady Alida had given him. But squirming under his shirt was a small, young monkey. (At first the man had tried to pawn a toothless old creature off on Talis, but he'd not spent his life on a farm and learned nothing.)

Feeling very confident, Talis made his way

through the crowd toward where he knew Callie was walking with that emaciated Frobisher. Talis was sure that all he had to do now was present the monkey to Callie and she would fall into his arms and everything would once again be all right. They would leave this fair and go to her hill and sit there and do nothing. She could spend the afternoon telling him stories and peeling peaches for him. And he'd like to tell her about his latest escapades in training. It would be nice to have her tell him he was great and strong and brave, as she used to do.

"Callie," he said, stepping in front of her, a smile of anticipation on his face. When she saw what he had for her, she was going to melt with gratitude.

"What do you want?" she asked coldly.

"I have something for you." From inside his shirt he withdrew the little monkey, holding it in his hands as it blinked against the light.

"Oooooh," Callie said, and reached for the animal, her face softening, just as he'd hoped it would.

"Talis! We have been looking everywhere for you." "Where have you been?" "You must escort us through the fair." "We want to see everything and only *you* can show us."

At the sound of the women behind him, Talis acted instinctively, shoving the monkey back inside his shirt, hiding the animal from the women.

"And I have been looking for you," he said, turning, trying to smile at the five women, all gorgeously dressed, all looking up at him with expectant eyes. *Why* did they have to come *now?* he thought. Three minutes later and Callie would have been his. "I will take you in —" he began then turned back to Callie, only to discover that she wasn't there. Already, she had taken Frobisher's arm and was walking away.

For a moment, Talis's head spun, not understanding what was going on. What did Callie want from him? What was wrong with her?

It was then that he began to understand some words he'd heard in the last few days: *coward* and *fight*. Will had said that Callie didn't think Talis loved her and Talis had laughed at him. "Have you ever *told* her you love her?" Will had asked. "Women always want words."

"Of course I have," Talis had said, but he hadn't been able to meet Will's eyes. Well, so what if he hadn't actually said the words? Callie knew how he felt. He let her know every day how he felt, didn't he? He allowed her to . . ."

What was it Will had said? "Women want more than to feed you and tell you how handsome you are. In all of Callie's stories, a man slays a dragon to win his lady fair. The man *works* to win the woman he loves."

At that moment, Talis looked at the phalanx of women coming toward him, and their glittering silk dresses seemed to be the scales of some magnificent dragon; their jewels were its eyes; the excited faces of the women were the fire coming from the dragon's mouth. And Allen Frobisher was the keeper of the dragon.

"Callie!" Talis called, running toward her — and the women picked up their skirts and ran after him. They had indeed been searching for him all day and now that they'd found him, they weren't going to allow him out of their sight.

"Callie, Callie!" Talis shouted again until she halted, an expression of disgust on her face.

Talis stopped in front of her and he was very aware of the women behind him, the insolent Frobisher in front of him, and in his peripheral vision, he could see Philip and James approaching. He did not, *not* want to make a fool of himself in front of all these people. He didn't want them laughing at him. He wanted to be a knight of great honor, someone looked up to by everyone, someone —

"What could you want with me?" Callie said, her voice dripping venom. "You have so many others waiting for you."

"Callie, I . . ." He swallowed. Then he took a deep breath. "I love you."

Heaven help him, but he was so nervous that the last words came out so loud he halted about fifty bystanders. And of course the women, Frobisher, Philip, and James, were riveted to the spot.

"Talis!" Callie said, her eyes wide. "People are staring." She was trying to let him know that this was something private, not something others should hear. They had always been careful to keep their feelings from others — at least they thought they did.

459

To his astonishment, Talis could feel sweat on his brow. He usually loved a crowd watching him; he was a natural exhibitionist and loved an audience. But pouring his most intimate feelings out for everyone to hear was not something he relished doing.

"I love you," he said again and this time it was easier.

Callie blushed. "I am glad," she said softly. "We will talk of this later. Now you had better leave. There are people waiting for you." She nodded toward the women behind him, then started to leave with Allen.

"No!" Talis said, making Callie look back at him. "I don't want you to go with him. I want you with me."

One of the women stepped forward and put her hand on Talis's arm. She was Lady Frances, a cousin to the Hadley family and quite beautiful. Lady Alida had secretly promised her marriage to this delicious young man, so she could not allow him to continue talking like this. "You must come with me, Talis," she said firmly.

"Yes, you must go with her," Callie said, starting to turn away.

For just an instant, Talis hesitated and Callie saw that hesitation. And in that flash Talis knew what it would mean to lose Callie. What did he care if these people heard what he felt in his heart? Heard that he loved her? What was anyone or anything without Callie?

"Callie," Talis said. "My love, my only love,

460

the love of my life. I love you. Do you not care at least a little for me?"

Callie was sure that even the soles of her feet were blushing. She'd wanted Talis to tell her that he loved her, wanted him to let those spiteful women know that he cared for her, but she did *not* want to be embarrassed in front of the whole village. "Please, Talis," she said, turning back toward him.

But he wasn't there. It was a second before she realized that he was walking on his knees toward her, his hands clasped to his heart. When she looked at him, he put his hands out beseechingly to her. She was so stunned she couldn't speak.

"Callie, my own true love, tell me you love me too or I shall die here and now."

"Really, Talis!" said Lady Frances, who, unknown to Talis, thought she was his bride-to-be. "You are making a fool of yourself."

"If to be in love is to be a fool then I am the most foolish of men. I will die a fool. Callie, please, you must tell me you love me."

Callie wanted the earth to swallow her up. To say they had gained an audience was an understatement. People were deserting the paid performers to watch this gorgeous young man make an ass of himself.

"Yes, yes, I love you," Callie said quickly and quietly. "Now get up from there and behave yourself."

Actually, now that Talis had started this masquerade, he was finding that he rather liked it. Every man near them — and there were more by the second — had a look that said, I've been where you are. And the women were looking at him as though he really were the slayer of the dragon.

Talis grabbed the muddy hem of Callie's skirt and raised it to his lips. "My beautiful Callasandra, I am not worthy to kiss this sacred garment."

"Then *don't!*" Callie said, snatching her skirt out of his hands.

"Talis!" Lady Frances snapped. "This is *not* proper behavior for a young knight."

"How can I act any other way if my heart is bursting with love? I can feel nothing but this pain in my heart because my lady love has not said she will forgive me. I fear, dear, ah, onlookers, that I have neglected her sorely. I have, oh please, will you forgive me, I have been enticed away from her by the radiant beauty of *other women.*"

"Can't blame him there," a man muttered, then yelped as his wife twisted his ear.

"Talis, please," Callie hissed at him. "Get up from there."

"Not until you say that you forgive me."

"Yes, of course I'll forgive you," she said hastily. "Just get up!"

"I must have your love *and* your forgiveness. I must —" At that he slammed his clasped hands into his chest and the poor monkey, who had been gratefully sleeping, let out a squeal and tried to claw his way out of Talis's shirt. Too bad he tried to dig through the skin side instead of the fabric side.

With a yelp of pain, Talis drew the angry little fellow out and offered him to Callie. He made this offer with great show, bowing his head, holding the monkey in his hands, Talis still on his knees.

At the sight of the little animal, Callie gave a bit of a smile.

"Go on," a man urged. "Take it."

It was Lady Frances's voice that scared the animal. "Talis, I have had enough of this! I am not feeling well and you *must* take me home! And get rid of that nasty thing." She only meant to push the monkey out of Talis's hands, but the poor animal had had enough mistreatment for one day. With a quick lash, he turned toward Lady Frances and bit her finger, drawing blood instantly. And when she screamed as though she'd been pierced with a lance, the frightened animal leaped from Talis's hands, jumped onto Allen's shoulder, grabbed a handful of his hair, then, when Allen swatted at him, the monkey vaulted onto a rain barrel, where he sat blinking at the crowd.

"Oh, Tally," Callie said, tears in her voice. "You can't let him get away."

It was at that childhood name that Talis knew he had won Callie back. And knowing that she was once again his gave him new strength. Drawing his sword in a dramatic gesture, he raised

463

it to his face, his nose touching the blade. "I will give my life to this quest, my lady fair. I will die if I do not bring this creature back to you. I will climb the highest mountain, walk across fire, swim oceans. I will —"

"Talk it to death, most likely," Callie said, making the crowd laugh. "Go on, lazybones, get the monkey!"

Feeling the happiest he had since arriving at Hadley Hall, Talis rose from his knees, tossed his sword to James, then started toward the rain barrel where the monkey still sat, looking as though it didn't know what to do. As Talis passed Callie, he lifted her hand as though to kiss it. "If I may, my lady? One touch of your sweet skin, one caress of your hand, one —"

He stopped because Callie, frustrated with his everlasting talk, grabbed his head in her hands and gave him a resounding kiss on the mouth. "Stop talking and *go!*" she said, pushing him away from her.

To the accompaniment of raucous laughter — by now there was no one at the fair who was not watching this unrehearsed drama — Talis started toward the stack of barrels. There were people on rooftops, climbing on anything, including shoulders, to better see.

"Sssssh!" Talis said loudly to his audience as he approached the frightened monkey, moving with exaggerated tiptoeing that the crowd found hilarious. "Please, dear little creature," Talis was saying loud enough to wake the dead (or, in his case, to reach the furthermost onlooker), "you must not run away. I need you to prove to my lady love that she is everything to me. I must show her how much I love her. I must —"

Lady Frances, sick of this idiocy, pushed her way through the watching throng. "Really, Talis, this is no way to behave. Lady Alida will be very angry with you."

"Ssssh," Talis said to her, his finger to his lips. "I must rescue this sweet creature."

"It is a nasty little thing and I —" Lady Frances broke off when she realized that everyone was watching them and that *she* was being seen as the villain. "Scat!" she said to the monkey, and the frightened little animal leaped from the rain barrel to the roof. And at that, she picked up her skirts and made her way out of the crowd.

For just a moment, Talis hesitated. The roof the monkey had climbed onto looked as though it might collapse at any moment. It covered a derelict stables, open-fronted, and inside was an ancient donkey chewing powdery hay. No one had bothered to repair the roof in years; there were holes in it, and other places that looked as though they might fall through at any moment.

But Talis thought again of the last months without Callie by his side, and he hesitated no longer.

"No!" Callie shouted, her hand firmly about his ankle as he climbed onto the third barrel. "Talis, this has gone far enough. That roof is not safe. You could be hurt."

Looking down at her, his eyes were not teasing;

they weren't the eyes of a man who was putting on a show for an audience. "I would rather die than try to live without you," he said, and the words came from somewhere deep inside his heart.

He had not meant for anyone except Callie to hear him, but in truth about half a dozen people heard, and his words were recounted to those who hadn't. It was rumored that three women fainted from the sheer romance of what he'd said, but then it could have been the closeness of the crowd.

However, Talis lightly vaulted onto the ridge-pole and began to balance himself along the steep pitch. He knew that if there was any strength in the roof it was along the main pole. If he so much as stepped onto the roof itself it would no doubt give way under his weight and he'd plummet.

Feeling like the rope walker he'd wanted to go see with Callie, Talis began to walk the pole, his arms extended, toward the little monkey sitting at the far end.

Callie thought she was going to die, her hands clasped to her chin, her breathing fast and shallow as she looked up at Talis walking along that ridge.

"Slowly, slowly," someone beside her whispered, and she saw that it was the rope walker, the man she'd seen performing. "He's got good balance. If he keeps his concentration, he will make it."

Talis did make it. He managed to walk all the

way to the end of the ridgepole, then he cautiously squatted down and reached for the frightened monkey. Since the monkey knew that people meant food, it did not run away. However, the creature was just out of Talis's reach, just barely at the end of his fingertips.

Below him, everyone in the crowd held their breath.

Callie, her heart beating in her throat, stepped closer to the roofline of the building.

"Planning to catch him if he falls?" a man asked, making the crowd laugh.

Yes, Callie thought. Yes, I'll catch him in my arms. The next moment, she gave a shout, "No!" as Talis lifted his foot from the ridgepole and started to step forward onto the rotten roof.

But Talis had a look of determination on his face, and when he had that look, Callie knew there was no stopping him. Cautiously, he took one step onto the roof, then another. At the third step, he reached the little monkey and it not unwillingly scampered into his arms.

In triumph, Talis held the animal up to show Callie, and she couldn't help clapping her hands in happiness. And the crowd gave one great shout of victory.

It was probably the vibrations of the shout that shattered what was left of the roof, sending it crashing to the ground — and Talis with it. One second he was on firm footing and the next he was sent sprawling into the dirty hay below him.

What made the crowd howl with laughter was

that Callie ran after him, as though she did indeed mean to catch him before he hit the ground. What happened was that Talis, Callie, and the monkey all landed in a heap together, next to the enraged donkey.

For a minute or two the old stables were alive with the screeches and screams of the monkey and the donkey. Callie's hair wrapped itself around Talis and somehow caught the monkey as though it were once again in its cage.

"Hold still!" Talis was shouting, trying to free them.

But Callie couldn't hold still because the little monkey was trying to tear her hair out by the roots, and the donkey was fighting them all for his share of the food.

All in all, it was the best play the townspeople had ever seen: romance, excitement, breathtaking spills.

When Talis and Callie were at last able to untangle themselves — and no one offered to help — Talis, with great ceremony, presented the pretty little monkey to Callie. "With all my love," he said loudly.

When she accepted the monkey, Talis made gestures that said that now his life could truly begin, then he led her out of the dirty stables and they headed toward the hill where her Poison Garden lay. Behind them the crowd laughed and agreed that this had been the best fair they'd ever attended.

36

Seventeen Years After Birth

1588

"I hate men!" Callie said with vehemence, brushing the monkey's tail out of her mouth as she spoke.

She and Dorothy Hadley were in what had once been the Poison Garden. It was still called that, but the character of the garden had changed under the care of Callie and Dorothy. It had been a whole year since Callie had first come to Hadley Hall, and after the first chaos of everyone finding his or her place, things had settled down. Callie spent her days taking care of her garden, with Father Keris happily dozing in the shade, a hoe near him in case someone should happen up the hill (after all, he *was* in charge, wasn't he?).

Two weeks after Callie had been sent to the garden, Dorothy found that she missed her very much, so gradually, Dorothy began to ease herself out from under Edith's rule and spend her days with Callie. In the last year, for some unknown reason, Edith had become more angry and more of a tyrant than ever, and, besides, Callie was a great deal more fun than any of her sisters.

Dorothy never told anyone this because they might laugh at her, but while she and Callie worked in the garden, putting order into what had been little more than a patch of weeds, Callie often told stories. Wonderful stories, stories of great romance without all the fighting that the jongleurs put in their stories. In Callie's stories the women were strong and courageous and brave and very often saved the hero's life.

Dorothy gave a great sigh as she weeded a clump of monkshood. "I would like to spend enough time with a man so I could come to hate him. As it is, saying that I hate men is like saying I hate cinnamon. It is too rare to make a judgment." As Dorothy said this, she glanced up at Callie, hoping for a compliment on her joke.

As always, curled around Callie's neck or her wrist or even sitting on her head, was the little monkey Talis had given her. Callie had named him Kipp, and the animal was so grateful for the kindness and love, not to mention good food, it received from its mistress that it never left her. When it was frightened it would sometimes scurry under Callie's skirt and cling to her ankle or knee. But, always, it was with her.

But Callie didn't laugh at Dorothy's witticism as she usually did. "If you knew them you would hate them," she said seriously.

Dorothy sighed. "What has Talis done now?"

"What makes you think my hatred has anything to do with him?" Callie snapped. "What makes you think *I* have anything to do with him?"

Dorothy gave Callie a look that said everything. Personally, Dorothy was beginning to think that loving only one man was like having only one food to eat. It became quite monotonous after a while. "You think of him, dream of him, live for him, your every thought, your —"

"Ha!" Callie said, but she turned away from Dorothy and attacked some wolfsbane with a hoe, her abrupt action causing Kipp to give a squeal and nearly choke Callie with his tail. "Well, if I did ever think of him, which I do not, it would do no good. He has no time for *me*. He spends all his time with other women. He dances with them, sings to them." She narrowed her eyes. "He *fetches* for them."

As Dorothy watched, amusement growing on her face, Callie began to parody Talis and the many women who surrounded him. Callie deepened her voice. "Oh dear lady, may I help you carry that very heavy needle? May I be allowed to walk behind you and caress the stones your feet have touched? May I be allowed to breathe the air that you breathe? May I please kneel at your feet and allow you to use my body for a footrest?"

Dorothy couldn't help giggling. Callie was so funny. Even when she didn't mean to be, she was quite amusing, which is why Dorothy spent her time with Callie rather than with her sisters. Also, there was something about Callie that attracted men; they liked her. Callie was completely unaware of this fact as her every waking — and probably every sleeping — thought concerned Talis, but daily, men and strapping boys found a reason to stop by the garden. Like as not, Callie would put them to work in the garden, which was why in a mere year she had managed to take something awful and make it into something beautiful.

Callie was now mimicking a huge woman walking, a great clumsy oaf of a thing, and then she was a bigger-than-life strutting man (who could *only* be Talis) looking up at the fat lady and rolling his eyes in ecstasy. He was telling her she is as dainty as a fairy, as lovely as a moonbeam, as delicate as dandelion fluff.

Callie jabbed at a harmless root with her sharp-edged hoe. "Talis has become a liar and an all-round worthless human being."

"I think he is just learning courtly etiquette," Dorothy said, but she did not tell Callie her true feelings. What was happening with Talis and Callie had something to do with her mother, Alida, but Dorothy didn't know what was going on. Why was it important for Talis to have lessons on every conceivable subject but not important for Callie?

"Etiquette is to tell some fat ugly woman that she is beautiful?" Callie asked, but it wasn't really a question.

"If she is also rich, yes."

"Then he *is* a liar."

Dorothy continued hoeing for a while. She had

become used to Callie's anger. If she was not with Talis then she was angry at him for not being with her. "Have you ever thought that Talis might marry one of these rich women?" Dorothy asked quietly. "For all that he is my father's favorite, he is a younger son. There will not be much money for him. Talis will have to marry wealth if he is to live well."

"Yes," Callie said, her voice sounding like death. "I have thought of this."

Dorothy took a while before she asked her next question. Part of her wanted to know what was going on, but part of her wanted to stay out of it. Unlike Edith, who never suspected anyone of ulterior motives, Dorothy always thought that what people said had nothing to do with what was true. "Has Talis told you that he wants to marry you?"

When Callie answered, her face was pale and she could barely be heard. "No."

At that answer Dorothy knew for certain that her mother was involved. She didn't know what her mother was doing, or why, but she knew it was her mother. Alida loved intrigue. Loved to tell one daughter something and another something else. Dorothy had seen it many times. If Talis was not telling Callie every day that he was working to marry her, then there was a nefarious reason.

Dorothy saw the way Talis looked at Callie, how he watched her whenever she passed. The most beautiful woman in the world could be in his arms, and if Callie passed, Talis would drop her. This was not just Dorothy's observation but every woman's who made a play for the beautiful Talis. All the women worked hard at taking him away from Callie. In truth, his love for another woman made him even more valuable, as he was unattainable.

So, if he hadn't spoken to Callie of marriage then there was outside interference. Honestly, Dorothy was terrified of her mother, but maybe she could help a little bit, because as far as Dorothy could tell, there was no reason why Callie and Talis shouldn't marry and produce half a dozen children — and her father could pay for it. Maybe if they did marry it would inject some happiness into Hadley Hall.

Dorothy hesitated at telling Callie a story because Callie was so very good at storytelling, but, tentatively, she started. "Did you ever hear how my third eldest sister got her husband?" She didn't wait for an answer. "She went to bed with a man."

Startled, Callie turned to look at Dorothy and waited for her to continue. Second only to telling stories, she liked to hear them.

Acting as though she weren't smiling throughout her body, Dorothy continued her story. It was pleasing to get the attention of a practiced storyteller like Callie. "By the time our second sister was married, we knew our father was never going to get husbands for the rest of us. He complained incessantly about the money a dowry and wedding would cost. Most of us were too young to concern ourselves with this, but Alice decided to take matters into her own hands. One night after a hunt, she chose a man, sent a small keg of wine to his room then, much later, climbed into bed with him. She had her maid, who she paid handsomely, run weeping to fetch our father, and there he found his daughter in bed with a man. The man was married to my sister before he was sober."

Callie took her time before answering. She had not missed Dorothy's point. "That would never work with Talis," she said slowly and it was obvious she had thought of this trick. "He has such a sense of honor. He says that a man cannot get married if he has no money. And, besides, he is not . . . interested in me. Whenever I get too near him, he turns away."

Dorothy tried to hide her smile. This was one aspect of love she did not envy. Callie always thought Talis did not want her, that he lusted after other women. But Dorothy had seen Callie stretch, her gown expanding across her newly formed breasts, and at the sight Talis's face would turn white with desire. Dorothy had thought that if a man ever looked at her like that once in her life, she might die happy. Well, truthfully, to be safe, she'd rather like to have most of the men on earth look at her like that.

But always, by the time Callie finished stretching, Talis had managed to turn away, and the next moment he would be furiously attacking another man in mock combat. As far as Dorothy could tell, Talis combated his lust for Callie with physical exercise — which is why he was always in a frenzy of motion, dancing, riding, hunting, practicing with his sword. Once, when Edith had said, "Does he never sit still?" Dorothy had laughed out loud. As long as Talis's desire for Callie was unquenched, he would never sit down. In fact he was losing weight. No matter how much he ate, it wasn't enough to balance all the exercise he was getting as he tried to overcome his lust for Callie. One woman said that Talis rose before dawn to swim in the icy river that ran not too far from the house. But that couldn't be true; no one could stand those frigid waters.

"Perhaps Talis needs a little encouragement," Dorothy said. "Maybe a push over the edge." Personally, she thought that the push of a feather — a feather guided by Callie — might break whatever hold Alida had over him. "Perhaps he needs the right place and time. If he . . . had his way with you, would his honor not force him to marry you?"

"Yes . . . ," Callie said tentatively as she pulled Kipp from around her neck and held him in her arms to stroke his soft fur. "Do you think he really thinks of me as a woman?" She wasn't about to admit to Dorothy how many times in the last year she had tried to get Talis to kiss her. But every time, he had pushed her away, saying things like "I cannot bear it" and "You will drive me mad." If he'd just *tell* her that he wanted to marry *her* and not one of those hundreds — nay, thousands — of women hanging around him, she would be happy. If he *told* her he wanted her she would be content, but he didn't. He said nothing.

Dorothy continued. "If one of your story ladies was in love with a man who was surrounded by beautiful women, what would your lady do?"

Callie smiled. "She would force him to look at *her*." She gave a malicious little smile. "Preferably naked."

Dorothy smiled. *This* was why she spent so much time with Callie. Callie had the courage to put into words what Dorothy felt. Perhaps it was because Callie had been raised on a farm, but at times she was so very . . . very unladylike.

"I think she would . . . ," Callie began as she started weaving another one of her stories. At the sound of that special tone in Callie's voice, Kipp closed his eyes in contentment and Dorothy opened hers wide in anticipation.

Once again Talis was standing before her and again Alida felt love run through her heart. It always amazed her that in the last year she had come to love this boy perhaps more even than her husband did. With each day she could feel her strength leaving her, and she knew that the old witch woman had been wrong: She would not live out another year. She hid this knowledge from Talis, but every day she coughed up more blood. Only the herbs Penella gave her kept her

477

from coughing in front of Talis.

Now, as he did every day, Talis was telling her about his great feats of that day, how he had excelled at this and that, how he was the best there was at everything. Alida would have thought he was bragging, but the truth, according to the reports she asked for, was that he was actually better than even he said he was. She liked that he told her all about himself, liked that he was her best friend.

Of course she refused to believe what that horrid old maid of hers, Penella, said, that Talis was telling her about himself to show that he had learned enough that now he should be allowed to marry Callie.

"He enjoys my company!" Alida had spat at her maid.

Penella had learned her lesson; she had learned that food and survival were more important than protecting anyone. So she kept her opinions to herself, but that didn't keep her brain still. Truthfully, Penella thought it was disgusting the way Alida flirted with Talis; no one with any sense would think they were mother and son.

On the other hand, Alida treated Callie as a mother would, always criticizing her, never wanting her to look too pretty. If Alida happened to see Callie and the girl's hair was unbound, Alida nearly had fits.

It was Penella's opinion that Alida was using Talis to make up for the way John had ignored his wife all these years and the way her children, sick of being bullied by her, came to her only when they had to.

"Come, sit by me," Alida said, motioning to the sheepskin at her feet. She loved to have Talis sit on the floor at her feet so she could run her fingers through his hair while he talked. His daily presence helped to make up for the fact that none of her own children ever came to see her unless commanded to do so. It was a bitter taste in Alida's mouth that her sons, whom she had done so much for, worked at avoiding her. As for her daughters, she sometimes thought they had no use at all for her. Sometimes she thought that Edith even hated her. And merely because Alida had saved her from marriage, that institution that in Alida's experience gave nothing but misery. Better to stay unmarried and in your father's house than to turn yourself over to a husband.

Only Talis came to Alida every day and talked to her as she lay alone and weak in her room.

"I want to marry Callie," Talis said softly.

Alida gave a great sigh. Now came the bad part. Every day the same thing. Every day he said the same words, asked the same question. And every day she wanted to tell him the *truth*. Talis was destined for greater things than to marry John Hadley's daughter.

"When you ask me if you may marry Callie, to me it means that you are wanting me to die, since you will be allowed to marry her after I am dead."

This statement did not shock Talis, since he

had heard it many times before. "That is not true. I want to marry Callie because I love her and I want to be with her."

"Will you not have enough time with her after my death?"

Talis did not turn to look up at her in sympathy at the mere mention of her death as he usually did, so Alida knew it was time to try another tactic. "Perhaps if she troubles you too much and you cannot keep away from her, I should send her to her father." At that Talis turned a face filled with horror toward her. "Although I would hate to do that. You have not seen what Gilbert Rasher is like. He is a brutal man; I fear for someone as delicate as your Callie to be under his rule."

"No!" Talis burst out. "Do not send her to him. I will stay away from her. I will do anything to keep her here." He turned his face away from her, not wanting anyone to see the look of desolation on his face.

Alida stroked his hair. "It will not be for much longer. I will be out of your life soon."

Cupping his chin, she turned his face toward hers, then smiled at him. "Come and read to me. Do not be sad in these my last hours. Soon I will be under the cold ground and you will be happy then."

Slowly, as though he were in pain, Talis got up and went to a shelf where Alida kept her precious books. As she looked at him in the sunlight, she knew how much she had come to love him, and she was glad she was going to be able to give him what she could. She was fading fast and her death was coming soon; she could feel it. But before she died she wanted to see Talis at court. How she'd like to see him with the queen. The queen would like him so much!

As Talis began to read to her, Alida stroked his hair. He'd soon forget the pale girl he thought he loved. In the glamour of the court, in the sunshine of the queen's smile, Talis would forget everything that had happened in his past. He'd forget those rustic farmers he'd grown up with; he'd forget that girl who was not beautiful or rich enough for him.

Yes, Alida thought, everything would work out well: Her own sons would inherit the property she had brought to her marriage, and this glorious young man would go to court, would entice the queen with his exuberance and love of life — just as he'd seduced Alida into loving him.

Yes, she thought, it was time for everything to begin. She must send for Gilbert Rasher today.

"And what do *you* care what I do all day?" Callie spat at Talis, her eyes flashing at him as though they were on fire. "What business is it of *yours?*"

Watching them, Dorothy felt sick with the sight. Never in her life had she seen two people more in love than these two; they were the dream of every girl growing up. Talis thought only of Callie; Callie thought only of Talis. Yet why did they not see what everyone else at Hadley saw clearly?

Now, Callie was, as always, hoeing in her garden, and, as always, there were five young men offering to "help." Two of the men were quite good-looking, and one of the others, the farrier's son, had a homely face, but from the neck down he was quite a sight to see.

The only person who did *not* see all this pulchritude was Callie. These handsome young men came to her, hoping to win the hand of a nobleman's daughter, yet all Callie saw was free labor.

But when Talis arrived, *he* saw his beloved surrounded by men, as though she were a queen with her courtiers.

The entire situation further convinced Dorothy that a woman should never love one man, at least not love him to the point where she could not even *see* the attentions of other men. Dorothy was sure that there could be a line between blind love and utter stupidity.

"You are under my care," Talis said stiffly, looking at the broad back of the farrier's son as he bent over a hoe. All of the men around Callie pretended they weren't listening, but they were. The only person not listening was Father Keris, who was, as usual, asleep under a tree. Even that made Talis fill with rage. Why did not the old man protect the two young women in his charge? And why did she *always* have to have that damned monkey clinging to her? Never mind that he had given it to her. It was just that . . .

"Under *your* care?" Callie said disdainfully, interrupting Talis's thoughts. "And who made you my keeper? You are never here. You are always with *her*."

It took Talis a moment to understand who Callie was referring to. Which of the many boring, ugly women who surrounded him was she jealous of? Not that he'd ever tell her, but there were times when he was so bored by their inconsequential talk that he thought he'd go mad. With Callie he could be himself, he could be lazy or sad or happy or silly or whatever he wanted to be. With these other women, he had to pretend to be what they wanted him to be. Always he had to be courteous and courtly and strong.

"My mother?" Talis asked, his eyes wide. "You are jealous of the time I spend with my mother?"

"*Is* she your mother?" Callie asked softly. "She doesn't look like you."

Talis was aware of the talk, but what did it matter whose mother she was? He could see that she was dying, could see that she was eaten with loneliness, and he knew that he was the only one to visit her voluntarily. He also knew that if he were allowed to marry Callie, he would probably do just what she feared and abandon her.

"She is —" Talis began then cut himself off. He couldn't tell Callie that Alida was dying.

"There is something you aren't telling me,"

Callie said, and he could tell she was on the point of tears. "We never used to have secrets from one another."

How very much Talis wanted to tell Callie everything that he had sworn to keep secret. He did not understand why he could not tell Callie that he wanted to marry her. When he asked Alida why, all she said was that Talis would never look at her again if he made it known that he was to marry Callie. And then Alida would have to die alone. How could he turn down Alida's last request? Wasn't it a mortal sin to refuse a person's dying request?

"Sometimes we can't know all there is to know about a person," Talis said, and even to himself he sounded pompous. He didn't want to keep a secret from Callie. It was very hard not to tell her how, every day, he had been begging to be allowed to marry her. Keeping this vow was the most difficult of all the promises he'd made to Alida.

Except for vowing to leave Callie a virgin. That was the worst. He wanted her so much that he could hardly bear to touch her hand. If she got too near him he had to get away from her as fast as possible.

One day Hugh had seen Talis as he watched Callie walk across a courtyard, her hips swaying. Afterward, Talis had spent three hours in a blind frenzy of activity. As Talis was dripping sweat, drinking from a gourd, and trying to get the image of Callie out of his mind, Hugh stepped beside him and said, "Your honor is battling against the lips and thighs and breasts of Callie. Do you *want* to win?" It had been all Talis could do to keep from collapsing into tears at Hugh's understanding — and at the provocative image of Callie's lips and thighs and breasts.

Now, here she was standing in the midst of all these men and complaining that *he* was not constant in his love for her. *She* was the one who was not constant. If she loved him, she should believe in him. He was with the other women because he had to be. Lady Alida — he could not call her his mother even in his mind; Meg was his mother — said he had to be trained as a knight before he could marry Callie, the daughter of a man who was related to the queen. Part of his training was learning to dance and sing and play the lute and all the other things that took so much time and involved so many obsequious women.

That Callie did not understand these things without being told angered him. He had told her he loved her; what else could he do?

"I must leave you now," he said abruptly. She was breaking his heart and she did not even know it.

Turning on his heel, he walked away from her, and did not look back even when she threw a clod of dirt and hit him in the back with it. Nor did he turn back when the laughter of the men standing near her rang out over his head.

For a long time, Dorothy lay beside Callie, listening to her crying. Or rather, felt her crying, for Callie was utterly silent in her weeping, poor little Kipp sitting beside her, twitching its head as it looked at Callie, sometimes extending tiny pink fingers to touch her tears. In truth, Dorothy thought Callie's crying was almost eerie, these nightly tears that came from somewhere inside her and found their way out her eyes. Once, in a failed attempt at humor, Callie had said, "It is my heart melting and pouring down my face. If I cry enough, I will have no heart left, and when my heart is gone my tears will cease."

Tonight they were staying in the little house with Father Keris. They'd learned to say that he was ill and they needed to nurse him back to health so they would be allowed to stay there instead of going back to the house. To both Callie and Dorothy it seemed that with every day, the atmosphere of Hadley Hall became more oppressive. It was as though a storm was building and would soon burst with such fury that they would all be destroyed.

So, whenever they could, Dorothy and Callie stayed with Father Keris, who slept through whatever they did or said.

"I cannot take any more," Dorothy said, sitting upright in the bed she and Callie shared, her fists pressed over her ears. "I am sick of *both* of you. Sick of you, do you hear?"

"Who?" Callie asked, sitting up, rubbing her

eyes, Kipp clinging to her waist. "I have no idea who you could mean."

"The devil you don't!" she said, shocking Callie into awareness. "Now you listen to me, Callasandra, you are going to *do* something about putting both you and Talis out of your misery."

"I have no idea what you mean," Callie said loftily. "Talis Hadley means nothing to me. Just because —"

She broke off at a vulgarity from Dorothy. "Talis wants you so much he is becoming flesh and bone. He cannot eat for wanting you so much; his studies are suffering. Yesterday he fell off his horse when you walked past him."

"Did he? I did not notice. If he did fall, I am sure it had nothing to do with me. I —"

Dorothy grabbed Callie by the shoulders and gave her a shake, ignoring Kipp's squeal of protest. She wanted to tell Callie the truth, that Lady Alida was behind whatever was going on and only heaven knew what her motives were, but Dorothy had a keen sense of self-preservation. It was better to leave her mother's name out of all this.

"It is Talis's sense of honor that keeps him from you and that is all. You should be proud of him, not angry with him."

"But I do not believe that. I do not believe Talis wants me. Why should you? Have you seen how beautiful Lady Frances is?"

"And have you seen how selfish she is? You do not think she is half as beautiful as she thinks herself."

Callie gave Dorothy a look of disgust. "Yes, and we all know how much weight a man gives to a woman's mind. Look you at Edith: plain face and a good mind but no husband."

"And me," Dorothy said softly, saying what Callie could not. "I know, do not say it. I am a very nice person, but I am not beautiful enough to have a man fight my father's stingy ways to win me." She would not allow Callie to comment on this very true statement. "But *you* have a chance! You have what my sisters and I want so much."

"You mean Talis? Do you mean that *I* have Talis? How could I have him when all the others —"

Dorothy repressed the urge to smack Callie for not seeing what was so plain. All Dorothy knew was that she wanted to get these two people together before her mother could do whatever it was she was planning. If it killed her, Dorothy wanted to see some happiness in this rich house. Too much gold and not enough love was her opinion.

"Now listen to me," Dorothy said, "and help me to form a plan. Do not tell me more of how Talis does not want you. Think of this as one of your stories and help me plan."

When Callie looked skeptical, Dorothy smiled. "You are right, this is probably beyond your storytelling abilities."

Callie's expression changed. "What story do you need? I will tax my poor brain and see what I can manage to create."

"All right, now listen to my plan."

It was hours before Dorothy got to sleep and Callie didn't sleep at all that night. In the morning both young women were smiling in conspiracy.

37

"I do not know why you would want *me* to ride with you," Talis was saying as he rode beside Callie into the woods that were John Hadley's private hunting preserve. "You have so many other young men to escort you wherever you go. I do not know how you tolerate someone as lowly as *me,* you with a father who is an earl, who is the relative of the queen."

Talis himself wanted to stop the words that poured out of his mouth, but he couldn't. Yesterday Callie had sent him a message saying she wanted to ride with him, and after his initial elation, he had begun to worry about being able to keep his vows to Alida if he were alone with Callie for very long. In the year since he had declared that he loved her — in a spectacular drama before the entire village, as he remembered it — he'd done his best never to be truly alone with her.

She was wearing a gorgeous cape of blue wool, with a big hood edged in white fur. It was almost as though she were trying to make herself too beautiful for Talis to be able to resist. Today he did not even seem to mind the furry face of the monkey peeping at him from inside the folds of her cloak at her waist.

"I am thinking of getting married," Callie said, looking at him over her shoulder.

For a moment, Talis couldn't breathe, but then his spine stiffened and he put his head up. "Yes, that is a good idea. You are getting old and you should be married."

"I agree. I would like to have children. Tell me, do you think I would be a good mother?"

How could his back have become stiffer? It seemed that even the muscles in his throat were tightening. "Yes, of course," he said.

"Good," she answered, smiling. "Today I thought we might go somewhere private and you might tell me what it is that a man and woman do to make babies. I do not want to go into my marriage as ignorant as your sisters. You are my friend and you must tell me *everything*."

Rage melted the stiffness in Talis's body. Turning in his saddle, he reined his horse to a halt and faced her, his face red. "You asked me to come all the way out here with you in weather that looks like a storm is about to break to tell you — to tell you about . . . about . . ." He was so angry he couldn't speak.

"Oh, I see," Callie said casually, kicking her horse forward. "You know even less than I do.

491

I was not sure, since you spend your life with so many women."

"I know everything!" he shouted, moving beside her. "I know all there is to know. But you . . ."

"Yes? What about me?"

What made him so very angry was the fact that she was half smiling at him, as though what she was saying was not the most horrible, the most despicable, the most — He broke off as he realized that she was teasing him, that there was no other man and she wasn't actually thinking of marrying anyone other than him.

He smiled at her. "Lady Frances has taught me all that goes on between a man and woman. Do you not think she is beautiful?"

At that he had the satisfaction of seeing Callie's face turn red with anger, then before he could stop her, she dug her heels into her horse's flanks and set off at breakneck speed. He'd made sure that she was given a horse that was more suitable for children than an adult, while he had taken a huge black monster that Lord John had forbidden anyone to ride. Talis had disobeyed because he wanted to impress Callie — if that was possible.

Just as Callie's horse went charging through the forest, a bolt of lightning split the sky and the heavens opened into a downpour. It was minutes before Talis could get his frightened horse under control and go after Callie.

When Talis found her, his heart leaped into

his throat, for his first thought was that she was dead. She was lying lifeless on the ground under a tree, the rain not yet penetrating through the thick leaves. To Talis, she looked like an angel fallen from heaven. In the fall from her horse her hair had come unfastened and now it lay about her in a heavenly cloud; her cloak was open and her gown was torn at the neck, exposing one bare, creamy shoulder and the beautiful, perfect round of one breast. After having teased her for so long about her flat chest, he had been fascinated to watch over the last year as she had made up for lost time. Kipp was near her face, and when he looked up he seemed to be imploring Talis for help.

Talis was off his horse while it was still moving. "Callie!" he shouted, running to her and pulling her into his arms. "Callie, my love. Speak to me. Callie, I will die if you are hurt. Please, Callie, please."

He was holding her body so close to his, her face pressed to his shoulder so hard that he barely heard her groan. When he knew she was alive, he felt his eyes fill with tears.

Pulling her face away from him, but still holding her so tightly she could hardly breathe, he stroked her cheek. "Callie," was all he could whisper, then began to kiss her cheeks and forehead and hair in relief that she was still alive.

"I am hurt," she managed to whisper.

"Hurt? I will take you back to the house. I will get the finest surgeon, the best —"

"My ankle. I am sure it is broken and my leg hurts. I do not think I can stand."

"My horse —" He had started to tell her that he'd take her back on his horse, but the skittish creature was nowhere to be seen. However, Callie's horse had been taught to stand and was —

"Where is your horse?"

"How would I know where my horse is?" she snapped.

Talis was still holding her, but he was looking about him with a frown. This was odd. He had purposefully chosen that horse for Callie because it was so safe. It was attached to humans and would never leave its rider stranded. In fact, one of the stable lads had joked that the horse could not be got rid of. So where was it?

"Oh, my foot, my foot," Callie groaned. "It pains me. And my side and my head also hurt."

The rain was coming down harder now and cold drops were penetrating the roof of the tree. With a squeal at getting hit in the eye by an icy droplet, Kipp scurried under the folds of Callie's cloak. Talis knew that they would need to get home soon. He must find one of the damned horses and get Callie back to safety as soon as possible.

Carefully, he laid Callie down on the ground and started to get up to look for the horse.

She sat up on her elbows. "You are more interested in your horse than you are in *me*?"

"No," he said hesitantly. "We need a horse

to get back to Hadley Hall. I must —"

"You aren't even going to *look* at my ankle?" At that she fell back against the ground in what could have been a faint.

Instantly, Talis was again beside her, again pulling her into his arms, and for a moment his mind whirled with thoughts. It seemed to make the most sense to find a horse and get back as soon as possible and have someone who knew more about injuries than he did look at Callie.

"Oh, Tally, it hurts so much," she said, limp in his arms. Pliable. Helpless. Totally dependent upon him.

With one arm still around her, he reached for her foot to try to look at her ankle. Callie was a bit smaller than other girls her age, and compared to Talis she was tiny, but even at that, he could hardly reach her ankle while holding her. In order to see her injury, he had to pull her skirt up past her knee just to see her ankle.

Oddly enough, there didn't look to be any swelling around the joint.

As he was looking at her ankle, trying to see the wound, Talis wondered why he had never before noticed that Callie had such delicate ankles, nor had he been aware of how gracefully her ankle curved into her calf. She wore thin, almost transparent hose that were made just for her leg and fit her like skin.

"My leg," Callie whispered. "Higher. My leg hurts very much. I think it is bleeding."

With a hand that shook just a bit, Talis raised

her skirts higher on her leg. When had she started wearing all of these female undergarments? If they'd been on the farm and he'd found out she was wearing delicate stockings, he would have laughed at her. These things would not hold up for even one afternoon's jaunt through the brambles.

But right now he had never seen anything as alluring as these pale pink stockings that stretched up Callie's shapely leg. Slowly, with his mind nowhere near his purpose of seeing whether or not she was injured, he held her upper body with one arm and lifted her dress with his right hand.

The stocking stopped just above her knee and was tied in place with the most extraordinary thing he had ever seen. It was a garter made of pink ribbons and white embroidered cloth; there were tiny hearts sewn onto the cloth. The garter was frothy and feminine and Talis had never in his life seen anything as fascinating as that piece of fabric. It was as though he could not take his eyes off it.

As though time were suspended, his eyes moved to above the garter and there he saw Callie's thigh. Just a few inches of skin before her skirt concealed her body. Her skin was as pale as spring sunlight, the curve firm, seeming to invite his hand to touch it.

As he lifted his hand, a loud crack of lightning brought him back to reality.

In one frantic, terrified movement, Talis dropped Callie to the ground and jumped away from her. "I must find the horse. I must find the horse," he said, and the water on his face was more sweat than rain. "I must get you back to the house. I must —"

For a moment Talis thought he heard some rather vulgar words come from Callie but he was sure that couldn't be true. If she'd said such a thing, it was probably just the pain from her leg, or maybe that damned monkey twisting her hair. Whatever the problem, he realized he had to do something *now*. Jumping up to grab the lowest hanging branch of the tree, he swung himself upward.

"What in the world are you doing?" Callie yelled up to him as he quickly and agilely began to climb the tree.

"I'm trying to see the horses," he called down to her.

It was at that moment that, coming from the other direction, Callie's horse appeared and she grimaced. "The only horse ever born that can't find its way back to the stables, and *I* have to have it," she muttered. Glancing up to be sure Talis was involved in his mad dash to the top of the tree, Callie ran across the grass into the rain to the idiot horse. It was looking at her as though it wanted her to take care of it — which it did.

Callie loved animals but she loved Talis more, so what she did, she did with a feeling of guilt. From inside her pocket she withdrew a little bundle of herbs from her own garden, a posy she had prepared for just such an emergency as this, and tied it to the horse's bridle. With one whiff of the herbs, the horse turned and ran in the general direction of Hadley Hall, and Callie, with Kipp clinging to her belt, scurried back to her place under the tree.

When Talis came down from the tree, Callie was reclining on the ground, which was growing damper by the moment. Talis saw that her dress was disarrayed so that one leg was exposed to above her knee, the other to midcalf. He knew it could not be possible, but it was almost as though her gown was torn more at the shoulder than it had been and now it seemed to expose more of her breast than it had. Was he being punished for having laughed at her flat chest of a year ago? Couldn't she have *stayed* flat? *Why* did she have to look so ravishingly desirably beautiful?

"Callie?" he said, then when she did not open her eyes, he fairly shouted, but he did not stoop and take her in his arms again. "Callie! We must get out of here. You are wet through and the rain's coming down harder. We must . . . ."

Gracefully, she opened her eyes and when she spoke she sounded as though she were at death's door. "I cannot walk. You must go and get help. Get . . . get Edgar, the farrier's son. His house is near here and he is strong enough to carry me back to Hadley Hall. He will not need a horse."

At that Talis swept Callie into his arms and

she snuggled her body against him, her face in his shoulder, her arms tightly about his neck. "You will harm yourself carrying me," she whispered, her lips against his ear. "Your back —"

"Save your breath; you need your strength," he said tightly. "I can carry you to the ends of the earth, if need be."

"Are you sure you need no help?"

Talis didn't bother answering that. However, it *was* miles back to the hall and the rain *was* coming down harder with every minute.

"What are you thinking?" she asked, managing to turn her body so her breasts were pressed against his chest.

Water was dripping off the tip of his nose. "That I'd like to know why that stupid horse of yours ran off. That was very odd. And I'd like to know why you insisted on riding this far out when I *told* you there was going to be a storm today. Anyone with half a mind could see that a storm was brewing, yet you —"

At that moment Callie was sure that if any man in history had ever been romantic, it had been an accident.

"Oh, Talis," she began to wail. "I am so sorry. I have been awful to you lately. Really awful and I wanted us to get away from everyone just to be alone. Like we used to do. I just wanted to tell you that I loved you and I am sorry that I have been so horrid. Can you ever forgive me?"

Callie knew that groveling from her was one of Talis's favorite things in life. Abject apologies often got her what pride could not.

"Well, perhaps," he began, blinking away rain that was cascading over his lashes, down his nose, and splashing straight onto Callie's face.

"I am sorry it all worked out wrong." She had to shout to be heard over the rain. "But I truly am in pain. Couldn't we stop? Isn't there any place we could . . . well, rest until this is over?"

"Are you talking about the farrier's again? Is *that* where you want to go? Would you rather —"

"No, of course not. Isn't there someplace near here?" she asked, trying to cut through the jealousy that was blinding him. She tried again to make him remember. "A hut or something? Someplace dry and warm."

"This is hunting land, you know that. Callie, really, I'd think you'd have more sense than —" He cut off as he had a thought. "Yes, there is a place near here. It's just a cellar and it has no door, but it's better than this."

Callie had to hide her face so he wouldn't see her smile.

"No!" he said, shaking his head against the rain. "It is better to get you back home."

At his words, Callie really did feel like weeping. "Talis, please, let's stop. It's raining so hard I can't see and I'm so cold."

"Since when has rain bothered you? We've walked for miles in the rain together. You love walking in the rain and now you're not even having to walk. I'm carrying you."

"But look at me, I'm soaked." She moved her

body away from his so she could show him her wet gown. She was not wearing a corset. In fact, she wasn't wearing much at all under the thin white woolen bodice of her gown, and as a result, the dress was almost transparent. "Look at me! Talis, you are *not* looking." But even in the rain she could see that his face was red. Obviously, he *had* looked.

Slipping her arms back around his neck, she pressed her breasts against him. "Please, if you know a place where I can get dry, please take me there. Maybe we could sit and rest. My ankle does hurt so much."

Talis didn't say a word but kept walking as though he meant to carry her to China.

"Oh, I see. You're afraid to be alone with me," she said. "How very flattering. I had no idea you thought I was so beautiful that you could not be alone with me. Some knight *you* will make! You can only keep your vows if you are not tested. Yes, I understand now."

Talis turned so fast Callie had to clutch his neck to keep from spinning away from him and Kipp dug his fingers and toes into her waist as he held on. It really was cold and Callie really did have on a very thin gown with almost nothing on under it. Had it not been for the concealing cloak she would never have left her room wearing so little. But it was all for a good cause, she told herself.

Minutes later they were in the little shelter built into the side of the hill.

501

When Talis had gently placed Callie on a clean, thick bed of new straw, and Kipp had delightedly begun to burrow into the straw, he began to look about him with interest. Even when Callie let out a loud groan, he gave her only cursory attention, but kept looking at the interior of the shed.

"What is wrong with you?" she snapped, getting more frustrated by the minute. Why couldn't he give his attention to *her?*

"Look you at this place," he said. "Mere weeks ago this was no more than a shack. There was not even a door, but now the place has fine new straw in it and it —"

He broke off as, behind him, the door slammed shut. When he ran to the door, he found that it was locked! Locked from the outside. He spent several minutes running his hands over the door, examining it.

"Callie," he said seriously, "something very strange is happening. This door has new forged iron hinges. The iron is not rusty."

"Obviously, someone was preparing the shed for use."

"If that is true, then why was the door standing open when we arrived? Rain rusts iron. And why isn't this place being used now?"

"Perhaps the people plan to use it tomorrow and some lazy workman forgot to close the door."

"What could this place be used for? It is too small for storage, too small for housing. And why would someone put a four-inch-thick oak door on a cellar that has a dirt and timber roof? The roof will melt before the door gives way. And, besides, this land belongs to Lord John, and since he bought it he uses it for hunting only. He has trespassers whipped."

"Yes, well," Callie said, her tone conveying how uninterested she was in what he was saying. "That must be it. This hut was to be used for a poacher-catcher. As a place for someone to spy from."

"Really, Callie, that makes no sense. A spy cannot 'hide' in a place with a door that can be locked from the outside. A spy would —"

"Talis! I do not know what this place is for. I do not know why someone has gone to all the trouble to put new hinges and new crossbars on the door on this place. I —"

Talis looked at her, his head cocked to one side. "I did not say the crossbars are new."

"Of course you did. And if you did not then I can see from here that they are new."

Talis was thoughtful. "No, the crossbars do not look new. In truth, the wood has been taken from somewhere else. Callie, it is almost as though someone wanted the door to appear old. They are new but look old. I wonder —"

For a moment Callie looked at him and didn't seem to have anything to say to his speculations. Then, she hugged her arms about herself and shivered. "Talis, I am cold." To emphasize this, she sneezed three times. "You stand there talking about that door while I am freezing to death."

Talis's face was very serious. "Yes, I know

503

you are cold and I will get us out of this. I swear to you, Callie, that I will get you home."

With her lips tight, she said, "You cannot get out of here. This building has stone on three sides and a hill on the other. The door is four inches of stout oak and the hinges are new iron. You can*not* get out."

While she was saying this, Talis had turned to look at her as though trying to understand what she was saying.

She gave him a hard look. "Now, I think the best thing for us to do is to prepare for spending the night here. In the morning someone will come to fetch us."

For a few moments Talis stood there, as far away from her as he could get in the small space, and seemed to consider what she was saying. Callie was so innocent, he thought. She still seemed to think they were children and they could sleep snuggled together with the guiltlessness of children. No doubt she imagined them together in the straw, holding each other and sleeping in peace.

But Talis had only to look at her and he knew that, on his part, there could be no innocence. Her cloak was open, exposing that white wool dress that clung to a body with many newly formed curves. If she had grown breasts could she not have had the courtesy to grow them a bit smaller? Every man in England was going to look at her and —

Best to stop those thoughts, he told himself.

Turning away, he looked back at the door. He had his sword with him so maybe he could somehow break the hinges. Or maybe he could cut his way out the door. Or perhaps there was a loose stone in the walls. Or —

At a sound from Callie, he turned back toward her. To his absolute horror, her cloak was puddled on the straw and she seemed to be unfastening her gown. She was leaning against the stone wall, standing on one foot in a way that made her hip jut out and her breasts thrust forward.

"What are you doing?" There was real fear in his voice.

She spoke to him as though he could see the obvious. "I am removing my wet clothes. I told you that I am freezing."

Logic, Talis thought. Filling the brain with logic would help him keep his head cool. "And how do you plan to get warm once you are . . . are unclothed?"

She halted with her hands on the ties of her gown, which was now unfastened to her waist. Did she have *nothing* on under that dress? he wondered.

Callie gave Talis a sideways look. "I had not planned that. I . . . we could . . ."

It was innocence on her part, Talis was sure, but Callie was fluttering her lashes at him in a way that made him think of a couple of ways they could use to get warm. "The straw!" Talis said gleefully, as though he'd just had the most brilliant idea ever. "You can burrow under the straw. Deep, deep down inside the straw. Very far down into it. The farther down into the straw you go the warmer you will stay."

"And what of you?" she asked softly. "Where will you stay to keep warm?"

"Me?" He gave a movement to show that his own comfort had not been a consideration to him. "I will of course spend the night trying to get us out of here."

Callie's face lost its calm, almost seductive look. "But Talis! You cannot stay awake all night! I have told you, the walls of this place are made of stone and the door is —"

At those words Talis knew that Callie doubted him. It was the first time she had ever done this, so it did not anger him. But her doubt of his abilities made him resolve that he *had* to show her he was able to take care of her. Also, it was about time he spoke to her with truth; he must show her that he was an adult, not the child she seemed to still think he was.

Going to her, he put his arm around her, then kissed her cold cheek. "Listen, my sweetheart, I have never failed you yet, have I? And I won't fail you now. I do not mean to worry you but I do not think anyone will come for us in the morning. We are too far away from anywhere. We might stay here days and no one would find us. Now, while I am fresh and rested, I must do whatever I can to get us out of here. Do you trust me?"

Callie let her body in its half-unfastened gown lean against him limply. "Talis, my love, it is not that I think you cannot get us out of here. If anyone could, you could. It's that . . ."

"Yes? What is it?"

"Nothing," she said tightly. "Go on, spend the night hacking at the door and tearing your hands on the stones. What do *I* care? What does it matter to me? Go on, go do your honorable deeds."

Talis had no idea what she was upset about but in the last year he'd never been able to figure out what was wrong with Callie. When she pushed away from him, she almost fell, but when he tried to help her stand, she pushed him fiercely. Her actions made Talis know that he had to get them out of there. He had to once again win her trust of him; he had to make her look at him with eyes full of belief that he could do *anything*. If he died trying, he was determined to get them out of there.

But an hour later, Talis had made no more headway in getting them out of their cold prison. Callie had tried to interest him in something or other that she was doing, but Talis was concentrating on his mission and didn't so much as look around. He knew that now she was buried up to her neck in the straw and she was angry at him, so angry that it was something he could feel, like the wet of his cold clothing. But the more he felt her anger, the more determined he was to get them out of their prison. He could bear most anything except Callie thinking he was incompetent.

A scream from her finally got his attention. Turning abruptly, he saw her flailing about under the straw. The monkey, asleep nearby, looked up in interest.

"Fleas!" she screeched. "There are fleas in here."

Instinctively, Talis took the one step to close the distance between them, just in time to catch a naked Callie in his arms as she rose from the straw as though she were some golden creature rising from the sea.

"Help me," she cried. "They are everywhere on my body. Help me find them."

For seconds only, Talis ran his hands over Callie's delicious body as he tried to rid her of the fleas that were, according to her, scurrying over every inch of her body.

But he could not stand such torture long. Pale, shaking, sweat on his forehead in spite of the cold room and his nearly frozen wet clothes, he jumped away from her. Then, as though he were some great animal of uncommon strength, he used his sword to hack a hole through the dirt roof. Dirt flew everywhere, great clods of it flying about until Callie had to put her arms up to shield her face, Kipp screeching in protest at his disturbed slumber.

When Talis had cut a space barely large enough for his body, he grabbed a beam and hauled himself out into the cold, driving rain. Within seconds, he flung open the door. But Talis did not look at Callie, still standing in the midst of a pile of straw that hid her naked body from the knee down. He kept his back to her.

Very sternly, as though she had no other choice, he said, "Callie, put your clothes on. We are going home."

"But Talis," she began. "I think we should stay here. I think —"

He kept his back to her. "Then I will go and get a horse and come back for you."

"You cannot. It is too far. It will take too long." There were tears in her voice.

"I will run."

"Talis, you cannot run all that way. It is miles."

He lifted his hands skyward. "Callie," he said in exasperation, "I could run for miles and days. Perhaps for years. I could run to the ends of the earth. I could —" But he didn't say another word before he began to run, run as fast as he could move to put distance between himself and Callie's beautiful nude body.

But he didn't have to run far for he found Callie's horse with its reins caught in some bushes, so he was able to return to Callie very quickly.

Later, after he was able to rescue her, Talis was quite proud of himself for what he had done. But for some reason Callie was so angry that she wouldn't speak to him and her unjustified rage made Talis angry. When did girls, people you could have fun with, turn into women, who were incomprehensible?

Their ride back to Hadley Hall had been in silence and Callie didn't thank him even once for rescuing her.

38

"And what are you smiling about?" James asked Talis as he stretched out beside him, Philip taking the other side. "In truth, you have been most pleased about something these last weeks."

When Talis didn't answer, Philip also began urging him. "Come now, you can tell us. We are your brothers."

Talis was lying on the bank of the river that ran not far from Hadley Hall, his hands clasped behind his head and looking up at the azure of the sky. Nearby Hugh stood with his horse as it drank from the river. All morning Talis had been training with his brothers, but there were times when he could hardly keep his mind on what he was doing.

"Tell us!" James demanded.

Knowing the value of making his listeners wait to hear the story — something he'd learned from Callie — Talis took a moment before he answered.

"Callie is trying to seduce me."

That was not what James and Philip had expected to hear. But the words made their minds whirl with the possibilities. They were always trying to seduce the girls who worked about the hall, and here Talis was saying that a woman was trying to get him to . . . to . . .

"What has she done?" James whispered, awe making his voice almost inaudible.

Talis's face had a dreamy expression as he looked up at the sky. "Locked us alone together in an old cellar. She'd had a new door put on."

James looked at Philip across Talis's inert form and wiggled his eyebrows. "Oh yes, I am sure this is true. If I see a shed with a new door then I know it is because a beautiful woman is trying to seduce me. Do you not also find this true, brother?"

"Most certainly. It is one of the certainties of life. A new door equals a lustful woman."

Talis was grinning broader. "Laugh all you want but she never stops. It is night and day." Images began to float through his head: Callie naked in the shed; days later holding her dress up to show her bare legs when she was crossing a pond that was hardly deep enough to cover her toes; the frequency with which she tore the tops of her gowns.

"Yes," he said happily, "Callie is trying to seduce me."

"How do you know?" "I doubt if she is." "You probably just think she is," his brothers replied in unison.

"Every time I look up, she is naked or at least

partially so," he said softly, and in his mind he began to list the things she'd done in these last weeks since the time in the shed. He would have died before he admitted that he had not figured out what she was doing that first time in the storm. But since then he had understood and driven Callie nearly mad with feigned stupidity. He was praying that the more naive he was, the harder she would try.

"Perhaps you 'boys,'" Talis said, to sound as though he were the older and wiser of the three, "would suggest to her that she rise from the sea wearing nothing but her hair. Or, since there is no sea near here, the cow pond would do as well. Yes, I would like that. Callie wet and wearing just her hair."

It was a moment before the other two could get their mouths closed. James recovered first. "I see. Callie is trying to seduce you but you, being the very strongest of men, have resisted all of her attempts."

"Yes!" Talis said fiercely. "I have not touched her."

"And this not touching her has been easy for you?" James continued, with Philip beginning to smile, seeing where his brother was leading.

"I am a man of honor," Talis said loftily. "I do not take what I have no right to."

"So *this* is why you haven't been sleeping," Philip said.

"And why you come from our lady mother's room in a rage, with tears in your eyes."

Talis didn't like anyone to think he was less than a man of great strength and nobility. "What you say is not true. I am immune to Callie's childish pranks, but she is female and I must allow her to do what she wants. I enjoy the sight of her but I can control myself. I will not touch her."

"Is this why you do not eat? Is that why your ribs are beginning to show through your clothes? Talis, brother, why do you not just take your beloved Callie to bed, then she will *have* to be married to you."

How many times in these last weeks that were so filled with pain and pleasure had he thought this very same thing? But a vow was something that must be honored. When he spoke, his voice was serious. "There are things you cannot know."

Philip was the first to speak and his voice was bitter. "We know our mother *very* well. She finds out things about people and uses their own weaknesses against them. Talis, you should protect yourself against her."

At these words Talis grew angry. Could they not see that their mother was dying? She grew weaker every day, but still not one of her children visited her without a summons. Only Talis visited her every day. And he was ashamed to admit it, but his brothers were right: Most days he emerged from Lady Alida's room with tears staining his cheeks. Every day Talis begged Alida to release him from his vows, telling her he could not take much more. In a lapse that he now regretted, he even told her the truth about Callie, that she was trying to seduce him. On his knees, Talis had begged Alida, telling her he wanted Callie so much, that he loved her more than he loved money or great deeds. Life would be nothing without her.

But Talis couldn't tell Philip and James any of this. First of all, he had to protect his masculinity and, second, he would not believe what they were saying about their own mother.

"There are things you do not know," he repeated stubbornly. "You should not talk about our mother like this."

"Then why can you not marry Callie?"

There was no answer Talis could give.

"He cannot marry her because that would make our esteemed mother jealous," Philip said. "Our mother has grown to love you." Instead of envy or jealousy in his voice, there was a sound of relief.

"I am glad she does not love me as much," James said. "When my mother loves someone she expects his soul in return."

Talis could not stay there and listen to what they were saying about a woman who had so little time left to live. But the worst thing was that their words were beginning to sound true to him. He went to stand by Hugh with the horses, stroking a horse and frowning.

"Love is all to a woman," Hugh said after a moment.

At first Talis did not hear him and when he

did, he didn't understand what he meant. He thought Hugh was talking about Lady Alida. "Yes, perhaps she does love me. I do not count that as a sin."

"No," Hugh said. "Not her. Your Callie. She is everything in this matter. Do not make light of her. That Callasandra of yours is full of pride."

"I *know* what Callie is like," Talis snapped at him, tired of all the advice and teasing he'd received that day. No one knew the truth of what he was going through these last weeks. On one side he had Callie doing her best to get him to make love to her, and on the other was his mother daily reminding him of his vows to God to leave Callie a virgin.

Talis knew that it was true that he was many pounds lighter and he hadn't slept but a few hours in the last weeks. Yes, he thought, Callie was indeed proud, but so was he. He, Talis, was very, very, very proud.

With a glare at Hugh to let him know that he'd heard all he wanted of his advice, Talis walked away from him.

"It begins," Alida said, leaning back in the bed and holding the letter to her once-plump bosom. "Gilbert Rasher is on the way to claim his son." Pausing, she smiled a bit. "And the groom has arrived."

Penella barely looked up from her chore of shoving Alida's clothes into the big carved oak chest at the foot of the bed. Wrapped inside one

516

of the garments was a small silver dish; later she'd return for the dish and add it to her growing cache of items. Should she ever again be sent away, she would not be without funds. Never again was she going to leave her welfare in the care of others. She explained her thievery by telling herself that the Lord helps those who help themselves.

"Your beloved Talis will not go with his father. His heart and soul are with that girl." As Alida dwindled in strength, Penella became bolder. What had once been love for her mistress was now disdain.

Alida hardly noticed her maid's insolence. Her mind was now fully occupied with Talis and providing for his future. "I have thought of that, which is why I have chosen a man for Callasandra to marry."

At that Penella gave a snort. "The boy will not allow such a marriage, nor will your daughter." Penella refused to pretend that that great, strapping, black-haired boy was Alida's son.

Alida lay back against the pillows and closed her eyes for a moment. "I am not so ill that I have lost all my senses. I do not plan to ask either of them what their wishes are. Before I die I mean to see Talis on his way to the queen, and I will do whatever must be done to ensure that. Now, come help me to look good, for the man is here."

"The man?" Penella said, trying to act disinterested, but she hated it when her mistress did anything that she had not told her about first.

"The man who is to be Callasandra's husband. I have found her one. Do not look at me like that! He is a good man, honest and kind. I have done what I could to console the girl for the loss of my Talis, so I have chosen well for her. He is handsome and intelligent. He is everything a woman could want."

"He is not Talis," Penella muttered.

Alida ignored her as she turned her face so Penella could comb the other side of her hair. She imagined that she looked like a fair, frail maiden, but in truth she was emaciated, the muscles in her face and neck mere strings, and her eyes glittered with her sickness.

"Is he rich?" Penella asked.

"He is now. I have given him much to marry Callasandra. He is to meet her and marry her in the same day."

At that Penella paused in her combing, but quickly resumed. It wasn't any of her business what Lady Alida did to her own daughter.

There was a knock at the door.

"Let him in! Go on, quickly," Alida said, making Penella give her a look of disgust. She was acting like a girl about to receive her lover. Had Penella not been treated so badly by her mistress, she might have felt sorry for her dying loneliness. But now she felt only repugnance at the woman's behavior.

Peter Erondell was indeed handsome, with dark red hair and a pleasing freckled complexion. He was not tall, but he was broad shouldered and strongly built. And when he saw Lady Alida he smiled at her without flinching, kissing her raised hand as though she were a beautiful woman instead of the stringy old chicken she was now.

"You are well?" she asked, fluttering her pale lashes at him.

Penella was glad she did not have to remain by the bed to see more of the display, but went instead to answer the door and admit Callie. Penella did her best to harden her heart to the girl, but even now, before Callie heard what was to happen to her in this room today, she had a haunted look in her eyes, as though she had already given up on life.

Penella knew exactly what was wrong with the girl because she had heard every word that Talis had said to Alida, as the ravaged boy had begged and pleaded to be allowed to marry this girl he loved so much. Since Alida had so very cleverly, so heartlessly not allowed the boy to tell his beloved that he *wanted* to marry her, Penella knew that Callie, like most girls, worried whether her love was returned.

Penella snapped her head around. It was none of her business!

"Here she is," Alida said, motioning toward Callie as she stood there with her head down, not seeming to care where she was or what was being done to her. "Is she not what I told you she was?"

Penella knew that any man would want Callie,

with her shapely body and her blonde hair peeping from under her cap. She was an appealing little thing.

But Sir Peter shocked both the women. "But this is the girl from the Poison Garden," he said. "This girl is the light o' skirt of young Talis." He turned an angry face to Alida. "Madam, you have played me false. I was given to believe I was to marry a virgin, one of your own daughters. This . . . this creature is little better than a harlot. All of Hadley Hall and the village know that."

With that, he turned toward the door, meaning to leave.

It took a great deal of strength that Alida did not have to spare, but she shouted, "No!" with so much force that she halted him.

"The girl is a virgin. I swear it. She will be examined and you will see. Please . . ." Alida said. "Have I not given you enough money? I have a thousand more acres in Scotland. I will give you that."

The man paused with his hand on the latch. "I will not marry a girl who gives birth to another man's bastard within six months. I will not be laughed at the rest of my life."

"I do not ask you to. Penella will examine her. She will tell you —"

"Do you think that I would trust your maid? No, she will be examined by my sister's maid. She is here with me. I will fetch her." At that, he left the room, showing Alida that he was eager for the match — if the girl proved to be a virgin.

Through all of this, Callie had stood by in wide-eyed silence, not understanding anything that was going on. But now she was beginning to understand. "No," she whispered.

Seeing that a storm was about to start, Alida waved her hand toward Penella. "Take her away to wait. I do not have time to hear her protests. Go, now, I am tired."

Penella clamped her hand on Callie's arm, but Callie jerked away from her and ran to the side of Alida's bed.

"What!?" Callie demanded. "What is going on? What do you mean to do with me?"

Penella did her best to harden her heart to the look of anguish on the girl's face. Had Callie been raised with this family she might have been prepared for the sudden and absolute decisions of Lady Alida, but Callie was not. She had grown up under the love and protection of two kind-hearted sweet-natured people, and that love had not prepared her for the machinations of a woman like Alida.

"What is it?" Callie wailed. "What are you doing to me? Please, please, I beg of you to tell me."

"The man you have just seen is to be your husband by nightfall."

Callie backed away from her mother until she was against the wall by the head of the bed. "No, this cannot be. I am to marry Talis."

At that Alida turned to face her, her eyes flashing brilliantly. "Talis!" she said with contempt.

521

"*You* to marry Talis? Whatever made you think such a thing could be? You think you are so clever, yes, do not deny it, I know what you have been doing. You *are* no better than a greensleeves for the way you have thrown yourself at the feet of that dear, pure boy. But thank the Lord he has more sense than to throw himself away on the likes of you."

Anger gave Alida energy. "How could you think yourself clever and not guess the truth? Everyone else has. Talis is not John Hadley's son; he is Gilbert Rasher's son. And you who think you are so important that you can disobey me, you are *my* daughter. You are merely the daughter of a lifetime peer, while Talis is related to the queen. Since Talis knows this, you think he would go to bed with you and risk impregnating you? If he had to marry you, all he could hope for would be to become a knight. But as Gilbert Rasher's son, he can go to court and marry according to his birthright. Do you not know how very proud Talis is? Do you not think he *wants* to marry into the royal family? His father wants to marry him to Arabella Stuart, and if he succeeds, Talis could become king."

Alida lifted herself up on the bed. "Do you hear that? King! But what would he have if he was forced to marry you? And make no doubt of it that if he did go to bed with you, his sense of honor would force him to marry you. And what would he have then?"

Stretching, she moved closer to Callie, whose

face by now was as white as parchment. "How can you be so selfish as to think only of yourself? Can you ask Talis to give up the possibility of being king in order to live with you in some farmer's hut? For that is what he would have. His true father is coming here now to claim him and everyone knows Gilbert Rasher hasn't two beans; his only wealth is in his son, Talis. If Talis refuses to go to court and claim what should be his, Rasher will cut young Talis off without a farthing. And my husband will be so angry he will give Talis nothing. All he will have left is that dirty farm he grew up on. How will you feel ten years from now to see your precious Talis bent and stooping over a plow, and knowing that only your lust and selfish motives kept him from the throne of England?"

Callie was too stunned to speak. Talis as king! It was how she had always thought of him, but was it what *he* truly wanted?

Taking advantage of Callie's silence, Alida waved her hand. "Take her away to await the man's maid."

With her hand firmly on Callie's arm, Penella pulled the girl into the little antechamber that adjoined Alida's room. It was in here that Penella slept and spied on her mistress. Painstakingly, she had bored a hole through the wall so she could see and hear whatever her mistress did.

Penella could not bear to look at Callie's face. Always pale, Callie now looked as though she were all eyes that stared out of hollow sockets, sightless, frightening eyes.

"Here, take this," Penella said, not unkindly. She had found that with a full belly each night, her former fear and even her memory of those years in the kitchens were dulling and she could once again afford to give kindness.

Callie did not take the wine Penella offered, but turned beseeching eyes up to her. "If you have any mercy in your soul, help me get out of here. Help me to go to Talis. I must see him."

"I cannot," Penella said with finality. She was not going to lose all that meant so much to her just to save this chit of a girl. What did the girl mean to her?

"Please, I beg of you," Callie said, clutching at Penella's arm.

"No!" Penella said sharply, twisting away and meaning to put an end to the matter.

"You do not know what you are doing when you deny me this," Callie whispered. "You do not know. Talis is my life. He is all to me. If I do not have him, I do not want life."

Penella crossed herself at those words, then gave the girl a stern look, the look of an adult who knows everything. "You are just a child and you do not know what you say. You think you love this boy but love is based on years with a person. This man your mother has chosen for you is a good man; he will give you many children and —"

"If I cannot have Talis's children, I do not want any."

524

"You have no idea what you're saying. Come, drink the wine. When you hold your first child in your arms you will be laughing over this." Even as Penella said the words, she did not believe them. This was no child talking of losing a childhood sweetheart. There was indeed death in the girl's eyes.

Callie collapsed on the small bed in the room, drew her knees into her chest and put her head down. "I wish I had burned up in that fire the day after I was born. I curse whoever saved me. I curse that person to the end of time."

At that epithet, Penella felt her body tremble. She did not know if she believed that a person could curse another throughout time, but if it were possible, she knew this girl was able.

Perhaps Penella was signing her own death warrant, but she could not stand by and let her selfish mistress have her way with other people's lives. "Take this," Penella said to Callie, handing her a silver candlestick, one that she had stolen from Lady Alida. "Take this and hit me with it, and when I am insensible, make your escape."

Penella knew this was the coward's way out, that being found unconscious and the girl gone put all the blame on Callie and none on her, but it was better than nothing. She had learned her lesson of protecting herself too well to risk everything now.

"Go on," she urged Callie when she hesitated. "You must do it now while she sleeps. She will awaken soon and your chance will be gone."

Callie hit Penella with the candlestick, but it was a blow that would not have hurt a kitten. But as the girl went running from the room, Penella took a small fruit knife and made a gash on the side of her head to give evidence that she could not have stopped the child.

"May the Lord watch over you," Penella whispered as she looked out the window and saw the girl running toward the woods behind Hadley Hall. She dearly hoped that she never saw either Callie or Talis again; she prayed that they would escape.

39

Callie did not hesitate as she made her way to the shed that she and Dorothy had so cleverly prepared for the seduction of Talis. But that day Talis — damn him! — had been even more clever than they; he had found a way out of the shed. Had Callie thought it possible for him to go through the roof, she would have had bricks laid atop it.

But Callie had not thought of that means of escape, and as a result she was still a virgin, a marriageable woman. If he were given a great deal of money as well as the assurance that no man had touched her, that red-haired devil would accept her as his wife.

As Callie ran, she paused only long enough to remove Kipp from his hiding place under her skirt and pull him to her waist, where the little monkey hung on for dear life. Callie's fear transmitted itself to him and he did not protest the bumpy ride.

When at last she reached the shed, she sat down

in the midst of the clean straw she and Dorothy had had taken to the shed, the straw she had meant to use for her seduction of Talis, put her head on her knees and began to call Talis to her. Only once, as children, had they used it in earnest, and that was when Talis had been lost when he was a boy. Many times they had thought the same thing at the same time, arrived at the same place at the same time, but they had only laughed about the coincidence. And if either was hurt, the other always came right away.

But now Callie knew that her very life depended on seeing Talis and seeing him *now*. He must choose freely. She must know that he loved *her* more than he loved anything else, and that included his honor and his pride. She knew she could not tell him of the marriage she was being forced into, for if Talis knew, his honor would force him to marry her.

And all her life, Callie would feel that she'd tricked him into marriage. But if he chose her freely, with no strings, no threats, then she would be justified in jeopardizing a future that could possibly be glorious. But he must choose her over everything else — including his honor.

Even as Callie sat there, using her mind to call Talis to her, she knew that his honor and his pride were everything. If Talis's hesitation were caused by another woman, she could fight her; she could wear revealing clothes, do things with her hair. But Callie had nothing so ordinary as a woman to fight; she had to fight what was inside Talis himself.

It was not long before Talis arrived, out of breath from a neckbreaking ride on a horse, his sword drawn. He looked dazed, as though he did not know what he was doing there, as he did not.

"What is it?" he demanded of her. When he saw that there was no blood dripping from Callie and that all her limbs were intact, his face changed from the fear he'd felt as the urgent, not-to-be-denied call inside his head, to one of annoyance. "Callie, I ran from my father at your call. Do you know how this makes me look? One minute my father is personally instructing me on the use of a sword and the next I rudely leap on Hugh's horse and ride away. I am sure they all think I am insane."

"Talis," Callie said, moving to stand in front of him. "I want us to get married today. Now. The priest in the village will do it. Everyone already thinks we are great sinners. He will be glad to save our souls by marriage."

"Is that what this is about?" Talis sheathed his sword. "Another of your attempts to seduce me? Callie, please, I love all of this but there is a time and place for everything." Turning, he started toward the door.

"No!" she cried, grabbing the front of his jerkin. "This is different."

He gave her a knowing little smile. "Different from all the other of your attempts to seduce me? Callie, my love, did you not think I knew

529

what was going on? I have known always. Every time."

Giving her a brotherly kiss on the forehead, he started to push past her. "Now I must return to my father and apologize."

She would not release him. "Talis! Listen to me. I know you knew and I know how you enjoyed the game. How could I not know something like that about you? But I swear to you that this is serious; this is different."

"How is it different? What has happened?"

To Talis's disbelief, he could see that Callie had no intention of telling him what had happened — if anything. He could hardly fathom it, but Callie was keeping a *secret* from him. Never had she done this before. Oh, she might pretend she was not trying to seduce him when she was, but now there was something that she was not telling him.

His back stiffened, and instantly, Callie knew what was wrong.

She *would* tell him, she thought. In spite of her better judgment, she would tell him all. She could not allow his honor to separate them. "Lady Alida —" she began, but Talis cut her off.

"Do you start on that poor woman again?" he asked. "She is dying. Can you not see that?"

"She means to marry me to another."

"Nay," Talis said calmly. "That is not true. There are things that you do not know of."

"Talis, do not be blind to what is around you. There are things that *you* do not know. Do not let your pride come between us. Let us be married today, now. If I am no longer a virgin no one on earth can part us."

With a knowing smile, Talis chucked her under the chin. "Then that *is* what this is all about. What did my lady mother say that has made you believe she means to marry you to another? Or did she say anything? I think this is just another of your ruses. Will the door slam shut again? Will I need to hack through the roof again?"

Callie's face was serious. "This is no jest. She has shown me the man."

"If she has said something to upset you, she was teasing you. She plans for us to . . . No, I cannot tell you. I have made vows to God."

"You have made vows to *her*," Callie said spitefully and even to her own ears she sounded jealous.

"No," Talis said seriously. "You do not know what has transpired. I have put my hand on the Bible. My honor is at stake. I have —"

"You have been used," Callie spat at him, all her anger at him coming to the surface. Why would he not listen to her? "*We* have been used. They care nothing for us, only what *they* want. They have used you against yourself."

"You talk in riddles and you could not know what you say. The people you speak of are my mother and father."

"You do not believe that. John Hadley is *my* father and that woman is *my* mother. Can you not see the truth?"

Talis stood looking at her, puzzled, knowing something was wrong but he could not figure out what it was. That Lady Alida was not his mother was no surprise to him. Whoever she was, she was a lonely woman and she had promised him that if he acted as a son to her, she would give him so much. And all of it would be for Callie — if Callie would just be patient. How very much he wished he could tell Callie what he was doing, what he had planned, but he could not. All he could do now was try to soothe her. Everything would be well in the end if she would only trust him. How could she doubt him?

"Callie, what is wrong with you? You used to be so soft, so loving, so . . . so sweet natured. Now you are —"

Callie glared at him, angry at his lack of understanding. She was fighting for her life. "Yes, once I gave love because I received love. But in this time in this house I have given but received nothing. You have stood by idle while I have been exiled, ridiculed, humiliated. You have cared nothing for me."

"You are wrong! You do not know what you are saying. If only you knew what I have done to help us to be together." With each word he could feel himself pulling away from her. How could she believe he cared nothing? How could she think he had not lived every minute of his life just for her? Did she not realize that what he did with Lady Alida was for her, for Callie?

"*What* have you done? Please tell me. I am waiting. You must tell me what you were doing when you were following after Lady Frances as though you were on a leash. You must tell me why you have . . ." Her voice lowered. "Why you have not asked me to marry you."

Talis knew that what he was going to say would hurt her, but pain now was better than breaking his vows to Lady Alida and losing their future. He had seen this Peniman Manor and he wanted more than anything in the world to give it to Callie, to see her there with their children.

"I cannot tell you," he said, hoping she would trust him.

"It is as I thought," Callie said. "Your pride, that damned honor of yours is everything and I am nothing." She turned away from him.

"Callie!" He grabbed her arm. "I love you. You are my life. You are everything to me. Surely you must know how much I want you as a man wants a woman. You must know how difficult you have made my life these weeks when you have . . . when you have appeared naked before me. You *must* know that I die with the wanting of you."

She whirled around to face him, her hair flying about her, almost as though she meant to strike him. "May you always love me and want me but never have me," she said, and her words sounded like a curse.

"Callie," he pleaded, reaching for her, but she drew back.

"Then this is your final word? You will not go now and marry me, even though I tell you that this means my life to me?"

"One of us must be sensible. I am bound by vows that make it impossible for me to be free. I cannot tell you of these vows or I would. You must trust me."

"Yes, I am to trust you but you are not to trust me. I tell you the truth and yet you do not believe me."

"Callie, my love, you are overwrought now. We should return and —"

"Yes," she said coldly. "You must get back to that father who is not your father, to that woman who is not your mother. You must get back to that glorious future of yours. When they put the crown on your head will you think of me?" With that she swept past him, Kipp running to catch up to her.

For a moment Talis stood scratching his head, not able to figure out what Callie was up to. This was, of course, merely another of her attempts to seduce him, but today she seemed more upset than usual. But he did not like what she had said. *May you always love me and want me but never have me,* was what she had said, and just remembering the words sent a chill up his spine.

Tonight, he thought, tonight he would see Lady Alida and demand that she release him from his vows. He could not stand what this separation was doing to him and Callie. Perhaps tomorrow he might take Callie and return to Meg and Will. But whatever Lady Alida said, tomorrow, he would go to Callie and tell her all.

40

"Have you heard?" Lady Frances asked Talis, her nose in the air, her head cocked in a way that Talis found very annoying. What nasty little thing was she going to tell him about Callie now?

"I have been too busy minding my own business to hear much," Talis said as he ran his sword edge across the big grinding wheel. With his training on the farm he was one of the few men who could achieve a proper edge on a sword.

"Your Callasandra was married to Peter Erondell not an hour ago."

"Is that so?" Talis said, without the least concern. What would those jealous biddies think of next? Of course it pleased him that they were fighting over *him* but, all the same, it could be most annoying. "And who is Peter Erondell?"

"Your mother brought him here. I heard that she had to pay him a great deal of money to marry that plain-faced girl. But little Callie went along well enough and said all her wedding vows without a word of protest. Even now she eagerly awaits the wedding night."

Talis had stopped sharpening his sword to look at Lady Frances. "You are a liar."

"I beg your pardon, sir, but it is true. She met and married him in one day. He is a very good match for such as her. She has done well."

There was, of course, no truth to this, and Talis could imagine how all Hadley Hall would laugh at him if he believed such lies as this. He had best play along with them and keep what pride he could manage. However, at even the thought of Callie marrying another, he could feel the blood pounding through his head so hard he could hardly think.

Carefully, slowly, he put his sword back to the whetstone. "And where did this fine wedding take place? Were there no guests? No feast?" Talis's head was so full of blood that he could hardly recall this afternoon, but he did remember that Callie had tried to make him think she was to wed another. But how in the world had she been able to get Lady Frances in on the trick? Now Talis was, no doubt, to go running to Callie in a rage and beg her to marry *him*. It would not work. He was not going to fall for her —

"Where is she?" he heard himself asking, then was horrified to realize that he was holding his sword to Lady Frances's beautiful white throat.

"You may kill me if you must, but that will not change what is," Lady Frances said with the utter confidence of a beautiful woman. No man on earth was going to harm *her*.

Frances smiled sweetly when Talis lowered his sword. "She is now in the chamber next to Lady Alida's, awaiting her bridegroom."

Talis left the woman there, her laughter ringing out behind him as he ran full speed into the house. All he could think of was that he was going to wring Callie's neck when he saw her. But at the same time he was flattered at this further proof that she loved him. Perhaps Callie was right and perhaps he should be more firm with Lady Alida; perhaps James and Philip and Hugh were also right when they warned him about Lady Alida, this woman who had said she was his mother — but was she?

There were too many thoughts in his head for him to sort them out as he tore up the stairs to the chamber.

Callie was alone in the darkened room, only one candle burning on the far side. She was sitting on the edge of the bed, and when he entered, she did not turn to look at him, but he could feel her misery. This time she was not joking; this was no trick.

Going to her, he knelt before her on his knees and took her hands in his — and his heart almost stopped. There was nothing in her eyes. Absolutely nothing. It was almost as though her soul were missing from inside her body.

Talis refused to think of what he had just heard. That is not what could be wrong with Callie. "What has happened?" he asked. "Is it Meg? Or Will? Have you had news from home?" As he said the word he realized that with Meg and Will he *had* been home, and now, more than anything in the world he wanted to go back there.

"Come," he said, "we will leave this place. We will go home."

Callie did not move. Instead, she put out her hand and caressed his cheek.

Taking her hand, he kissed the palm. He might be unable to think, but he was still able to feel and what was in her poured into him. "What have you done?" he whispered, some part of him knowing, but almost too frightened to hear the words.

When he looked at her, he knew. He knew. He knew that she had done what she had threatened.

What ran through him was more than rage. It was white hot hatred. Hatred, the other side of the coin of love. Rising, he went to the window to stare out sightlessly. "You have married another?" he said, his jaw tight with his anger, his sense of betrayal, the full extent of which had not yet hit him.

Mutely, Callie gave a nod, her eyes on her hands.

A thousand words ran through Talis; a thousand visions of the two of them together as children, as adolescents. He saw her as she was the day she fell face down in the pig pen; he saw her sitting in an apple tree, her bare legs hanging down. He saw her last week standing naked in the straw. He saw her with their children. He saw all that he had done to make a future for them, to win them a place to live.

"Why?" was all that he could say. Thousands of words and thousands of dreams condensed into one.

"With this deed of mine I have given you the world," she said. "Your father can make you king."

At first this made no sense to him, but then he remembered things that Lady Alida had said to him, about Gilbert Rasher being related to the queen. She had talked to him about this more than once. But Talis had not thought much of it. She had even once asked if he would like to be king and Talis had laughed at her. "I want only Callie and what is mine," he'd said and had never meant anything so much as he meant those words.

Now, looking at Callie, his lip curled into a snarl. "You know me so little that you think I would want such as this? Do you think I would want to give my life to a country when all I want is . . ." He could not say the words. As he looked at her he knew that he was looking at another man's wife. *Wife!*

"You did not want me," she whispered. "I asked you and you did not want me."

Talis was so angry he could feel his entire body trembling. And so he told her the truth. His vows to God no longer meant anything to him. What did he care about his immortal soul if he lost

540

Callie? He told her of his vows, how he had worked so hard to win Peniman Manor for her so they could live together there with Will and Meg.

"But you could not wait for me," he said. "You could not trust me, or believe in me. You . . ." He could not speak; could not bear to be in the same room with her. He had lived all his life for her and she had betrayed him.

"So now you have your husband," he said, his voice beginning to break. He could not think of anyone else touching Callie; could not bear the thought.

"May you never love anyone but me," he said and strode from the room.

It was an hour later that it was discovered that Callie was missing. Lady Alida set the household to trying to find her. When it was discovered that Talis was also missing, it was at first assumed that they had run away together.

But it was Dorothy who was sure that Callie and Talis were not together. When she heard what her mother had done, she was furious. Breaking Callie and Talis apart was like splitting a house down the center; neither half would be able to stand alone.

When Dorothy saw Penella in a state of agitation, she crossed herself, for she had an idea of what the maid was going to say.

"Where is she?" Dorothy asked.

"It is my fault," Penella said and she was nearly

insensible. "I should not have interfered. God has punished me. It is my fault. I should not have stopped the fire."

Dorothy gave the woman a shake. "Where is Callie?"

"The fire. The fire," Penella kept repeating. "I could not wake her. She had died there twice."

When Dorothy saw that the maid's hands were black with soot, Dorothy knew that Callie must be in the old burned tower. She did not like to think about the second half of what Penella was saying.

It seemed to Dorothy that all of Hadley Hall was in chaos. Her father had found out that his wife had done something to anger his precious Talis and was shouting at everyone.

"Where is Talis?" Dorothy shouted at Hugh over the noise of her father's bellowing.

When Hugh looked at her, Dorothy wanted to shrink away, for Hugh's eyes were bleak with despair. "They have killed the boy's spirit. They should have taken a knife to his throat, it would have been kinder."

"Where is he?" Dorothy demanded.

"He is in the stables. But it is as though there is no one inside him now. As though he is no longer alive."

Holding her skirts up, Dorothy began to run, and once she reached the stables, she had to elbow her way through the crowd to get to Talis. She didn't care that people snapped at her or told her to mind her own business.

"Come," she said to Talis, holding out her hand to him.

Three women pushed her away, but Dorothy pushed them back in a way that was fueled by necessity. "Come!" she commanded Talis.

As though in a trance, he stood up from the little stool, took her hand, and left with her. When people began to follow them, Dorothy yelled at them to get back and they obeyed her.

They were still quite some distance from the old burned tower when Talis put his head up, as though he heard something in the cool night air. The next moment he dropped Dorothy's hand and began to run to the tower, leaving her behind him.

Taking the steps two at a time, Talis ran up to the top. This tower was where so many things had happened to the two of them. Here they had been saved from death, here they had laughed together when he had sent her headdress and corset flying over the parapets. Here they had been happy; here they had lived.

Callie was sitting on the parapet, her hand hanging limply to one side; when she heard him, she did not turn.

"Callie," he said, flinging himself onto her, his head on her breast. "Callie, what have you done?"

She put her hand on his head, feeling the curls of his hair, but already there was no life in her hand, no life in her body. "I am giving you freedom," she whispered.

He was crying, his tears wetting her bosom. "I never wanted freedom. I want only you. Callie, please don't leave me. I cannot live without you."

"Yes," she said. "You can live without me. You must live *for* me. You will be a king. You will be the greatest king the world has ever seen."

"No," he said, looking up at her, his eyes huge with tears. He knew without being told that she had taken something from that hideous garden of hers. With each second he could feel her life ebbing from her. "I do not want to be anything without you. Why did you not tell me? Why did you not —"

She put her fingers to his lips. "It is over now. Talis, I loved you. I loved you with all my heart, with all my soul. I could not love you more than I did. But I feel that it was not enough to make you love me in the same way. I feel that I failed somewhere."

"No, no," he said. "I loved you. I loved you more than —"

He could see that Callie was past hearing him. He could see that the breath was leaving her body.

How was he to live without Callie? What meaning would life have if he didn't live it with her? He thought of years without her laughter; years without her there to tell him he was wonderful, that he could do anything, be anything.

"I am nothing without you," he whispered. He could feel her life departing her. As though someone had stuck a needle into his vein and his blood was flowing from him, with her approaching death, he could feel his own life leaving him. Half of him, he thought. She was the other half of him and now one half of him was dying.

Carefully, he pulled her nearly lifeless body into his arms, then climbed on top of the parapets. He did not think about what he was doing. There was no need to think.

As he pressed his lips to Callie's, she opened her eyes and looked into his. She did not have to look down to see that they were on the edge of the stone wall and it was many stories down to the ground. "No," she whispered, but there was no strength in her protest.

With what was left in her body, she flung her arms about Talis's neck and kissed him. And when he stepped off the wall into the open air, she did not break her connection to him. She kept her lips to his until they hit the stones below.

John Hadley arrived in time to see his beloved son crash onto the stones, then stood in stunned silence as he looked down at the two young bodies, so tightly entwined that he could not tell where one body began and the other ended. At Callie's feet was the broken body of the little monkey, her beloved gift from Talis.

When John put back his head, the cry he let out could be heard echoing off the hills miles away. "No, God no," he cried, flinging himself on top of the two broken people.

Two innocent young people had died because they had loved too much and others had loved too little.

41

Upon hearing that Talis was dead, it was as though both parents gave up the will to live. Alida lingered for little more than hours before she died.

"Hell is richer now," Penella had decreed, making no attempt to conceal her hatred of her mistress.

Overnight John Hadley became a broken man, aging before the eyes of everyone.

But there was a gloom over Hadley Hall that even the deaths of the two young people could not explain. There was more than death about the beautiful house with the old, ruined castle in the background.

"It is the absence of love," Hugh Kellon said, just before he rode away forever. "For a while there was love in this place and we all felt it. Before they came we had resigned ourselves to the absence of love around us, but those children awakened us. They made me remember sweetness I thought I could not remember. There was not a life they did not affect."

It was true: Callie and Talis had affected everyone. With her mother gone, Edith lost no time in swooping up the available Peter Erondell; she was married to him before he knew her name. Then she quickly found husbands for her other sisters. John stayed in the background; he was an old man now and he did not care what happened to the money he had so carefully hoarded all his life.

Penella lost not a minute in setting herself up as housekeeper to the broken John, and soon Hadley Hall was run with more efficiency than it ever had been before. And she easily persuaded John that Alida could not be buried at her precious Peniman Manor. She had used that rich estate to entice and threaten; she was *not* going to have it in death, since she would not give it in life.

With Talis and Callie gone, there was no soul left in the house, or in the family. As Hugh said, there was no more love left. One by one the children left the place, not one of them wanting to remain near their father or Hadley Hall.

Gilbert Rasher never came to the hall; never even saw his son as an adult. On his way to claim his son and make him king, he and his other sons were set upon by brigands and killed when they refused to give up the few coins they carried with them. But then, there were very few people at Hadley Hall who knew he was to have come and given revenge to Lady Alida, so Gilbert Rasher was not missed.

It was three years after the deaths of the children that Penella demanded that John do something to commemorate the deaths. In their memory, John had a chapel built, a chapel of great beauty, with a coffered ceiling and marble floors. In the east end was a large marble monument. Lying on tasseled pillows of the purest white marble were full-length statues of Callie and Talis, a little monkey twined about Callie's ankle. Their heads were turned toward each other, their hands clasped, their eyes gazing into each other's for all eternity. Above their heads doves held a white marble canopy open, as though the viewer were seeing something that was private and should not be seen.

Below the statues was a brass plaque that said:

BORN IN THE SAME HOUR
DIED IN THE SAME HOUR
APART IN LIFE
TOGETHER IN DEATH

Part Three

42

I was crying when I came out of my trance, and for a moment I didn't recognize the two people bending over me. One was a young man with an oddly dirty face. Under what looked like very cheap makeup streaked with sweat, he was pale.

"We thought you were a goner," he said in an accent that showed he hadn't bothered much with school.

"You *were* dead," whispered a pretty girl on the other side of me.

Turning, I looked into the eyes of Edith, the woman who had been my elder sister in the Elizabethan Age. With difficulty, I remembered that now she was called Ellen and she desperately wanted a husband. No wonder, I thought, after all she'd been through with her lying mother.

I started to get up but felt faint and fell back onto the hard little couch. When had they invented upholstered furniture? And why did I seem to remember carriages that had no horses?

"Catherine," Ellen/Edith said, "we must get

home. It's late and you've had a . . . a difficult day."

I guess committing suicide does tend to make one tired, I thought as I allowed her to help me up. Not to mention a hypnotic trance so deep I may have died. The young man was already by the open door, obviously very anxious to get rid of the two of us before he was accused of murder.

I wasn't much use as I allowed Ellen to put me in a carriage and take me back to her brother's house. I stood still, in an exhausted daze, while the maid undressed me and put me to bed. I was asleep immediately.

When I awoke it was morning and I felt much better, although ravenously hungry. My memory was slowly returning to me. I seemed able to remember all of it: my life in New York in 1994, my Edwardian life, and my life with Talis.

After ringing for the maid I let my thoughts wander, as I did when I was plotting a book. I wanted to remember everything.

Now I understood Tavistock's old nanny's hostility to me and my inexplicable desire to make her love me. Aya was Alida, in truth my mother. In this Edwardian life, she finally had Talis for her son, in a manner of speaking. At least a nanny was fairly close. And Tavistock no doubt kept her here because Talis had died believing that Alida had his best interests at heart.

Tavistock's uncle Hubert was Hugh Kellon, still trying to get us together after all these years.

Smiling, I looked up at the underside of the bed canopy. Dorothy was Daria, still listening to my stories, still wanting to have lots of men. She'd gotten her wish of making men adore her. No man ever ignored Daria. And we had been friends for centuries.

With a grimace I thought that although I'd not met her, Fiona *had* to be Lady Frances. I felt sure that she had been chasing my man for a few hundred years.

When my maid entered with a tray she placed over my knees, I kept looking at her very hard. Had I known her in the past? As far as I could tell, I hadn't.

"Will there be anything else, madam?" she asked.

"No, nothing. I feel much better after a night's sleep."

At that the maid smiled. "You have been asleep for two nights and a day. His lordship gave orders that you were not to be disturbed."

After the maid left, I ate everything on the tray and was tempted to eat the flowers in the vase. Two nights and a day, I thought, smiling. No wonder I felt as though I'd slept under a thousand pounds of blankets.

As I finished the food, my husband came into the room. For a moment I trembled with emotion as I looked at him and remembered all that we had been to each other. He had not wanted to live without me and I would not live without him.

"I am glad to see that you are better," he said formally.

I knew now what he was really like, how vulnerable, how soft he was inside. Like me, I thought. People think I'm hard-hearted and cynical, but I'm not.

"Tally," I said without thinking and reached out my hand to him.

He did not take it. "Now you have forgotten my name."

"No, I haven't. It's just that —" That what? That I know so much more now? "Tavey, I want us to try again. We love each other. I know you love me. You have always loved me and you always will."

For a moment it looked as though there were tears in his eyes, but he recovered himself. "Yes," he said in a harsh voice. "I have always loved you but you and I cannot . . . We cannot . . ." When he couldn't finish the sentence, he turned and hurriedly left the room.

"Yes," I said aloud to the silent room. "I know. We cannot."

"May you never love anyone but me," is what Talis had said.

"May you always love me and want me but never have me," was what Callie had said.

Nora had told me that curses were involved in keeping my soul mate and me apart and it was because of these curses that we did not trust each other in this life. And unresolved differences in Edwardian times were why we couldn't find each other in 1994.

After what I had seen in the Elizabethan Age, of how other people manipulated Talis and Callasandra, I was ready to forgive and forget.

"I hereby rescind my curse," I said aloud, half in jest, but there was an odd little tightening of my skin that made a chill run through me. I think curses said for real were stronger than curses removed in jest.

So how did I remove the curse?

My first thought was that I wished Nora were here to tell me what to do. Did the removal of curses involve crystals and little dolls that looked like a real person? How about dead frogs and powdered unicorn horns?

While I was entertaining myself I noticed that a newspaper had been placed in the pocket of the breakfast tray. I've never read newspapers much, but when I moved the tray to the side, I noticed the date. The eighth of June. For a second I wasn't sure why that date startled me so much, but then I remembered.

Today Tavistock and I die. Today someone kills us or we kill ourselves and my body is never found.

At that thought all humor left me. Murder is serious.

The question uppermost in my mind was, How can I stop these deaths? And if I can't stop them, how can I get out of here before they happen?

I remembered something Nora had told me. "You will be very happy together. But you have many things to learn before you find him."

Learn, I thought. What was I to learn? That past lives affect everything? That you shouldn't put a curse on anyone's head no matter how angry you are?

As I lay there it came to me that I knew what I was to learn: Love is everything in life. Nora had been right: I wanted to marry Steven because I was afraid I had only a few fertile years left and if I was going to marry it had better be now. I hadn't actually loved Steven. Proof of that was that I thought he was perfect. Tavistock wasn't perfect. In fact he was about as imperfect as a person could get. He was vain, arrogant, proud, and he thought I was an extension of himself. All in all, he was horrible.

At that thought, I put my hands over my face and began to cry. Maybe he was awful, maybe he was exasperating and unfair. Maybe he expected a thousand times more from me than he gave, but he was *mine*. He was mine as no one else had ever been or ever would be.

"May you never love anyone but me," he'd said and I didn't and I wouldn't.

"I *must* get rid of that curse," I said aloud. "I must!"

But how? I knew nothing about getting rid of curses. All I knew was how to tell stories and entertain people. Now if this were one of my stories, I thought, smiling. If I were writing this I'd —

I sat bolt upright in bed. "That's it! Stories

are my talent and I must use that God-given gift to figure out what needs to be done. I must —"

I was out of bed in a flash. Just like Scarlett, I got my strength from the land. In New York, when I needed to think I went to Central Park and walked. Walked for miles. Now I must dress and go to the garden and figure out what my heroine — I — must do to rid herself of this curse.

Four hours later my legs were tired, but I had a plot, no, a plan. All I needed was a little gunpowder, some cosmetics, hair dye, and a whole lot of luck.

As I walked back to the house, I wasn't wishing, I was praying.

43

Adam Tavistock, Lord de Grey, rode the horse as though he were part of it, his long legs gripping the sweating sides of the animal as it leaped over hedges and ditches. Mud spattered him; brambles tore at his clothes and tree branches swiped at his face. But he didn't care as he urged his horse on, faster and farther. If it were possible, he wanted to escape himself. He had a feeling that what he would like to do is ride so fast and hard that he left his very soul behind.

But where would he go? he wondered, for no matter how hard he rode, he couldn't stop his thoughts. Where was there to go? Into the waiting and willing arms of Fiona? Sometimes when he looked at her he was enraptured with her beauty and he wanted her very much, but most of the time he nearly fell asleep in her presence.

She's so beautiful she doesn't need a sense of humor, he thought as his horse sailed over a tall hedge. She'd never had to make a man laugh; never had to entertain anyone. Just the sheer presence of her was enough to satisfy most people. All she had to do was sit and that was enough. No one seemed to care that she never listened. But then she never had anything to say, so why should she learn to listen?

Yet Tavistock was planning to marry her. Why? he asked himself, knowing that the answer was that all he wanted was to make Catherine jealous. Catherine seemed to hate Fiona, truly hate her. When Tavistock had first seen the beautiful Fiona he hadn't paid much attention to her, only noted that she was extraordinarily pretty, but he had never thought of possessing her. He hadn't thought of making her his own any more than he would have taken a painting off the wall of a friend's house.

What had made him interested in Fiona was Catherine's animosity, her instant hatred of the woman. And for some odd reason, Catherine seemed to think that Tavistock was passionately interested in the divine Lady Fiona. Catherine's unfounded jealousy had made Tavistock take much more notice of the lovely Fiona than he would have otherwise.

The horse leaped at a stream with steep banks, lost its footing on the other side and almost fell, but Tavistock's sheer willpower and his expert handling of the reins kept the animal on its feet.

He loved Catherine, loved her with all his heart. Four and a half years ago he had seen her at a garden party at his aunt's house. He had taken one look into those blue eyes, one look at that white-blonde hair and he was lost. Never since had he cared about any woman other than her.

But things had gone wrong on their wedding night. Very wrong. Very, very wrong. As much as he wanted her, he couldn't make her his. Catherine had been so innocent that she'd not known there was anything wrong. She had loved the way he'd caressed her naked body, loved the way he held her. After hours of touching and kissing, she had not understood why her husband had slammed out of the room in a rage. He knew that Catherine felt that she had done something wrong, but she had no idea what.

The next morning he'd told himself that his inability had been due to wanting her so much, loving her so much that he was in pain. And it was due to the unfamiliarity of her. Perhaps if they knew each other better he could relax around her.

So he had spent time with her, traveled with her, laughed with her, confided in her, but all that did was make him need her, make him love her more than he had when he'd first married her.

He wanted her so much. He ached with wanting her. Everything about her enticed him: the way she walked, how she spoke, what she spoke of. The way she held a teacup made sweat roll down the back of his collar.

After a year of living near her and being unable to consummate the marriage, he knew he had to get away from her, so he began to travel, began to stay away from her, hoping that not seeing her every day would free him from what he felt for her.

And there were other women. He had to prove to himself that he was still a man. He left Catherine in the country and spent his time in London, drinking and seducing women. Never did he have any problem with any of them. Only Catherine made him feel less than a man.

Somewhere during the three years of their marriage — if it could be called such — he'd started to tell himself that their problem was her fault, not his. There was obviously nothing wrong with him, so it must be her.

His Uncle Hubert had been concerned about Tavistock spending so much time away from Catherine. "Women get into mischief when they have no one to occupy their time," he'd said. "You should give her a few children to take care of. Keep her busy in bed." He had not understood Tavistock's angry reply and subsequent storming out of the house.

When Tavistock had seen the way Catherine reacted to the lovely Fiona, Catherine's jealousy had touched something deep within him. He didn't like himself much for it, but he wanted to hurt Catherine, just as she was innocently hurting him. He'd begun to mention Fiona at every opportunity. He told Catherine of Fiona's perfume, of her clothes. He suggested that Catherine ask Fiona how she made her hair so soft. With every word he spoke, he saw Catherine grow more and more angry, until, at last, her anger matched Tavistock's.

But everything backfired when Catherine wrote those letters. He knew very well that she'd never had sexual relations with any man, not him or anyone else. She was too closely looked after for that. Whenever Tavistock returned from a trip, he called her maid to him and asked for a full report on every minute of Catherine's doings. Her greatest pleasures seemed to be in patronizing opera singers and buying pretty little ornaments from some Russian émigré.

Tavistock knew very well that she had written those letters to make him think she was desirable. She'd never say so, since she was as proud as any man, but he knew what she was after. Catherine wanted him to realize that other men did like her and want her, just as he seemed to want Fiona.

But Tavistock had some pride of his own, and he couldn't very well explain to Catherine that the problem was him and not her.

Everything would have blown over if it hadn't been for Aya, his old nanny. She had always been very possessive of her charge. When Tavistock was a child she used to pinch him to make him cry before she presented him for the obligatory 6 P.M. visit to his parents. It didn't take too many appointments before the visits were suspended; his parents did not want to be bothered with a screaming, runny-nosed brat in the drawing room every evening. When his parents instructed the nanny to bring the child back when he was old enough to have learned some manners, Aya had what she wanted. Her sweet little Tavey was hers alone.

For all that Tavistock could fool other people into thinking that his little wife bored him too much to remain at home, Aya knew the truth. She knew that Tavistock was obsessed with Catherine. From the moment he had first seen Catherine, he had thought of no one else. Only she was on his mind. Aya knew that Catherine had stolen Tavistock from her in a way that only deep love could, and this made her hate Catherine.

Tavistock pretended that he didn't know how Catherine's letters became known to the public, but he did. In a naively clumsy way, Catherine had "accidentally" left the letters lying about so he could find them. Truthfully, he had enjoyed reading them, as he always enjoyed her stories. Catherine could go to the most boring, ordinary function in the world and come away with truly hilarious stories. When they were first married he would sit through a tea party with some old crone pouring tea and talking endlessly about her garden. It would be all he could do to keep from nodding off. But later, when he and Catherine were driving home, she would entertain him with her accounts of all sorts of subtle things that had happened during the tea party. Catherine told of big-nosed, bony daughters who were dying of love for him. Her "proof" was the way the girl had handed Tavistock a teacup and the way she had asked if he wanted milk or lemon. When Catherine described the gathering to him, Tavistock always felt that he had attended a different party than she had. Where had he been when all this happened? He came to look forward to what Catherine told him had happened much more than what did happen.

But after the first year of their marriage, when Tavistock's anger had gradually increased, Catherine had stopped telling her stories. She'd said, "When I am unhappy, there are no stories in my head." After that he'd started traveling and staying away from her.

But he always came back to her. He missed her so much when he was away. When he was away from her he felt that part of him was absent, as though he'd left part of his body or his mind in another place.

So why could he not perform in bed with her? He had no idea, but no matter what he tried, nothing happened between them.

So Catherine had tried to get his attention by writing letters that said she'd been seduced by every man in England. Tavistock had read the letters and laughed, but then Aya mailed two of the letters to the newspapers, and that had stopped the laughter. She mailed some of them to the wives of the men who Catherine said she'd had torrid affairs with. She sent others to the men whose names were at the top of the letters.

Tavistock didn't know who was worse, himself or the men who knew that they'd never touched

Lord de Grey's pretty little wife. Each man liked for others to think that he had cuckolded the man who often made their wives weak-kneed with lust. There wasn't a man in the salons of England who hadn't heard a wife or mistress mention the beauty of Adam Tavistock, or the virility he exuded when he walked across a room. Not one man hadn't heard how Lord de Grey looked at his little wife so hotly her hair might catch fire, and why didn't *her* husband look at *her* like that?

The letters gave these men an opportunity to get back their own. Often, they denied having touched the pretty little blonde, but they all said the words in a way that actually said they were lying, that they were being noble and trying to save the woman's honor.

So what did Tavistock do to save his own honor? Did he remain married to Catherine, unable to make love to his own wife? He would rather like to have children. He'd like to have a son to carry on his name, then he'd like to have some girls who looked just like Catherine. Girls to tell him stories and look at him as their mother did. The only thing he could think of that would be better than having Catherine would be to have half a dozen Catherines.

But that wasn't going to happen. He was never going to have children with her.

Coldly, after the letters were sent, he had made the decision to divorce her. And who better to marry than the lovely Fiona? Appearing with such a beautiful woman on his arm would show the world that he was still a man, even though his wife had humiliated him in front of that world.

But every time Tavistock thought of marriage to Fiona, he felt sick. He *wanted* Catherine. Wanted her with all his being. But he couldn't take her.

The horse, tired now, stumbled again, but Tavistock kept pushing the animal. He had ridden this way many times and he knew the way well. Soon he would come to the road, then turn and start back to the house; he had reached the end of his property.

Catherine, he thought. Catherine, Catherine, Catherine. What could he do with her? What would he do without her?

He thought he would die when the doctor had told him that Catherine had fainted twice and he felt sure that she was in the family way. "Find out," Tavistock had snapped, then drunk half a bottle of brandy while he waited for the doctor to return.

When the doctor told Tavistock that his wife was still a virgin, the look on the man's face was all Tavistock needed to see to know how the outside world would view him if this information became common knowledge.

When Tavistock had confronted Catherine with knowledge of her virginity, she had shouted at him in a way she'd never done before. In fact, in the last few days she had been different. Not so frightened. Not so shy. She didn't look at him with eyes that begged him to be nice to her, to pay attention to her, to love her. She didn't seem to be asking, What did I do wrong? Why don't you love me?

He didn't think it could be possible, but he seemed to love this Catherine more even than he did the other one. Maybe his inability with her stemmed from her goodness and her innocence. Maybe he thought he was soiling her by committing such a carnal act as lovemaking.

Even to his own ears, he knew that was a pile of cow manure. The truth was, he had no idea what was wrong with him.

He was so deep in thought that when he came to the pile of logs and rocks in the road and his horse balked, he hadn't the presence of mind to catch himself but instead went sailing over the head of the animal, landing on his back on the hard ground.

It took a moment to clear his head from the fall. Dazed, he sat up on his elbows just in time to see his horse disappear over the ridge toward the house. The animal knew the way home well, since this was the spot where he always turned, here at the edge of his land.

"Damnation," he said, trying to stand but finding himself so dizzy he almost fell again. Stumbling a couple of times, he made his way to the pile of brush and rocks, thinking that he'd have the hide of the person who did this. Why would anyone put a four-foot-high pile of rubble in the middle of a road that is used every day? he thought. Someone could be —

He didn't think anymore because he heard a sound, a zzzzzt that piqued his curiosity. Leaning over the largest log, he looked toward the source of the sound. He saw a tiny bit of light, a fuse that had been lit and was burning toward a cylinder that seemed to be leaking gray powder.

"Gunpowder," he said aloud, then turned away just before there was a burst of light and an explosion that almost deafened him. A flying rock hit the back of his head and he remembered nothing after that.

"Where am I?"

"Hush," a woman's voice said in an accent he didn't recognize, but it sounded decidedly uneducated. "You just rest now and I'll take care of you."

It was pitch dark in the room and he could see nothing; his head hurt so much he thought death might be the only way to end the pain, and there was a roaring in his ears.

"No! Keep your hands off the bandage," the woman said. At least that's what he thought she said. It sounded more like, "Keep yore hans off'n the bandin's."

Tavistock was too tired to try to figure out what was going on as he dropped his hands to his side. "Am I blind?" Blindness would seem to be a suitable ending to his worthless life.

"Just a little explosion, is all. A bit of gunpowder, that's all. Nothin' to worry yore little self about. Here, honey, you jist drink this and you'll feel better."

The bandage was tight about Tavistock's eyes as she lifted his head, her arm under his neck, the side of his face pressed into her soft bosom as he drank the warm liquid from the rough, thick cup. "What is it?" he asked dreamily, for he rather liked his face against her breasts. She didn't seem to have bothered with a corset.

"Willow bark tea," she answered, "the precursor of aspirin, laced with some dark rum." She mumbled something about not knowing if aspirin had been invented yet.

That statement should have engendered some questions in his mind but he couldn't seem to think what they were. "Who are you?" he whispered.

"Your guardian angel, honey," she answered. "Who would you like for me to be?"

"I can't think that I'd want you to be anything other than what you are," he said as he ran a hand up her arm.

Abruptly, the woman dropped his head on the hard bed, making sparks of light fly through Tavistock's head and eliciting a groan from him.

"Don't you have a wife?" she asked and there was anger in her voice. "Don't you have a wife who spends a lot of time alone while you go tomcatting around the world?"

Her slang was unfamiliar to him, but he understood the gist of what she was saying. "She doesn't —"

"So help me, if you tell me she doesn't understand you, I'll hit you with a poker."

At that Tavistock laughed. "I'm afraid she understands me too well. May I have more of that drink of yours?"

This time she did not hold his head but held out the cup to him at arm's length. In his blindness, he had to flail his hands around to find the cup.

When the woman was silent, he listened to hear where she was, but the roar in his ears was too loud to hear anything clearly. Something about her intrigued him. "How did I get here? Please, you must tell me everything."

"I brung you," she said in her odious accent, but he was disliking it less with each swallow he took of the warm liquid in the cup.

"No," she said softly, and he felt the hard cot move as she sat beside him, "you tell me all about yourself. Why was you ridin' that pore horse so hard? You nearly killed it."

He gave a snort of laughter that made his head hurt, but the pain was easing with the help of the magic elixir in the cup. "If I started to tell you the problems of my life I'd never stop."

"I am a good listener," she said softly, forgetting to speak in the exaggerated accent she had been affecting. Tavistock didn't seem to notice.

There was something about the strangeness of the situation, his blindness, the warm room, the softness of the woman in spite of her attempt at coolness, that made Tavistock want to talk.

"Have you ever loved anyone so much that nothing else in life mattered? Loved someone so much that you couldn't eat or sleep or work?"

"Yes," she answered and he could tell from her voice that she did know. "The person is your reason for living."

"Yes, she is."

"Ah," the woman said. "Your Lady Fiona."

Tavistock smiled into the darkness that surrounded him. "Fiona. She is nothing. An empty shell. I own pieces of jade with more soul than she has."

"Then who?" the woman whispered. "Surely not your wife. It is common knowledge that you plan to divorce her."

"Yes, I love her and only her."

"Then why . . ."

"I must," he said fiercely, which made his head hurt. "I must. I must. I —"

"Ssssh," she said and again pulled his head to her breast, but this time she stretched out beside him. To his shock, Tavistock felt her slim bare legs next to his. "What is wrong?" she whispered into his ear, and her soft voice combined with the roar that was there made her voice seem far away and not real.

"I cannot make her mine," he said, knowing that he'd never said the words to any other person in his life.

"Cannot . . . ," she said, moving her hips against his side, her lips on his ear.

In the last few years he'd been to bed with

573

several women, some of them renowned for their expertise in lovemaking, but he'd never felt the flush of excitement that this woman was sending through him.

"You seem like you could do anything you wanted to do," she practically purred as she rolled off the bed.

Tavistock had no idea what his hesitation was, but there was something holding him back from taking this woman. Abruptly, with a quick gesture, he tore off his blindfold. For a moment he could see nothing and for a moment's panic, he thought he truly was blind. But then he had a vague impression of a one-room cottage, a tiny fire in a brazier in one corner. Little furniture and that of the simplest, crudest sort. Outside the one window the darkness of night; the oak door heavily bolted.

As Tavistock's vision began to clear, he saw her standing to one side, legs spread wide apart, hands on her hips in a truly provocative pose. His vision was fuzzy, blurred even as he wiped his hands in front of his eyes. She had on a red blouse that barely covered her breasts, a wide red and black sash at her tiny waist, then a full black skirt that was pinned up high on one thigh, exposing one bare leg.

"Will I do?" she asked insolently, her red lips drawing back in a smile that made chill bumps rise on his skin.

Part of him told himself that he should not touch her, that she probably had a husband lurking in the shadows and she planned to seduce him then blackmail him for all she could get. He didn't like dealing with women like . . . like her, but there was something about this one that he found irresistible. No doubt his attraction to her was because he couldn't see very well, heard things as though they were at a distance, and —

He broke off as she moved toward him. "What kind of lover is a gentleman like you?" she asked, sliding her body toward his. "I'll bet you're too uptight to even take your clothes off. Do you throw a lady's nightgown over her head then do your business and leave?"

"Yes," he said, smiling, eyes closed as he felt her body move on top of his. "Only the lower classes know about love," he said facetiously.

As she put her hands on his shirt front, he opened his eyes to look at her, at the black, black hair floating about her face, hiding most of it. In the flickering, dim light of the fire she looked almost like Catherine, his beloved wife, but then he always imagined that every woman he was attracted to was Catherine.

She startled him when she tore his shirt open, buttons flying across the room, one sizzling as it hit the fire in the brazier.

For a moment he didn't move as she straddled him, then ran her hands up his chest, her nails over his stomach. "Come on, pretty boy, can you make love to a *woman?*"

Tavistock knew he had never been so excited

in his life as he reached up and entwined his hands in the woman's abundant hair and pulled her lips down to his. And after that he had no more thoughts at all. He was blind not from a blast of gunpowder, but from the lust that took over his body. This woman seemed to be all that he'd ever wanted in his life, and he knew that he'd die if he didn't take her. There were no more thoughts of the consequences of his action, but just his overpowering need for her.

He had always prided himself on being a skillful lover. Since he was always in bed with women other than his wife, he knew that they would talk and compare him to their other men. Such gossip carried responsibility with it, so Tavistock knew he had a duty to have the women say that he was a lover of great tenderness, a man who thought a great deal of his partner's satisfaction.

But with this woman, he wanted her too much to think of anything but his own needs. But she met him more than halfway. As he tore her clothes from her body, he felt his own being taken from him. Her enthusiasm matched his.

Within seconds they were both naked and he lost no time on the niceties of lovemaking. What he felt for her was primitive, a hunger that had to be fulfilled.

When he entered her, he was vaguely aware of the tiny membrane he encountered and he heard her little yelp of pain, but he was too far removed from the basics of earth to think what this meant. His need of her was such that it took only moments before he was ready to spill his seed inside her.

When he did come inside her, it was like nothing he had ever experienced before. It was like part of him died, but as though part of him were given life again. The release he felt was as though he'd been waiting for this all his life. It was the end of something; the beginning of something.

He was trembling from head to foot as he held her to him, wrapping his whole body about her; there were tears in his eyes, but he didn't know why.

"I did it," the woman said. "I did it."

For a moment Tavistock was disoriented, not remembering all that had happened to him before the last minutes. Oh yes, something to do with gunpowder and a woman with black hair. When she tried to extricate herself from his arms, his first response was to hold on to her, to never release her. "No," he whispered, and wanted to beg her to never leave him.

"It's all right," she said as she began to kiss his neck. "It's all right now. It's over. The curses are finished."

His head still hurt; his eyes were still foggy and his hearing was dull, but he knew that voice. Grabbing her shoulders, he held her away from him to stare into her eyes. Under the smeared makeup, beneath the black hair, he saw Catherine.

For a moment he was angry. How could she

play such a trick on him? What was his *wife* doing dressed up like a slut? What was —

It took a bit but he realized what had just happened. He had just made love to Catherine, to the woman he loved. There had been no physical problem. "But how did you —"

She put her hand over his mouth. "Do you *really* want to talk?" she asked.

At that he laughed, grabbed her to him, and the next moment his hands and mouth were all over her — as hers were him. Had he not drunk a great deal of rum, had gunpowder go off near his head, and been hit on the head by a rock, not to mention falling off a horse at full speed, he might have spent some time asking her just where the hell she learned all that she seemed to know. But then, on the other hand, he wasn't fool enough to stop what she was doing to his body to ask questions.

He had always known that making love with Catherine would be wonderful, but it was better than he'd imagined. He could not, of course, tell anyone, but it was almost as though he could feel both parts of their lovemaking. It was almost as though her mind were his and his was hers. If a thought passed through his mind, she acted upon it, and he seemed to intuit what she wanted and needed.

They made love all night, moving from one position to another with such familiar ease that it was as though they had made love many, many times before. They seemed to know all there was to know about each other.

"I feel as though we have always been lovers," he whispered.

"Never," she answered. "Never in the history of time, but we have wanted each other for so many centuries that we know everything. We are making love to ourselves."

"Yes," he said, not understanding her, but at the same time understanding every word she spoke.

Being in bed with her made him feel free. With other women he was aware that he had a reputation to uphold. He must at all times appear knowledgeable and experienced.

But with this black-haired Catherine, he could be . . . well, experimental. Would this feel good? he wondered as he picked her up, turned her around, and sat her down on the rampant evidence of his desire for her.

"Oooooh, nice," she said, making him laugh as he ran his hands over her breasts, then down her flat stomach, his hands spanning her little waist.

Later, as he collapsed against her for the fourth time in as many hours, he started telling her how much he loved her.

"Still going to marry Fiona?" she asked innocently.

At that he gave her a whisker burn on her soft neck that made her squeal.

"Will this come out?" he asked, holding her hair up and referring to the color. There was light coming through the window and his vision was clearing more with every hour.

"Do you care?"

"I love you whatever color your hair, but . . . It is nice having a little variety."

"You!" she said and rolled on top of him.

The next moment she was clasping her head in pain.

"What is it? Catherine? What is it?"

"No," she said. "No, I don't want to go back. I want to stay here."

"Of course we can stay here. Oh, you mean you don't want to go to the house. If you don't want to go —"

"No!" she said sharply, her eyes shut tightly, and it was as though she were talking to someone else. "I don't want to go back."

When she looked up at him, there was agony in her eyes. "It is Nora. She is calling me back. She says that I have done what I needed to do and now I must return. She says that I do not belong here. Don't let her take me."

He didn't understand what she was saying but he knew that she was frightened. And if she was frightened then so was he. Wrapping his body about her, he held her as tightly as he could without breaking her bones. "I will let no one take you. You are mine."

"Yes," she said, "I am yours and only yours. I have never loved anyone but you. Not in all my lives. Even the ones I spent without you."

He didn't bother trying to understand what she

meant, but just held her, as that was what they both needed.

"Don't let her take me. She is calling for me. She means to take me away from you."

"I won't let her take you."

"No, you don't understand. She will take my spirit, but she will leave my body. Oh, Talis, don't leave me. I have lost you too many times."

"You won't lose me this time as I will go with you. I will always stay with you."

Pulling her head back, she looked at him. "I wish I had time to explain everything to you. Take care of Catherine. She is me and she loves you."

"You are Catherine; you love me," he said and was frightened at her words, which made no sense. It was almost as though she believed that she was dying. "I will not allow you to leave me."

"I am not Catherine. I am Hayden Lane and I live in another time and place, but I love you there as much as I love you here. Hold me tighter. Hold me. She's getting stronger. Make her leave me alone. I don't want to go back. I want to stay with you forever."

He held her, caressing her hair and trying to pull her body into his while he talked to her calmly and with all the love he felt. "I will not leave you. Wherever you go, I will go with you."

"Swear it!" she said, her voice muffled from her face pressed against his chest. "Swear it on your immortal soul!"

"I swear it," he said softly. "I make a sacred

vow to you and God. I will go with you wherever you go. I will never leave you. Never."

And it was with those words that Hayden began to feel herself growing weaker. Her spirit was leaving Catherine's body. She protested in her mind, protested out loud. She tried to reason with the voice of Nora in her head, the voice that was growing stronger by the minute.

But she knew that she was losing when she heard Milly's voice. "Hayden, please wake up. We, love you and need you. Please come back to us. Please don't die."

When Hayden tried to speak to Tavistock, nothing came out of her mouth, and she could feel his body fading from her arms. She screamed, "No!" but everything went black and for a moment she was in no body.

The next minute Hayden opened her eyes and she was lying on a chaise in Milly's Texas living room and staring into the eyes of some very frightened people.

No one said a word when she turned her head away and silent, hot tears began to run down her cheeks.

Part Four

44

"Catherine was attached to you and didn't want to be separated. Like Siamese twins who share one heart. When you returned, she tried to stay connected to you. Her body could not live."

What Nora meant was that *I* had killed Catherine. When I left Catherine's mind, she had clung to me — and a body without a spirit dies.

"And what of . . . of Tavey?" It hurt even to say the name.

Nora looked at me a long while before she spoke. "You are soul mates. You are the same. You are one."

"That's all very romantic," I said, "but just exactly what does that mean?"

"Truthfully, I don't know. Perhaps his spirit stayed there and waited for you."

"You mean *he's* the ghost of Peniman Manor?"

"Possibly. Or he could have followed you here." She narrowed her eyes at me. "You made him swear he would return to 1994 with you. Perhaps he did."

Obviously, she had not liked my using what I had learned about curses and vows holding true across centuries, but Nora's displeasure seemed a small price to pay for getting back my soul mate.

I sat there with my mouth opening and closing as I tried to understand what she had said about Tavey following me. I couldn't quite do it so I just whispered, "Tell me."

Nora smiled, since I guess she understood my shock. "Catherine's spirit left her body when yours did."

"You mean she died."

"In a manner of speaking."

I was so eager to hear the story I didn't even interrupt to comment that dead was dead, no matter how I spoke of it.

"When your . . . When Tavistock felt you leave the body, he couldn't bear to live without you. I don't know what happened next. Maybe his spirit clung to yours and followed you?"

Nora's eyes showed bewilderment, and I realized I had come to depend on her answers to my questions. Now I had fallen into uncharted territory and was on my own. Everything that was most important to me hung in the balance, and without her guidance I felt bereft — orphaned.

"Do you think he's inside me?"

Nora laughed. "No, his spirit would have been put inside the body of the man who he is in *this* life."

Oh good, I thought, and didn't bother to understand. I was sick of voodoo. I wanted flesh and blood. "How do I find him?"

"You must wait for him to find you."

I said a very nasty word and got a chastising look from Nora. "Sorry," I mumbled, "but I *hate* to wait."

"You think I don't know this?" Nora said with heavy sarcasm.

But it was my turn to be smug. I sent her thoughts that told her that if it hadn't been for my inability to wait I wouldn't be receiving Jamie/Tavey/Talis for another three lifetimes.

Nora smiled in answer to my silent thoughts. "Nothing ever happens that is not meant to be."

"Oh. So now I guess I'm to believe I was predestined to return to Edwardian times even though you told me not to go."

"How else did your Lady de Grey die if not from your spirit leaving her body? She was not murdered as your history books hint, and if there is a restless spirit in that house it is not hers."

I think that if I'd strangled her then it would have been justifiable homicide. I was to receive no credit for ingenuity; everything was predestined.

Oh well, I thought, who cares who takes the credit if I get my Tally? "How will he find me? When?"

Nora gave a little shrug and there was apology on her face. "I don't know."

"You don't know," I said flatly.

She nodded.

"But you *do* know he will find me."

"No," she said, somewhat exasperated, then she calmed. "You have . . . shall we say, changed things and my visions of the future are a bit, well, confused."

I couldn't help smiling at that, since Nora usually seemed to know and understand everything.

As I opened my mouth to ask one of my neverending questions, she put up her hand. "I cannot answer what I do not know. But if he is meant to find you, then you can lock yourself in your apartment, see no one and yet I know he will appear."

"Only if he delivers from the deli," I said, not believing a word she said. I couldn't imagine Tally as a delivery boy, yet delivery people were the only ones allowed into my building. Twenty-eight men guarded my apartment every minute day and night. *How* could he come to me? *I* would have to search for *him*.

"Can I put an ad in the paper?"

"Which paper?" she asked. "Which country? What language?"

"Oh." I remembered her saying that I must be willing to accept my soul mate in whatever package God had made for him. "With my luck he'll be a nine-year-old transvestite," I muttered.

Nora laughed. "Somehow, I doubt it."

All I could do now was go home and wait. As I gathered my things I turned back. "What happened to Catherine's body?"

"The old man, Jack . . ." She looked at me as though waiting for something.

"Yes," I said, only at that moment realizing who he was. "He was John Hadley's spirit, wasn't he?" I paused a moment. "His conduct in the Elizabethan Age lost him everything, didn't it? He lost his money, his prestige, his family, even his healthy body." Just thinking of what had happened to him made me vow to behave myself in this life.

Nora nodded, pleased with my memory and insight — or at least that's how I interpreted her nod. "Jack found the bodies together and thought they'd committed suicide, so he knew they wouldn't be allowed to be buried in the churchyard. He took Catherine's body away and hid it until after Tavistock's funeral. Then, secretly at night he dug into the grave and put Catherine inside the coffin with her Tavey. Their bodies sleep together forever."

"Just as they did in the Middle Ages," I said softly. "Born together. Died together."

I couldn't say any more as I left Nora's office and walked slowly home, thinking about all that I'd been through and had learned.

I kept myself busy while I waited. I spent a great deal of time with Nora, pestering her for all the information I could pry out of her. Then I put my researching abilities to work. First of all, I found the tomb that had been made for

Callie and her beloved Talis.

"One of the finest examples of Elizabethan sculpture ever made," a guidebook read. "Exquisite carving. Dare we say, sensual?" an art critic wrote.

Something that made my head fill with happiness was to read that the marble figures had not been desecrated with graffiti. In the seventeenth century a fire destroyed most of the village and half of the church. Because of this, the church had been shut up and vines had grown through the windows, covering the area where the statues were. Hermetically sealed, as it were. It wasn't until the early twentieth century, when the church ruin was destined to be pulled down, that the statues, in near pristine condition, were found. The National Trust stepped in and restored what they could of the church and protected the beautiful marble sculptures.

While I waited I collated the information I had gathered from Nora and what I had read, added what I had experienced, and managed to turn in a six-hundred-page book on past lives to Daria. She was so happy that I hoped she wouldn't notice that the book didn't have an ending. Needless to say, she noticed, but she didn't bat an eyelash when I told her that I didn't know what happened to the end of the story because it hadn't happened to me yet. There was a tiny silence on her end of the telephone, then she said, "Let me know when you're ready." Her trust in me was enough to make me cry.

While I continued to wait for Talis, I continued my research. I looked up what happened to Peniman Manor, the place that Alida had held over so many heads as a reward for doing what she wanted done. When I was in Catherine's body, before I saw what had happened with Talis and Callasandra, I hadn't realized that Tavistock was living in Peniman Manor. Thinking of how that rich place had been used as reward/punishment, I could believe that Cathy and Tavistock could never have been happy there. If any spirit haunted the place it was Aya/Alida's. When I read that the contents of the manor, all the paintings and furniture I had seen, had been put in storage during the First World War and the house used as a hospital, I was glad. When I read that on the night the war ended, some careless man, drunk with happiness, had accidentally set the place on fire, I was almost relieved. It would take a fire to cleanse that place.

I called an estate agent in England (real estate to us Americans) and started searching for a thatched cottage that had been a farmhouse in the Elizabethan age. It wasn't all that difficult to find and, somehow, it didn't surprise me that it was for sale. I was long past being surprised by anything. I bought it for £120,000, about $180,000. Cute little farm cottages with medieval origins aren't cheap, but I knew that under the floorboards were six jewel-encrusted goblets and a silver candlestick, all of which Meg and William had stolen from the Hadley family. I was going to see my name on a plaque in a museum as a donor, and I was going to have a holiday cottage in England.

Speaking of Meg and Will, I called Milly in Texas and told her that I desperately needed to see her. I told her that I was so depressed I couldn't write. She was on a plane for New York almost before I finished the sentence.

Then I called my dear publisher, William Warren. It was easy to make him move. All I said was, "Another publishing house is offering me lots of lovely things." We made a dinner date immediately.

I wasn't home when Milly arrived at my apartment with her suitcase. I'd left her a note saying I'd meet her in the dining room of the Plaza Hotel, then gave the headwaiter a twenty to show Milly to William's table.

I would have liked to have hidden behind the palms to see the faces of Milly and my publisher when they first saw each other, but I knew I'd be caught, so I stayed in the apartment and waited with my most smug smile ready.

I got a little worried when Milly didn't come back that night, and the next day when she still hadn't shown up or sent word, I was angry as well as worried. I called my publishing house and was told my publisher had not shown up that morning nor had he called in with an explanation for his absence — but that wasn't unusual, as publishers do what they please.

By the second night when Milly still hadn't

returned, I was ready to go to the police. Then I got a fax from Milly at 3 A.M. She and William were in Las Vegas and they were leaving any minute on their honeymoon. She hoped I was well and I was not to worry. She'd tell me everything when she returned.

"Ha!" I said aloud, laughing. "I'll tell *you* everything." At last Meg and Will were together again, and I was the cause of it.

I was very proud of myself for what I had accomplished, but the weeks turned into months and still I heard nothing from Tavistock. I was bugging poor Nora until I think she was ready to paint a few 666's on my living room floor and start chanting in order to get rid of me.

As for me, I was ready to give up hope. I found myself bursting into tears for no reason at all. Was it better to have loved and lost than never to have loved at all? I dreamed about Jamie, about Talis, about Tavey. I thought about them all the time as I stayed in my apartment and waited. But with each day that passed, I became more sure that Talis was not going to appear on my doorstep.

Then one afternoon I told myself that I had to start living again. I couldn't keep disassociating myself from the rest of the world. Maybe Jamie was waiting for me just outside my door. Maybe —

I filled the tub full of hot, scented water and soaked myself clean, my hair slicked down with some peach-scented stuff guaranteed to make it like an angel's. I carefully shaved my legs, then rinsed my hair, got out of the tub and slathered my body with some ridiculously expensive body cream. When I was finished, I knew that no flower garden smelled better than I did, but I refused to allow myself to acknowledge the fact that I had no man to nuzzle my neck and tell me how good I smelled.

Wearing nothing but a thick terry cloth robe, I opened my apartment door to get the mail that was brought up to me every day. Since I live on the top floor of the building, the elevator opens only to my apartment, and no one is allowed up without first being announced. So when the elevator door opened, I gasped in surprise.

"Excuse me," the man in the elevator said in such perfectly spoken English that he had to have studied the language rather than grown up speaking it. "I think I have the wrong floor. My colleague is on floor eighteen but this is —"

He broke off because of the expression I was wearing as I stared at him. He was tall, at least six feet, and he was no blond-haired blue-eyed westerner. He had the kind of golden brown skin that usually meant a Mediterranean origin, and I doubted very much that he had grown up with the same religion that I had.

All in all, he was one gorgeous package. I looked into those dark chocolate-colored eyes and nearly drowned. In those eyes I could see Tavistock and when I looked really deeply, I could see Tally. And maybe if I looked really, really deeply, I could see myself. I could see the man who was the other half of me.

He started to say something but he didn't say it because for the third time in my life I fainted.

45

"Are you all right?" he asked.

I was lying on my couch in my own living room and he was sitting by me, a cold washcloth in his hand and he was pressing it to my face. With his other hand he was smoothing back my damp hair, fresh from washing, and he was looking at me as though he meant to memorize every inch of me. Had I not been through what I had, if I had not known who this man was, I would have been frightened. A stranger caressing my cheek and neck with the back of his fingers, his thumb running over my eyebrow, then down the side of my nose, was not something I would have willingly allowed.

But this man was no stranger. I knew all there was to know about him, except maybe a few things about this life such as his name and where he came from. But those things didn't matter. This man was mine and had been mine throughout time.

I watched him as he looked at me. Would he

remember me? Was the spirit of Tavistock just under the surface?

Abruptly, he seemed to come out of his trance. "Forgive me," he said, sitting up straight. "I must introduce myself. I am Tariz —" He said several other names but I didn't hear them. The sounds of his name were made in his throat, and as he sat by me, his hip touching mine, I felt every syllable of his name as he pronounced it. Tariz was all that I needed to know. Talis, Tavey, Tariz.

"You are not well," he said. "Perhaps you should see a doctor." His honey-colored skin paled and his voice whispered, "Perhaps you are with child."

"No," I said, smiling. "No baby. I'm not married. Not engaged. I am free."

Tariz didn't say anything but just kept looking at me intensely. "You will think I am a crazy man, but it is as though I know you. It is as though I . . . I don't know how to say it. It is as though I recognize you. Can you understand such a thing?"

"Yes, I understand perfectly."

"You will laugh, but it is as though I know things about you. But that could not be, since we have never met."

"What do you know about me?" I asked.

He smiled softly and I thought my heart would melt. "You are afraid of high places and you like . . ." He hesitated. "You like small animals." He glanced at a candleholder on the table behind me. "You like monkeys and you . . . You do something." He ran his hand over his eyes. "You tell stories. You tell wonderful stories. You make people laugh. No, you make *me* laugh. You . . ."

He trailed off as he looked at me, his big brown eyes growing larger, his skin turning paler by the second. "I think . . . I think —"

I'd never seen a man faint before but I was afraid I was about to. I scurried off the couch, pushed him against the back of it, then went to fetch some brandy. Except that I didn't have any because I don't like brandy, so I poured a little Mandarin Napoleon in a glass and took it to him.

"You must excuse me," he said, sitting up straighter. "I am sure it is, what do you call it? With the airplane."

"Jet lag." Or century lag, is what I wanted to say.

He was wearing a dark suit, which made his hair and eyebrows even darker, and more than anything in the world I wanted to touch him. I wanted to tell him everything there was to tell about us. I wanted to feel his arms around me.

"Why are you looking at me like that?" I asked, wanting to force him to tell me what was in his mind.

He smiled and he had straight, even, beautiful teeth — and his mouth was something that made me ache. My robe was gaping open but I didn't bother to close it. With even the tiniest hint from him, I'd have flung it to the floor.

"I do not know you," he said softly, "and you do not know me. But, somehow, I do know you. I know all that is good and all that is bad about you."

"Bad?" I said involuntarily.

He smiled. "You have a temper, I believe."

"Only when you don't do what I want you to do," I answered. "I'm perfectly reasonable when you do exactly what I want when I want you to do it."

Considering that we had just met, this should have been an incomprehensible statement, but he smiled and said, "Yes, I know. Your will is very strong."

He took a deep breath and looked down at the tiny liqueur glass he held. I was sitting on the edge of the couch, about eight inches away from him, and the distance seemed almost intolerable.

"I am new to your country," he said softly. "I have arrived only yesterday and I was to meet a man here in this building."

"On the eighteenth floor, but you pushed the wrong button."

He lifted his head and looked at me. "No, I think I pushed the *right* button."

"Yes," I whispered. "You pushed the right button."

He looked back down at his glass and I could see a vein pounding in his neck, a neck that I longed to kiss. The air between us was like a bolt of electricity that stayed charged and grew stronger with each moment.

"I have come from my country to your country to talk to your people, your president, about misunderstandings between your country and mine."

"A diplomat," I said, knowing how very talented Talis would have been as a diplomat. He was so likable that he could make enemies at ease with each other.

"I do what I can," he said modestly, then gave me a piercing look. "You are not one of these American women who is tied to a company and cannot move, are you?"

For a moment I didn't know what he meant, but then my heart gave a little flutter. "I am completely mobile. I write for a living and I can live anywhere."

"Good," he said, smiling, then started to say something else but hesitated as he carefully put the still-full glass of liqueur on the table beside the couch.

"Why do you, ah, ask whether I can travel or not?"

"You would think me mad if I said what was in my heart."

"No I wouldn't!" I said fiercely, praying he wasn't just going to ask me out to dinner.

When he looked at me his eyes were on fire and my heart leaped into my throat. "I do not know how or why, but I love you. I love you with all my heart, with all my soul. It is as though I have been waiting for you, searching for you all my life."

All I could manage to say was, "Me too." And now, I thought, we tear each other's clothes off, and I made a bit of a move in that direction.

But when he looked at his watch, my heart fell. How could I have forgotten his meeting? He was here in America for a very important reason: peace between two countries, uniting two philosophies of life, maybe even trying to prevent a war. How could one fainting woman stand up against that?

"I am very late now, but I will finish my meeting by four o'clock. At that time I will return here and we will go to get married."

My mouth fell open until my chin nearly hit my chest.

"You will not faint again?"

"I . . . Well, no, I don't think I will. But . . . married?" For the life of me I couldn't think of anything to say. "Couldn't you delay your meeting for a while?"

At that he stood, and there was a twinkle in his eyes that I had seen many times on Talis. He knew very well what was in my mind and he was enjoying my exasperation. He put the tips of his strong fingers under my chin. "I will not touch you until you are legally mine. And then I will not allow you out of bed for the first six months." He kissed my forehead. "And by then you will be too heavy with my child to go far."

I could feel my knees buckling. There was only one thing I wanted as much as I wanted this man and that was to have our baby.

"Now go and dress and I will come for you in two hours."

I couldn't bear the thought of his leaving. What if he didn't return? What if I'd just made him up? What if — "It takes three days to get married in America. We'll have to wait. We can't —"

He kissed both my cheeks in the way of Europe or the East. "I will make a few calls. There will be no waiting." He kissed my neck but did not pull me close to him. I knew that he felt as I did and that if we got too close we would not be able to pull apart.

"Do you have any more questions?" he asked, his lips by my ear.

When I didn't answer, he held me at arm's length, but all I could do was shake my head no. No questions. None at all. He was mine and I was willing to follow him to the ends of the earth.

"Then give me your passport. There will be arrangements to be made."

With shaking hands, I pulled the blue book from my desk drawer and handed it to him, then watched as he opened it. "We were born in the same year," he said, "the same day."

I just nodded as I followed him to the door, then stood there in silence as the elevator arrived.

"Do you doubt me?" he asked, his hand on the door.

"Never. I trust you. I believe in you."

"And do you love me?" he whispered.

"With all my heart. With all my soul. From the beginning to the end of time."

"Yes," he said as the elevator door shut softly. "Yes. It is the same with me. I have loved you always."

"Yes," I whispered. "Yes."